DATE DUE   OCT 04

DEC 18 '04			
APR 3 0 05			
AUG 2 4 05			
NOV 0 2 05			
18 Dec 07			
12-03-08			
8-5-14 S			
GAYLORD			PRINTED IN U.S.A.

China

China

ALAN WALL

Thomas Dunne Books
St. Martin's Press ❦ New York

I am grateful to the following for their continual assistance and support: Gill Coleridge, Ann Denham, Steven Denham, Geoff Mulligan, Anthony Rudolf, Bernard Sharratt, and the staff of the London Library.

THOMAS DUNNE BOOKS.
An imprint of St. Martin's Press.

www.stmartins.com

Library of Congress Cataloging-in-Publication Data

Wall, Alan.
    China / Alan Wall.—1st U.S. ed.
        p. cm.
    ISBN 0-312-32779-X
    EAN 978-0312-32779-8
    1. Family-owned business enterprises—Fiction. 2. Inheritance and succession—Fiction. 3. Conflict of generations—Fiction. 4. Parent and adult child—Fiction. 5. Fathers and sons—Fiction. 6. Pottery industry—Fiction. 7. Jazz musicians—Fiction. 8. Aged men—Fiction. 9. England—Fiction. I. Title.

PR6073 .A415C47 2004
823'.914—dc22   2004041876

First published in Great Britain by Secker & Warburg

First U.S. Edition: June 2004

10 9 8 7 6 5 4 3 2 1

To Theresa
Clare, Michael and Ann
With love

And so things proceed in their circle.

Niccolò Machiavelli, *Opera*

China: China plate, hence mate. One who is close to the heart.

A Dictionary of Cockney Rhyming Slang

Bye Bye Blackbird

'Ladies and Gentlemen, please welcome once more the legendary Zeno.'

This announcement, uttered into a rasping mike, syllables distending draughtily into a buzzing PA system, elicits hardly any interest from the sundry drinkers and conversationalists scattered around the smoky tables of the Barley Mow. The boys climb on to the dais: Paul, Reg, Dove, Breezer, Pete and Theo. Which is another way of saying Zeno, a jazz sextet not notable so far for its worldly success. A scattering of applause, thin enough to initiate the appearance of an apprentice juggler at an orphans' party, accompanies their brief ascent, for they do have their devotees, a tiny group of followers who know precisely how good Zeno can be when they're all blowing on a good night, but these disciples have managed to keep the secret to themselves with a degree of success that might baffle the CIA.

Then the boys begin to play and those chosen few with ears to hear realise that the sound is oddly and unpredictably beautiful. Not for the first time they are flying tonight. None of them knows why, but they are. Sometimes it happens. They turn to each other with the graciousness of ancient musicians in a dark Viennese concert hall and nod in ritual acknowledgement of an unpremeditated fact: they are playing jazz now with a sudden fractured beauty that should undoubtedly be recorded or broadcast over the airwaves. It isn't, though. These unmelodic words on an unscored page will have to stand as solitary tribute to that evening's entertainment. The legendary Zeno. Their name isn't even written on water, only on the scrollwork of cigarette smoke that drifts towards them each evening and then drifts by.

Afterwards they stand in silence at the bar, each with a drink before him.

'Not bad, that,' Breezer announces finally from behind the mighty brushwork of his beard. He swiftly lifts the bottle to his mouth; a stray green missile penetrates a hillside of bracken and heather. 'So what's happening with the tape, Pete?'

'I've sent it to the *North Putney Gazette*.'

'The *North Putney Gazette*,' Breezer says slowly, scratching the oatmeal thatch that camouflages half his face. 'We couldn't maybe aim a little higher, could we? *NME*, *Wired*, *The Sunday Times*?'

'Tried them all. Didn't even bother to send the tape back in the envelope provided.'

'So we've cut our losses and settled for the *North Putney Gazette*.'

'I happen to know a bloke at the *North Putney Gazette*.'

Breezer turns his vast shape towards the diminutive figure of Pete, Zeno's piano player and the editor of the *Streatham Clarion*.

'And how many blokes are there normally at the *North Putney Gazette*, Pete, out of interest?'

'One.'

2

'So we needn't worry about the receptionist having her period the same day that our tape arrives, then.'

'Exactly. No problems with internal office communications at *NPG*.'

'Readership?'

'Small but select.'

'A bit like Zeno's fan club, by the sound of it. We've obviously got a lot in common – Zeno and the *North Putney Gazette*.'

'I'd say we've both been equally scrupulous in avoiding the vulgarities of success, the excesses of fame, the kind of filthy degradations that so often accompany a life of notoriety.'

'I think I can feel another bout of nausea coming on. Must be all this talk of fame, Pete. Always did give me the vapours. Anybody fancy another drink?'

'Yes,' five voices say in unison; their first chorus since laying down their instruments. Zeno: together once more.

'Nothing wrong with our timing anyway,' Breezer says as he bangs his empty bottle on the bar. 'Maestro, please – the musicians are dry after their labours.'

Half an hour later they all set out on their different journeys home. Breezer the saxophonist gives Theo the trumpeter a lift, and drops him down in the centre of Wandsworth. Once back in his flat Theo walks over and opens the window to try to get rid of the smell of Dettol and detritus, then he takes the trumpet from its case. The notes drift upstairs and down. Below him, Kosta's Kebabs has already closed for the night. Above him Mrs Trevelyan is watching television but she doesn't mind the sounds of *Bye Bye Blackbird* commingling with the late night news. That must be the new young man who moved in the month before. By himself, but then nobody seems to stay married for long these days. Not that anybody would be wanting to start a family in this place. She likes the way he plays ballads, as a matter of fact. He gives them a quality that chimes well with her mood in the evenings. It reminds her of some trumpeter she heard when she was a girl, though she can't remember his name any more. And you can recognise the tune, which is more than can be said for most of what passes for music these days. She even hums along for a moment, when the man on the screen starts talking about football. And outside in the permanent roar of the traffic the occasional pedestrian looks up to see where the slow trumpet solo is coming from. *Pack up all my cares and woe, Here I go, singing low . . .*

Finally Theo puts down his instrument and wipes his lips with the back of his hand. He walks over to the telephone and picks it up, hammering in the numbers of what had been his home until a few weeks before. He listens to her voice, her well-rehearsed and tolerant voice.

'It's Theo,' he says to the answering machine. Is she lying in bed as it records as she so often used to? The big wooden bed with the giant duvet. No smell of Dettol or detritus in that room, only a fragrance of freshly laundered linen and perfumed hair. 'I just wanted to have a bit of a talk with you about money.' He can see her sceptical smile as she hears the words. Even asleep she'd still be smiling at the notion that Theo should want to inaugurate a discussion with her about money. 'In case there's bills or anything that needs settling, Jill . . . Anyway, I'll phone again tomorrow.' He rings off. Tomorrow then. Tomorrow he will see his father. Tomorrow he will broach the topic of finance with the old man. Tomorrow he will do the one thing he hopes might possibly save his marriage. He picks up the little Dictaphone that lies on the table and brings his lips close to the tiny metal grille, as though it really were a miniature confessional and he a penitent homunculus come to kneel before it.

I'm not even sure why I've started making this tape for you, dad. Twelve hours from now I'll be seeing you and asking for money. You must owe me something, surely. Even if it's just a courtesy, after all these years, for the fact that you killed my mother.

The Missing Heron

The following day Theo rose late as usual. He boiled a kettle and poured the scalding water into a cup containing a spoonful of instant coffee. He lit a cigarette and walked over to stand in front of the picture he had hung on the wall, one of the few possessions apart from his trumpet and his tape machines that travelled with him wherever he went.

A framed black-and-white photograph: Charlie Parker playing alto sax with Miles Davis standing behind him, taken at the Three Deuces in 1948. Theo didn't know how many hours of his life he'd spent staring at it. Now he stared once again and tried to think himself back into that club. This was the high-point of Be-bop's musical cubism. All black-and-white.

Spectral streets; New York City at midnight in the snow. Mists of decomposition and possibility, needles of aerial antennae rising on the roofs above them, Bird's appetites already outrunning his ability to pay for them physically or financially. Artie Shaw said jazz had been nurtured into life from a whisky bottle, sustained on marijuana and was now dying its slow death on heroin. Drastic stuff, Satchmo called it, who made sure he had his own blaster at least once a day, innocence itself compared to the junk wasting those spectral apparitions on street corners. Parker was still glowing up there in the photograph, glowing with a lot more health than his pale spectator today in Wandsworth, but it wouldn't take long before he'd be on a panic again. Playing all night, then off to Minton's at nine to play all morning and then swerving away to find the man for another fix. Even Dizzy couldn't help any more – the other side of my heartbeat, he'd called him. The music was fast, fractured, difficult; this modern malice, Satchmo called it. 'Sounds like they're all trying to find the right note.' For every note they actually rested on they played a whole scale gratis. Theo wished he'd been alive then, even though it would almost certainly mean that he'd be dead now. Surely a price worth paying. Anyway, it was time to go and see his father. Time to beg.

Less than a mile away the wind blew across Trinity Road and veered over Wandsworth Common, slapping the faces of sundry suburban runners, flesh-tight in black and yellow Lycra. It distractedly lifted the manes of sniffing dogs on their myriad faecal quests and finally snatched a handful of dirty leaves from one of the autumn trees which fretted the sky with shattered Gothic tracery; thence to deliver that year's cast-offs with a brittle clatter against the first-floor window of an Edwardian house on the far side of Bolingbroke Grove. Behind that window, face as pale as a winter moon, Theo's father sat and stared.

A single-decker bus, the 319, stopped to beckon aboard all those intent on travelling towards Sloane Square. The weather had been shedding its grey complaint throughout the morning; inkwash skies maintained a promise of incipient rain as the bus thrummed up the road. After raising his face briefly to the clouds, he bent his head once more to stare at the object on the table before him.

It was a mug. Its misshapen features bespoke the early years of the Industrial Revolution, a survival from modernity's infancy when the pistons of raw-limbed machines thumped up and down in oily mania; one of the first, clumsy makings of our age. The old man looked at it gently as a father might gaze upon a crooked child, finding in its gauche asymmetry sufficient cause for celebration.

As he went downstairs to the kitchen he murmured to himself once more how glad he would be to see the back of the twentieth century. Now what was there left to be said of it? That it had fired repeatedly into the crowds with lethal intent and not simply watched the bodies as they fell but, uniquely in our brief and murderous history, recorded this latest *lapsus* on film? The same century that set out to fathom the intricate secret thread of life had also arranged at last for its utter destruction. Even though it hadn't happened. Not yet anyway. It was possible though and therefore, like all possibilities, an inescapable terminus in some region of the mind. The scenarios for apocalypse kept multiplying: thermonuclear, chemical, biological. That was always assuming the Darwinian goddess, that blind idiot called nature, wasn't already fashioning a virus sufficiently potent to wipe her billions of children off the face of the earth. The only thing that troubled him was this: although they'd almost finished with the twentieth century and the old millennium, had anyone really the faintest idea how to get started in earnest on a new one?

Watch him now as he makes his way, curved and quirky as a question mark, to his kitchen: an old man, what is left of his cropped hair entirely white, fidgeting ever closer to the edge of his days, already inches shorter than he was in his prime. He feels that he has grown familiar with death, which is why he can address that grand black finale, that dreary self-important little hiccup, with a colloquial familiarity verging sometimes on contempt, at other times on love. And yes, he'd grant you that without the modern ethic he so casually disparaged with all the eloquence at his disposal he would most certainly not be alive to whinge and witter as he did today. One heart attack, a spastic colon, an alien plastic hip, not to mention a whole host of minor adjustments to nature's original intentions. Nature left to herself had arranged a premature fatality, so he'd long ago lost any urge to wax sentimental about her, brutal, fecund bitch that she undoubtedly was.

He sat in his favourite chair by the window and looked out over his garden. It was large by the standards of the neighbourhood and had now grown long-haired and verdant, topping the heads of midnight cats who fought it out through this expanse of bonsai jungle, their cries seemingly from some unexplored limbo of the heart, a discordant music of chainsaw and banshee. Whenever he heard it in the night he found the sound chilling and exhilarating by turns. The swing had rusted since the days when it squeaked with his son Theo's pleasure, just as the room above his head had long since ceased echoing with the boy's cries. That dream he always had. That terrible dream.

Over these last few days the autumn russets and ochres, and the leaves breezily entangling themselves outside his window, had almost tempted him to share their mellowness. But now the weather was turning and now his son was about to arrive: Theo, his errant boy, who had kept alive his mother's beloved features as ghostings in his own physiognomy; and whom Digby Wilton therefore loved with all his crooked old heart. Or so he always told himself.

The curious theatricality of his son's knock. A veritable tattoo. Repeated twice. And there he was. Theo. His only child, except of course that he wasn't a child any more but a man in his forties. Still oddly beautiful for a man all the same, the living proof of his mother's physical distinction even if he had started to look a little battered of late. Theo had bad habits and Digby fretted that he wasn't so much a replica of his beautiful wife as a dittograph: the repetition of an unwanted character, a chip off precisely the wrong part of the old block.

'Given the tides today, shouldn't you be at work?'

'Been suspended,' the younger man said quietly. He looked seriously short of sleep and had lost even more weight. His father had thought that life with his new wife Jill might have quelled at least some of his appetites, but it certainly didn't look that way at the moment. He hoped they were not already quarrelling.

'What was it this time?' Digby asked as they walked through the house together. He was far from sure he really wanted to know.

'I tried to add a little colour to the commentary, that's all.' This son, having so far bungled all his vocations, from being a jazz musician to running a ceramics gallery in Fulham, an enterprise that had failed so spectacularly it had ended with nine months' imprisonment, had now been reduced to the status of part-time barman on a Thames cruiser. He was also periodically requested to speak into a microphone from a prepared sheet. Topographic details of London's rich and varied history. The commentary. They had arrived in the living room.

'A little colour, Theo?'

'I said the new Tate building had finally made use of the old giraffe house; apologised that the cupola of St Paul's wasn't revolving this week. That sort of thing.'

'Very droll. Out of interest, in your other capacity as barman had you perhaps . . .'

'I'd had a sharpener. Maybe two. I wouldn't say no to a drink now, to be honest.'

His father was hardly in need of this information since Theo, as far as he was aware, had never said no to a drink since he was fourteen years old and undergoing his first expulsion from school. He made a gesture towards the corner where the alcohol was kept and told his son to help himself. He watched him as he poured, oblivious as usual to the concept of a measure. He had his mother's almost liquid grace of movement as well as her facial profile. He could have been a serious athlete, so one of his priestly games masters had informed Digby during Theo's brief sojourn in that particular place of learning. But he'd preferred drinking and smoking, which was why he was now lighting up. Digby went and opened a window. He didn't understand his son. Never had. How such a luminous intelligence could be the instigator of so much self-inflicted damage was beyond him; as was the fact of such prodigious talents so prodigiously squandered. But none of this prevented his fatherly concern.

'You're not driving, are you?'

'Lost my licence six months ago, dad. You must remember.'

'Of course I do.' Of course he did. His son, with characteristically reckless generosity, had offered to drive one of his musical friends home after the pair of them had been boozing all evening. His friend, having leapt out at the traffic lights, had slammed the passenger door but not hard enough apparently. A few streets on Theo was cornering with his customary exuberance when the door flew open knocking a female pedestrian off her feet. She was in fact only slightly bruised but Theo had been most solicitous, chivalrous as always with the ladies, checking her wounds, manipulating limbs to see nothing was broken and finally breathing into her face with relief. And when the police had arrived he'd breathed into their faces too. Then at their request he'd breathed into their breathalyser. A little harder if you don't mind, sir. They had whistled in wonder at the speed with which the lights on the box flicked from green to amber to red. Two and a half times over the limit, the magistrate had announced. A three-year ban; a £2,000 fine; and perilously close to getting banged up once more.

Theo drank his vodka with a look of distraction, a look which was almost contemplative in its purity. Digby only kept vodka in the house for Theo – he loathed the stuff himself and was more than happy to eschew its scorching Russian intensities. Gin was surely a more British way to take comfort from the bottle. His bright blue eyes stared unrelentingly at his son and heir. Had things turned out differently Theo might now have been in charge of the family pottery business. But things hadn't turned out differently, it being in the nature of things not to, and there was no longer a family business for anyone to be in charge of. For although the company still carried the name Wilton, its true owner these days was entirely unrelated to any Wilton from the Potteries, being in fact a Mr Takashima from Kyoto. So things proceed in their circle.

'Did it happen this week, Theo?'

Theo shrugged. It was a gesture he had adopted during his adolescence. It was neither a yes nor a no; it appeared to signify a fundamental doubt as to the validity of the question or possibly even the questioner. It had always provoked Digby to quiet fury. He went over to the drinks table and poured himself a gin and tonic.

'So I suppose the only money you've got coming in is from Jill's work at the paper and . . .' He couldn't bring himself to say it. Theo was staring out of the window towards the swing where so many years before he had sailed through the air. Back and forth, back and forth. Jill and money. Money and Jill. Perhaps negotiating an advance on the old man's mortality might allow the different factors of their lives to be once more reconciled. If he was ever to get back underneath that big duvet in Wimbledon, he was going to have to arrive with some kind of tribute.

'Playing the trumpet, dad. That's what I do, remember.'

Although it had been the one constant feature of his son's life for twenty-five years Digby couldn't talk about it. It had gone on too long. He often thought it the main ingredient in the boy's ruin. Had he been better at it he might have made his fortune and had he been worse he might have realised the limits of his gift. Instead he was somewhere in between, scurrying across a wasteland of perpetual possibility and surely too old to be still waiting for the sound of opportunity knocking. Did he want money? Was that why he was here? Was that the only way he could make a contribution to his household? Was he calling upon the old ancestral debt? If so he could stop shrugging and ask for it. Politely. It still stung Digby to remember how he had once given Theo a cheque, had spontaneously signed over a substantial figure with several noughts at the end, made out jointly to him and his new wife shortly after their marriage, and Jill had returned it the next day with a curt note explaining that if they'd needed his assistance they'd surely have seen fit to mention it. Jill could be difficult, there was no doubt about that, and she had always been particularly difficult with her father-in-law, whom she appeared to hold personally responsible for Theo's substantial quotient of emotional oddities, addictive tendencies and *ex gratia* personality deformations, not to mention the death of his mother, but he still wished them a peaceful and successful marriage, even though they hardly ever came to see him together. Apart from anything else their union appeared to be his one chance of ever coming face to face with a grandchild. To that extent Theo was responsible for whatever was left of the old man's future. Could that really be described as a wise investment, he wondered?

He stared in silence at his son's bleak face, the delicate blade of a nose set between the beautiful dark eyes. And a sprouting mass of black hair to set off the consumptively white skin beneath. Victoria. All black-and-white. His wife had given their son her face. Digby tried to lighten his own countenance, to glow with easygoing fatherly warmth – don't get angry; don't, whatever you do, get angry, remember what happened the last time you did – but his facial default-setting had been melancholy all his life, descending in subtle shades of gloom to the unquestionably sombre and minatory. His large blue eyes always seemed to stare unblinkingly as his lips turned downwards at the corner from long-irreversible habit, and his slow and measured breathing was frequently indistinguishable from a sequence of exasperated sighs. Vicki had often remarked upon it. Even his lovemaking could seem like nothing so much as the frantic gestures of a man in a black rage. He could sometimes claw Vicki so hard he left bruises. At least she had done the same to him. They'd kept soothing creams and ointments about their bed in little white pots. What a long time ago all that seemed now. The only thing that furrowed his flesh these days was the sharpening blade of the years, rehearsing their final coup.

Theo looked at his father's face. A judge at a hanging, he thought, and it's not hard to work out whose neck's going to be stretched. The sentence had been passed so many times before. I can't ask him, he thought. I can't. He fingered in his pocket the tape that he had brought. The legendary Zeno. His trumpet-playing on it, as all who had heard it had been ready to acknowledge, was superb. He had imagined handing it over to his father, even inserting it into his ancient machine, as the old fellow made out the cheque that might save his marriage; had imagined saying, 'Now do you see why it was worth staying with it, dad? You never did understand how good I was, you know.' But what could you say to someone who still thought Miles Davis fluffed his notes on *Kind of Blue*?

'If there's anything I can do, Theo.' His son shrugged his famous shrug and then finished his vodka. Ten minutes later they were shuffling towards the door. 'It would be nice to see Jill again. The two of you together, I mean. I often pray you'll both . . .'

'Don't,' Theo said coldly. He didn't like being prayed for, particularly by his father, who was no saint himself. He could keep his piety for the scrupulous examination of his own conscience as far as Theo was concerned. Murderous old delinquent. He could devote his twilight years to bringing to mind what he had done to his own wife, to Theo's mother.

And sit counting his money as the shades of extinction gathered about him.

'How is Jill?' the old man asked, nervous now of overstepping whatever boundaries Theo had decided to set for him today.

'Probably better off without me.'

'Without you?'

'We've split up, dad. I've moved out.' Theo was genuinely astonished at the tear he saw rising to his old man's eye. He could only remember that happening once before.

'So where are you living?'

'I've rented a flat down in Wandsworth.'

'You could have come here. There's plenty of room. There's still *your* room.'

'Then you'd have had to listen to the sound of my trumpet. And you wouldn't have wanted that, now would you?' He fingered the tape in his pocket as he stared into his father's face, which seemed in that instant so old and frail and defeated that he briefly relented. 'How's *China* going, dad?' This question was delivered in a much softer tone, in a final gesture of filial civility as he opened the door.

'It's going,' his father said wearily.

'Still haven't found the Coleridge letters then?'

This was something of a family joke and Digby didn't even bother to answer it. Of course I haven't found the Coleridge letters, the old man thought. I'll never find them, will I? And now it looks as though I'll never find myself face to face with a grandchild either.

A minute later the door closed and his son was gone. So he hadn't asked for money, after all. Penniless but proud. Something else he inherited from his mother then. Though she'd managed to extract enough pennies from him, if the truth were told.

China. Or to give the volume its full title: *Wilton Bone China: Two Centuries of Family Tradition.* By Digby Wilton, MSc. The old man himself.

Theo walked across the Common in the direction of Wandsworth. He couldn't be bothered going back to the station. He looked out for the heron by the pond but it was nowhere to be seen. As he reached Trinity Road he stopped and stared over at that squat brick fortress where he had been locked up for nine months. It could pass for a particularly secure warehouse of elephantine proportions or even the prototype of a concentration camp. No flamboyant rustication; no Gothic portals. This was the industrial face of incarceration: Wandsworth's correctional facility which had numbered among its guests Oscar Wilde and Ronnie Biggs. He felt as though a block of ice were moving slowly through his intestines. How he feared the prison; its hard rooms, its inconsolable and semen-stained dreams. Buggery and thuggery. A sheer geometry of human waste no sociometric calculus could ever compute. He wouldn't be going back there again. No, he'd rather give the grave as his return address. He had watched once from inside as that missing heron flew over them all and had known then for the first time in his life how a man can truly envy an animal.

As he walked past the bank in Wandsworth he halted. He stared at the machine in the wall and pondered the possibilities, but he had done it too often over the last six months, pressing his card in while it flashed on the screen: WHICH SERVICE DO YOU REQUIRE? You pressed CASH, NO

RECEIPT, and waited. You could hear the whole building as it started to think, electronically clicking away, considering your prospects darkly before resolving itelf in regard to your biography and credit rating: SORRY. THIS SERVICE NOT AVAILABLE. INSUFFICIENT FUNDS IN ACCOUNT. He couldn't face the green menace of those letters on the quietly hissing screen, the buzz of accusation that accompanied the message, whichever street corner you received it on. He had no idea what was in his account but was reasonably certain the figure would be preceded by a minus sign. Why couldn't his father have given him some money, simply put his hand in his pocket, no questions asked? It was hardly as though he was short of the readies himself. The old bugger wanted for nothing. What was he saving up for at this point in life? Why did he always have to stand on ceremony? Why, just for once, couldn't he . . . But no, he thought, let it go.

In fact he had lost his job on the boats six weeks before but then he seldom lasted long in such positions. The relationship between his income and his outgoings, always a tricky equation at the best of times, had once more become vertiginous. This cessation of income had led to the final breach with Jill; well, that plus the fact that he spent most of the cash he did actually earn from his music in the company of women other than his wife. The musician's life, ah yes, but now that musician's life had to be funded minus Jill's salary. He stopped dead on the pavement and thought hard for a moment.

He went back to his flat. First he tore a piece of white paper into a rough circle and wrote on it: *Tax Applied For.* Then he rummaged in the holdall that contained the meagre documentation his life still afforded. He found his car keys and the registration documents. Then he stepped into the tiny bathroom, brushed his teeth and swilled out his mouth with a peppermint wash to kill the smell of the drinks which his father had so graciously provided. Thanks, dad. After that he went down the steps and back outside. He took the next bus heading towards Wimbledon.

His car was parked outside his house, except that it wasn't his house any more, was it? It was now once more entirely Jill's, as it had been when he'd first left prison to join her there. The car had not been moved for six months and was covered in dust. Jill naturally detested it, preferring her ancient Deux Chevaux for its snail's-pace ecological sound-ness; its peaceable velocity in the face of any local fauna. Hedgehogs had nothing to fear from a world filled with drivers like Jill. The motorways would soon have been cleared of their mounds of bristly little corpses. Theo had noticed the month before that the tax disc had expired. One more legal liability he had decided to ignore. He now stuck the circular white paper message in its place.

Sitting in the driving seat for the first time since his licence had been revoked he prayed the car would start. It did so at the second turn, good car, and he started to drive, punctiliously, courteously and with exaggerated caution. Thus did his black BMW 323i make its way first to a car wash at the edge of Tooting and then up the Merton Road until it finally pulled over on to the vehicle-crammed forecourt of the dealer's where he'd bought the motor in the first place; the dealer where his jazz-playing companion and fellow band member Reg now worked.

Reg looked as though he'd lost even more hair in the last week. He had so little of it now that you noticed each lonely elegiac tuft as it disappeared from the denuded hillsides of his skull. His melancholy, loping figure topped by his great domed head was in no way enlivened by the single flashing earring he wore with what he must have hoped was gypsy panache. A costive smile briefly tortured his features as he caught sight of Theo.

'I'm afraid we don't have any Rollers in at the moment, sir.'

'Well, you'll be needing this Beamer then. For your more discerning clients.'

'Selling it?' Theo couldn't help noticing that Reg didn't seem exactly thrilled at the prospect.

'Not much use to me, is it? After my three-year ban. This isn't me driving, by the way, Reg. I'm somebody else. See if you can get me a decent price from the old man.' Reg shook his head dubiously.

'He's not in much of a buying mood at the moment, Theo.'

'He was in enough of a selling mood when he took my money.'

'It's not been a bad motor, has it?' Theo was forced to admit that in fact it hadn't. 'I'll try then. No guarantees, mind.'

Mr Thompson finally emerged from his grubby little office looking spherical and distressed. He said a perfunctory hello to Theo, then there was the usual scratching of the head, the troubled intake of breath, the expression of practised incredulity as he made his sceptical way from boot to bonnet. He offered him twelve hundred pounds. 'Only because you're a friend of Reg's.' The rotundity of his brown-coated body was echoed by the rotundity of his face. White hairs sprouted from his fleshy nose. They quivered as he sighed, considering the absurd dimensions of his own charity.

'Fifteen hundred,' Theo said. 'I bought it from you for three thousand. That was only eighteen months ago.'

'I'll go up to thirteen hundred but no higher.'

'Cash,' Theo said.

'You've got the logbook?'

'It's here.' Mr Thompson peered over at the windscreen and then gave Theo one final forensic look.

'*Has* the tax been applied for, out of interest?'

'No.'

Finally with the money in his pocket Theo went to see the Hungarian at his house in Fulham. There he collected £50 worth of hashish and with this buttoned securely into his inside pocket a sense of well-being came over him as he stepped back out on to the street. Who needs fathers anyway? Though a wife might still turn out to be a good idea. He looked up at the sky, threatening rain as it had all afternoon, and smiled. What should he do now? He bought the local papers and decided to go home and read his way through the classified ads, to see if there was any employment going for a trumpet-playing jailbird. But *en route* he stopped at the pub in Wandsworth. The fat man and the thin man were standing at the bar; the fat man and the thin man were always standing at the bar, and they always stood on the same corner, always adopted the same pose – so how did *they* make a living? – the fat one wearing a tight T-shirt that showed his beer gut to its best advantage; he'd obviously invested a lot of money in that belly of his over the years. No point being shy about it. He finally spoke.

'I was reading in the paper about President Clinton. This old girlfriend of his says that when he was at Oxford he never slept without his saxophone in the bedroom with him. Now what do you make of that?'

'Maybe he used it as a penis sheath. Like that one Gerry used to bring down the pub before he got sick.'

'Gerry's a hypochondriac,' the fat man said dismissively. At which point the thin man changed his demeanour. He spoke more quietly.

'He is dying, you know.'

'Oh, I know he's dying,' the fat man said easily, 'but he still exaggerates it.' They ordered another drink. The fat man spoke again.

'Do you remember Terry?'

'Terry.'

'Married Tom Biddle's sister.'

'Oh, Terry.'

'Except that she only stuck it for six months with him and then ran off with old Alf Rudge's son, who's obviously giving her whatever young Terry wasn't, because she's still there.'

'Didn't have enough ginger in him to keep her frisky.'

'Maybe. Anyway, Alf's son's a bouncer at that big disco round the corner, the one that's always getting busted for drugs. And the other night I'm walking home up the road there and I see Terry sitting in his old Land Rover outside the disco. So I went over and looked in through the window. He's got two big tears streaming down his cheeks. Those new street lights made them glisten.'

'Sodium.'

'I thought the new ones were tungsten. Anyway I tapped on the window and Terry opens it and I look down and see he has a bucket between his legs, a big metal bucket filled with some kind of white liquid. I said, What's that then,

Terry? Bleach, he says. What do you want a bucket of bleach for at this time of night, Terry? You wouldn't by any chance be planning on seeing Alf's son, would you?

'He turns towards me, still with the tears in his eyes, and this amazing look, this expression . . .'

'Lovelorn.'

'Eh?'

'Lovelorn. Alf's son's still shagging his wife, when all's said and done. He'd be lovelorn. Stands to reason.'

'Whatever. And he says, I don't want to blind him, you know – I just want to turn the fucker white.' There was a pause and then the thin one spoke.

'Wasn't all that bright, was he, young Terry?'

'Oh, couldn't spell tit backwards.'

Even as he walked into the flat it hit him again. What was that smell? It seemed to emanate from the carpet, a combination of its sundry deposits over the years and the various disinfected attempts to clean it. Theo opened the window. Now the rush of the traffic from the road below would have made it difficult to hold a conversation with anyone else in the room. But there was no one else in the room. He looked around him at the cheap furniture with its balding fabrics and leprous leather patches, the horrible little vases on shelves, the kitsch white prancing horse cavorting on the mantelpiece. This was one of those cheap rented flats that was entirely non-absorbent of the human personality. All it absorbed of humanity was the stuff you would have preferred it to flush away.

Zeno's gig that night was in colour, Walter Sickert sludge-browns, so at least it provided more information from the spectrum but it seemed to Theo that it had moved further from reality than the black-and-white image he'd been studying earlier, or the black-and-white sounds that played constantly inside his head. He wished himself back into the age of monochrome. He missed the chiaroscuro of cigarette smoke rising into the spotlight's beams, the *film noir* sunsets, black stockings, white thighs. He couldn't use colour; daylight and springtime were no use to him at all. He didn't know what to do with them either in his music or his life. Shadows and nocturnes, those were his numbers. He hardly noticed the other boys in the band that night. Breezer, Dove, Paul, Pete and Reg all did their best to blaze around him, but he just concentrated on his chops whenever they came. If he thought at all he thought of Jill. He thought of himself. He thought of that empty flat with the curious smell in the middle of the traffic tangle that was Wandsworth. When he arrived back he phoned straight away.

'Theo,' he said.

'It's late.' She was in bed. 'What do you need to talk about so late into the night, Theo?'

'I went to see my father today.'

'Didn't ask him for anything, did you?'

'He gave me a vodka.'

'*A* vodka, Theo?' He didn't need to reply. 'Did he confess?'

'No. Actually, Jill, I didn't phone up to tell you that. I wanted to talk to you about money.' She started to laugh.

'Money. Ah, yes. I listened to your message last night. You need to discuss the division of your estate, do you?' This was Jill's competent, ironic voice, the one she used all day at the newspaper.

'I sold the car, Jill, that's all. What I mean is, I have some money . . .'

'Then put it somewhere safe, Theo. Hide it in a biscuit

tin. Stuff it in the rafters. Leave it with a friendly band leader. Just don't, whatever you do, keep it in your pocket. You know what happens to money that ends up in your pocket.'

'If there's any bill you need settling . . .'

'It's over, Theo. All over. No good getting prudent now, putting away savings for the housekeeping. You never did before, did you? Whatever you do, it won't make any difference. It wasn't the money anyway, sweetheart. I got used to being the one who paid all the bills a long time ago. It's everything else you did. And just because you're feeling lonely all of a sudden doesn't mean you'll stop. We both know that. The only way you could ever be faithful would be to go back to prison and even I don't wish that upon you. You're who you are. Better just keep on playing the trumpet now. So save your money for the life that lies ahead – you're probably going to need it. And in the meantime I need my sleep.' She rang off.

A moment later, Theo picked up his battered Dictaphone and pressed the record button. There was an edge to his voice.

What was it you always used to say to me? How quantitative changes, if they go on long enough, always become qualitative changes: water grows colder by degrees then suddenly it's ice; hotter by degrees and suddenly it's steam. Well, a marriage grows sadder by minutes and hours and days and suddenly it's a divorce. Did you ever notice?

I suppose it's a shame that I had to lose my wife before I finally came to see things with such clarity. It suddenly strikes me that I've eaten nothing for three straight days, so busy has my mouth been swallowing my pride. And last night I had to improvise a long lament, dad, on the trumpet of course, on the theme of my own stupidity. *It harmonised with the sobbing of the water pipes. So even as I sound my depths the plumbing has to go and join in. It chorused in B flat, if my ears weren't deceiving me. A good key for the blues, that's for sure. Most melancholy of all the signatures. I'd at least hoped for that celestial choir you once told me about, not the gurgle of the water pipes. Water pipes and the throttling of motor cars on the road down there. So tell me, where's the music of the spheres gone now, old man? It all sounds like devilish discords to me. Filled with flatted fifths. The funeral music of New Orleans — those hymns of lamentation. Psalms of comfort and condolence. In the old days even the devil wept. I think we're going to have to get the boys on this one: Pete, Dove, Reg, Paul and Breezer. We could do it as a twelve-bar. It's not as though she's the first of our wives to bite the dust, when all's said and done. Maybe marriage and jazz just don't mix. So let's do what they did in New Orleans and turn it all into music. Then we'll be in the same place they were, won't we? Sitting on top of the world.*

Then he took the tape out of his pocket, the one he'd intended to give to his father that morning as a token of his achievement, and he put it in the recorder. He kept pressing the forward button until he came to his favourite track. *Pack up all my cares and woe, Here I go, singing low.* There's nothing wrong with this, dad — this is good. So don't you ever ask me to apologise for my life. For my life or my mother's either. What have you ever done in all your years that made as good a sound as this, Mr Potman?

Archaeology

Digby. Dig. Be. They seem contradictory don't they? After all, the digging usually starts when the being ceases. To be or not to be – to dig instead. To lie in cold obstruction and to rot.

Digby, Theo's father was well aware, was a formal sort of name, more easily spoken in the courtroom or Land Registry Office than between the sheets but most attempts to shorten it had created as many difficulties as they'd solved. Digs he particularly detested. Victoria had finally disposed of the problem entirely by never calling him anything but *Love*. *Love* she would say enticingly, somehow riding the circular vowel at the word's heart as though closing her moistened lips ever so gently on his soul. *Love* she'd whisper with her perfumed breath and the merest flick of her tongue and he would say yes. Whatever it was she wanted he said yes. So expert had she become at unguents and powders that he could still smell the mysterious traces she left in the air as she went from room to room. She was training him even then to hunt after her ghost. Diana and her invisible hounds – how dogged he had become in pursuit of those invisibilities. God how he missed her. He even missed her screaming at him, pounding on his chest with her fists. He even missed the silent rages that seemed to go on for years. He missed the clawing of her nails in the small of his back. He missed her tiny murmurs after their mighty rows. He missed her.

They had met towards the end of the war. Digby's war had been an undistinguished one. A host of physical problems even then, particularly his defective sight, had somehow precluded him from any of the more heroic missions, so his greatest contribution to the defeat of Fascism had been a stint of junior quartermastering at Aldershot. He had been glad to get into uniform all the same, even though it had been suggested that wartime production schedules at his family firm in the Potteries might well have excused him military service. He could have kept his head down and helped produce Utility Ware for the country's wartime needs. But he didn't want to be excused. Nor did he want to have much to do with the various young women occasionally presented to him as potential brides. A man with a mighty inheritance, or what had seemed so once, can find himself popular with women when he comes of age but he can't help wondering from time to time if it's him alone they yearn for. The Staffordshire daughters paraded before him were, he had little doubt, practical enough creatures beneath their hesitating smiles. But Digby had in those days sought from womankind what he had finally come to feel God alone could provide: absolute love. A language of love without a conditional mood, without any of the mazy manoeuvres of *if* and *perhaps* and *but*. Young men search it out in women; old men settle for the Almighty, since the deity's embrace is often the next big one they're expecting.

Wilton Manor was set in its own sloping grounds behind ornate black gates a few miles outside Stoke. In his early years he had occasionally escaped but with invariably unhappy results. He could still remember with a vividness that abolished the sixty-odd intervening years his first attempt to get out there and mingle. He had ended up in what was known as the refreshment room of the train station where he was at least out of earshot and more than a stone's throw from any of the local ragamuffins, who were only too aware he was the son and heir to a local pottery family, living in a fashion very different from that of their own immiserated rookeries. He was brooding in *Brief Encounter* mode on the possibility of random romance when he found himself staring at an elderly woman hunched inside her overcoat, who sat down with a deep plate, the contents of which struck him as indescribably disgusting. Fish had been mixed up with lumpy mashed potato and the whole sunk in a pool of milk. She picked up the sugar dispenser and started shaking it with vigour over the dish. The sweet snowstorm fell and fell until the sizeable dispenser was empty. Then as her final preparation for the feast before her she carefully removed her false teeth and placed them on the table. He was already going through the door when she sucked in her first noisy mouthful. Back to Wilton Manor he went, grateful once more for its iron fences. For a while anyway. Whatever he had to endure at home suddenly seemed mild compared to what he might have to endure outside.

So he liked the anonymity his uniform afforded him and was happy to continue wearing it during his few days' leave in Hastings. He and his Aldershot friend Charles had decided on a trip to the seaside and had met two girls, one of whom was Vicki, daughter of a Maltese who owned a fish and chip kiosk down on the seafront. The war was over now in all but name and the right side had won. There was an air of celebration about. People who had barely met behaved as though they had known each other for years. So on the second night Charles who was short, almost as short as Victoria, had swapped coats and hats, stockings and trousers with her so that Digby could smuggle her into the lodging house. And when Digby removed Charles's coat and Charles's trousers he'd found something very different from Charles underneath. *Love* she had said to him, using that word for the first time: *my love.* Her heavy vowels pulled him down through their loops. That night Victoria had shrouded his future with possibility. And best of all she'd had no idea who he was. Just another young man in uniform. My love: she said it over and over again with a curious, compelling melancholy in her voice, even once to his astonishment silently weeping. He was touched to have touched a woman so deeply, to have sounded her warm darkness and known that whatever had prompted her to lie with him it wasn't his money because she hadn't known he'd had any. Perhaps she had wept at losing her innocence; wept at all that she had given up to him on that first night.

To dig and to be. Perhaps they weren't so incompatible after all. He stood for a moment meditating on the tygs and other Cistercian ware in his glass case. They'd been dug out of the ground hadn't they? And as for himself, what was left for such an antique crock amongst the antique crockery? He was half-ghost already. One more curator of time's detritus.

The doorbell rang. He wouldn't answer. He remained absolutely motionless as he always did when not wishing to disclose his presence, as though his chameleon stillness might permit him to evade the door-stepping harassment of the benevolent. The letterbox lid snapped open.

'DIGBEE. It's me.'

Daisy. Daisy Gresham. The only one who could come in without an appointment.

'Have you been brooding again?' she asked from the other room as he made her coffee in the kitchen. He himself had given up coffee as one of his few concessions to an ever-burgeoning prostate gland. 'It would be better if you gave up the gin and the wine,' his doctor had said. 'I think I'll give up the coffee, thanks,' Digby had answered.

'How did you know?'

'You leave a kind of wreath in the air whenever you brood.' He carried the coffee through and gave it to her. She stood by the french windows as he sat back down in his chair.

'Anything in particular,' she asked, 'or is it just life in general?' She could never help smiling at his funeral-parlour gravitas.

'My son came to see me yesterday and that always gets me thinking about the past, though I suppose the truth is I don't need much prompting these days.'

'Not in trouble again, is he?'

'I'm afraid Theo's always in trouble; it's just a question of precisely how much of it he's in. I'd hoped his wife would sort him out. She seems like the sort of woman who sorts men out. She did a pretty good job of sorting me out whenever I was foolish enough to open my mouth. But instead of sorting him out, she seems to have thrown him out. It's only two years since they were married. So it seems that Theo now spends his days in a rented flat in Wandsworth, no doubt playing jazz for all he's worth and when he's not doing that he'll be doing something even less financially rewarding.'

'That's right – he's a musician, isn't he?'

'A criminal trumpet player.'

'He plays that badly, does he? Just as well they never criminalised incompetent acting or half my colleagues would probably be in chokey by now.'

'It wasn't actually the noise he made on the trumpet they put him away for.'

'Inadequate embouchement?'

'No, I should think that's perfect, given all his years of practising with different sized bottles.' It wasn't that Digby objected to drinking. He drank. Almost everyone he knew drank. But Theo *drank*.

'And what's Howard up to these days?' he asked.

'He's an internet journalist – a founder member of the Radix Group.'

'You'll have to explain. I'm afraid I haven't kept up.'

'It's all about how we're destroying the planet. How international capital will be the death of us. Money, I suppose. He disapproves of it so much he can't bring himself to make any and feels obliged to get rid of mine as quickly as possible.'

'Ah, then we have more in common than I'd thought.' Digby couldn't help noticing that Daisy, who was famously pale to begin with, had of late turned even paler. Her face looked as though milk pulsed behind the skin instead of blood. As she stood staring out at his overgrown garden she appeared to be in a state of utter abstraction, her hand fluttering like a demented moth around the white candle of her face.

'I've no idea where he is at the moment. Mind you, at least he hasn't ended up in prison yet,' she said, 'though to be honest it wouldn't surprise me if he did.'

'We could compare notes,' Digby said. 'My son got

married while he was in there. I'm not sure it did much for him otherwise. Does it ever do anybody any good, I wonder? Life inside seems to be ten parts retribution to one part rehabilitation. Maybe getting married in there was part of his punishment; it certainly looks as though it will be now.'

Daisy Gresham. When he had seen her through his side window ten years before, after she had first moved to the neighbourhood, he had thought he was hallucinating. After all it couldn't be: not *the* Daisy Gresham now living in symmetrical proximity in the house to his left. It was the sort of prospect adolescent boys grew moist at the thought of, and old men never entirely escape being adolescent boys: they simply carry that incarnation along with so many others inside them. A man is a nest of Russian dolls shrinking all the way back to the embryo. Digby had even thought sometimes he would have liked it better if he'd been constructed from the same hardwood. With a gleaming shellac finish; anything to be less porous.

And here she was, on her way towards sixty now but lovelier than ever. Her blonde hair, pale skin, blue eyes and slightly hooked nose had etched themselves into the minds of a generation of men. She was dressed in tight jeans and a red pullover baggy enough to reach her knees. She wore oversize white trainers, one of which had a hole in the toe. She was carrying a large canvas bag. He remarked once more to himself how beauty so easily transforms slovenliness into casual grace.

That evening Digby, who had sworn off ever again watching live television, went to the shelf where he kept his videos. He took out *Noah's Rainbow*, the film from the late

Sixties which had established Daisy's reputation worldwide. One more sex goddess to disrobe alongside Julie Christie, Brigitte Bardot and Susannah York. In *Noah's Rainbow*, which was a more spectacular re-run of *On the Beach*, she had been the new Ava Gardner to Chuck Hill's Gregory Peck, except that in the famous scene where the first two stars faded into soft-focus in the hotel room, the camera lens evidently melting with passion along with the viewer, as the boozy boys below sang *Waltzing Matilda*, in *Noah's Rainbow* Daisy had left nothing to the imagination. While the bombs were being racked up to turn the world into a thermonuclear desert, her dance of the seven veils had pushed through to the end and the camera had then malingered over every part of her anatomy like a bridegroom inching his way over his new possession – including her small but perfect breasts and the tiny red buds of her nipples, so different in every way from Vicki's. As a result Digby could now never look at her in her clothes without also seeing her without them, such being the power of the cinematic image. So he sat back once more and waited for the end of the world.

Radix

Daisy Gresham stared at the telephone with a look of growing hostility until she finally picked it up and poked in the numbers with her delicate index finger. She was phoning her first ex.

'James, it's Daisy.' She could tell within seconds of his starting to speak that there was somebody there in the room with him. A certain coyness in his tone, the sense that he was turning and smiling to another silent and smirking presence, was inescapable. James had made quite a lot of mileage out of the fact that he had once been married to Daisy Gresham. It seemed to make other women curious. Perhaps they thought something of her glamour had once rubbed off on him and might in turn now rub off on them. So why not slip your clothes off, darling, and find out? She could never summon the right words to describe how much it irritated her, this notion that she might have become his vicarious procuress, so that now in the posthumous years of their marriage she was still a supplier of flesh for his fornications.

'Do you know where Howard is?' she said, interrupting him. 'I'd like to know because he's my son, that's why. Because he took off from here two months ago without any mention of where he was going and I haven't heard a word since ... Yes, I know he's a writer. Well an internet journalist, whatever that means but ... Will you please stop laughing, James. I'm phoning you because he's your son as well as mine. You have somebody there with you, don't you? I always know when you're playing to the gallery. I've often thought you were the one who should have gone on stage.

'I am calling you, James, since you ask, because I thought you might be able to help. Howard after all has your features, your voice. He has perfected the same public-address system belch. He leaves his dirty socks on the kitchen table, so maybe Lamarck was right after all and acquired characteristics can be inherited. And since these days you both seem to date girls of more or less the same age ...'

James had rung off. Daisy replaced the telephone slowly, stared at it for a few moments in silence then said softly, almost lovingly, 'Bastard'. She resolved to do what she had otherwise not done for over six months: she would ascend to the loft where her son Howard sometimes stayed free of charge whenever the fancy took him.

As she opened the loft door she caught it again, that unmistakable reek of unmarried young men. Women spend half their lives trying to remove it. Howard wasn't even that young, when she came to think of it. He was nearly thirty: James's age when her son had been conceived. You might at least have taught him something, James, she thought. Passed on some sort of family heirloom, if only to show him how to snap frisky young doxies in the buff. She really did feel she'd done enough in regard to Howard's reek over the years; felt it was time for another woman to step in and waft the odours of rutting and hibernation from this particular sett. The pine bed in the corner was a cumulus of dirty sheets. And the computer screen on the table was glowing. Did he never switch it off? Who was paying for the electricity around here? Books, pamphlets and papers were scattered everywhere across the floor and the walls were plastered with ragged posters. Save the Earth. Eat the Rich. The WTO Kills Children. Down with the IMF. RTS. Planet Earth Not Planet Inc. Greed Is Swallowing The Earth's Ozone. Anarchy UK. There Is No Third World: There Is One World. She stared for a moment at the photograph of a tall young man in combat fatigues and boots, his face covered with a bandit's kerchief, then turned back to the table and read what was on the computer screen. It was an e-mail to a colleague of his in America. She stared hard at the last three words typed out in capitals: THAILAND GREAT ANAKH. What on earth did that mean? Then she sat down before the screen and, using the expertise Howard himself had imparted to her, keyed the word Radix into the appropriate box and pressed Return. She sat and waited to see what revelations might follow. And, scrolling her way through the *Radix Manifesto*, she started to read:

Money is the world's intelligence. Whether it's a voucher for the company store or some grand gold coin bearing the monarch's head – this is how the world makes its decisions. We can lament it, comrades. We can denounce it on the streets. But floating here together in the noosphere we can see clearly how the history of the world is the history of money and the way those who have it buy up the present and future of those who don't. These are the facts, however melancholy or triumphant we might find them.

In our university libraries we sit examining the ruins of a civilisation and what we're looking at is money. In the solicitor's office signing the documents that close a marriage we soon find that they're all about money too. All your nights of love must now be computed and accounted for, the same as in a Paris brothel – in the end it all comes down to who gets what and who pays whom.

Money is intelligence in the other sense too, not merely the mechanism whereby the world makes up its mind day by day, second by second, whether on electronic screens or in wads of grubby notes, but also the medium of information; how we finally receive the news that seals our fate, both the good news and the bad. Some people who stayed at home in Germany throughout the First World War could ignore the slaughter at the front entirely, even receiving mighty premiums as the blood poured out and the screams grew louder. The real intelligence only hit home when the great inflation started. That's when money really began to talk. The country might have lost its pride, its military prowess, its young men in their hundreds of thousands, but only when inflation finally wiped out its savings was the triumph of Fascism assured. And so, net-navigators, cyber-souls, founding members of the first true International, money is the world's intelligence for the very simple reason that the sum total of its transactions demonstrates the global state of play at any single moment. It's the harbinger that brings us details of the next big thing to happen in life, however much we might wish it wouldn't. Ages of gentility learned how to disguise it, sticking a Georgian facade between the effluvia of the street and whatever profits were accruing in the counting-house behind it. Or even to hide it entirely: in Bath some of the houses along Royal Crescent have servants' doors set inside their wooden casings. After the hirelings had gone through them even their existence could be safely forgotten, for the doors closed so flush into the surrounding woodwork that the joints became invisible, although one discreet tug at a bell-rope would soon bring them running back.

The purpose of Radix is to ask this simple question: What is the price of a man? Wergeld, it used to be called. Insofar as this price changes between the first world and the third, then that is the measure of the barbarity we still refer to as our civilisation. These days the door the hirelings disappear through bears the name of another country but nobody doubts that the labour is global, the profits international. And if such exploitation is criminal, which we all know it is, then we in the first world are criminals one and all, because in truth there isn't a first world, a second world and a third world. There is one world.

Digby stared at the invitation which had landed on his mat and the features of his usually inexpressive face grew pink with a vivid sense of alarm. For apart from Daisy, the welcome neighbour to his left, he had another, less welcome neighbour to his right.

Jonty Merriman was uxorious. Indeed Digby often felt that the intensity of his neighbour's feelings for his spouse verged on the macabre. No sooner had her eyelids started fluttering in the morning light than Merriman was at her side proffering a cup of steaming hot tea. Should she so much as sneeze he would have her hemmed in by a baffle of cushions while he spooned medications into her mouth. She was his junior by over twenty years, but he was the one who played nurse.

And as if all this weren't enough Merriman was an avid amateur photographer. He had converted one room in his house to a studio and another to a darkroom. His speciality, inevitably, was taking photographs of his beloved's naked body and since she was no more gifted a model than he was a portraitist the end-product tended to display their joint incompetence to truly striking effect. Digby had learnt over the years to blank them out somehow from his field of vision, these prodigiously enlarged prints which would otherwise have distracted him from any coherent train of thought: Merriman's wife leering backwards over her haunches; Merriman's wife apparently attempting to unscrew her own right nipple while wearing an expression which Digby could only interpret thus: the *summum bonum* of all existence peaks no higher than such a moment of total self-exposure, preferably experienced in front of a Hasselblad.

It was evidently inconceivable to Merriman that anyone might find his younger wife's physical charms, her spot-lighted womanly attributes and the entry-point to her fecundity, less hypnotically alluring than he himself did. He was never far from her image, even when the model herself had strayed from home.

So when Merriman's doting old mother came to stay she would make a great show of exuberantly dusting throughout the house, thus providing herself with the excuse she needed to drop the standing pictures face down on their tables and shelves while turning the hanging ones discreetly to the wall. Then Merriman's wife's eyes, supposedly approaching ecstatic climax or sliding vertiginously away from that recent cataclysm, would briefly and blessedly stop following you around the room like Lord Kitchener's on the Great War recruitment posters. Merriman had once winked complici-tously at Digby while this motherly iconoclasm was going on, as if to say – The old, eh? Those ancient constraints of the mind still in place after so many years – seeming to mistake his aged parent's sound aesthetic judgement for mere prudery.

Jonty was hideously robust. His unseasonally tanned face positively gleamed. He approached every pleasure life afforded with the sort of hearty gusto that could sometimes put Digby off his food entirely.

Digby would often watch him out of his study window, dressed in a luminescent track suit, jogging around Wandsworth Common then halting to stretch and lean and sashay back and forth, finally dropping down prone to get started on his press-ups. Jonty evidently had no intention of getting any older if he could help it. Digby could still remember celebrating his forty-ninth birthday with him three years in succession. The man had simply decided that he wasn't prepared to be fifty – he was too young to be fifty. Allegations that he had reached that age he regarded as unworthy of detailed refutation. He was a great believer in free choice, was Jonty, and had a particular distaste for all outdated powers, principalities and bureaucracies, so he obviously found it frankly ridiculous that Time should dictate to him in this way without any prior consultation. And to help him hold Time in its tracks he employed whatever potions and magic tinctures needed applying to his body. When Digby had first met him he'd had a perfectly respectable thatching of grey hair, then one day it had all disappeared, replaced instead by a sort of glistening black helmet.

'Your hair, Jonty,' he'd said, startled. 'What happened?' Jonty had winked and then followed the wink with a lascivious grin.

'You'd be astonished what a good sex life can do, Digby.' Jonty then tapped his neighbour's largely bald pate with an apodictic finger. 'Yours might even start growing again, if you get my drift.'

And Jonty had taken great delight one day upon discovering that Digby's fortunes had originally been built on the production of bone china.

'Then we're in the same business,' he'd cried, trium-
phantly making for one of his desk drawers and pulling out a
glossy colour brochure which he proudly placed in Digby's
hands. Digby read the title on the cover: *The Merriman
Museum of Miniature Collectables*. Then he started turning the
pages, staring with a morbid fascination at Jonty's product
line. There were enough thimbles to deck out a giant
centipede suddenly given to needlework, and whole panora-
mas of 'miniatures of classic pottery from historic collections'.
Digby felt a mild sensation of discomfort, not dissimilar to
the sort usually induced in him by looking at photographs of
Jonty's spreadeagled wife, but this was surely the pornography of commodities; the items gleamed at you come-
hitherishly in all their provocative unreality. The only thing
standing between you and their possession was money.
Digby wondered what on earth he was meant to say in the
face of such lavishly displayed fripperies; such a glittering
array of gimcrack baubles and fatuous bric-à-brac. But he had
temporarily forgotten that he was seldom obliged to say
anything at all with Jonty, since Jonty was so confident of
eliciting the requisite responses from the world around him
that he was more than happy to supply them himself, should
those responses not be swift enough arriving.

'Bang on the money, this stuff, eh Digby? I've nearly
finished the new catalogue. I'll put one aside for you.'

'Very gracious of you, Jonty.'

'Just being neighbourly.' Then La Merriman had arrived,
dressed as usual in clothes that evidently cost a small fortune,
every single item of which was at least one decade too young
for her. The twenty years between herself and Jonty appeared
to give her a sense of perennially vouchsafed youth. But
Jonty was now heading towards sixty, so his wife's teenage

clothing tended to elicit from her neighbours the inevitable remarks regarding lamb and mutton.

Digby, still with the invitation in his hand, went quickly to his writing table, took out a card and pen and wrote: 'Dear Jonty, How kind of you to invite me to your soirée. Unfortunately, I have for the last few days been suffering from a troubling indisposition which my doctor tells me is certainly infectious, and which can apparently be particularly distressing if contracted by any woman over twenty-five . . .'

There had already been one knock on the door that day and Digby had ignored it. So when the next bout of knocking started he was more than happy to ignore that too, until the letterbox snapped open and he heard Daisy's unmistakable voice.

'Well?' she asked after he had finished reading a few pages of the *Radix Manifesto*, which she had printed out in its entirety on Howard's Hewlett-Packard. If her son chose to compose anarchist manifestos in the parental home she felt the owner of that home at least had a right to read them. Digby turned back to the beginning and considered the title once more. 'Why is it called Universal Wolf?'

Daisy threw back her head and recited:

> *'Take but degree away, untune that string,*
> *And hark what discord follows. Each thing melts*
> *In mere oppugnancy; the bounded waters*
> *Should lift their bosoms higher than the shores,*
> *And make a sop of all this solid globe . . .*
> *Then every thing includes itself in power,*
> *Power into will, will into appetite,*
> *And appetite, a universal wolf,*

So doubly seconded with will and power,
Must make perforce a universal prey,
And last eat up himself.

'I taught him that when he was a boy,' she said proudly. 'It's from *Troilus and Cressida*. My Stratford Cressida was acclaimed, you know, Digby.'

'I seem to remember,' he said vaguely, turning through the pages once more. 'Did you also take him to Bath, out of interest?'

'I did indeed. He was delighted about those invisible doors back then, though he doesn't seem any too pleased about them these days, does he?' Suddenly Daisy's face chilled with concern, her snowy pallor scaling down to permafrost. 'And I suppose when it comes right down to it all that stuff about solicitors' offices and turning love into alimony is about me too. Not, I hasten to add, that I ever got too much in the way of cash out of my various husbands, bless their pointed little heads. I always seemed to be the one paying the bills as I remember it.'

'This is written by Howard is it? It's not actually signed.'

'Well it certainly sounds like him – it's the same sort of thing he talks to me about. When he bothers talking to me at all, that is.'

'Then I would have to say that whatever else the *Radix Manifesto* is, it appears to be an extended letter from a son to his mother. Might I keep it for tonight, do you think, and read the whole thing?'

So it was that Digby spent the evening reading the *Radix Manifesto*, and as he read he came to feel that Howard's lengthy address wasn't merely directed at Daisy but at him too, even though the two of them had never met.

His own book was effectively finished but Digby kept tinkering with the chapter 'Wilton Bone China in the Age of Coleridge'. Here he had confronted his conundrum: what precisely is the relationship between art and finance, or to put the matter another way, how can you measure the distance between a nation's soul and its wallet?

The company that still bore his name, Wilton Bone China, had gone from strength to strength after his departure, if you defined strength merely as success in the market place. You can still see its creations any day in the malls of London. Perfect objects in their way, with their faultless finishes and infinite shades of beige. As expressions of a culture though they made it very difficult for Digby to end his book on a positive note. His elegiac tone kept shifting imperceptibly into sardonic rancour. He could barely bring himself to look at them, those insipid little ladies with long dresses and bonnets. Moist-eyed spaniels that might have turned even Landseer's stomach. One delicate bimbo with a wand, he was confidently informed by the 'certificate of authenticity', represented the Queen of the Fairies. She wouldn't have lasted two seconds in the company of Puck or Oberon let alone Cobweb, Moth and Mustardseed. They would have eaten her, starting with her fleshy morsel of an upturned nose. If there were ever to be compiled an iconography of blandness then these lifeless confections would surely reign supreme within it. But they can be found in their thousands in the shop windows of Knightsbridge and Piccadilly. They gleam away quietly under expensive lights. Prettified gargoyles; icons voided of all sanctity or adoration; acres of disinfected kitsch. And purchasers still queue up to hand over notes in large denominations so they might carry them back as treasures to their homes. Authentic products of the

Potteries. So that's how it ends, he thought. Wilton Bone China: two centuries of family tradition. I suppose my old company's ended up having more in common with Jonty's scam than I'd care to think. Or was it ever thus?

He sat in his favourite chair and watched as the wind blew Theo's old swing back and forth. Perhaps the *Radix Manifesto* which had so unexpectedly landed in his lap could help him come a little closer to the heart of these questions and then he might finish his final chapter and his first, which would really mean that he had finished the book for in all other respects it was written, but Digby did seem to hesitate before polishing it off entirely, not least because he had managed to convince himself that when the last comma was shifted into place, the last t crossed and the last i dotted, he would die.

Dove

Theo arrived at the place in Balham where they were playing that night. He stood and looked around him. There was no one else there yet except for Dove, over in the corner in a world of his own as usual. Theo ordered his drink and gazed across at Zeno's guitar player. You only had to look at Dove to see how he'd got his name. Five foot two, with a small head and cropped hair, its colour somewhere between albino and blond, he moved with the rapid precision of a bird, and his face was so delicate it appeared to have been assembled from a canary's skeleton, using doped tissue for skin. He had once been something in the City though nobody was quite sure what; a sharp-eyed monitor of money's glittering career if not actually one of its protagonists. He had always lived with his mother in an enormous flat off Earls Court, which had been bought by Dove's long-dead father decades before. The first time Theo had ever met Dove's mother was at five o'clock in the evening and she'd been drinking gin. The second time he'd met her had been at ten in the morning and she'd also been drinking gin, with an air of distracted gentility but with something like methodical rigour nonetheless. Theo had joined in, happy to provide her with moral support. On both occasions she had been propped up on a

sofa with a shawl wrapped about her shoulders. Dove, it had
soon become apparent, had been barman, cook, attendant,
nurse. His mother was a highly intelligent and well-read lady
with white hair and delicate features like his own who, since
the death of her husband thirty years before, had apparently
divided the day between alcohol and oblivion, though the
line between the two might sometimes waver. Dove was
utterly devoted to her.

So when he came in one morning to find her growing stiff
where she lay, her thin lips already a pale blue, he broke
down. He managed to have her decently buried then he
went under. They said that he wept for the better part of a
week. The drugs slowed his tears to a trickle but did not
actually stop them. When his eyes finally dried, still shaking a
little and mildly sedated, he had made his way back to his
office in the City but he somehow couldn't find the
wherewithal to resume that life of arithmetical surmise and
calculation and ended up instead as an attendant in the
National Gallery where he contrived as much as possible to
spend his time in the little room containing the Vermeers.
Theo had once sought him out there and they had sat in
silence for five minutes surrounded by those evocations of
captured stillness, a portrayal of homely stasis that contained
all the noise in the world and then transcended it. Dove was
entirely still here too, all his usual avian twitches and twitters
gone amidst such achieved perfection: Dove at peace then,
framed in meditative quietness. Theo took the point.
Somehow those paintings did manage to stare down all the
turbulence and trouble of London's vortex spinning immediately beyond the museum's walls. And Dove himself seemed
to be translated into the language of their haunting serenity.
His silent smile asked Theo what might be the cost of such

stillness. As if Theo would be likely to know the answer to that. He'd even started laughing at the ridiculousness of the question as Dove had continued to smile at him in silence, a beatific monk in his cell of contemplation smiling his smile of wisdom at the latest worldly ordinand.

Dove's guitar-playing, so often dementedly speedy, had now become beguilingly slow, curiously detached and thoughtful, giving the impression he was playing from a great distance, at some much quieter gig, one the rest of the boys had never as yet quite made it to. His hero had always been Tal Farlow. He had even tried to imitate Tal's style but this had proved impossible. So many of that saintliest of guitarist's licks had been dependent on the span of his vast hands; Dove's tiny fingers had had no chance of imitating the chord voicings. He had once bought a miniature guitar hoping the Lilliputian fingerboard would provide him with the opportunity to gain Tal's stature in his own little world. It didn't though and Dove had returned to his beloved black Les Paul with its curiously liquid sound, notes like unpricked bubbles rising through the netting of the clef. And he had finally developed, once his mother's death had led him at last through the elephant's graveyard of memory and extinction, a spider-fingered dance over the strings which was entirely his own, unexpected scales curiously scattered in their distribution, reminding Theo sometimes of bats at twilight: an eyeflitter of bats queering the lengthening shadows.

And now he had been taken over by a woman who was bigger than he was, though to be fair everyone was bigger than Dove: even children on their way to school towered over Zeno's hyper-sensitive, guitar-playing midget. The other members of the band heard rumours of her peremptory activity, her not-to-be-challenged authority, in the occasional asides he would make: 'I can't do that night, sorry – Jennifer's bought tickets to the theatre' or 'I won't be at those gigs, Jennifer's booked us both a holiday that week'. All the boys resented Jennifer whom they had only ever met for a few minutes each. She was too big for him, too old for him, too bossy, too predatory, too sober, too normal. Dove, it seemed, could provoke the possessive element in people who otherwise didn't have anything to be possessive about. People who didn't possess a thing could soon come to feel that they at least possessed him.

One by one the others turned up. Reg the drummer. Paul the bass. Pete the pianist. And Breezer, tenor saxophone. Here they were then: Zeno, the legendary sextet. After a while they took a final swig of their drinks, shuffled up there and began. There was always a lift when they started, however unpromising the circumambient din. The human traffic in and out continued noisily. The pub was a vast lung filled with smoke, occasionally wheezing in a little fresh air as the door opened. They did their usual set. Breezer played his not-quite-solo version of *If You Were the Only Girl in the World*, adapted from Sonny Rollins, just to get things going, then followed with some heavyweight pantherish numbers from Dexter Gordon. Paul plucked away at his evergreen version of *Goodbye Porkpie Hat*. He was so devoted to Mingus that he'd named his cat after him. Dove did his tender version of *Somewhere Over The Rainbow*. Pete's fingers danced lightly over the keyboard on *It Might As Well Be Spring* and Theo ended by playing *Bye Bye Blackbird*, as he always did. They all noticed that Reg had started playing the drums with a renewed ferocity, as though he were trying to rupture the skins. Obviously having a hard time of it with his latest Regina, whoever she was. Then at the end money was shared out in six directions and the equipment stacked away before they stood for a final drink at the bar. They all stared over at Pete who was now deep in conversation with one of the female regulars, a stout middle-aged woman with a large, gnarled face.

'Looks promising,' Paul said, in his lugubrious Yorkshire tones.

'Likes his women heavily gigged, does our Pete,' Reg said, with what struck Theo as an unaccountable note of envy.

'You're not seeing what he's seeing,' the Breezer said.

'What's he seeing?'

'Reinforcements. Double-supports. Whalebone and elastic. Invisible rigging.'

'The woman herself is just the pretext, you mean?'

'The clothes-horse on which he hangs the accoutrements of his desire.'

'Christ, Breezer, you've been thinking this one through, haven't you? You're wasted on those kids you teach, mate. You should have your own psychiatrist's chair.'

'Pete intrigues me. I think if we could study him properly we'd all have a better notion how our minds worked. And our bodies.'

'What, men you mean?'

'Men. He does what we all do: he just takes it to its logical conclusion.'

'You mean the police station?'

'Well, he's only been there once, to be fair. He never did a bona fide stint inside like you, Theo.' They all sipped for a while before they fell to talking once more. This particular night Breezer was in didactic mood, something that was far from unusual. He was after all a physics teacher in Battersea, so he spent most of his working days being didactic with someone. And now he was lecturing Zeno.

'A quarter of a century ago Miles said that jazz was dead; that it had become a museum. Well, Wynton Marsalis is the curator. He's note-perfect – he knows how the song ends before it even starts. But jazz made itself up, the same way America made itself up, and now Wynton's coming at it from the far side of invention, after everything's already been done. His music never sweats. Think of the oceans of lyric perspiration that came out of old Louis when he was really blowing up there. But Wynton's dry; dry as a bone. I'm telling you, he doesn't sweat.'

'Wynton did sweat in the beginning though,' Dove said intently. 'I saw him during an early performance and he was sweating then.'

'Maybe.'

'No, honestly, Breezer, he did. I saw him. I was up very close and he was definitely sweating.'

'All right, for fuck's sake. All I'm saying is he doesn't sweat now.'

'But he does that classical stuff half the time these days, doesn't he,' Dove continued, not to be deflected from his defence of Marsalis. 'You probably wouldn't want a man sweating too much in a classical concert with his white collar and everything.'

'You know, Dove, there are times when fairmindedness if you take it far enough can become positively unreasonable, and you take it too far, mate. It starts to be . . . I don't know.'

'A form of tyranny?' Pete offered, having returned from his brief courtship and now once more unquestionably the editor helping to find the *mot juste* for the final edition.

The boys in the band turned and stared at the tyrant Dove

then, all five foot two inches and a hundred and ten pounds of him, as he smiled serenely back at them.

That night in the car Breezer was still itching with it, the injustice of Dove's perennial even-handedness.

'I think Dove's great, Theo, you know that, and both of us know Zeno could never have a better guitarist, but he can be an argumentative dwarf sometimes, can't he? A sort of miniaturised Goebbels with a smile. Why does he always have to be so *nice* about everybody? It's fucking unnatural.'

'He speaks very highly of you, Breezer.'

'Does he?' Breezer said, turning away from the road to look at Theo.

'Always. Thinks you're brilliant. Says if there were any justice in the world you'd be on the telly with that sax of yours.'

'Well, bless his little cotton socks. I take it all back.'

The Breezer's mighty hands, hairy and adipose, spun the driving wheel of his Land Rover this way and that and London's nightlights bleared by. The car juddered every time he engaged a new gear.

'Thought it might be the clutch,' he said. 'But I've a feeling it's electrical. It seems to be firing on three cylinders till it gets over three thousand revs, then it cuts in with the fourth. Could be the plugs, I suppose. Maybe one of the leads. Any expertise in this region, Theo?'

'None.' Theo's eye was caught by the copper bracelet the Breezer wore around his left wrist, to siphon the arthritic vapours that might otherwise rot his big bones. Breezer was the biggest of the band. His caftan was the size of a small tent. Coltrane's *Ascension* was harrowing the air inside the car. This was Breezer's true hero in his disintegrative, mystic phase. At some of the shrilling shrieks of the horn Theo felt as if razor blades had been blasted across his brain. Breezer himself, like Theo, was still stuck resolutely inside the song – he hadn't escaped into this stratospheric wilderness of self-expression. Good thing too, thought Theo. Trust the song. The song says it all.

'Funny that Pete should end up as the only one amongst us pulling at gigs. Doesn't that strike you as funny?'

Theo shrugged. Nothing much struck him as funny at the moment and Pete was welcome to his Oedipal pursuits as far as he was concerned. Obliterating the distinction between sex and social work wasn't Theo's notion of a good night out.

'The last time any of the rest of us made it was when you were screwing that little piece in Battersea.'

'We were screwing each other.'

'Well, that sounds very PC, Theo, but as a DIY man my knowledge of screws suggests that something's got to drive its way into something else.'

'Find a more mutual way of putting it, Breezer.' The big man pondered, scratching his thick beard roughly while he drove with one hand.

'All right then, that little piece in Battersea you were two-way adapting.'

'Makes us sound as though we were running AC/DC.'

'No, I've never suspected you of that. With Pete, I'm not so sure. I mean, that crease in his Levis. In my experience when a bloke feels he has to be *quite* so fastidious . . . And the one he was chatting up tonight could easily have been a bloke underneath that dress. Straight from the boilermaker's union . . . You actually spoken to Pete recently?'

'Said hello. Didn't want to interrupt his jive with the raven-haired madonna. What's she called again?'

'Dot. So you haven't actually spoken?'

'What about?'

'The future of the band.' *The future of the band.* Theo had never even contemplated any such concept. The band was there and they were all in the present. Wasn't that enough? The future and its contemplation, its increments, its penalties, was something he tended to do his best to avoid. Particularly at the moment.

'The future of the band,' he repeated vacantly. 'What about it?'

'Just something that seems to be on Pete's mind. Whenever he's not playing piano or trying to bed one of his surrogate mothers, that's what he goes on about. You all right, by the way, Theo?'

'Why?'

'You seem a bit distracted somehow.'

'Jill chucked me out.'

'Ah.' There was a pause. Theo saw a boat's navigating lights somewhere out over the dark water of the Thames. 'Any chance of you creeping back in through the cat-flap?'

'Don't think so, Breezer, to be honest. Not this time.'

Jill

That Friday evening Jill stood with her mother in her parents' large kitchen in Kensington. They had eaten early so they could pack and be ready for their journey the following day. Her father still planned trips as though she were ten years old: early bed, early breakfast, off on the road by seven-thirty. They were only going to Kent, for God's sake. Her parents had decided it would be good for her to 'get away' for a few days. Her mother, who was washing the plates while Jill dried, turned to look at her daughter and sighed. She often sighed at her these days and Jill very much wished that she wouldn't. Her mother was sighing as she always did at the list of catastrophic relationships her daughter had already managed to notch up. She didn't take after either of her parents in that department, and that was for sure. She'd met Theo shortly before his imprisonment which, in her mother's view, the girl had seen as some sort of provocation to romantic loyalty. Getting married with him still locked up, indeed. A hard-nosed journalist on weekdays she might be but it was Mills and Boon all the way at weekends with her sundry menfolk. Seemed to switch her brain off after the first kiss. Until she finally turfed them out. What had caused her to develop this fascination with unsuitable and signally unsuccessful musicians? For Theo had certainly not been the first. There had been a flautist with a wonky eye for a time, then a vegan soprano saxophonist from Cleethorpes. She'd even had some chap who played cowbells; or was it a vibraphone? Admittedly they were the sort of people her work obliged her to meet, but she didn't have to take them home and tuck them up in bed, did she? You'd have thought she'd been studying their profiles long enough by now to know precisely what to expect.

Jill had only had one single cohabiting relationship before Theo, one of those modern variants on marriage where they at least shared the same house for a few years, and that had been with a wacky if affable young man called Alex. Alex played lead guitar in a characteristically unpromising band known as The Quarks, and Jill had seemed for a while greatly taken with his musical monomania, druggy drawl and leather fetishism.

'Why Quarks?' her mother had asked him when Jill had finally brought her boyfriend over to Kensington to introduce him one afternoon. 'Is it something to do with sub-particle physics?'

'It was James Joyce's word for thunder in *Finnegans Wake*,' Alex had replied. Then, opening his mouth wide he had roared: 'QUAAAAAAAAAAAAAARK! Jimmy thought it was the noise God made when he was in a temper.'

'Oh,' Mrs Simpson had said, startled by the fearsome racket of Alex's exposition which had been sudden and very loud indeed. 'I still don't quite see the relevance . . .'

'That's because you haven't heard our stuff, Mrs Simpson,' Alex said, then leapt up and started hammering on the table, while accompanying his rhythmic palmistry with his own percussive cries: 'Ba ba ba dah dah ba dah dah. Ba dah DAH

DAH. QUAAAAAAAAAAAAAAAARK.' The knives and
forks finally stopped rattling and Alex sat down again
grinning at her. 'Get Jill to bring you and the old man to one
of our gigs.'

'Yes, I really must do that. I'm sure Mr Simpson would be
absolutely fascinated.'

'Your old flame Alex was sweet in a way,' her mother
now said to her. Anybody seemed sweet these days
compared with Theo, though she'd liked him well enough;
it was hard not to like him. Marrying him was something else
altogether. 'But you have to admit there was something a
little odd about the way his head was wired up.'

'What do you mean, mother?' Jill asked. The twirling
Chinese lantern shed a scatter of luminous peelskin across the
parquet floor.

'What do I mean?' her mother repeated meditatively,
lifting her hands briefly from the soapy water. The suds were
seafoam on her fingers, bubbling prisms breaking up one by
one. 'Well, as I said, he was very sweet. But he was obviously
barking, darling. And those tight leather trousers he wore
didn't leave much to the imagination, did they?'

'What started you off thinking about Alex?'

'Oh, I was just reminiscing about your love life, that's all.
You're sure this time? About finishing with Theo? I mean,
you are actually married to this one, you know.'

'I'm sure.'

Now it was Jill's turn to ponder. She remembered the first
time she had ever heard Theo play. She was doing her yearly
feature on the musical life of London's pubs. The sweet tones
of his sad trumpet contrasted satisfactorily in her mind with
the bellicose riffs of Alex's supercharged guitar solos, with
which she had by then grown bored, as bored as she had

grown with Alex himself. Alex had wielded his axe (as he always called it) as though it were a prosthetic extension to his penis, swivelling out from his hips and seeding the air around him with the speedy blur of rock's ectoplasm. But Theo held his trumpet like a golden chalice. He tipped it upwards gently as though trying to drink the last melancholy drops from the grail, and then he sang a song with it – subdued, half-defeated, meditative. All his melodies were heavy with gravid thoughtfulness. It was as though they had to move so tenderly to avoid hurting themselves, as though one note never exactly knew where it might turn to find the next.

Jill knew enough about jazz to be able to hear the influences behind this sound. In the fullness of his yearning tone there was something of the early Satchmo's ballads, though without anything of that legendary attack and bite. In the hesitations of his trumpet's breathing, its troubled modulations, sometimes a hint of Chet Baker. But in his refusal to race the notes, to play those vertiginous and dizzy scales so many jazz players sprint up and down, it was Miles Davis all the way. In the intonation, in the troubled, melancholy tone it was all Miles Davis without, as it were, Miles Davis. Perhaps because of this he never fluffed a note or played a clinker. There was accuracy as well as decorum in his serpentine progressions. Emotion. Its eggshells. Somewhere at some time he had learnt to tread softly. But he could never follow Miles in his offhand insouciance, even though he certainly agreed with him about using no vibrato: what's the point, after all – you're going to shake enough when you're old. The birth of the cool and maybe its death too, in the way Miles made the muted horn breathe, for what a chill breath it could sometimes be. Ice steaming in its heart.

But Theo wasn't cool. In fact he could sound so warm in his tones of measured regret that his fellow musicians wondered at times whether he was playing jazz at all, despite the flattened notes, the changes he moved through, the substitutions, even the modes he sometimes employed in imitation of his master. He had a tendency to deliver his songs straight, eloquent, honest and straight, for he loved the melody lines of old standards and made his way across them with the focused intensity of a high-wire artist on the tightrope. When he played, say, *Bye Bye Blackbird* he was invariably so entranced by the shift to the seventh in the middle section that he could never bring himself to do anything elaborate or sophisticated with it. He simply put his heart and soul into caressing the notes.

'We're a jazz band, Theo,' the saxophonist had said to him one night. 'So don't you think we might jazz it up a bit? When you do those ballads I sometimes think you'd be better off with Mantovani behind you, instead of us.'

'The song says it all,' Theo had replied, because that was what he believed. The song said it all.

And when Jill had heard him that first evening playing so many quiet ballads, *Embraceable You, I Cover the Waterfront, Someday He'll Come Along, She's Funny That Way* and, astonishingly, since she could never have imagined a jazz band playing it, *Slow Boat to China*, with his notes triste and languorous at the same time, seeming to calm the impatient rhythms of the rest of the band with the weighty pace of his considerations, she had felt touched by him before he'd even spoken a word to her. In fact she had been touched by his eyes more than once that evening, his hungry look had stroked her face, her neck, her breasts. She had been both flattered and embarrassed at the same time, as she turned away to write her notes. She knew he would come over to her table as soon as the set was finished. It was as though they'd already silently agreed: the song says it all. So trust the song.

And the first time they'd lain in bed together he had said to her, 'I could tell that you heard the songs, you know. I could tell by the way you moved your head that they'd touched you. I can't understand people music doesn't touch. Sometimes you finish playing and all you can hear is this wall of laughter and shouts as though someone's throwing noisy smoke at you. Do you think they even listen to the music in their own houses?'

'They might just use it for sexual wallpaper,' she said. She was naked beside him.

'Sexual wallpaper,' he repeated. 'Christmas baubles. Bunting in the bar.'

'Noise to fill up the silence. But just as long as somebody hears, Theo.'

'To play at all you've always got to believe that one person hears, at least one person. You know, I could never make love to anyone who couldn't hear the music,' he had said and Jill had believed him. It certainly wasn't true, though. Theo could make love to just about anything bearing a female shape when the mood was on him. And, as Jill was to discover once his sentence was over, that mood seldom went away for long. He did his number with women as fluently as his numbers on the horn. She had the funny feeling that, while he was saying the words, he actually meant them. But maybe all womanisers were like that. She'd misread Theo. She'd once assumed that only a little bad luck stood between him and fame. Could that be true? Was he really as good as she'd thought when she first heard him? They say love makes you blind, but who knows whether it might also affect your hearing?

When she had brought Theo home, precisely one month before his arrest at the Koré gallery, the reaction had at first been enthusiastic. Theo had been on his best behaviour and had groomed himself convincingly for the occasion – for when Theo was good he could be very good indeed. Her mother had fallen for him almost as quickly as Jill herself. This was in the early days when he had so effortlessly, so sweetly celebrated Jill's mind and body, particularly her body, her own small, compact, fully-fleshed little body; when he had seemed so permanently eager to find himself once more between the sheets with her, that it simply hadn't occurred to her until much later that he might have grown used to celebrating every body that came his way with something like the same enthusiasm. If celebrate was really the right word: more and more it seemed to her that it wasn't. Whatever drove Theo on it certainly wasn't joy. What was it? Something to do with his father and mother had left him always on the move, terrified of being trapped. But then, she supposed, if your father sets about killing your mother it must inevitably unsettle your domestic expectations to some extent. Had it not been for the way that spell of imprisonment had given her his undivided attention for nine months would they ever have married? Now she would never know. And, curiously, she was no longer entirely sure she greatly cared. It can be very liberating, finally deciding to move on. Or even to move someone else on.

'All done,' her mother said, as she put the last plate away. Jill stared into her face, rounder now than it had been once and with a growing web of creases about her green eyes, and she wondered if that would be the shape of her own face thirty years down the line. 'Looking forward to the trip tomorrow, darling?'

'Yes, mum. Whitstable again.'

'Whitstable. Just like the old days. We can have a lovely meal in that restaurant next to the harbour. I'm sure you've done the right thing, by the way. Finishing with Theo, I mean.' She paused for a moment. 'I suppose your generation decided to go for the excitement.'

'How do you mean, mum?'

'Well, our lot were brought up to choose reliability. And it worked, on the whole. Certainly did for me. Though I'd have to admit that whole years could sometimes go by without too much happening in the way of physical contact or, well you know, any of that sort of thing. So I suppose some might say it's really six of one and half a dozen of the other, the whole business with men and women, I mean – paying your money and taking your choices.' Jill caught her mother's eye and something about her well-worn expression of tragic resignation started her laughing, thereby provoking a mild eruption shortly afterwards from Mrs Simpson herself. And once they'd started neither of them could stop. So that was the way they were when Mr Simpson leaned his slightly baffled face around the kitchen door – his wife and his daughter hugging one another and gasping for breath, tears of uncontrollable mirth streaming down their faces. The prospect of the family's first divorce had evidently made his womenfolk merry.

'Come on now, girls,' he said firmly. 'We haven't even got to Whitstable yet.'

NPG

Pete arrived at the pub and threw the paper down on the bar. 'There,' he said. They all stared at the copy of the *North Putney Gazette* that lay in front of them. 'Success. Turn to Page 12.' So they did and all across the Arts Page was a feature about Zeno. They leaned over one another's shoulders to catch glimpses of themselves in the photograph, reading out the more pleasing phrases : '. . . brilliant . . . unknown perhaps to any but a few . . . that won't last long . . . a subtlety of interpretation that surely deserves a recording contract . . . if some A and R man wants to make his name . . .'

'This make it easier?' Pete asked as he took out another five copies from his bag. Each member of the band hunted through his individual copy for references to himself. Theo was particularly pleased: 'To take on the mantle of the early Miles Davis might seem reckless, but Theo Wilton's playing achieves such lyrical subtlety that surely the master himself would have approved.'

They looked up finally and grinned at one another. Breezer raised his glass of lager high. 'Today the *North Putney Gazette*. Tomorrow the world.'

'And it's got us another gig,' Pete said. 'Just down the road from here. Looks like I'm not going to have to desert you boys after all. So, is anybody going to order me a drink for all my trouble?'

Five-sixths of Zeno surged forward to the bar then to buy their piano player anything he wanted.

Smoke and Mirrors

Digby stood in the doorway to his kitchen and stared. In one of the tricks time had started playing on him he saw it once more, not as it now was, tidy and spruce, its bottles and bowls in neat arrays, but as it had been years before when Victoria had still inhabited the place and Theo was a small boy. He could see her as vividly as if she were standing five feet from him, the miniature perfection of her person framed bizarrely in the tatterdemalion chaos all around, a freakish hinterland of ruined foods and homeless smells. He had seen men who'd been to war reduced to silence for minutes at a time at the sight of that kitchen. A cave from some unidentified mythology, it was easy to feel that something without a name must lurk there working up an appetite, but an appetite for what? The meals, he'd had to admit in fairness, were invariably wonderful in their anarchic Mediterranean manner, though frequently intermittent and always unpredictable. Never anything fried, particularly not fish and chips. Her early days in Sammy's Fish Bar had provided her with a lifetime's antidote to that English speciality. Theo in those days ate with a savage undistractibility as though civilisation had not yet been invented. For him, at that stage, it probably hadn't. And when Digby came to think of it, it didn't seem to be making too much of an impression on him even now.

Escape the present, however briefly, and time collapses, shedding all dictatorial perspectives. So Digby travelled on in his head back to Stoke. He had in fact only been back there once a few years ago to do a little research for his book. He had not enjoyed the trip. Stoke didn't seem to have improved in the intervening years. It was less dirty but only because there was less work. The bottle ovens had now gone. They had closed their great mouths on the city, putting an end to the occluded skies, the bad black breath of industry's halitosis. It had been dirty all right but its dirt had talked serious money. At times it had even raised its voice, rather grandly, to leave vast public buildings with classical façades as proof of a certain probity of purpose, a stony compensation for the countless broken men with their charred lungs and exiguous earnings. Now the town itself looked as though it had stopped breathing. Even Wedgwood's Etruria had long before vanished, converted into a retail park, a marina, a leisure centre. One single kiln remained as a *memento mori*, its heart unfired for over half a century. Digby had gazed and pondered and remembered how the chimneys of Wilton Bone China would once cough their smoke into the sky when the firemouths were baited. Fragments of pottery tooled up by archaeologists had allowed us to piece together civilisations from thousands of years before. Its resistance to corrosion and rotting meant it outlived the corruptions of swamp and sand, the ravages of arid wastes and stormy deluge. It survived and whatever remained of its crazing spiderweb on history's shattered glaze led you on through dark corridors, to show what had been lost and found again millennia before, to show us where we'd all got started, and yet this town that actually made the stuff had lost its own shape and identity in less than half a century; had lost the marrow of its meaning and found nothing else with which to replace it, no new bone for bone china, only old bone for ossuaries: they at least never stopped their necessary trade. A few of the big consolidated names remained though Wilton Bone China itself had long before moved far away, but there was no longer a bottle oven to be seen on a skyline once crammed with them. Electricity couldn't fill the void that had been left despite its flashes and its bleeps and the way it made the constellations fade at night.

In his memory it had all been canals and railways and pottery chimneys but when he had finally gone back there it had seemed to be all roads now; roads and cars and utility buildings offering cheap food and night frolics, and the occasional deconsecrated chapel up for sale. He had found the graveyard and laid flowers on the resting place of his mother and father. Something to decompose above their decomposing bones. Something else he'd surely never do again, though his own bones felt as though they'd be decomposing soon enough.

And Digby had been unable to walk those streets without thinking of Uncle Freddie, his father's younger brother and the tutor of his own early years, for they had once walked them together so often.

He'd simply arrived one day when Digby was four years old and had never again left until Digby was on his way to university. Never left, that is, except for his intermittent 'trips', from which he returned either utterly drained or exhilarated to the point of mania. There would be nothing for it then but more walks about Stoke, an endless peripatetic tutorial. For it was Uncle Freddie who had provided all the crucial years of Digby's education; who had taught him most of what he knew about languages, science, poetry and history with a memorable potency which had never entirely left him.

He'd cut a distinctive figure back in the Potteries in those days. With a black coat that stretched almost to his feet and his slanted beret perched on his head, his tall, thin figure – he was an inch or more over six foot – and his pale bony face with the wire-rimmed spectacles and pebble lenses, gave him the appearance of an unworldly and slightly alien priest. He wasn't really so unworldly, though; Digby discovered that soon enough. He spoke four languages fluently. He followed all developments in the modern sciences with the keenest interest. It was rumoured (everything of any real importance about Freddie seemed to be rumoured) that he *had* once studied for the priesthood in Rome or perhaps Lisbon, though sometimes he spoke as though it might have been Paris or Oxford, before difficulties of some unspecified sort had beset his training. Spiritual, intellectual, sexual? Nobody really knew except Freddie and he certainly wasn't saying. He had an encyclopaedic knowledge of heresies and a great fondness for the grand heresiarchs. If you study them with care, he would say, you'll discover the shape of the human mind, all its desires and deceits, every corkscrewed oddity of which the benighted heart of man is capable, though these are in fact infinite in possibility and each, however sordid, is unique – like the crystals forming snowflakes. He had soon passed on to Digby an unallayed devotion to the work of Blaise Pascal, whom he would frequently quote from memory in the original French, also the writings of Lord Acton whose lectures at Cambridge he claimed to have attended in his youth. He described them and Acton himself with such vivid recall that Digby believed him, though as the years passed he became aware that Freddie often appeared to be describing other lectures he had attended at the universities of Oxford, Durham, Edinburgh, Paris, Berlin and Rome, and it struck even the youthful Digby that it was unlikely that his curious uncle could have gone to all of these places for any length of time. But Freddie's claims, like the Church of which he spoke in *ex cathedra* tones, while never actually attending any of its services, were universal.

What a sight they must have been on the streets of Stoke, the tall, thin, priestly figure in black and the young boy hurrying along beside him, for Freddie's gait was as brisk as the swift torrent of words that poured from his mouth. The smoke from his Turkish cigarettes, supplied exclusively from a shop on the Charing Cross Road and delivered in small, scented wooden boxes once a month, left its trail in the air behind them. The local inhabitants would occasionally sniff it as they passed and turn back curiously to look at the pair of them. Amidst the skyfuls of smoke in that smokiest of towns, the wispy traces from Freddie's foreign cigarettes were distinctive. The faintest elegiac whiff of the Ottoman Empire.

From the top of Century Street, one of their frequent stopping points, Freddie would wave his arm towards the vast array of bottle ovens in the distance all spewing their smoke into the sky.

'If I were Virgil and you were Dante, I would now introduce you to one of the circles of the Inferno. I do wonder which of them you might opt for, Digby. You've hardly had a chance to refine your taste in sin as yet so I dare say you might find yourself temporarily nonplussed. Instead I suppose I'll have to take you home for tea. To the sinless mansion of your progenitors.'

He would sometimes insist that they walk around the various public gardens like Hanley Park.

'Victorian grandees built these for the pleasure of their proletariat,' he said, 'so the poor grimy fellows could grab a mouthful or two of air before the next shift.' They would walk for hours up and down the populous streets, with Freddie stopping to stare with shameless curiosity at clutches of children holding one another's hands and walking along the pavement. They giggled at the oddity of his dress as he continued to peer at them through his small convex lenses. Digby had often wished he could disappear entirely from these scenes but Freddie was invariably oblivious to the commotion his presence created.

'Beneath the smuts and the fog and the filth,' he would say loudly enough for the whole street to hear, 'desire continues here as uncontrollably as between the silk sheets of palaces, Digby. Another of life's little mysteries. These people will never make a revolution, whatever the scholastic epigones of Doctor Marx might argue. But they will continue to produce marvels. Do you know, I do think I might be in need of a drink.'

In the Jug public house on Jug Bank, by the side of the blacksmith's, he would down four pints of beer in such quick succession that Digby wondered at his capacity. He had obviously practised elsewhere; in point of fact, it wouldn't be too long before he would be practising at Wilton Manor. Afterwards they would walk once more along streets where the washing was hung out in a cat's cradle of lines from one terraced side to the other, sometimes almost dragging the wet and heavy cotton sheets along the cobbles. Freddie's indiscretions became even louder when he had some drink inside him. If he'd been overheard by any of the working men they might well have beaten him for the lordly condescension of his insults. He and Digby were trespassing in any case, stealing intimate images from the parish of the others' streets, just as the workers would have been if they'd been caught uprooting shrubs from the grounds of Wilton Manor.

'I would have thought the polluted air deposits as much filth on their garments as their strenuous scrubbing has just taken off,' Freddie would flute merrily, lighting another Turkish cigarette. He snorted out smoke plumes of a delicate violet. 'My surmise would be that they'd be better off submerging themselves in the canal fully clothed, though I can see that might be a little chilly in the winter months. Now imagine if Ophelia had drowned in a canal, Digby; you can see how irrevocably that would have altered the play, can't you? Curious the associations a single word can bring along with it, you know. One would be hard put to imagine Lear on a tram, for example, or Othello on a bicycle or Lady Macbeth in a haberdasher's shop choosing a warm vest to keep out the pesky northeasterlies. You only have to think of Oedipus picking up a prescription for his suppurating sockets and you're done with the tragic perspective of Sophocles for ever. The world of the plays has been banished to another world, another language which can't contain it without translating it into something else entirely. And yet the funny thing is that one can always imagine almost any Pope at any time in a brothel. However ascetic, they always seem perched on the cusp of corruption. Odd, really. It wouldn't in any way contradict our faith to find them in there, merely point up a few of its darker precepts. The fact that even priests can be found stripped-down for concupiscence is a sort of tribute in a way to the perennial truths of the Roman creed. Eucharist and confessional are at the heart of the Church. The need to feed the spirit combined with the acknowledgement that it is continually outrun by the flesh and its dark desires.' Then back they would go finally to the silent shadows of Wilton Manor.

Sunlight had to fight its way into Digby's childhood home. And once there it was not always treated as a welcome guest. Rooms made of mahogany may famously reflect every sound but they can swallow the sunlight entirely. Vast drapes and deep brocades conspired between them a pre-Copernican conspiracy: the universe, it seemed, was not heliocentric after all. Galileo might as well have got on with polishing his telescope and eating his spaghetti because sunshine, on the hill outside Stoke to which Digby and Freddie returned after their erratic excursions, was an intermittent presence, so intermittent as at times to seem almost as alien as Freddie's priestly garb. The notion that all life depended upon it would have sounded scandalous in most of the gloomy, echoing rooms of the Wilton family home. Such a notion might well have deserved the name of heresy. Digby could still hear the parrot-squawk of Uncle Freddie's high-pitched laughter through its corridors and the scraping of his consonants on the stone walls. 'I rather think the Holy Office was right to try to scotch any such idea before it caught on, don't you, my boy? The sun at the centre of our planetary system, indeed. A few months spent lodging in Stoke would have put that uppish little Eyetie right.'

'I want to take you to lunch,' Daisy said later that day.

'Lunch,' Digby repeated, as though the mere sound of the

word was a bell tolling. Daisy noted how he seemed to recoil in a tone of mild alarm at any invitation whatsoever. What a curious old man he was.

'Well, you're always making me things here, little bits of this and that while you pour me wine and I thought that if we were going to have a chat about international capital and the new movement my son's organising to overthrow it, we could at least pop out for an hour.'

'But where to, Daisy?'

'How about that pub, the one they've given the silly name to?'

Digby's face darkened another shade. He could still vividly recall the last time he had been there. It was just at the edge of Wandsworth Common, a mere five minutes' walk from his house. He had sat nursing his drink, inundated by music of such aggressive and repetitive squalor that it had seemed no more than a punitive sequence of electronic grunts and vocal howls. He had thought of the Bacchae, immured as he was in smoke and fury; thought of the rationalist Pentheus, his head soon to be removed from his body in an ecstasy of unreason by a clutch of ululating and demented women, one of them his own delirious mother (Freddie had read *The Bacchae* out loud with him when he was eleven).

When mercifully a tune would occasionally emerge out of this cacophonous rut, living proof that order could be born from aleatory couplings in primeval soup, it was invariably backdated by a minimum of thirty years, thus confirming Digby in his increasingly antiquarian instincts. All the great modern artists and potters had been antiquarians or primitives. How many pictures of cars and boats and trains did Picasso ever make? He'd employed pretty much the same subject matter as the Etruscans. His own beloved Jakob had made pots as though he were doing it two thousand years before, utterly undistracted by the noisy clutter of modernity. Now a new age is arriving, he thought; a new millennium is about to be announced and it looks, astonishingly, as though I'm going to be in it. What will it be? What novelty will it put before our eyes? How much more modernity can modernity take? Or will it start rolling backwards at last?

He had gone to sit outside and only then had noticed that the pub had been renamed. It was now the Faith and Firkin. This pseudo-rustic fatuity did nothing for his good humour. He'd sat at one of the rough-hewn trestle tables as far as possible from the blaring jukebox within. He had been there for less than five minutes when a young woman with a baby arrived at the next table. A moment later her companion came out with the drinks and Digby had gazed at him. He was a man in his twenties wearing tight torn jeans and an exorbitantly battered leather jacket. His hair was dyed a vivid scarlet. A single silver safety-pin dangled from his left nostril and as he sat down he belched. This was not an inadvertent belch. He seemed to put considerable effort into extending the toad-croak for as long as possible, as though he were trying to turn himself inside out. It was a declamatory belch extending all the way down to his chest; a self-satisfied manifesto of a belch, and Digby found himself wondering what the self-advertising belcher thought he was saying to the world with his windy and noisome grunt. As though hearing his silent thoughts the young man had turned to him and grinned crookedly. One of his front teeth was missing.

'All right, old fella?' he'd called. Digby had bowed as graciously as he could manage then and leaving his drink unfinished had slowly walked back home to contemplate the mysteries of youth and age.

'Are you here, darling?' Daisy said, rousing him from his reverie with a gentle finger on his cheek.

'I don't think I could face that pub, Daisy, to be honest.'

'Let's at least have a walk on the Common then.' But Digby had given up on that too. The last time he had gone out there he had been stopped in his tracks, mesmerised into a brief paralysis, by a crow eating dung. There had been something about the glint of its eye – the emperor crow strutting about above his kingdom of corpses and *merds*. He started to tell Daisy about the crow.

'So nature's turned against you as well, Digby.'

'The crows aren't really the problem. My eyes have always been bad and with so many' – he tried to think of a delicate way of expressing it – 'tantoblin tarts placed in my way . . .'

'Tantoblin tarts?' Daisy said. 'Oh, you mean dogshit. Yes, it does sometimes seem to have pretty much replaced the grass, doesn't it?'

'You know, Daisy, one day I was out there and some mutt stopped in front of me, right in front of me, to deposit the most atrocious pile of . . . I'm not even sure what it was. It's what you'd get if you pulled the plug out of the world's sump. A woman – dressed up in wellies, tartan headscarf and sunglasses, which struck me as a trifle optimistic given the meteorological conditions at the time – comes striding up, large as life and twice as natural, and trilled, "Teddy's got worms, I'm afraid." She seemed positively cheerful about it. Since then I can't even hear the word beige without mephitic vapours seeming to rise up from the cellar.'

She had started laughing, bending the whole of her delicate body forward from the midriff and turning her face up to the ceiling, and he couldn't help but remember the scene in *Noah's Rainbow* where Chuck Hill saw her through the restaurant window doing exactly the same thing. The first time he had ever seen her. He had fallen in love there and then. Digby found himself wondering if she made love off-screen in the same way she made love on it and if so which had come first. In *Noah's Rainbow* it had been lyrical, choreographed, infinitely yielding and gentle. Was that the way she'd been with her exes?

Suddenly Daisy stopped laughing, stopped so suddenly in fact that it was as if the script demanded it. But if there was a script then Digby hadn't seen it. Now she sighed instead and the sigh was even more beguiling than the laughter. Where had she learnt to sigh like that? In bed or at RADA? To the invisible and unreal touch of the camera she responded with reality. Or an appearance of reality so compelling that it was indistinguishable from reality. Where that left reality, Digby had no idea.

'Then I'm coming over with some lunch for you. No, don't start arguing. I'll be back here at one. Do you have some wine?'

'I always have wine, Daisy, you know that. I keep claret for you and vodka for my errant son. Though it has to be said that you come far more often than he does.'

'Then I will come again and we can talk.'

And come again she did, with cheeses, thin slivers of Parma ham and French bread.

'What is it, do you think, this modern affliction?'

'Plenty's desolation?'

'So you read Howard's manifesto then.'

'Yes. I thought your son put it rather well. We swallow and swallow our expensive fare until we're the ones vomited out.'

'He says that's what we're doing with the planet, you know. Vomiting out so many fumes that the sky has a hole in its head. The ozone layer. Shakespeare's universal wolf is getting fatter. He explained how with global warming that passage is literally coming true:

> *And hark what discord follows. Each thing melts*
> *In mere oppugnancy; the bounded waters*
> *Should lift their bosoms higher than the shores,*
> *And make a sop of all this solid globe . . .*

If the ice-cap melts and the oceans rise whole islands will disappear.' Then they both fell silent for a while.

'Digby, did you ever go to Thailand in your pottery days?'

'Once.'

'Did you come across a place called Great Anakh?'

'No.'

'I've looked in the atlas and there's nowhere with that name.'

'One of the early rulers?'

'I thought of that. But it doesn't seem to be in any of the books.' Then Daisy reached into her large canvas bag and pulled out a number of objects. She laid them on the floor. A gas mask, a balaclava, a black cotton kerchief and sheets of computer print out.

'What do you make of these?'

'Where did you get them?'

'I found them in Howard's room.'

'Ah.'

'What do you think they might be for?'

'Confrontations with people who use tear gas, the sort of confrontations where you'd prefer not to be recognised?'

'That's what I thought,' she said. He remarked to himself again how she was the physical antitype to Vicki; thin, wispy and blonde, where his wife had been short, fully-fleshed and black-haired. Theo had her hair as well as her eyes, though he didn't seem to have inherited much of her flesh these days. Daisy picked up one of the sheets from the floor.

'You always seem to know these things, Digby. So tell me, what is thermite?'

'Thermite,' Digby said confidently, remembering his pottery-related chemical training from all those years before, 'is a mix of fine aluminium and iron oxide.'

'What's it for?'

'It was often used in the repair of heavy ironworks, among other things.'

'What other things?'

'Well, it produces an extremely high temperature on combustion. Around three thousand degrees if memory serves. At a push you can use it in explosives. The rudimentary sort. Home-made variety. Precisely what Jock Lewes used in 1941 in the early days of the SAS to blow up enemy airfields.'

'Were you in the SAS, Digby?' At this question Digby began to laugh uninhibitedly, something she could not remember ever seeing him do before. His crooked teeth were clearly visible in the rictus of his mirth. The blue vein on his forehead throbbed. The involuntary grimace of his features as he chortled disturbed her. There seemed to be some dreadful memory of violence in it.

'No,' he said, when his chest had finally stopped heaving, 'I seem to remember they called it something else at the time, but I wasn't in it anyway. I was in Aldershot, squinting at inventories and handing out boots and army blouses to disgruntled squaddies.'

'Are you going to Jonty's soirée, by the way?'

'Certainly not. I'm far too ill, as you can testify. You've witnessed how the latest pestilence has laid me low. The plague man has been with his bell. He painted a cross on my lintel. I'm surprised you were even prepared to step over the threshold.'

'You're a malingerer, Wilton, and you'll come to a sticky end one of these days.'

Cryptography

Thailand Great Anakh. Daisy had already been to the local library. She had hunted through the *Encyclopaedia Britannica* and a clutch of weighty guides about the Far East. Nothing. She had even phoned up the Thai Embassy to see if they could help. Nothing again. Great Anakh appeared to be no one and nowhere. So why did the phrase keep recurring in all of Howard's communications? Whenever the story started to get interesting, it would break off and there would be a single message: See *Thailand Great Anakh*. She keyed it into his computer: *Thailand Great Anakh* and the words flashed up as she clicked on: *Greetings to the law*. Every time she keyed the words in, she received the same message. Greetings to the law? Why, she wondered, could her son never say precisely what he meant? Or even precisely where he was, if it came to that. Ungrateful little sod.

She picked up the photograph from the table and looked at Howard's face. There was so much of James in his features. She went back downstairs and walked over to a shelf crammed with framed photographs. She picked up the portrait of James she kept there, taken the week they were married. What a brilliant smile he'd had back then. It did seem a bright decade in retrospect. Sometimes, as she peered down along the unreliable corridors of memory, even luminous.

Daisy had a professional interest in images, particularly the sort created for public consumption, whether they were to be hung on a temple wall or in a gallery or even filtered through the riddling smoky beams of a cinema projector. After all, she had been turned into one. It was in fact the process of being turned into one that had led to her meeting her first ex, Howard's father, James: James Oldham, Photographer. Domiciled, in those days anyway, in Chelsea. She had been playing Miranda opposite Gielgud's Prospero at Stratford and her freshly acquired agent had insisted on some portraits of her which could perhaps afford to be a little more striking than the standard, stagy ones commissioned by the theatre itself. Off she had been sent to London, to a mews studio off the King's Road, an enormous studio – since the first floor had been taken out to give space for booms and lighting fixtures overhead – which carried over its smoked glass door the name James Oldham.

There had been a thrill to it back then, she could not deny it. By that stage in the late Sixties James's name was often mentioned along with Bailey, Donovan and Lichfield. He had already photographed Twiggy, Julie Christie, Jean Shrimpton, the Beatles and the Rolling Stones. He appeared frequently on that new and seemingly indispensable creation of contemporary humanity, the chat show, talking sometimes of his broken heart, his problems with amphetamines and barbiturates, the burden of celebrity, the unfathomable conundrums of his multiple affairs since, as he so amusingly explained, many of the models who took their clothes off so as to enable him to point his varied lenses in their direction did not necessarily rush to put them back on again. Some he ravished; some he impregnated; one or two he even married. And into this den of promiscuous rogues and charming shysters the nineteen-year-old Daisy had stepped. Alice had fallen down her riverside hole once more, into the hallucinogenic underworld.

For the truth was that Daisy had been innocent. However much her naked body had subsequently become the very image of the breaking down of boundaries, whether celebrated or reviled for the breakage, she had at that point had little enough notion what was going on all around her. Her father, a solicitor in Shropshire, had been a man of such rigorous and unrelenting propriety that he had even gone bald with an evolutionary predictability dependable enough to let his neighbours count the passing years by the number of his falling hairs. She'd had the impression that his courtship of her mother had been about as exciting as watching the paint dry on a thatched cottage in Wem – though much, much slower. She could not remember a single instance when instinct had ever triumphed over calculation in the household of her girlhood. And now here she was in the famous studio of this famous playboy of the western world. As she walked through she saw a slim but pneumatically thighed and breasted model stroll off to put her clothes back on.

James had taken one look at her and decided to give her the treatment, to make an image of her so compelling that even she soon half believed its authenticity. He took her out to dinner in London. The following week he travelled up to Stratford to see her Miranda. Soon enough they became lovers and his images of her were scattered through the glossy magazines. It was a brave new world. She met whoever he met, even once gazing with hypnotised distaste as he contrived the glamorous menace of Reggie and Ronnie Kray into front-cover material as the boundaries between movie dreams and actual mayhem – *bona fide* knife-in-the-eye slaughter – grew ever more confused. Then off to another restaurant, another nightclub. They had married after a year and Daisy often felt that she had never entirely recovered from her marriage to James, though it had seemed to do little more than provide further lumber for his own consuming fires. And he had left her not only with their son Howard but also with that image of herself she had never since escaped. Beneath the coquettish invitation of her smile he had conjured enough of her breasts, heartbreakingly small and enticing, somehow eternally pubescent in the studio's swampy shadows, to make a million men want to reach out and touch them and to make Daisy herself wonder if they still had anything to do with her. They had become exotic accoutrements to fame. Her own body had started on its curious journey of public estrangement from her mind.

Then it had been Hollywood in the Seventies. Studios where you were offered marijuana in silver dishes as you walked through the door. Francis Ford Coppola. Michael Cimino. Martin Scorsese. Jack Nicholson. She could still almost taste the rich air of those days, its tang of brilliant and metallic unreality. Grand schemes; sums of money so vast they made money itself seem meaningless. Then finally guilt. Back to London she had gone, back to one final great attempt to live with James, an attempt that had produced Howard but hadn't saved their marriage. Another marriage, an utter disaster. And then suddenly there was no husband at all, only a little boy. Who was now a big boy of no known location. Thailand Great Anakh. She would go and see Digby. In his morose presence she increasingly took comfort.

Was it simply because he was one of the few men she'd ever met who simply had no interest whatsoever in laying a finger on her? He had renounced the world and all the flesh within it. He didn't even watch television or read a newspaper. Her neighbour, the bent and sardonic monk one house to the right.

Digby stood in the room of wonders and looked around him. It bore a striking resemblance to a room in Wilton Manor. In fact, it contained many of the same beautiful objects. The magical room from Staffordshire had been translated to the edge of Wandsworth Common.

'Do you know what this is?' Freddie had asked as the youthful Digby had stared about him all those years back. He'd shook his head.

'It's a wunderkammer, that's what it is. This is your father's room of wonders. And one day it will be yours.'

Treasures. Antique porcelain; sculptures; figurines. A gallimaufry of endearingly ugly debris from the Industrial Revolution. Coins from two thousand years of history. Freakish objects collected over a century from sundry beaches. And round the four walls hung David Jones's engravings of 'The Ancient Mariner'.

Freddie had spoken sitting on the large mahogany table as though giving a tutorial and Digby felt as if he could still see the creeping vines and herbaceous borders of a Staffordshire garden instead of Wandsworth Common, which was what really now lay beyond his current windows. And the harsh complaint of the crows as they bickered in their high trees drifted across here, just as it had there.

'During the Renaissance the princes of northern Europe started to construct for themselves an extra chamber in their palaces, and this they called the wunderkammer, a room to be filled with mirabilia – miraculous objects that generated wonder, oddities and splendours which had issued from nature's left hand: surreal fossils, mandrakes, corals, uncannily misshapen antlers. At its most banal you might well call this no more than a cabinet of curiosities. The well-endowed but enervated mind always requires narcotics of one sort or another. I myself can vouch for that, Digby, though I suppose we'll have to leave your vouching till later. In one sense it was just another trophy room to stand beside the kunstkammer next door which was filled up with heraldic medals, memorial shields, ivory reliquaries. But before long it became a kind of tabernacle and I suppose in some almost indefinable way the prince became a priest. Have you ever thought much about the function of the priest, Digby?' Uncle Freddie needed no answers from his pupil and seldom waited for any.

'Well now, when Jesus blesses the bread and wine, when he signifies that the divine body is present in these humble necessities he abolishes the distance of exoticism for ever. You need no longer go to the holy mountain, you see, for the simple reason that you are already standing on top of it. This was what came to be known as the sacramentalising of the diurnal. At about the time of the Reformation though, the world of sacrament and mystery began to be replaced by a world of inward intensity and the spectacle became subject to experiment; and so, soon enough, Thomas was no longer satisfied with pressing his fingers into Jesus's wounds, he now had to flay him entirely on an autopsy table with a whole cloud of witnesses in attendance. They attended not the body of the victim, or at least not merely that, but the vindicating speech of the scalpel-bearer. The miraculous that had once accrued about the saints in their aureoles returned once more to inanimate objects. And that's the way tabernacle transmuted into wunderkammer. But filled no longer with the daily objects of Christ's consecration, remember that. This holy of holies had to be filled now with distant objects, for the measure of their fitness for inclusion was precisely their distance from the ordinary. All mirabilia are excluded by their very nature from the genus of mundanity. The wondrous was now a calculus that separated viewer and object. I'm lecturing you again, aren't I, Digby? Should I go on or do you really need sunshine and laughter and a ball to kick, like those normal boys beyond the iron gates?' Once again, he didn't wait for a reply.

'It didn't take long before wunderkammer and kunstkammer became one, and men were employed to improve upon the artistry of nature. As I said, the high priest of this endeavour was the prince but this particular magician's enchantment arose not from within – it had to be brought to him from far away. He needed to be a man of great resources. Once he had brought all these objects together within the constellation of his well-nigh illicit curiosity they shone more brightly than they ever could have done in their separate locations. It was as though they'd been destined for his possession; as though they needed him to write their biography. The collector was born, Digby, so what wondrous exempla could not actually be found on distant mountains or beaches had to be fashioned anew and in the imperial workshops the artisans were soon labouring to provide mirabilia for the wunderkammer.

'Some of the greatest collectors – Ulisse Alrovandi in Bologna or Ferrante Imperato in Naples – were also scientists and during the course of the Enlightenment the objects of wonder which were still travelling under the rubric of the word "natural" start to be graded into scientific rows and hierarchies. They ceased to be a mere matter for wonder and became instead comparative. Amazement gave way to taxonomy. They found a new life, a uniform one funnily enough, inside inventories. All collections have an irresistible pull towards the encyclopaedic, you know, and since all collectors are trying simultaneously to abolish distance and time, they're driven to acquire everything that fits the shape of their obsession. One single escaping object could threaten the entire edifice for it's managed to flee the safety of the collector's gaze. To be thus is nothing but to be safely thus. Consequently, as the Enlightenment progresses, it's left with no alternative but to turn the world itself into the wunderkammer, to replace all sacred distance by the relentless proximity of intellect. Worship gives way to rational appraisal, benediction bows down before examination.

'Look at Emperor Rudolf at Prague and his collecting frenzy. He gave himself over entirely to scholarship and close observation, surrounded by paintings from the hands of Dürer and Bosch, visited by Tycho Brahe and Kepler, supplied day and night with elaborate instruments by his artisans and goldsmiths. There's a whiff of the sacred about it all. But by the end of the eighteenth century the scientists and curators had so much ceased to be priests that they were in danger of forgetting the grail itself. The sacred was becoming distrusted, even discounted.' Freddie paused finally in his monologue. He looked troubled.

'So what happened to it?' his young student had asked.

'To what?'

'The sacred.'

'Two things, I suppose,' he'd said then, with an uncharacteristic hint of hesitation. 'Disenchantment and romanticism. An utter scepticism about what we are and where we came from on the one hand and a destructive indulgence in it on the other. Wonderful objects are after all invested with our wonder, maybe even primevally, and that might be precisely why they shine. The gleam emitted by the imagination is an electrical charge which might be bright enough to cover the whole universe with enchantment. But without it . . .'

'Without it?'

'I don't know. You end up with what your old man's doing these days with Wilton Bone China. You must presumably have noticed the insipid little fairies which presently constitute a substantial part of your forthcoming patrimony: a supernatural that nobody believes in. The pornography of commodities. That's much more threatening to the soul than the pornography of bodies, you know. Time we went for a walk, I think. And time I had a drink: the easy route to wonder.'

When Daisy turned up later that day Digby led her for the first time to the room.

'It's rather beautiful, Digby. What is it?'

'It's my wunderkammer.'

'You'll have to explain.'

'My Uncle Freddie would have explained it all to you far better than I can. This is where I study how we turned the world from a place of enchantment to a place of manufacture. How we went from magic to industry and hardly even noticed. These days it's where I try to fathom where and how the wunderkammer lost its wonder. How China came close enough to us to become Wilton Bone China. I suppose it's a bit like sitting in the ruins of a marriage trying to remember the exact date love climbed over the wall.'

'I've certainly been there, Digby. And look at all those lovely engravings of 'The Ancient Mariner'. I recited it once, you know, at a benefit. Never could understand why he had to go and kill that bloody albatross. Why Coleridge, out of interest?'

'My great-great-grandfather corresponded with him,' he said and smiled wearily. 'A rather one-sided correspondence, as far as history's concerned. I'd better give you a glass of wine, Daisy, then you must tell me all about the Merrimans' soirée.'

'So,' he said sitting down opposite his famous neighbour once more, 'how did it all go?'

'Just as well you didn't come, really. It was a bit crowded. I popped in for what I thought was a quiet drink at my neighbours' but by the time I arrived they seemed to be holding a durbar. La Merriman was distinctly wonky.'

'Squiffy you mean.'

'Well, totally pissed actually. Do you subscribe to the Freudian line on parapraxes, Digby?

'I don't go along with Freud at all, I'm afraid. He seems to assume that people can't choose between good and evil, whereas it's the basis of my religion that they don't have any choice but to choose. I tend to put my trust in angels and ministers of grace. Apart from anything else their consultation fees are lower.'

'The old bugger's very good on parapraxes, all the same. But I don't think we're going to need to summon up the spirit of Sigmund with a ouija board to fathom the goings-on in La Merriman's unconscious. She took me by the arm when I arrived – maybe just to steady herself – and she said, "Let me get you a Fuck's Bizz, darling." If I'd been a chap I'd have jumped on her there and then.'

'Maybe that's what happened between her and Jonty all those years ago.'

'What, she offered him a Fuck's Bizz, you mean?'

'And he accepted her offer. One way of inaugurating the romantic attachment. Might it not merely have been an innocent spoonerism, Daisy?'

'Not according to Doctor Sigmund. There's no innocence in his world, no fire exit to the random or the accidental. We're always signifying away like mad, even when we're only getting a bit of shut-eye. But there's no need for subtlety, analysing what's going on with Lady M, as she hovers about with that hideous smile cracking her Max Factor and her Do-Roger-Me-If-You-Need-To micro skirt and black stockings. Oh by the way, Jonty was most solicitous after your health; he asked me to give you this so as to help pass the hours during your recovery programme.' Daisy reached deep into her bag and pulled out a glossy brochure. She laid it on the table: *The Merriman Museum of Miniature Collectables. Autumn Special Issue.*

'He apologises that there's nothing royal in it.' This was a reference to what Jonty felt was an unfortunate thinness in the Merriman Collection's recent bone china royal commemoratives, for not a silver jubilee or golden wedding, not a pearl or diamond anniversary ever escaped his notice. Though not English himself, Jonty had registered early that the normal processes of the universe appeared to go into a temporary reverse in the British Isles whenever a scion of its royal family started nudging towards nuptial ritual and the possibility of procreation. An actual royal wedding involving bona fide human beings who were still demonstrably alive, sound in body if not necessarily in mind, could prompt an emblematic mood of near dementia. Every face, however remotely connected to the distant regal spermatozoon and ovum, however faint and remote the genealogical trace of a dynastic physiognomy, could then appear on some cup, saucer, plate, teatowel, goblet, bracelet, hologram, eternity ring, cufflink, tie or recessed plastic locket. The proponents of commemoration, amongst whom Jonty ranked high, were well nigh totalitarian in their zeal. Money grew agitated and excitable whenever a prince drew near the satin bedsheets. Ledger books would be impregnated even if the princess herself were not. Profits and headlines; bunting and palaces. Champagne and tiaras and honeymoon suites. Jonty loved it all – his joy was unfeigned – for this he knew was where his bread was buttered, and royal butter was invariably of a rich and golden sort that drips over the edge of even the poor man's crust. He didn't feel there'd been enough of it all over the past few years. Didn't feel the royals had exactly been doing their bit. His living depended to a considerable extent on their zest for weddings, funerals, coronations and lengthy commemorations of all the above. Daisy let him glance for a minute at the full-colour pages and then continued.

'Later on we were all taken upstairs and shown their new remote control curtains. There's a switch at the side of the bed. Press it and the curtains close.'

'This is a necessity for the up-to-date modern home, is it?'

'I suppose it's in case they get taken short, caught unexpectedly in the throes of passion, starkers on top of the candlewick bedspread. No time to hurtle over and pull the curtains, you see. Not with the moment of ecstasy so imminent. You've seen those photographs of Tessa the same as I have, Digby, so don't start looking coy. By the way, Jonty's hair has been renewed once more. It is now a glistening sable.'

'He's been at the bottle again,' said Digby. 'Never would have thought eternal youth could be purchased so cheaply.'

'Oh, I shouldn't think it's cheap.'

Meteorology

Digby stared out of his window at the sky above the Common. It was starting to make dark promises. Vicki's Maltese mother had been convinced that the different weather forecasters on the television gave out different sorts of weather, according to mood and temperament. The microcosmic climate inside their heads was an ineluctable prompt to the macrocosm of wind, tide, sunshine and rain going on outside; the heavens merely did as they were told.

'Oh not *heem*,' she would complain as she saw the features of that day's weatherman on the box. 'Now we get rain. Rain rain *rain*.'

Digby had at first assumed this was ironic, a meteorological hoax shared by the family, a fragment of frisky Maltese vaudeville, but he'd realised his mistake after chortling merrily first time around. Vicki's mother had fixed him with her well-practised evil-eye look. There never did seem to be much in the way of irony in Vicki's family. The menfolk in particular took a dim view of it. It didn't prompt laughter, merely morbid, scowling scrutiny, the fish-fryer's hostility congealing slowly round its object. Digby had come to the conclusion that his wife's brother and father took any manifestation of sardonic dissonance, that constant English register, as a personal affront to their Maltese manhood. Subtle self-deprecation from maritally related males was neither more nor less than a dynastic blade aimed at their testicles. If English men needed to mutilate themselves daily on the sharpened flint of their own self-mockery then they must obviously be permitted that curious indulgence, but the Maltese were having none of it. No Abelards in their manly crew.

'Eees not so *funny*,' Vicki's mother had hissed, sibilantly surfing the words while jabbing her crooked finger in the air. Arthritis. 'Weather here not funny for poor Sammy.' This was a reference to potential fish and chip sales in the kiosk below. Rain invariably reduced the quotient of seaside strollers queuing up to eat heavily fried foods out of last week's newspapers, while sauntering along the promenade. Sammy's establishment boasted no tables. Two greasy Formica ledges under narrow windows on either side of the door permitted you if truly desperate to eat there, swiftly and in silence, as you watched the traffic nose-to-tailing it outside or ran your fingertips up and down the containers of vinegar and salt, their dimpled plastic skins beaded permanently by condensation, topped with squat black nozzles.

'But the weatherman doesn't actually make the weather,' Digby had said gently, merely stating what he assumed to be the obvious. The response had been swift.

'So why it always rain when this one come on then?'

Digby had fallen silent at this. Mediterranean peasants, he'd thought. They'd burn that poor, benighted weatherman at the stake if they could get their hands on him. And that would teach him not to turn the skies black and the streets liquid in vengeance for his wife's headache last night, wouldn't it? They're probably convinced he stands dead-centre in a pentangle chalked on the studio floor, just off-camera. Dear God, he'd thought, I might as well have married into a cargo cult.

Over the years he learnt to avoid the old woman, who sank ever deeper into her hoydenhood and who always regarded him with the utmost suspicion whenever he entered a room. He did wonder what she might have sounded like in Maltese. In English her voice hit a pitch somewhere between a howl of pain and a squawk of displeasure. Everything she said, however trivial, was pitched at the top of the vocal register. If her voice was to be trusted then every perception endured since arriving on these shores appeared to have prompted outrage. Digby found it a matter for astonishment that anyone could stay cross so consistently and for so long – for a whole lifetime in effect. And he could never work out what it was exactly that she was so cross about. Could it really be because her daughter had broken with family tradition and refused to wed a Maltese fish-fryer, choosing instead the heir to an English pottery company? Could marrying upwards out of your class really be *so* offensive? After all it was hardly as though he'd plucked her from a volcanic rock in the Mediterranean, Perseus to her Andromeda; she was already here, lurking in one of England's damper corners, waiting for someone to come along and help shake the rain from her brolly.

But Sammy, Vicki's father, had grown ever more confidential. He was particularly fond of reminiscing with Digby about the war, though since one of them had spent it counting buttons in Aldershot and the other frying fish and chips in Hastings, Digby could never understand why. War experiences: that was the theme Sammy most liked to descant upon. Digby didn't really think of himself as having had any war experiences, or only the same ones everyone else had had. Dullness and discomfort were what he remembered rather than daily danger. He told Sammy this but Sammy smiled a smile of disbelief: he'd got wise by then to the English strategy of self-deprecation.

'Honestly, Sammy, I spent most of my time making sure a lot of chaps had decent underwear. I was shouted at, I grant you, and I learnt how to march up and down pretty briskly, stamping my feet with a gun on my shoulder. That was my contribution to the war. They didn't actually want me shooting at the enemy because with my eyesight I'd certainly have missed and probably hit our own commanding officer instead. Never even really saw the enemy except when the V2s flew over my head. Then I just waved before I ducked like everybody else.'

'They saw the enemy in Malta all right,' Sammy rasped. You must have needed a powerful telescope to watch it all from Hastings, Digby thought, but he kept the thought to himself. As far as he was aware the fish and chip shop had stayed open for the duration of hostilities though the black-out had posed a few problems. Probably designated an essential service, and why not? Sammy had drawn a little closer. 'You know in 1942 a submarine called *Rorqual* sailed to Malta filled with carrier pigeons. You know this, Digby?'

'No,' Digby said, wondering why he too had lowered his voice. Sammy's corrosive intimacy.

'Well it did. But trials no good. Pigeons wouldn't leave the boat. They couldn't get them out. Even threaten pigeons with a court-martial but still they wouldn't go. You know what this mean, Digby?'

'No.'

'It mean the pigeons had more fucking sense than we did,

my friend.' At this Sammy threw his arm about Digby's shoulders and laughed loudly. 'A lot more fucking sense.'

'You had a good chat with dad,' Vicki had said later as they drove home.

'Yes indeed.'

'What did you talk about?'

'Our wartime experiences.'

'He'd have liked that.'

Next time he can show me his medals, Digby thought. In fact the whole of Malta had been awarded the George Cross for its bravery during the war years but did that still apply if you'd spent all your time cooking fish and chips in Hastings? He thought of Sammy's final words to him before parting.

'Remember, Digby, sniff on the onion and you'll cry.' An old Maltese proverb no doubt though no less true for that.

Daisy had made a decision. But there was a problem. The problem was her two cats, Dylan and Django. The woman who cleaned for her was off for a few days and Daisy's sister Beth was out of the country until the following week. Nobody to feed them. She couldn't face asking Jonty, she certainly wouldn't have wanted him in her house prowling about, and if Tessa even tried to stroke them she'd end up cutting their throats with her extended, razor-sharp nails. Tessa's fingers weren't so much working digits as erotic accoutrements, designed for the night shift in Soho rather than the washing-up. Jonty's torso must be striated, she thought. It would have to be Digby, but she knew without asking that it wasn't a task he'd relish.

'But I don't go out, Daisy, you know that.'

'It's only next door, for God's sake. It's not as though I'm

sending you to Van Diemen's Land. A military veteran like
you can surely make it next door to feed the pussies.'

'Just take a look at me: I'm bent.'

'Might you perhaps exaggerate your disabilities?' She
leaned forward from her chair and placed a comradely hand
on his knee. She had started laughing. 'I mean, just a little,
Digby?'

'No, my disabilities are more than capable of exaggerating
themselves, without any help from me. You've seen me
hobbling about here: I'm positively buckled.' He stared at
the hand on his knee. He had never before noticed how
small it was. Nails like tiny violet shells.

'You're not buckled, Digby, you're not bent and you're
not buckled, do you hear? You're stooped. Peter O'Toole
has stooped all his life – for all I know he might even have
got started pre-natally, a stooping foetus, but I've always
found Peter a most attractive man. Anyway, Dylan and
Django happen to be very fond of stoopers. They find it
easier to see into their faces. They'll purr with satisfaction
while you bend over them.' He sulked for a while and when
he walked over to put the kettle on he tried to make sure his
gait looked as valetudinarian and asymmetric as possible, but
she finally charmed him out of it.

And so it was that with the greatest possible reluctance
Digby agreed to feed Daisy's cats, allowing her to climb into
her Morris Traveller early the next morning and drive up to
North Shropshire where James now lived in a rambling
farmhouse close to the Welsh border. She had not phoned
him for she knew that if she did he would do everything in
his power to prevent her from coming. He might even be
putting a new model through her paces and she could still
remember vividly how engrossing an experience that could

be. Memory like an elephant, haven't I, she thought. She would simply arrive, then he'd have no choice but to discuss the matter with her. Her anxiety about Howard would be addressed one way or the other, and if she couldn't turn to the boy's father in her hour of need, then who could she turn to?

Five hours later she arrived on the hillside outside Oswestry where her first ex now chose to live. She was the one who'd introduced him to the area; they'd taken holidays up there, in her own childhood county. It still struck her as mildly improper that he should have gone to live there, having first divested himself of the locality's native daughter.

Dilapidated white stone walls, half of them ruined, surrounded the farmhouse itself. Dark hills rose up behind it. Sheep and goats were the only flocks you'd have farmed up there. Agile creatures, unencumbered with vast udders. James kept a curious menagerie but you could hardly call it farming. He was still very much the photographer, however far he'd strayed from Chelsea.

He opened the door and to her annoyance seemed entirely unfazed by her arrival.

'The mother of my child,' he said. 'What a pleasant surprise.' He was still very much James but there was no denying that he was older. The once-dark hair had grown long again, rurally ragged and unkempt, but it had turned entirely grey. She wasn't sure she didn't prefer it. And his ever-so-trim body had slackened and slumped, particularly around his waist-line which was no longer the thirty-two inches in diameter it had been on their wedding day.

'Can the old tart come in then?' she asked and he opened the door wide with a flourish.

They moved through the rooms towards his kitchen. She

kept her eyes open for any young female shape flitting about but there didn't seem to be one.

'Alone, James?'

'Sorry to disappoint you. You'd be surprised how many of my days are spent in solitude.'

'How did you ever end up here?'

'I had thought you'd brought me to the place.'

'I might have brought you to the place. I certainly didn't leave you in it.'

'Do you remember the hills?'

'How could I forget?'

'Come on. I'll take you for a drive. Have a quick coffee first.'

Still the same old green Bentley. Once it had been a new green Bentley but that was over forty years ago. Sitting in the driving seat in those days he'd looked sleek and ridiculously successful. Now he looked stately; genteel in a slightly shabby manner.

'You're a lot more faithful to cars than you are to women, James.'

And as he drove, with what felt like the velocity of a rally driver, over hills, through villages, some with Welsh names some with English ones, the territory of so many oscillating battles over the years, so many routine slaughters, he played his ancient tapes of Dusty Springfield. The valleys went by vertiginously, slopes were climbed with maximum torque in second. A dun mare or a brindled cow would share a slanted field with a ruined caravan, its metal panels warping and rusting in the prevailing rains. Ribbons and clouds of mist scrolled up wooded escarpments as the wildlife conducted its shameless transactions, glimpsed cinematically through the speeding window. Crows took their roadside meals wherever they could: smashed hedgehogs; spine-snapped rabbits; flattened grouse; despoliated pheasant; annihilated shrews; a badger disconsolately dumped in its pelt as though pondering its next move. Animals round here were far more likely to die with a tyre-mark across their heads than a bullet through their hearts or a hound's tooth in their gullet. The crows' mighty and unfastidious beaks scraped the carrion from the tarmac as their eyes, black and shiny as a policeman's boot, stayed alert, fluttering away as the car bore down on them then settling back in its turbulent wake. There was even once a magpie on the white line in the middle of the road, hammering into the neck of a fox with the efficiency of a mechanical digger. As it looked up into the oncoming traffic its beak was redly luminous. Then they saw a crow which had got its timing wrong spatchcocked over the road surface. Which creature ate the crows, Daisy wondered; which species took the carrion-bird as carrion? Dusty was singing how the only man that she'd ever loved was the son of a preacher man.

'I couldn't really believe it when I first heard she was a left-footer, you know.' His Dusty was not the short-haired gay icon of later years but the back-combed blonde, the mascara'd and Max-Factored vamp of the Sixties, shifting her glistening, stockinged legs back and forth on high heels and belting out one hit melody after another with unfathomable potency. 'But then it started to make a kind of sense. A man's heart in a woman's body. The strength of that voice. Just listen.' Dusty had by now moved on to the next track and was singing how she thought she was going back to the times she used to know in her youth. Her melancholy husky voice matched the weather as whirlpools of rain corkscrewed the buffeting winds. The car didn't slow. She felt the G-force as they cornered. By the time they descended the next hill Dusty was lamenting that silver threads and golden needles couldn't mend that heart of hers. Her brother Tom was singing with her on that one, keeping their harmonious grief in the family. The pills and booze hadn't mended her heart either. Simply made its brokenness more visible as the lenses and the microphones closed in. Trees sped by, the hedgerows blurred, the webbed air was now entirely soaked, a membrane of fine cottonwool doused in chloroform and Dusty had moved on again. She was explaining how she didn't expect love now. In fact she sang how she didn't expect anything much at all. Then the great whooping cries came as she asked us to believe her. You didn't, of course, any more than she did herself. Whence the tragedy; whence the wrenching heartache in that mighty unassailable voice.

'Didn't you once photograph her?'

'Once.' They geared down into a village and James pulled over into a leafy lane.

'You didn't notice anything at the time?' she asked and he turned upon her his old-fashioned look. A frown of schoolmasterly disbelief. It had always made her laugh but his latest wrinkles made it more convincing somehow.

'She didn't actually lez up while I was changing lenses, no. She was a singer, remember Daisy, not an actress. Want to look round the church?'

'The *church*, James?' Her astonishment, however theatrical its expression, was unfeigned. He was already half-way out of the car.

'I'm doing a book on old English churches with Crispian. Didn't you know?'

'I don't think you could have surprised me more if you'd told me you were about to marry into the royal family.'

'I've done enough marrying for one lifetime, Daisy. More than enough if the truth be told.'

'Well thanks, husband.'

Later back at the farmhouse he took her into the room he used as his studio and showed her some of his recent work.

'The photographs are so quiet, I didn't know you could take such quiet photographs.' They struck her as almost reverential. 'You've been spending time in the silence at last.' He was staring at his own images with his head cocked to one side.

'I got so tired of the chatter, Daisy. The endless chatter of the big city. God, but they do go on. So I thought I'd have a go at photographing silence for a change. And somehow it seemed so easy: the insides of the churches just seeped into the inside of the camera. All the stones round here leak shadows. And I usually have the place to myself, you know. Nobody queueing up to worship much any more.' Prayerful James, Daisy thought, but said nothing and simply continued smiling. Life never ceased astounding her.

She ran a hand over the silk surface of the prints; vast stretches of oilskin-black imprinted from the chiaroscuro of the naves. James has discovered the darkness along with the silence, she thought, and fallen in love with it. Such a creature of light he'd once been too. Flash-guns in his eyes, always in pursuit of another brilliant creature making its way from studio to bedroom. Maybe he was just getting old. And if he was, then she must be following in his wake speedily enough.

He did make a lovely stew though. She couldn't remember him ever cooking when they'd lived together. Now his ramshackle kitchen had brought out the farmhouse chef in him. Rich stew; home-made bread; fruit salad. It was positively wholesome. And there was as ever excellent claret. That's how she'd acquired such a taste for the stuff. They told each other stories they both knew; mocked people they both liked; fell silent at times in recollection.

'You've become domesticated, James. Any idea where your son might be?'

'Yes, as a matter of fact, I think I do. Well, where he's just been anyway. A letter arrived this morning.'

'From?'

'Seattle.'

'What's he doing there?'

'Protesting. The same as everybody else. The population of Seattle appears at present to be made up of those running the world and those who think it's high time someone else took over.'

'Might a mother look?'

'I can't think why not.' He went and found the letter.

The Speakeasy
Seattle   *Tuesday 2 November, 1999*

Dear James,
I think I might be paying you back soon.
All the cameras here have unfriendly eyes. No matter.
The people united will never be divided. If you're horizontal enough,
all the verticals in the world can't cover you.
Remember, only lime mortar.

Thailand Great Anakh.

Howard

'When did he start calling you James?' Daisy asked, unhappy with the usage.

'A few years back. We thought it was more grown-up.'

'I hope he doesn't expect to start calling me Daisy. What's he got to pay you?'

'Loans.'

'You should tell me, James.'

'Do you tell me, then?'

'No, I don't suppose I do. Lime mortar?'

'Repairs to the farmhouse. He feels very strongly about it. What's environmentally responsible and what isn't. He's probably right.'

'Horizontal? Vertical?'

'He explained it all once but I can't remember exactly. It's about structures of authority. The groups he moves in don't have any. There's no vertical axis of command. Only horizontality. An equality of communication.'

'This is Radix?'

'I suppose so.'

'Do you know what Thailand Great Anakh means?'

'Absolutely no idea.'

She stayed the night. After he had shown her to her room he came back ten minutes later with a cognac in each hand. That was the way they used to do it.

'How about it, Daisy? Just for old times' sake.' Only in his presence did she ever remember how much she liked him. Telephone calls and letters merely served to increase her fury. But there in the room together the old affections returned. The only creatures who ever shared her bed in London these days were her cats. The wind was banging at the ancient window casing.

'Only if you promise to help me find Howard.'

'I promise.'

In the morning she stood looking out at the trees and the valley as he started to wake raggedly behind her. Rogue winds were vexing the trees. She turned to look at him, mussed and dishevelled in his torpor.

'Horny old bugger aren't you? Was I as easy as that the first time?'

'The first time I didn't even need to give you a cognac.'

'And now I suppose it's time for the little lady to make breakfast.'

The Noise of Time

Howard still didn't return. Nor did he contact his mother. But she started following events out there with care. Normally she had little use for newspapers except for checking the theatrical reviews, but now she noted the events as they flashed across the front pages of the red-tops or blinked out from television screens. G8 summits, WTO congresses, IMF get-togethers, tear-gassed streets with bodies strewn across them, the shouting, the smoke, the shattered windows, shops turned inside out, their innards scattered over pavements and the sense that those inside the zones of power must be shielded by steel, truncheon and gun from those without, from that black bloc in masks and scarves crouched menacingly beyond the walls of the citadel or even those dressed in turtle-suits, merely dancing a dissenting dance. Globalisation. polar caps of control separated by an equator of discontent. And between them both oceans of confusion. Computer screens scrolling page after page of hieroglyphic code. If you could only understand these ciphers, it seemed, then the dirt of your life would transmute to gold. If you couldn't every day was mortgaged, the hours of sleep and waking calculated, accounted, amortised. Not even death could absolve your debt for you. Whole countries for ever in hock, not to other countries, nothing so concrete as that in landmass or topography, but to transnational entities vaster than any bank, entities that money passed through as tides passed through the oceans, controlling the element that generated them.

As for Digby, he had given up on the news the way other old men finally stop cycling or playing golf. After four decades of standing on the shoreline of the twentieth century he decided he'd had enough drenchings from the filthy modern tide. Heard enough, seen enough. He couldn't cope with any more information. He had in any case by that stage placed the management of his financial affairs entirely in the hands of his long-term brokers Moffett and Son. Old Jeremy having now retired had left the firm in the hands of young Tony, though with a personal pledge to Digby that he would keep a close eye on things. Make sure his ancient client was dealt with properly. Each year the company informed him what they were doing with his money and each year there was a specified yield on his investment, sometimes more than the year before, sometimes less, and that was pretty much an end to the matter. His own involvement counted for nothing in any event and never had done, so what difference could it make whether or not he continued to monitor humanity's doings? In fact he had received a letter some time back from Tony Moffett informing him of an enhancement of his investments. Something promising higher yields. Communications; that sort of thing. A fundamental structural change in the pattern of money-making. He couldn't even remember what it had said exactly. Who knows the real pattern of money in any case? So what's the point of worrying? It never was worthwhile. He had signed the form as he always did and returned it in the pre-paid reply envelope provided.

Anyway, with no reason to torture his mind further with what was going on out there, the rise and fall of empires, the enduring misery of the poor, the garish insolence of the rich or the relentless couplings of celebrities, he had called it a day, cancelled his newspapers and had never since switched on a television channel. What was the point in following so sedulously who's in, who's out, which scurvy politicians the glassy cyclops eye is focused on, and whether they choose presently to be known as Guelphs or Ghibellines? Digby had also been developing a problem over the years, one he thought might have a medical origin. Time was making more noise than it ever had before.

Even while Vicki had still shared the house with him this extraordinary sensitivity had grown worse each month. The creak of a floorboard, the buzzing of a fly, the yawning of an opening door, seemed to stab his brain with the force of a spear. So his wife's raucous voice swooping suddenly out of the nest of silence both discomposed and displeased him. He had frequently told her so.

'Now you want me to be silent as well as miserable? Why did I ever marry you, you loveless English ———.' The last word she'd uttered was one she occasionally employed, plucked he presumed out of her father's rich vocabulary of Maltese curses. He had memorised the syllables and the next time he had met Sammy he'd asked him what it meant. Sammy had stared at him for a moment in silence then said, 'Potmaker.'

But it continued even after her departure. Finally he had sought medical assistance. The doctor had expressed his puzzlement in the face of Digby's complaint. He thought it *possible* (he extended this word in pronouncing it to convey the minuteness of the possibility) that the combination of his

medications could produce the extreme sensitivity of which
he spoke. In particular a fleering of the brain by certain
sounds, an intense sense of discomfort that his mind was
being stripped of its skin by noises he simply couldn't escape:
the noise of the age itself, the noise of time accelerating with
the fearsomeness of its own momentum. *Mens Marsyas*, the
doctor had suggested as a classification, hoping presumably to
raise a smile and failing. Giving it a name, however
whimsical, was one thing but what was to be done? The
doctor shrugged to convey his ineffectuality in such impon-
derable matters or possibly even his boredom with them. So
Digby had started to take his own precautionary measures,
the first of which was to dispense with the television and its
lurid technicolor roar. Enough of the sound of time emitted
from that dictatorial contraption to deafen anyone. He kept it
now purely for the playing of videos, most of which were
black-and-white anyway (except for those featuring Daisy),
black-and-white constituting in Digby's opinion a more
reasonable amount of information for the eye's appraisal. Too
much data merely engorged the mind, obliterating thought,
engulfing the faculties. The world surely wasn't ready yet for
colour television; it had barely finished blinking at Renaissance rainbows. Technology was once more racing ahead of
any use perception might put it to. The videos he had come
to think of as historical documents rather than the plastic
excrescences of modernity. Inside the camera obscura of their
black casings awesome images had been trapped before they
fled. He watched them intently as he might have studied
shadows dancing on the wall of a cave.

And so when a form had next come through the post
requiring him to renew his television licence he had thrown
it in the bin. Several more such forms arrived in ever more

admonitory colours – he threw those in the bin too. After all, he wasn't actually watching any television programmes, was he, so why then must he pay anyone for the privilege of doing so?

Anyone didn't come into it though as he was soon to find out. To use the word anyone was to employ the anthropomorphic principle in a region where it didn't apply.

Some months passed before a man turned up one day at his door. Digby had intended to ignore the knocking but it went on. And on. Finally with undisguised irascibility Digby had opened up. This man, a besuited figure in his thirties, a bland embodiment of officious anonymity, had directed at Digby the sort of smile he detested, a smile that said: I have a form of power, you know. Not much power I grant you but enough to bring some discomfort your way if you should choose not to smile back. It turned out that he was an inspector from the television licensing authority. He asked Digby if he could see his television licence. Digby informed him that he could not.

'Do you possess a colour television set?'

'Yes, as a matter of fact I do. But I use it only for viewing videos most of which, as it happens, are monochrome.' The man smiled again and Digby almost closed the door in his face. It was a smile that seemed expressly designed to provoke violence.

'If you possess a television set then it is illegal not to possess a television licence too.'

'But I don't watch any of it, not the BBC and not ITV either, do you understand? So why should I pay you people for producing pornography and ruining what's left of the English language when I don't even tune in of an evening? Please go away.'

'You're breaking the law, I'm afraid . . .' he started but Digby interrupted him.

'And you're trespassing. Now get off my property before I set the dogs on you.' Digby slammed the door shut and then thought better of it and opened it wide once more. 'Get yourself a proper job, why don't you? You should be ashamed of yourself, harassing elderly householders like this.'

The man stepped briskly away up Digby's driveway, a minatory smirk still disfiguring his features into a rictus of derision, and after a brief correspondence which gave Digby the unerasable impression that he was confronted by an electronic sphinx which didn't even pause to hear the answer to its riddles, or a hydra with a new head sprouting every time he lifted the telephone, after appealing in vain and with increasing exasperation to his solicitor, he had been fined £300 and forced to buy a licence under threat of further fines or even imprisonment. He had been reliably informed there was really no alternative except chokey and he thought one jailbird in the family was enough at any one time. The payment of this fine still grated with him like sharp metal cutting the fatty tissue of his brain whenever he considered the matter, which was often. In fact it hurt his mind daily. It had injected his heart with even more rancour than had been there before. To be forced to pay for his right to listen to the age's meretricious junk when he had no interest in even switching the wretched palaver on. Was there really a statutory obligation to be a conduit for such stuff? No chance then to evacuate the beach where the filthy modern tide deposited its flotsam. Three hundred pounds. That was the price of his attempted escape. Three hundred pounds: the price of a semi-detached house in Stoke when he was a boy.

Another iniquitous swindle. Another entrapment in the age's fatuity.

So he responded with something close to alarm when Daisy dropped the newspaper on to his table later that day.

'I don't use these things any more, Daisy, you know that,' he said pushing it away from him fastidiously. He didn't want to hear the news or read it either. He didn't want to know about anything that was *new*. Some politician on the front page appeared to be promising equity and contentment to the world's huddled masses. How very old the new had started to seem.

'Come on, Digby. You can at least give me the headlines; tell me how much worse the world's got in the last twenty-four hours.' Digby pulled the newspaper back towards him by its corner as though he were handling a soiled rag. There was a man who had killed himself by hanging while dressed in women's clothing. Was that what she wanted to know about?

'Sounds promising,' she said, as she chopped salami.

Digby stared at the paper lying on the table before him with a look of profound distrust. Uncle Freddie's lengthy induction into the laws of grammar and lexicography had made him a stickler for proper usage from an early age and the last time he had made his way through a national newspaper he had merely marvelled at the quantity of errors. The misuses had been prodigious: confidant and confidante, blond and blonde, disinterested and uninterested, dilapidated in every usage that had forgotten the stony lapis at the heart of the word. Enormity he had long before given up on but he still noted, for his own morbid satisfaction, all uses of fortuitous for fortunate, jejune for young or gauche, and refute whenever rebut was intended. He started to read the article all the same. She hovered above him briefly staring at the dead man's photograph, grinning into a future that had now disappeared. Something she'd noticed about her own image: how it carried on smiling even after you yourself had long since stopped. But he had started reading. She'd nailed him. Soon enough she'd have him back out on the Common. She felt strongly that Digby's total retreat from the world was to be deprecated. One of these days she'd even have him quaffing away again at one of Jonty's soirées. Not that she was excessively fond of the news herself. And her sister Beth, a lifelong teacher, had dispensed with her television entirely, having grown tired of shouting 'Special Needs' at people mangling the English language, people who couldn't make it to the end of a sentence without falling off, only to discover afterwards that they were running the world.

'Was it very sordid?' she asked casually.

'Very.'

'You can fill me in, Digby, while I labour away at your lunch. You do like olives, don't you?' She didn't wait for a reply.

'They appear to be unsure whether it was suicide or auto-erotic self-asphyxiation.'

'How do you do that then?' Digby read a little further in silence before speaking again.

'It requires the starvation of the brain's oxygen supply. You put a ligature around your neck. Apparently it heightens sexual pleasure.'

'I think I might have to take your word for that. Do you want butter? That was not a reference to *Last Tango in Paris*, so don't get anxious. But then you probably never saw that, did you?'

'I never did. I think I might have given up on the avant-garde by then. My devotion to the artists of modernity never went down well in the Potteries, even though I'm still devoted to a number of them. But no butter, whichever way you were planning on administering it.'

'I'm not the district nurse, darling.'

Digby had made his way over to the shelf where he kept the *Oxford English Dictionary*, all sixteen volumes of it including the supplements. He tried to look up auto-erotic self-asphyxiation but the nearest he could get was auto-eroticism, which appeared by comparison positively benign. Once more he could only marvel at how the speed of linguistic development constantly outstripped the scope of lexicographers to map it.

'What a very curious way to die,' he said. 'What is it, women trapped in men's bodies?' Daisy was taking a sip of her wine. She had of late started helping herself.

'Not sure I've ever met one of those, to be honest. Met plenty of men trapped *outside* women's bodies, and they often seemed to think the body they'd been trapped outside was mine.' She looked across to realise Digby was blushing and continued quickly: 'I do remember a few fellows on the stage who seemed a lot keener to get into lady's clothing for the performance than to hurry out of it again afterwards. Anyway that's enough about Mr Auto-Erotic and his self-asphyxiation. Pound to a penny he was completely off his onion anyway.' Then she became contemplative and silent for a while. Digby looked on her features admiringly, wondering why he seemed to have spent so much of his life in a state of emotional rancour instead of celebration. Too late to make up for it now, that was for sure.

'So where's Howard?' Digby asked to rouse her from her reverie.

'Buggered if I know.'

Improvising

*Pack up all my cares and woe. Here I go, singing low. Bye bye
blackbird.* Theo was aware that words didn't always mean
exactly what you expected them to mean. You have to be
careful in trying to understand what people say: he had learnt
that much in prison, if nothing else. 'Violence does my head
in,' his cellmate had said to him one day, and Theo had felt
touched somehow that this man (in for GBH) with whom
he'd shared the daily intimacies of family epistles read out
loud and the stench of shared faeces, this man had come to
see that it was no good smashing people up; that that was no
way to put humanity right about things. But Theo had been
mistaken. He soon discovered that this was not what Lee had
meant at all, for Lee was in fact quite happy with violence.
He used it habitually to deck his opponents and certainly had
no moral objections to it whatsoever, even as a means of
communication with complete strangers who had caused him
some momentary irritation on road or pavement, in bar or
supermarket, but it *did* do his head in. The frenzy it required
of him emotionally meant that he always needed medication
afterwards. Not that he had any objection to medication
either; in point of fact he was an enthusiast for the stuff, the
more of it the better – powders, pills, assorted resins – all

preferably mixed with hard liquor. He was if anything something of a connoisseur though very much a tooter not a shooter, for he never pinned up, but he did think a man should be in a position to choose his own medication, his cocktail of uppers and downers, crystal sharpeners and blurring smokes, rather than having dosages dictated by the fellows in white coats.

'They always sedate you,' he said to Theo once, spitting out the words. 'Sedatives is about where their medical knowledge starts and ends. Pacify the fuckers. Give 'em another bottle of sleepers. If they'd been doctors during the war we'd have lost. I'm telling you, Theo, our armed forces would have lost to Hitler. They'd still be claiming compo for the bombing of Dresden while our wives and children cleaned out their fucking toilets.' He had flexed his patriotic fingers then and Theo had once more noted the tattoo on his knuckles: ACAW. He had asked Lee what the letters stood for, imagining they might be the initials of a particularly treasured wife, girlfriend or child, or just possibly the acronymic slogan of a religious cult, for the murky waters of Lee's mind ran deep. His cellmate had smiled his foxy smile.

'All coppers are wankers,' he had said at last as though revealing the arcana of an ancient religion to some fresh-faced devotee. Theo could see how apposite the statement was, given Lee's continuing dialectic with the forces of law and order but he couldn't help wondering if he might not merely have memorised it, rather than having it needled in indelible inks on his right hand. And Theo had later noted for himself how badly violence did Lee's head in when his cellmate nutted a screw he felt had spoken to him disrespectfully one too many times. Lee had gone into a decline which had lasted for weeks, so Theo was told, for

Lee had by then been taken from their joint cell to another, tighter place and Theo only heard at a distance of Lee's regret for the screw's shattered spectacles and flattened nose. Theo had missed him in the cell; found himself pondering the scale of his curious companion's mental disturbance; wondered how many sleepers a day he was on now. Poor Lee: mad as a fish, engulfed by the rolling tides of life's tempest.

So Theo knew that words didn't always signify exactly what you thought they might. All the same, he took the copy of the *North Putney Gazette* out of his pocket and once more read the paragraph about his playing, and in particular one phrase that he couldn't get out of his head: *It's a danger of course, as the trumpet player must be well aware by now, playing music from inside a dead man's shadow.* Theo wished he'd elaborated a little more on the nature of that danger. The cost of discipleship? That was what his father had always recommended; well, he'd accepted the recommendation. Except he'd decided to follow Miles instead of Jesus. As it happened, he thought he'd been better at following Miles than his father had at following *his* chosen mentor. At least he *sounded* like Miles. When his father opened his mouth it certainly didn't sound like the Sermon on the Mount. Or could it be something to do with the potency of shadows? But that was the only potency he had; that was why his music always came out sounding black-and-white.

Anyway, no gig tonight. No need to take care of himself. Time to chase the blues away. Choose his own medication in a free market with a pocketful of money, itching fingers and a lepping heart. Lee would have been proud of him. A man who's got his legs, a man on the out, should make the best of things during his brief sojourn among the liberties of London or what's a heaven for?

Whatever enthusiasm the infant Theo had once shown for his food it had indubitably waned of late. As he had recently confided to his Dictaphone he had not eaten for days. In fact he had barely touched food for over a week. This was not as catastrophic as it might sound for many alcoholic drinks are much more proteinaceous than might be expected, and although essentially a devotee of distilled spirits Theo took in enough beer and wine here and there as he punctuated his journeyings to ensure that he was provided with some basic sustenance. The local brew was Young's, a nourishing old-fashioned sort of beer, and given that Theo diluted his vodka at intervals with fresh orange juice he had at least one source of vitamins to provide some balance in his liquid diet.

Breasts. Breasts and thighs. Mouse-down. Softened heather covering the mouse's cave. How liquid and warm, the mouse's throat. Who could ever have expected it to swell enough to swallow a man, moistening the body's little engines with love's spittle? He wished himself back into Jill's bed, now that he had been expelled from it. But if not hers then it would have to be someone else's.

Theo was already high, his mind's chemical altitude twinned as usual by electric sensations from below, new ones this time, body and mind entwined in worshipful psychosis. Nothing in the wreckage of his present life viewed in any way objectively could have led him with any logic to this state of serenity but he didn't care about that. Never had done. Theo had convinced himself that the hash in some way balanced out the booze. He knew this might be difficult to prove in medical terms but he was sure the dope herbalised and rendered green all the arid land which the scorched-earth policy of his drinking had lain waste. (He had been unable to maintain this balanced intake only for nine months in the last fifteen years, but then that was the thing about prison: you really had little choice but to drink less alcohol and take more drugs.) So having already started out this day with a substantial blast of the Hungarian's weapons-grade Afghan hemp, he now felt fortified enough to make his way round some of Wandsworth's pubs. He had already appeased the element of air; now he would partake of the element of water, the fire growing brighter within him all the while. And as for the element of earth, that he thought would have him soon enough, for Theo was nothing if not holistic.

The centre of Wandsworth, defined once by the fast flow of the tiny River Wandle, is now defined instead by the ceaseless flow of traffic through its heart. The river has almost disappeared, cooped in by concrete sidings, acknowledged by the merest bump in the road at the edge of Young's brewery and a small paved space edged with spruce, demarcated greenery where the rummies gather, their plastic bags clanking with bottles and cans.

He stood by the bar in the Brewery Tap and stared through the plate glass doors of the shop at the models of shire horses, the antiquated beer bottles and the framed pictures of draymen cheerfully waving. There were sweat-shirts and hats emblazoned with the brewery's logo: a handsome ram in profile. What a wholesome business drinking seemed.

After that he found himself in the Spread Eagle with its Victorian engraved glass and little bookcases containing leatherbound volumes of Dickens, cluttered with sepia photographs of life at the turn of the century. Alcoholically speaking this was Young's town. Here the emblem of the ram held sway. The only thing all these pubs had in common apart from the beers on offer was the traffic flowing past their entrances – cars, lorries, vans, buses, motorcycles. It was true that the occasional horse-drawn dray would clatter and clop along from time to time but it always looked as though it had emerged from the brewery to enter the one-way system of the wrong century.

He saw his face floating in the mirror behind the bar. 'It must be awkward, Theo, I can see that,' Jill had said to him one day. 'To look like that. To learn so early on that women won't say no.' He'd never thought about it much. It's only if and when the world starts saying no that a fellow need ponder the reason it ever said yes in the first place.

He sat with his drink before him, cigarette in hand, staring at the large leaded windows as the autumn sun blazed through, skittering against the Victorian mirrors with their decorative etchings, even rendering the arms of the leather chairs briefly brilliant. Suddenly he was in the centre of an immense pool of light. The traffic had stopped entirely for there was no longer a sound to be heard nor a single movement around him to register. He had no notion how long this silent and translucent moment lasted. Only when the traffic started up again and the sunlight once more shattered into splinters in the mirrors did he realise that it could have been no more than the pause between red and green at the traffic lights. Time's slowing down for you, Theo, he thought. Who knows, maybe it might actually open up and give you space enough to escape through.

Back to the bar. The two men stood leaning against it smoking. Theo now noticed for the first time that the short bald one, who was at least fifty, had a gold earring in each ear. Their words seemed to be scrolling on balloons inside Theo's head; at times even just above it, the way they float about in strip cartoons.

'So, you knew Horace then?' said the thin man to the fat one.

'Oh, I knew fucking Horace,' the other said, taking a lengthy pull of his cigarette before speaking again with great deliberation and an undisguised note of hatred. 'Horace Johnson had the luck of the nine blind bastards. The only time he ever got run over it was by an ambulance.'

'So what do you reckon I should give him?'

'Well if he was a rabbit I'd say myxomatosis. But since he isn't, maybe a gas mask.'

'A gas mask?'

'Last time I saw Horace I told him he could make a serious contribution to solving the problem of air pollution.'

'How?'

'How? That's what he said, How? I said, I'll tell you how, Horace. By stopping fucking breathing, that's how. Only a thought.'

Like most womanisers, Theo needed one woman constantly at base, to venture out from and then return to later. A still centre for the turning world. He needed a wife whatever her legal status. Now he didn't have one any more. Not one who'd let him through the door anyway. By the time the evening came round, and with the prospect of that empty rented flat in Wandsworth hovering before him, he decided to make a visit to someone he knew in Fulham. She opened the door and looked him in the face. Late twenties. Slender but spotted and ragged, her grubby blue jeans in need of replacement. Her short brown hair hadn't been washed for a while – it was matted in places. A child's insistent cry arose from somewhere inside. She did not smile.

'Nice of you to keep in touch, Theo. I thought you'd

settled into married bliss. Sure you have the time, are you?'
All the same she opened the door wider to let him in.
Women seldom turned Theo away. Even Jill had had to gear
herself up for a month or two before announcing his
expulsion. The great advantage of Theo, she'd explained to
her mystified friend Sue, was that if the worst came to the
worst you could always simply look at him or take him to
bed. It could be expensive but it was still satisfying. And
wasn't that the usual male line on women?

He rolled the joint while she settled the baby to sleep. The
child's father had cleared off a year before. She couldn't
afford a baby-sitter so her social life these days was limited.
When she came back into the room he lit it up and handed it
to her. By the time they were in bed they were both
communing solely with their own delirium. Theo dreamed
his old dream, adrift in some distant galaxy whose enormous
coloured globes kept crashing towards him. He counted
them. He multiplied them. He subtracted them. Somewhere
among the data and the calculations was a single beautiful
equation, one handsomely disproving the existence of both
paradise and inferno, but he knew that when he woke he
would no longer be able to put the numbers back together
and this anticipation terrified him. He felt as if he could save
the whole world if he could only remember that equation, if
he could only memorise the numbers and masses and
velocities of those vast coloured planets, but they all moved
too quickly.

But something else happened to him that night which had
never happened before: nothing happened. She had been so
exhausted and blitzed she'd barely noticed. But Theo had
noticed all right. Was it because the dream had come back?

Or had he left his manhood in that house in Wimbledon where his wife was now refashioning a life without him?

In the morning, wretched and wasted, his low as symmetric in its intensity as his high had briefly been the night before, he left the house early while she was still sleeping, having placed a few notes from his wallet on the table at the side of her bed. *Pour l'enfant.* He turned at the door and looked back at her head on the pillow. Her spots were getting worse. They had flared into a dingy mottling across her forehead. She never saw sunshine. The next time he came he'd remember to bring some orange juice to mix with the vodka. The girl was vitamin deficient. She needed to get out more. He tiptoed next door and peered into the cot where the boy was sleeping, then he went back into the bedroom, put his hand into his pocket and took out another £10 note which he laid on top of the first two.

Over he went to the flat in Wandsworth. Once inside he rolled another joint, as a damage-limitation exercise (take it easy – remember you've a gig tonight) and went to bed. Only at the end of the day after the gig was finished and after making his way home through the filthy weather did he finally extract the Dictaphone from its drawer, press the record button and start to speak.

I don't know what it means, dad, but the dream's come back. My famous dream, the one that always had me screaming. I remember how you'd come and lift me up. It was always you for some reason, never mother. And then you would carry me through into your bedroom and put me down between yourself and her. And I always knew if you'd been having one of your rows. I could tell because when you had, it was as though there were miles between you two and I was lying in the middle. I'd have to reach both hands out both ways.

You probably don't remember Dinah, dad, though I introduced you once. American. Wore enormous floral dresses and battered brown sandals. You remarked upon it. Wholemeal woman, you called her. Had long dark hair half-way down her back. Always quoting Blake. She positively quivered with sincerity. Into palmistry, phrenology, vegetarianism, astrology. You obviously found her intolerable. Gave her a talk on Original Sin.

Somewhere she'd come across that story about the fox and the hedgehog. And this had made a big impression. In fact she told me after we'd been to see you that you were a hedgehog and I was a fox, and this was the source of all our misunderstandings.

The fox, you see, knows many things but the hedgehog knows one big thing. And she asked me what the big thing was that the hedgehog my father knew but I couldn't tell her. And I still don't know. The only thing I remember saying was that you were so fierce in the few things you did believe not because of any inherited credulity or superstition but because you found it almost impossible to believe anything or anyone. Was it mother who did that to you? Who made you lose faith in all the possible sources of information? Was that why you had to go and kill her?

But something struck me last night. Do you remember the last time we all drove down to Hastings together? I remember it because, lying amongst the usual squashed hedgehogs at the side of the road, there was also a dead fox. I told you, dad, but you weren't listening. You were driving in that fierce way of yours, the way you did so many things and you weren't listening. It only occurred to me just now that however many things or even perhaps the one big thing the hedgehog and the fox knew between them, neither had been smart enough to get out of the headlights while the opportunity remained.

Now the phone's ringing and I'm not going to answer it. It won't be someone offering me money, that's for sure. It will be whatever agency has been selected to inform me about the latest debts arising from my life. And they must be getting desperate to start phoning at this time of night. What's it all gone to pay for then? The way I play the trumpet. Worth every penny.

The phone rang and rang but there was no answer. Out around the stews of Wandsworth, Digby thought. I dare say my son has gone a-wooing. Or he's blowing his trumpet at a pubful of inebriates. Another night spent molesting the silence. Either way, he obviously doesn't really need my money after all.

Digby walked over to the window and pulled back the curtains to stare out into the night. The wind was veering and backing with a brutal whimsy that at times slid towards hysteria. Dustbin lids were taking flight. Car alarms were self-activating into their relentless electronic duotones. The cats had fled the little jungle of his garden as the weather harried itself into skittish dementia. The night had finally gone mad.

Koré

Over Digby's mantelpiece was a framed postcard dated 1948 though printed long before. It showed Stoke and its bottle chimneys, the skies occluded entirely by industry's fumes. So black was the photograph that the legend it carried – GREETINGS FROM THE SMOKE – had simply been reversed out in white. Daisy pointed to it one day and Digby took it down and slid it from its frame so that she could see the exquisite copperplate on the reverse, which read: *In the smoke of the gunnes let us entre the gate,* a quotation from Hall's Chronicle.

'What does it mean?' Daisy had asked.

'It was a challenge to me. One that I rose to, in fact. I think it might have led to my ruin.'

'You don't look very ruined, darling. I still don't know what it means, though.'

'I think my Uncle Freddie, who was the one who wrote it, was asking me one of his favourite questions: what is the price of money? He was fond of pointing out that the money we have ourselves always seems hard-earned, whereas everyone else's appears to have been acquired far too cheaply.'

'Uncle Freddie?'

'My teacher. My mentor. The one who led me through the smoke. We wouldn't put up with all that smoke now, would we? Not here anyway. I suppose we still permit it elsewhere.'

'In the third world we positively encourage it, according to my son. Higher productivity there matters more than anybody's life. It's one of the things Howard keeps going on about.'

'We used to be our own third world. The price of a man,' Digby said, almost to himself, remembering the words in the *Radix Manifesto*. 'Could that be the same thing as the price of money, I wonder?'

Daisy had picked up another framed picture. This was a photograph of Digby on his wedding day, tall, thin, bespectacled, smilingly overwhelmed by the occasion. And there beside him was his small, young, black-haired bride.

'So that's Victoria. She was very beautiful.'

'Yes,' Digby said, hardly glancing at the picture, 'yes, she was.'

'Doesn't look exactly English.'

'Maltese.'

'What happened to her, Digby?' He paused for a moment before speaking again.

'According to my son, I killed her.'

'And did you?' Daisy didn't know whether to smile or not. Digby himself wasn't smiling.

'*Yet each man kills the thing he loves.*'

'Oscar Wilde. *The Ballad of Reading Gaol*. There's a recording of me somewhere at the BBC reading that. Always thought the line sounded better coming from a woman, actually.'

'Why?'

'Well, we're the ones who know what it means.' She had picked up the photograph of Theo in her other hand and was comparing the two images. 'Theo has her face.' Digby was staring out of the window at the garden and the swing. 'So how did he manage to end up in prison then, your son?'

'I set him up for it, I suppose. The first thing you must understand about my family, Daisy, is this: no good deed ever goes unpunished.'

Not all Theo's memories of prison were negative. He'd grown fond of some of his fellow inmates – Gerry, for example, who put his own comeuppance down to no more than the need to better himself. Gerry was a lifter, trapped in the same upwardly mobile vortex that affected everyone in a materialistic society, criminal and non-criminal alike.

'With Woolworth's, I was fine, Theo. Up in the morning. Daily trips down there. Sell the stuff off at night in the pub. Could be a long day sometimes. Wasn't big money but it was steady. You know what did for me, don't you? Ambition. The Tower of Babel all over again. There I was making a decent living, nothing flash, but I had to go and raise my sights higher, didn't I? So first it's Dixon's, then Peter Jones and John Lewis, Harvey Nicks, and finally Harrods. Always working my way upward. Toy Department, Pen Department, Clothes Department. At the end of the day even that's not grand enough for yours truly, is it, so I end up lifting in Jewellery where there's probably more security than punters. And that's how I got nicked. It's the oldest story in the book though, isn't it, Theo? Man reaches out for the stars and ends up floating around in the shit.'

Theo had merely nodded in agreement, touched as he was by Gerry's philosophical *rapprochement* with his fate. And for any pundits who imagine prison is not an effective deterrent Gerry might well have stood as a living rebuke to their liberal notions. For he had resolved upon his release to be foolish no more with his God-given talents: not another day of his life would he squander once he was on the out – from now on he would stick to lifting from Woolworth's, and Woolworth's alone. You knew where you were with Woolies. Such work was neither glamorous nor exotic. Merely a quiet living for an honest old lag who'd retained something of his morality and dress sense in a world gone wrong. Amongst the labyrinthine codes of honour in the prison Gerry was a traditionalist, a conservative with a small c. His was the steady and predictable sound of a Salvation Army band on a street corner when the rest of the world is down in a cellar playing free-form jazz. On hearing about some of the goings-on out there these days Gerry would shake his head at the sheer anarchy of it, the chaos, the randomness, the gratuitous offence given, the pointless violence perpetrated. 'There's no need for that sort of thing,' he would say gravely and the others would nod and murmur in agreement. 'I don't see why anyone has to go around just *causing* trouble. Do unto others as you would have them do unto you.' Gerry was a great Bible reader. He put the decline in the world of crime down to the number of youngsters either on the brown or charlied-up. What was wrong, he wanted to know, with good old-fashioned English beer? It had after all been the sustenance of generations of honest thiefs. And one day, when he judged the time to be right, he had turned to Theo and asked him: 'How d'you end up inside then, Theo?' And, taking his time over the matter, Theo had told him.

Digby had resolved to give Theo the benefit of his expertise since he undoubtedly did have some. His own departure from business had probably taught him more than any success might have done, for he had learnt something at least about the relationship between art and industry. He had put Uncle Freddie's precepts into action and discovered that they could not be acted upon; not in that particular way. Not in that society at any rate or at that precise time. Ledgers and ledgermen don't show much flexibility in such matters, since zeros along the bottom line lie heavily on the modern mind. So it was to come about that Digby Wilton was pensioned off from Wilton Bone China, so that the rest of his colleagues could get on with producing all the items he most detested.

There would be furious rows in his family home after Uncle Freddie had gone off on one of his famous trips. In pursuit of the marvellous, as he always said; that's where Digby had first got the idea from. And he would come back with some examples of modern marvels, some unexpected items for the manor's wunderkammer, even though it was only Freddie who ever referred to it in this way. Unlike Digby's father who had stayed behind to run the company, his uncle had fought in the Great War. Whatever else was in dispute about his past, this much was not. He had been wounded at the Somme. This gave him a certain prestige. Since then he appeared to have made full use of his share of the family inheritance, for he was one of the shareholders of Wilton Bone China, to the intense irritation of Digby's father who was prepared to accept his brother's role as tutor to his son, even though it had been very much his wife's idea not his, but who felt that he should stay out of the running of the business. But Freddie would turn up for board meetings, his lanky, languorous figure draped over a chair while he smoked a Turkish cigarette and listened with a look of intense boredom to the latest production figures. Then he would come back home and put Stravinsky on the gramophone. Digby would sit with him as they leafed through the latest art magazines and he pronounced judgement upon Picasso, Matisse, Modigliani. Digby loved those sessions, which never received a name in the admittedly somewhat informal syllabus that shaped his early life. Digby's father would occasionally come in, take a look over their shoulders at whatever picture they were pondering and walk straight back out again. Once Freddie arrived back from a trip with some plates from Paris bearing vivid, avant-garde designs. These he had taken to a board meeting to suggest that the company start making something of the sort. The argument was still continuing when they arrived back home in the evening.

'We'd never be able to sell them, Freddie,' Digby's father said at the dinner table, with an unmistakable note of weariness. He just wanted the subject to go away. He seemed to have little tolerance for Freddie and his eccentricities, unlike Digby's mother who often seemed to prefer the company of her brother-in-law to that of her husband, but then he was around all day. 'There's no market here for stuff like that.'

'Then create a market for it,' Freddie replied, pouring himself another glass of red wine from the decanter. 'Shake a leg, Charles, and raise the aesthetic level of the populace round these parts. Otherwise what are you for?'

'I think you might usefully ask yourself that question,' Digby's father replied crossly, his lips tightening. Digby wondered briefly if he was about to acquire a new home tutor. Or finally end up in school.

'I think all that Freddie is trying to say . . .' his mother began but she caught his father's expression and stopped. She turned her sad brown eyes back down towards the table.

'Couldn't we try at least one modern design, dad?' Digby piped up, not realising how angry his father had become beneath his impassive features.

'You can spend all day looking at the latest *objets d'art* from over the Channel with your uncle here,' his father said, raising his voice a little, which he very rarely did. 'But just remember this, my lad: without the daily grind that Freddie so casually disparages you might both have to go and join *them*.'

This was the way he always referred to the poorer people beyond the gates and as he indicated their location, down the slopes of the little park that surrounded the house, beyond the iron gates, they fell silent to consider the appalling prospect. Then Freddie started to laugh in his high-pitched squawking way and Digby's father left the room. Freddie stared at him after he had gone as if silently asking a question, and Digby knew with absolute certainty what the answer to that question must be: that when his time came he would put into action all that his father wouldn't or couldn't. He would use the factory he was destined to inherit to make some real art. He had too. Hadn't made much money from it though.

Somehow Digby had managed to talk Freddie into letting him go to the International Surrealist Exhibition at the New Burlington Galleries in London in 1936, although his tutor's trips away had previously always been a solitary business. Digby had found it all highly intriguing but certainly not shocking. In point of fact he was never to find any surrealist image shocking in the whole of his life, nor had he ever had any trouble understanding a single one of them from that day on. Indeed he had often felt in the presence of such images merely that the world made sense at last, that someone had managed to discover the hidden circuitry beneath the expected clatter of appearances. After all, the steam engine *did* come through the wall of the living room. Digby had heard it every night as it shafted its way up the gradient a quarter of a mile from Wilton Manor. And feet did become part of the stone on which they stood, contaminated with the geological chill of the millennia. Anyone who'd endured a winter in Staffordshire could vouch for that.

It was the sophistication of surrealism that Digby was to come to find disconcerting, not its primitiveness. He felt the game being played might be a little too elaborate to satisfy those more rudimentary yearnings art must stay connected to. A few years after the war he had seen the pots by Hans Coper and something connected. Here the form really was as primitive as the conception. Primitive wasn't the right word though – it was primal, not primitive. You could put it on a table or just as easily hold it up to the moon and pray. Then at an exhibition in London he saw Jakob Kirk's pots, met the man himself and knew immediately what he must do: he would produce such work in whatever quantity it was possible to produce it without losing its identity. The potter's hand would have to touch them all. Shapes like this had once been as common as the knives with which people ate and there was no law he knew of that said they could not be so again. He had found his life's work. He still had Uncle Freddie's words ringing in his ears: 'When you take over, Digby, you'll show them what can be done, won't you? Use industry to make art, just for once, instead of crushing it. Just imagine the excitement you'll cause.'

And that was exactly what he had set about doing. And where he had failed. It had been a mistake to attempt to produce the stuff in the same place, on the same premises where industry produced its commodities. His enthusiasm, his devotion, had perhaps produced confusion. He'd misunderstood the limits of the possible there. But he still believed that it was possible to sell it. To the discerning few. And that was why, in an attempt to redeem his son from the obscurity of his failure as an unknown trumpet-player and to make up for the departure of his mother from his life, he'd dreamt up the idea of Koré, a ceramics gallery in Fulham. They'd done it too between the two of them and stocked it with the very finest contemporary pottery. Much of it was from Digby's own collection but he had known exactly where to go to find the rest.

They'd even had sales that first year, too. Digby felt that he had finally done something to redress his failure with the Potter's Hand, and as an added bonus he had made his son employable in the process. During the day Theo was a gallery owner and in the evenings he could play his trumpet. Who could have asked for more? For twelve months after the opening Digby had begun to feel something he'd given up ever expecting to feel again: happiness. He didn't actually realise what was going on of course and looking back on it he was pretty certain Theo hadn't known what was going on either. Even the judge had said as much during his summing-up. Whether he should have known was another question altogether. Looking back on life we should have all known a lot better, shouldn't we?

As so often with mischief, it had all been a matter of contiguous geography. Ten minutes' walk from Koré was an old converted bakery. Although it wasn't a public house it served drinks. If it was a club it was one with no official membership, no entry cards, no signing-in book and seemingly no hours of closure. Its workings were as baffling to the Inland Revenue and the VAT inspectors as they were to the general public. Technically speaking the place had no name because technically speaking it didn't exist. But it was known to its users as Doug's, a reference to its owner and presiding spirit Doug Fitch. Fitch's curriculum vitae had apparently been dictated on the boundary between the mysterious and the murky and whenever it was written down, invisible ink had had to be used. He had undoubtedly spent some time detained at Her Majesty's pleasure, and if he could justifiably claim on the positive side to have given considerable assistance to the Metropolitan Police and their miscellaneous inquiries over the years, they could have pointed out with equal justice that he'd needed to be arrested each time before eventually agreeing to do so.

Doug's walls were covered with large paintings of extremely dubious provenance. School of Rubens, School of Canaletto, School of Rembrandt. It all looked impressive though, as did the exquisitely pornographic etchings in his toilets. A fellow could get serious ideas in there before returning to eye up his companion for the evening. Some of the clientele were just locals who had come to know Doug over the years, and probably to like him too, for despite his slightly sinister limping gait and the remains of a razor slash down his right cheek he could be very good company when the mood was on him. Some of the visitors were truly alarming. Doug's occluded activities still went on here and there and many a fugitive figure came and went to assist him in the prosecution of his duties up and down the land. The truth was that there was probably nothing you couldn't acquire from Doug's; it was just a matter of talking to the right person on the right evening and offering the right amount of money.

It didn't take long before Theo ended up there doing some serious late-night drinking. And Doug took an interest in the newcomer. He even started going round to the gallery and peering in the big pots that stood about on the wooden floors. Then he began turning up with his associates. In fact it wasn't long before Doug Fitch was spending as much time round at Koré as Theo was spending round at Doug's. Theo was flattered, even a little baffled. Doug would arrive with bottles of vintage wine and tell many entertaining stories; Doug's friends would then tell more. On hearing that Theo was a jazz trumpeter he had arranged for Zeno to play various gigs for his clients. This had gone down very well with the boys. Dove, Paul, Reg, Pete and the Breezer all reckoned Doug Fitch was a good thing. Everyone agreed that the relationship between Doug and Theo was one of genuine warmth and mutual assistance, but it transpired later that Doug had been deriving considerably more from it in the way of assistance than anyone had guessed.

One of the few things Doug Fitch genuinely feared in life was a drugs bust and the consequent dark trouble it could entail for his unorthodox establishment. For this reason he forbade all taking and selling of dope on his premises. But it would be naïve to imagine that this meant he didn't continue buying and selling the stuff. He had, after all, to consolidate his position in a constantly changing market. It wasn't as though it was easy to break even out there. When he had walked around Koré and peered into those deep pots, and once he had realised quite what a relaxed regime Theo presided over, joints upstairs, wine downstairs in the gallery, the owner occasionally playing his trumpet while visitors milled about at their own meandering pace, Koré had instantly recommended itself to him as a useful rendezvous.

The police had never entirely lost interest in Doug; in fact they frequently trained a wary eye in his direction. They'd even sent a few undercover boys round to his place to see if they could insinuate themselves into his confidence. Doug could always sniff them out. He could smell any copper a mile away and he would soon make it plain they weren't welcome. But there was a recent associate of his, Martin Fylde, in whom the police had a particular interest. Small and dapper, double-breasted, short-haired, respectable-looking Martin, they reckoned, after some close observation, was attempting to establish a new network of heroin distribution across London. And they were right.

Thus did it come to pass that when the drugs squad, after trailing Fylde for several weeks and noting how often he appeared to drop in at the Koré gallery, finally raided Digby's pride and joy, they found many substantial foil-wrapped packages lurking at the bottom of two of Jakob Kirk's larger and narrower pots. They were not visible in the darkness of the pots' interiors, which was why Martin and Doug had had two lever-clasps especially adapted for their own personal use. Telescopic devices that slipped easily into a pocket. All it needed then was for one of them to distract Theo for a while, never a difficult task for anyone at any time, and the other could either deposit or retrieve packages in a matter of seconds. The great advantage of the arrangement from Doug's point of view was that it was all happening on someone else's premises, not his.

Even the judge had admitted that Theo had been more of a fool than a rogue. But he felt the right message had to be sent out all the same about the sale of hard drugs, given the scourge it had become amongst the present generation. Hence Theo's sentence, subsequently reduced to nine months for good behaviour.

'They fitted you up good and proper, didn't they?' Gerry said when Theo had finished his tale. 'Good and proper, they did.' Then Harry had come by, jabbering away to himself as usual. Gerry had shaken his head with the gravity of a general disappointed at the calibre of his latest recruits: 'Can't do his bang-up. It's already in the post for that one.'

Shards

The trial attracted a certain amount of attention. It must have been about this time that Digby had decided he didn't want to look at newspapers any more. He'd already seen enough of them for one lifetime, but not before his attention had been drawn to one of the red-tops by a zealous friend. 'Tarr Talks Straight' was the column. In exploring whether or not to sue over its veiled allegation that he had covertly financed his son in a life of drug-dealing, Digby had found out more about the Tarr in question than he could reasonably have wished. Toby Tarr had a strong sense of his own privacy and the necessity of its protection. As for anyone else's, its invasion was merely a matter of profit as far as he was concerned. He felt without ever having examined the matter much that he was entitled to his own privacy and at a push to anyone else's too. The privacy of others, turned inside out in one of his columns, was invariably lurid, sometimes hilarious and frequently a little tragic. If those others didn't take the same legal steps he himself did to prevent the poisonous trivia of their lives leaking into the press or taking to the airwaves like a malignant virus, so much the worse for them. It was like leaving your car unlocked or forgetting to cancel the milk when going on holiday for a fortnight. Ask for trouble and you'll get it. In Tarr's case many of those who didn't actually ask got it anyway. Enough to make a few of them think of suicide for a while.

His short-sentenced prose chimed perfectly with a prevailing mood of self-righteous thuggery. He mimicked an illiteracy of sense and sensibility with considerable success. He had learnt along with many others to pretend that his arts degree from an ancient university had been a brief and mistaken interlude in an otherwise impeccable curriculum vitae of brothel-visiting, beer-puking, foul-mouthed debauchery. He even claimed to have nicked a few car radios in his adolescent years, as lads invariably do. Any failure by the national team left him gutted in his column the following day, though no one who knew him could recall him ever attending a football game. He was dutifully appalled if any member of the government, the royal family or the armed forces should be discovered using recreational drugs, though his own consumption of white powder in his early days on the paper had been sufficiently legendary to earn him the sobriquet of Tobe the Tube from the pool of hard-drinking subs. And he employed the word 'shag' in his pieces at least once a week to show that he was an ordinary bloke, a four-square, no-nonsense man of the people. A fellow of average emotions, unexceptional opinions and regulation appetites. Just a geezer like any other despite his degree from Oxford, his detached house in Surrey, his Mercedes convertible and the £150,000 a year (plus expenses) he expected to bring in from his acres of blokeish prose. He had adapted to the requirements of the age with considerable agility. He was a man of his time. He'd even briefly considered a tattoo but heard reports that the process could be painful. Toby's editorial line on pain was that it was best inflicted on others. Those who actually volunteered for it were probably SM perverts, who should be kept well away from Boy Scouting or the teaching profession and who needed (well, let's be straight about this and cut out all the wordy crap) a straightforward, honest-to-goodness shag.

To the extent that Tarr was full of the age's waste products, which he most assuredly was, his mental detritus was the *Zeitgeist*'s too. In any case, the ceaseless shower of money aspersed him: holy water for unholy times. His mother, still alive and sprightly in Richmond, lamented that her son's locution, those vowels she had made sure were of an impeccable pedigree, had now turned estuarine. She occasionally saw him on television and her pride at his appearance there was radically offset by his pantomime cockney diction. Had he ever spoken like that during his upbringing she'd have stopped his weekly allowance until he gave up any such ludicrous pretence of proletarian genealogy. For such a clever young fellow he seemed to take a particular pleasure in sounding off like a wretched little ingrate. The only thing that could be said about his speech these days was that it wasn't quite as repellent as his prose. When she occasionally read Tobias's column, and it was very occasionally indeed, she gave thanks that his father, a serious and cultured fellow, was six feet underground.

Come off it, Potman

That had been the title of the piece and probably the most distinguished phrase in it, if you were scanning with an eye to either vocabulary or taste. Digby had felt as though he'd been forced to strip naked in the centre of Trafalgar Square. He would wake in the night thinking he could hear the press-rooms humming as the furies yawned and stretched to their fresh themes. Such catalogues of sorrow and catastrophe in the daily chronicle. But soon after that it was all over and Theo was safely ensconced inside Wandsworth Prison. During the very short conversation they had had prior to his incarceration, his son had made it plain to Digby that he still held him personally responsible for the death of his mother. So much for that particular scheme of redemption then. And Digby didn't feel as though he could defend himself with any honour. How can you disparage a mother to her son?

The one missing figure at the proceedings had been Doug Fitch.

One of the snouts the squad were using at the time happened to owe Doug one, and he'd made a very discreet telephone call to Fulham half an hour before the raid. By the time the officers rushed into Koré, Doug Fitch had been well on his way to Victoria Station.

The day after the trial Doug had woken at five, hepped-up and raddled from the night before. He'd had to remind himself that he was in Spain now, not London. He would stay there for a while since he had absolutely no intention of joining Martin Fylde behind bars. He felt bad about Theo, it had to be admitted. Hadn't expected him to have to do porridge. But a man so feckless and unsuspecting, so ready to open the door to the fox and show him round the hen coop, was bound to end up getting fixed by somebody, wasn't he? If it hadn't been Doug it would have been Jack or Jim or Harry, almost certainly someone who'd have stitched him up worse. And his sentence wasn't all that long whichever way you looked at it, given that he wouldn't be serving more than half of it, any more than anyone else ever did these days. Being inside might even teach him a thing or two. After getting up to pour a pint of chilled water down his throat, to rid himself of the feeling that he'd spent the previous evening eating parrot-soiled sandpaper, it hadn't taken Doug too long to get back to sleep. Then other things had come along to occupy him, new international projects and innovative schemes, and he was never to think much of Theo again.

The Mysteries of Capital

'Did they actually have Chinese take-aways in those days?'

'Well, they had them in China, obviously.' There was a pause.

'Malcolm's son was in here last night.'

'Oh yes.'

'Full uniform job.'

'That's right, he joined the army, didn't he?'

'Didn't he though. Going on and on about his basic training and how it nearly wiped him out.'

'Heard it can be a bit gruelling.'

'Lost a stone in three weeks, apparently. But he's a young man. Joined the armed forces. Anyway, I told him. I said, it's only pain, Trevor, that's all. I mean, pain never hurt anybody, did it?'

Theo stood at the bar and listened as the conversation continued. He wasn't standing in the pub in Wandsworth but he might as well have been. Then he saw Paul arrive. Paul was the least communicative of the band and Theo sometimes thought he might like him the best. Blond and bearded, he never let slip his stance of flinty Yorkshire isolationism. It was as though his mind remained at the top of a moor awaiting the next blizzard, even though his body had long ago moved away to Britain's populous sump in the South-East. He played the double-bass with ascetic scrupulosity, as though an unneeded note would promptly lead to bankruptcy. He had, for as long as anyone could remember, been writing a novel.

'Won't be commercial,' he would say lugubriously. 'Probably won't even get published.' To that degree if no more he had been prescient. And so he continued to look askance at anyone whose books accrued into self-advertising piles in bookshops; vulgarians prepared to perpetrate the indignity of being interviewed by Melvyn Bragg on prime-time television. And he played on with Zeno, all his most distinctive riffs borrowed from his beloved Mingus. Like the shapes of crystals, each player had defaulted to his own unique setting.

Theo bought him a drink.

'How's the old man?' Paul asked and Theo shrugged. Paul was the only member of the band ever to have met Digby. As it happened they shared a crucial area of research. For Paul, prior to writing his interminable and unpublishable novel *North*, had for years been engaged on a thesis entitled 'Industrial Utopia'. Before becoming Zeno's latest addition he had been living in a house built of millstone grit by the architect Ingram Lapish one hundred and fifty years before – three small bedrooms, kitchen, rudimentary living room – where he had spent his evenings in research and his days working at the local Workers' Educational Association. This had been two hundred miles north in Saltaire, the model industrial village created by the Victorian worsted manufacturer Titus Salt. Realising the spendthrift under-utilisation in the northern woollen trade of both the goat's fur and the llama's, Salt had developed machines to produce and refine mohair and alpaca, becoming immensely wealthy in the process. So he'd constructed a workers' paradise and Paul had arranged to live in the heart of it.

The papers had mounted up on the table before him. He'd stared at them and they'd stared back. He had originally moved there in a mood of cynical curiosity but now his feelings about the buildings and people surrounding him had ceased to be so simple. They had in fact become complex to the point of being at times well nigh unfathomable. The title of his thesis had been intended to carry at least a rumour of irony – the notion that some mighty Victorian industrialist could really provide the perfect living environment in which his workers might thrive and prosper, materially and spiritually, had seemed to him so self-evidently contradictory that he had considered his case proven before the work had even begun. The village where he'd been domiciled was surely capitalism's window-dressing; a gleaming mask of alms-giving, widow-comforting, child-educating, worker-nurturing beneficence with which to confront the world while it made off with the loot through the back door. Made off with the whole world's scattergood prodigality.

Paul had come to wish that he had never moved into the village at all, then he might have kept his prejudices intact and simply finished his thesis which had grown longer and less sure of itself by the day, riddled now with parenthetical queries, cumbered increasingly by lengthy quibbling foot-notes and ambiguous appendices. Paul had once thought he could see right through Sir Titus Salt and his conveniently profitable paradise on earth. But as he stood each day before the founder's statue on the green he began to feel as if that stony buccaneering figure of northern manufacture, that dispenser of proletarian accommodation, education and hygiene on an industrial scale, was staring instead right through him, asking which of them was truly of a scale to encompass the other. What's it all about, Paul? the statue of Titus had begun to ask each day and Paul had started to mumble in his answers.

What was it all about? What was he doing there? Trying to trace how humankind had signed the landscape all around him with the oppressive weight of its reality; had mounted it, scoured it, channelled it, scorched it, built cities on it, veined it with railways, roadways, canalways. Had ruined it in its own image. Sometimes the ruin was beautiful, at other times hideous. Anonymous labour in prodigious, profligate, inestimable quantities lay behind it all.

The history on which he had been raised at school, a chronicle of crowned heads and pageantry with a murmurous background of distant slaughter, he had rejected in its entirety – such genitive progressions of fecund misery, with the emblems of heraldic arms atop them. He'd set himself the task instead of identifying, insofar as identification was possible, the feet that had made the first footpaths, the hands that had raised the packhorse bridges, the dry-stone wallers, their slabs and slates mortared together by air and skill, the same anonymous hands that had attended the shuttles and looms with a ghost-like rapidity of disembodied movement. The documents of these people weren't in any muniments room, for they'd never managed to muster a single muniments room between them in all their years. Their documents were the land itself, the mines they had burrowed, the buildings lifted up towards the skies with bruised and calloused fingers, fossils of the industries that had at first nurtured and then at last killed them, and Paul was the geologist hunting after those remains. He fervently wished to reconstruct these lives as palaeontologists had reconstructed dinosaurs from the scattered bones the earth held in its keeping. For it hadn't been so long ago and such souls had been our own kith and kin. Indifference, the last oppression of all, seemed to him one final insult from the far side of the grave.

So he pressed on, trying to express all this somehow. Thesis in the end was abandoned for novel and now the novel lay pretty much abandoned too. He couldn't find a structure. Structures needed to be solid but the modern world had contrived things so that all that is solid melts into air. He couldn't find a contemporary shape big enough to fit Titus Salt into. But when Theo had mentioned the work his father had been presently doing on *Wilton Bone China: Two Centuries of Family Tradition*, Paul had shown an uncharacteristic enthusiasm in his wish to meet him. Theo had arranged it, just the once, and the two of them had drunk tea and spoken of Ruskin and Bradford and the Potteries and Stoke. Paul had liked the old fellow; he liked all dignified and articulate old men of whatever class, however dubious he was of the system that nourished them. He didn't do much writing any more. He had taken a job teaching at a polytechnic in Middlesex, which had recently been renamed a university. He didn't like it much; felt that he'd escaped one type of factory up north only to end up in a different sort down south. Factories of hands; factories of brains. And in the evenings he did the one thing he really could enjoy by playing double-bass with passion and exactitude.

'Give the old man my regards, would you?' he said as the other members of the band started arriving and they shuffled off to set up the stage. 'Tell him Paul said to take care of himself.'

Kropotkin's Children

The road was sleeping. The bright eyes of the big houses had darkened and closed. An occasional car hummed along in the distance but even that had a dreamlike quality. That's when the explosion occurred. That's when Daisy's garage roof flew off the garage walls with such velocity that it crashed down twenty yards away as the neighbourhood's windows shattered inwards, shards flying through the air of living rooms, children screaming as they woke, women turning with bloody streaming faces, weeping silently at the bewildered men beside them. The blast was so loud it made even the windows on the other side of Wandsworth Common tremble. So loud that Daisy woke up sweating and moaning from her recurrent dream, to hear no more than the sound of the wind outside, and swore this time to get this matter resolved once and for all. She would have to call upon Digby's chemical expertise and what was left of his military discipline; there was simply nothing else for it.

'Well, he's right,' Digby said later that morning as Daisy finished reading out a section from the *Radix Bulletin*. 'The precursors of nitroglycerine *are* unstable. Without proper controls and monitors it's the molecular equivalent of filling one half of a pub with Rangers supporters and the other half with Celtic, and then providing them with unlimited supplies of alcohol all night. What you might call an explosive situation, Daisy.'

'But now, listen to the last bit.' She lifted up the final sheet of the print-out and delicately bit her tongue. Then she started to read: 'It would most certainly not be a good idea to have this material stacked for example in five-litre plastic containers in a garage, where the temperature and humidity can vary wildly from day to day according to random fluctuations in the weather.'

'Also true,' Digby said. 'Pretty obvious but nevertheless true.'

'You don't go out much do you, Digby?'

'Hardly at all. Except when my cleaner's son Desmond drives me to mass or to consult one of my professional advisers. Or when I have to feed your pussies.'

'How do you fancy breaking your fast again?'

'Not much.'

'It wouldn't be far you'd have to go, *mon vieux copain*.'

'How far?'

'Just to my garage.'

'Why would I want to go to your garage, Daisy?'

'So that you could have a look at a stack of five-litre plastic containers, all filled with some sort of dark liquid, and tell me whether I really need to stop being so sentimental about that absent son of mine and just phone the police.'

Digby had managed to venture out to feed the cats without any notable ill effects. So, after making sure he was well wrapped up, buttoned and muffled and hatted, Daisy had led her elderly neighbour into the chill December air.

As they stood there together on the garage's cold concrete floor Digby turned and looked into Daisy's eyes. He had a sudden vision then that made him smile. It was of both of them being blown to smithereens in an instant, except of course that he was watching this spectacle from a distant camera angle, the way he so often seemed to look at Daisy. She started smiling too. Now they were both on film.

'No, we're too old to do Bonnie and Clyde, Digs.'

'Please, Daisy, don't ever call me Digs.'

'I suppose it does make you sound like a particularly insalubrious Australian criminal.'

'No. Damp accommodation in Bognor Regis. I stayed there once.'

He edged forward cautiously and finally unfastened a cap from one of its plastic containers. He sniffed. For some reason, while all his other senses had rotted away, his sense of smell had remained in full force, feeling if anything even more acute. Was that possible? It seemed to him that the modern world all too frequently stank so God alone knew what the ancient one must have been like. A withering of that particular sense might have represented something of a blessing. But not today. He sniffed again and reasonably sure of what his nose was telling him dipped a finger into the murky brown liquid. Putting the finger to his mouth, he licked. Daisy looked on with her own fragile finger pressed to her almost bloodless lip. Once more Digby, entirely confident now, poked his finger deeper into the plastic container and stuck it in his mouth. He sucked on it contentedly. Finally he turned back towards her.

'Tell me,' he said, 'does that son of yours ever make home-made beer?'

★

'I think I'm going to kick the little bugger down the stairs when he gets back from wherever he is.'

'I don't think making beer at home's a crime as yet. But give them time and I'm sure they'll find a way.'

'No, but why is there so much information about explosives on the Radix website?'

'I don't know,' Digby said, handing Daisy a glass of the claret for which she had such a taste. He now placed a weekly order through Desmond's mother. He went and poured a gin and tonic. He felt curiously self-satisfied. He had after all handled himself with the sang-froid of a bomb-disposal expert. He turned and looked at Daisy. Her face had closed. Suspicion, he thought: the narrowing of the eyes, the sour and quizzical appraisal. It comes to all of us sooner or later, my dear. Sooner in his case. It rather suited Daisy. Fitted perfectly into the filigree lines about her eyes. Sorrow, the old lacemaker.

A few moments later they laid all the print-outs over the floor in a final attempt to fathom what Howard might be up to.

'And in another column he has listed everything under this heading: Chemicals not to be Kept under any Circumstances in the Home. Now what does that mean, Digby?'

'Either precisely what it says, I suppose, or the precise opposite. It could be precautionary advice of a sound nature or what I believe the priests of my Church refer to as an antinomian suggestion. Your son could merely be trying to ensure that his fellow demonstrators are abiding by the law. Or he could be trying to encourage all of us to break it. Difficult to tell with the young these days, isn't it? But let's not jump to conclusions about what your son is up to. He's at least entitled to be treated as innocent until proven guilty.'

Meticulous Digby had then sorted the sheets which Daisy had shuffled towards incoherence in her search for a phrase here or a paragraph there which might incriminate her absent son. He put them into sequence and started reading from the beginning. She let him get on with it. After an hour or so he looked up.

'You haven't really read this, have you, Daisy?'

'Well, bits and pieces. It all makes me so cross whenever I get started.'

'All the stuff about chemicals appears to be a lengthy and, I would have said, very knowledgeable book review. And this section here seems to be some sort of editorial.'

'Editorial?'

'If this were all printed on decent paper and bound together I'd have said it was the proofs for a magazine. Is that possible?'

'A magazine? What, something like *Vogue*, you mean?'

'No. Not like *Vogue* exactly. What did you say your son did again?'

'He's an internet journalist.'

'Then this must be his internet journal. Or the proofs for it anyway. Whenever it gets really interesting this phrase recurs.'

'Thailand Great Anakh?'

'That's the one. It keeps saying, *See Thailand Great Anakh.* Have you tried that?'

'Many times.'

'And what does it say?'

'*Greetings to the law.* I'm going to phone James.'

'Your first ex?'

'Howard's father and my first ex.'

And while Daisy went next door to get her phone book

Kropotkin's Children

Digby continued reading the editorial of what he could only assume was the Radix Group's planned internet journal.

May Day

Amongst the costumed zanies, the kilts, the sarongs, the antlered heads, the shifting focuses of countless eyes still blurred with last night's dope, the bony hands reaching out and sometimes shaking, amongst a Dunsinane of home-made wooden whistles fluting their celtic laments, two young women dressed entirely in alien, flashing silver foil, wrapped up in fact like turkeys for Christmas, their eyes daubed a vivid green, their hair twisted into silver spikes, sang a song about the one and the many. At least that's what I think it was about. The many was what we were; the one what we were expected to become. And for those of us who choose not to, expect penalties. Newspapers and pamphlets were handed out from every corner, sometimes in exchange for money and sometimes not, their typography and graphic design bespeaking a cherished unprofessionalism, embodying whatever is the opposite of slickness, the orthography inept, the syntax dependably wonky. Children, blissfully unkempt, dug holes in the grass. A man with dreadlocked hair, and boots like the pair Van Gogh portrayed inside a peasant's cottage, stumbled about offering an amiable grin to anyone prepared to receive it. Another man on high stilts stomped up and down, his brass-buttoned red jacket festooned with slogans about the iniquities of hunting, a stuffed fox wearing a golden crown tucked under his arm. That wore a royal grin too.

This I soon realised was a crowd of unglobalised people. No one here had been homogenised. Or if they ever had been they certainly weren't any more. The nearest they came to homogenisation was when a small group, unanarchistically shaped into a phalanx and draped in black, smashed up a McDonald's along the road. Then came the homogenised response of the police with their baton charges and their pincer movement of civil containment, which is in fact most uncivil when experienced by those actually being contained. Someone else had been throwing stones so obviously we must be punished. If globalisation is an invisible factory that girdles the globe then these people are its rejects, its self-proclaimed cast-offs, who make themselves useless for the universal project by the flamboyant misshapenness of their individuality. They are the human debris the big machine cannot employ or process through its intestines. As I left the demo a traveller came up to me and gave me a paper rose. I smiled my thanks and turned to stare at it. I suppose it had been constructed in the corner of a disused field or an ancient car park somewhere, behind the dirty windows of a fifty-year-old bus that would otherwise long before have been scrapped, given our ceaseless mania for the demolition of commodities. After all, the new commodity can only flourish if the old one is destroyed. For commodities the son can only dance on the father's bones. The consumer society is founded on the notion of a disposable world: we now have the means to trash all the reality we have inherited, then we can simply make ourselves a better one.

Like the hat on the traveller's head the rose was touchingly misaligned. At the bottom the stem was torn into papery ganglia, signifying tiny roots.

'Just make it grow,' she said to me before taking her small child by the hand and leading him away. And that was the beginning of Radix. This journal of liberation was conceived that day. Through the artifice of our technology a new reality may at last grow that isn't artificial. A new reality that recognises the validity of an older one and so doesn't need to demolish it merely to make space for its own development. Not everything humanity makes becomes a commodity. Some artefacts, asymmetric in their integrity, refuse that status.

Unlike the rose Radix doesn't even need to use paper to find its form and spread its message and so the forests can remain standing.

In the next house Daisy had got through to James.

'Why didn't you tell him to phone me?'

'I did.'

'Well, he hasn't. Did you ask him what Thailand Great Anakh means?'

'Yes.'

'And what did he say?'

'He just started laughing and rang off.'

Closing Time

One of the things that had most intrigued Paul when he had talked with Theo's father in his big, redbrick house at the edge of Wandsworth Common was the old man's total immersion in John Ruskin. He'd been doing research for that period of the company's history at the time and he'd been very thorough indeed in his reading. He didn't so much quote Ruskin as use the dead man's words as though they were his own.

'He taught us that we utter the values of our time not just in our books but in our artefacts and buildings. But don't ask me what we've actually learnt from it. Do you think Ruskin would feel any better about the things around him if he were alive today?'

As Digby said this Paul had thought of the mill in Halifax where his father had worked all his life until they'd closed it down. They'd all thought it was bad enough working at the mill but they were soon to discover that not working at the mill could be even worse. It had had its own grandeur about it, there was no denying that. Victorian architects had taken all the lessons they needed from the Romans. Now it had all been broken up into flats and prettified. The great machines no longer hummed day and night inside it. Instead there were window-boxes filled with flowers. Not only do we speak our age, it seemed, but we can even come to rephrase it entirely in terms of elegy and metamorphosis, heritage and self-congratulation. Paul was soon elbowed out of his reverie by Breezer's rant. It had obviously not been a good week at the school over in Battersea; the atoms and molecules had failed to gain easy access to the minds of the young and Breezer the frustrated physics teacher was getting a few things off his chest before the gig.

'I can't work out whether he's a tosspot or a twat.'

'Now these are subtle distinctions, Breezer. We're navigating deep waters here,' Pete said.

'There's a pretty sizeable difference, you know.'

'Between a tosspot and a twat?'

'Exactly. Terms of abuse need to be used with some precision. Old Ted behind the bar there is obviously a fuckwit, possibly even a dickhead, but I don't think anybody'd want to call him an arsehole, do you? That would be to overstep the mark.'

'You should write a book, Breezer. All these scholarly distinctions. Most people aren't aware of the fine gradations available to them in profanity's lexicon.'

He'll be blowing hard tonight, Paul thought, making a mental note to ensure that he did not end up at any point south of the big man's rear. For the Breezer had acquired his name through an indelicate attribute. Nobody would ever play behind him because of the truly prodigious blasts of flatulence he expelled on an average night. Even Paul, who had once worked on a farm in the Dales for three months in his late teens and had grown used to the interminable farts emitted from lowing ruminants as they pumped industrial quantities of methane from their rear ends into the atmosphere, even he had been startled by the seemingly inexhaustible amount of wind permitted egress through the saxophonist's fundament. However hard he blew through the mouthpiece of his horn, a greater gale always seemed to blow from the other end. It was as though there was a bellows in there with stereo outlets. This trait had earned him, among the musicians who'd had the privilege of sharing his stage, his affectionate sobriquet. The Breezer. Occasionally on particularly noxious evenings when he'd been on the beans and lager he became Force Nine. Tonight Paul resolved to stay well out of the wind tunnel.

'Roger Pringole,' Paul said quietly.

'That wanking lickspittle country gobshite fucking toad,' Breezer intoned, with evident sincerity.

'He's standing behind you, Breezer.'

'What?'

'He's presently about nine inches from your left ear, mate, pointing north-northwesterly.'

Breezer turned slowly in his chair and stared up at the towering figure of Roger Pringole, legendary radio producer, smiling darkly down at him. Breezer's trademark scowl transmuted swiftly into his most ingratiating smile.

'Hi. Rog. How's it going, man? I'd been meaning to call you, funnily enough. Got another tape we've just finished. It's great, actually. Thought you might be interested. You coming to the gig?'

'No,' Pringole said, his dark smile unaltered. 'I live round the corner. Just called in for a pint.' And as he left Breezer never took his eyes from his back but started to speak once more.

'Dandyprat. He's a media tart, isn't he? Just a fucking tart.

Nothing wrong with tarts, don't get me wrong. But at least the girls in Vienna back in 1945 got a pair of silk stockings for their knee-trembler down the alley; all he gets is two minutes on *Newsnight* being continually interrupted by somebody called Jeremy.'

There was a jazz renaissance going on. New names had been suddenly inflated like brightly coloured balloons at a party: Tommy Smith, Courtney Pine, Jason Rebello, Steve Williams. They lifted off and flew away, but the problem was that the boys from Zeno were still exactly where they'd been when they started: doing crappy gigs round London. Adding their distinctive timbre to the alcoholic fumes of a variety of boozing holes. Nothing seemed to change much except that time passed and everyone grew a little older. They'd also got a lot better, working their material over the years until it was second nature to them. And Theo, after he came out of prison, had played like an angel. They had listened in wonder. They thought his time inside would probably produce what resting boxers call ring-rust, but the opposite had happened. He had learnt to think his music instead of simply playing it. It came out of his head and his heart and only then through the trumpet. Sometimes they all played so well they applauded each other. But not enough people noticed. They had their devotees, but they never added up to more than six or seven a night. Why couldn't they make more people notice?

The boys themselves noticed that while they themselves made their way around the cafés of Stoke Newington, the cellars of Islington or the newly sprouting bistros and loose-boxes of Clerkenwell, glamorous gigs hosted heavy sets by hot young musicians. A new species of gilded British jazz was dazzling the bright eyes of the glittering people. Stylish new hornmen were blowing them away. Some of these musicians had even reverted to tuxedos, so as to emphasise the formality and gravitas of the occasions. But Zeno's gigs weren't glamorous and they were advertised if at all only by black-and-white photocopied A4 sheets crookedly pasted on to dirty windows. LIVE JAZZ THIS FRIDAY, they announced: DON'T MISS THE LEGENDARY ZENO. Posted beside this now was the spread from the *North Putney Gazette* but even so you could almost hear the murmurs of perplexity: the legendary *who*? A potent sense usually obtained of last night's unemptied ashtrays, a urinous aroma, the posthumous presence of dead drinks on the air. Too much anticipatory excitement at such venues was well-nigh impossible either for the performers or the listeners. Zeno still managed to get a burn going once they were on, but they knew that what they needed was somebody there who might take due notice and write it all up in the press the following day. Where were they, the A & R men, those elusive creatures? All elsewhere apparently, getting blitzed in a manner more suited to their suits, their salaries, their status. Even the grunge in Zeno's world too often seemed *déclassé* grunge, not the potent and occluded grunge that writers for Sunday newspapers suddenly discover has transmuted overnight into the latest golden fashion. Some nights, more and more nights if the truth were told, they were playing gold. But where was the gold they should be receiving in return? But then Ruskin, as Paul often told the other members of the band in satisfaction, had taken a very dim view of the role gold had played in the history of humanity. Not, as he had to admit, that the old fellow would have been likely to think much more highly of

Zeno. Or would he? They seemed to have left it a little late to ask.

Theo walked over to the piano where Pete was sitting. The squat blue dispenser on which Pete occasionally sucked was perched above the keyboard. Theo had taken a couple of tokes once while Pete was in pursuit of some hefty, careworn woman in a headscarf, just to see if there was a hit of any kind in it. He had squirted and sucked. But nothing. Just chill vapour and a hint of hospital wards. If that was Pete's idea of a good time he wasn't surprised all his women looked like cashiered nurses. Anyone younger would have been bound to clear off in search of a bigger rush. It was about as exciting as kissing the nozzle on a vinegar bottle.

Pete was constantly running to fat and occasionally arriving. Then he would starve himself for weeks, barely speaking to anyone except to look up with an occasional growl from his Diet Coke and mutter, 'Filthy. Filthy. This pub's filthy.' A great many of the pubs they worked in *were* filthy. People smoked in them and let their butts and ash fall on the table and the floor. The more drinks were drunk, the more drinks were spilt. They ate untidily leaving fragments of what they didn't consume mouldering on greasy plates. Pete in his ascetical mode observed such things with punitive vividness. He would stare about him with a permanent look of pained incredulity.

(Breezer's obesity was altogether less problematical. Each additional year brought additional pounds to his weight. He shrugged, ate another burger, drank another pint, ran his hand through his ragged beard and cheerfully farted. 'The fat buggers are having a hard time of it,' he'd say, with a note of elegy in his voice. 'They used to be emperors, kings of creation, the envy of every emaciated churl sleeping down below in the straw. Now they're sneered at. Why? Just because everyone can enjoy a good meal nobody's actually supposed to bother eating any more. The sign of wealth these days is being able to order your food in unlimited quantities then leaving it all on the plate untouched. We've produced the first generation of anorexic millionaires.')

Sniffing on life's onion and weeping, Theo thought. Now where had he once heard that? From the same mouth that had said it was bad luck to badmouth creation while saying the devil's paternoster?

Pete was a very accurate, if somewhat mathematical, pianist and he was also of course the editor of the *Streatham Clarion*. Through the interstices left in his life by these two occupations he pursued his interest in antique lingerie and historic corsetry. Theo smiled down at Zeno's fastidious piano player, observing Pete's neat ginger hair and understated freckles. Pete was the only genuinely neat one in the band. The others might dress up from time to time but Pete was structurally neat. You knew without asking that the towels in his home were all properly folded and put away. He even ironed his Levis until they had a crease in them, for God's sake. And he looked calm at last; he seemed to have finally overcome his recent traumas. He was sitting at the piano going through his sheet music lost entirely in his own thoughts. What was he brooding on?

It seemed that Pete had once found a book, *Creative Nude Photography*, hidden away in a dark corner of his parents' attic, and had been startled by the apparent willingness of women from his father's generation to take off all their clothes in wheatfields. He'd never met any girl he could imagine doing that these days. In fact he couldn't remember ever being in a wheatfield with a girl, let alone a naked one.

It had started him thinking. What had effected the change? A shift in the climate? Or was it something to do with a switch in the design of hosiery? He had gone with that last idea. Women's clothing once upon a time had been cunningly designed with an eye to lengthy and elaborate removal. A labyrinthine approach to a mystery. But no more. Now their expensive clobber seemed intended to abolish the mystery altogether. Why? Was that another mystery or merely the disappearance of a mystery? He had begun researches stretching back at least a generation. Hence the personal encounters that so bemused his fellow band members at their gigs. He'd presumably also thought he could extend his researches on a weekly basis by staring in the window of Seeland's antique lingerie shop window in the arcade, with its esoteric webs of inflammatory retro lacework and its stern rebukes of reinforced rubber. (He obviously preferred an element of severity in amongst the frills and fripperies. It was the sense of linen, whalebone and elasticated bands fighting back the great sea-surge of flesh that appeared to tickle Pete's fancy.) He certainly wasn't prepared to let such investigative opportunities pass without a struggle, despite the unwarranted abuse he always received from the middle-aged manageress if he happened to linger for more than a quarter of an hour. Lingerie of all words, of all worlds, was surely there to linger in. He had explained all this to the police, who had felt obliged to make their perfunctory inquiries after the third telephone call from Mrs Brookes saying he was putting off some of her elderly customers. Even by their own undemanding standards at the time there were barely grounds for an interview, let alone a prosecution. But down to the police station he had gone. Pete was advised to keep his interests a little more to himself, which he had promptly done. But they had, to a man, given him a knowing smile, had the boys in blue. He'd felt they'd been on his side really, which was why he'd received a mere caution and an admonition not to loiter further in the temenos of that shop of sacred mysteries. Fortunately the matter had never reached the pages of the *Streatham Clarion*, but then since Pete was editor, sub and (more often than not) sole reporter, that was perhaps hardly surprising. Anyway from then on he'd had to make do with direct mail catalogues from warehouses in the Midlands. When he wrote requesting another one he always signed himself Mrs. The recent advent of the internet, a newly acquired twenty-two-inch colour monitor, and a detailed list of websites for the discerning purchaser of practical female underwear, had all represented something of a blessing, if not exactly an advance, in Pete's otherwise uneventful life.

'All right, Pete.'

'Hi, Theo.'

'You looked miles away.'

'I was just thinking about some arrangements.' Theo didn't want to enquire any further as to what they might be. He looked around him for clues but none of the women in the pub looked old enough.

Zeno were playing in Wimbledon that night. Of all their numerous unwelcome gigs, this was the least welcome. It wasn't the noisiest place they played but it was the one with the most boisterously interventionist clientele. They liked to make requests and as the evening wore on and the drinks went down they even liked to get up and sing their requests themselves, while the combo provided its merry accompaniment behind them. *My Way* was a particular favourite, as it invariably is with all egomaniacal failures substantially the worse for drink. Then there might be *The White Cliffs of Dover* or *Daddy Wouldn't Buy Me a Bow-Wow*. There appeared to be some long memories in Wimbledon and they all became activated in this fug of boozy bonhomie.

'Why doesn't he just buy a fucking karaoke machine?' Breezer had once asked, a little more loudly than he should have. 'We're supposed to be a jazz band.'

'We're also supposed to be earning money,' Reg had said sourly. Bizarrely, they were paid more here than at any other venue. And so they continued to turn up and do as much serious music as possible before nine o'clock, knowing that after that it soon became party time, a squiffy, semi-imbecilic jamboree which simply had to be endured. It was during the interval, anticipating this next dreaded stage of the evening, that Theo looked up from his drink to see a familiar face across the table from him. He felt as though the past had emerged from the smoky murk, as though a coelacanth had swum up out of the waves to the side of his rubber dinghy, announcing the dinosaur depths still surging around him.

'Hello Shelagh. Fancy seeing you here.'

Theo's spell inside had made him unemployable in many sectors of the economy, and so like other inmates before him he had found work with small groups of informally organised builders and also behind bars – the sort where drinks are served, that is. Zeno's pay, even when they were fully gigged, had to be divided by six; all the others had daytime jobs. Theo tended these days to go for jobs where the pay was always cash-in-hand; where documents were seldom presented; references rarely requested or provided. And you always stood a good chance of meeting other miscreants of either sex. In fact there was one pub in the centre of Wandsworth he could no longer patronise, since his work there had brought him into intimate contact with Shelagh, whose womanly charms he discovered, though too late to save him his job, he had been sharing daily with the landlord. In the same room, presumably even between the same unlaundered sheets though obviously at different appointed hours. Shelagh had some personal standards to maintain, even if she did need an unusual amount of emotional affirmation. And Theo finally had to leave before finishing his lunchtime stint or even collecting that day's pay. Sadly his spell in the nick had taught him nothing of the ancient arts of self-defence.

'Hello, Theo.'

'You've changed.'

'I was a brunette. Now I'm a blonde.'

'You used to be raven-haired, as I remember.'

'I still dye my roots black though, Theo, the way you used to like them. Look.' Her fingernails, daubed a hallucinogenic purple, dug into her scalp to reveal the original sable still sprouting dyeless from her head. Dark-haired Shelagh, the one he'd laid hands on all those years before, still lurking underneath the blonde. A drowned coal seam of desire. A survival from the murky deep.

'Aren't you in the wrong pub?'

'No, I can't go back to the other one now either. It was all a bit of a misunderstanding, to be honest. Have you got anything on for later tonight?'

Theo thought for a moment. He seemed uneasy.

'Not exactly. Why?'

'It's just that I'm between places and if you could put me up . . .'

At the end of the gig they tried to sell some tapes. Breezer had had a new cover printed for them. Thought it might make all the difference.

'Tapes of Zeno,' he called out. 'Only six quid. Why not give one to your friends.'

'Why not give one to your enemies,' Paul asked, ever the lugubrious Yorkshire salesman. 'Why deny them the pleasure just because you can't actually stand them? Who knows, give them one of these brilliant tapes and the next time you meet up, they might strike you as slightly less detestable.'

The Breezer looked at him.

'Ever thought of taking up door-to-door encyclopaedia-selling, Paul? You've obviously got a gift for this sort of work, mate.'

The Breezer gave Theo and Shelagh a lift back. He was glad to see Theo with a bit of female company again. It wasn't natural him living all alone in that flat down in Wandsworth. Breezer had been divorced himself. He remembered how it was the worst thing that could possibly happen to you. It had been even worse than when he'd had his saxophone stolen; even worse than realising he couldn't make a living out of playing his horn; even worse than the time he'd picked up a dose of the clap from some housewife in Maidstone. But you did survive. He'd survived, and so would Theo. He'd wanted to tell him this but couldn't find the moment or the words, so he was glad that Theo had started finding it out for himself.

The big man had recently made himself a fish pond in his Battersea back garden. This he had filled with small golden carp but the existence of both pond and fish had recently come to a heron's attention and Breezer was making threatening noises about the situation as he drove.

'Eats any more of my golden carp, there'll be trouble.'

'You can't hurt the heron, Breezer.' There couldn't be all that many herons around Wandsworth and Battersea.

'I've hung up old CDs on threads from the bushes. They catch the light from different angles. To be honest, some of them make a better sound than they did when I used to put them in the CD player. But the fucker gets wise to whatever you do within a week.'

'You can't hurt the heron.'

'But it's one of those elemental conflicts, isn't it? The heron's interest versus mine. He's got a vested interest in eating my golden carp and I've got a vested interest in making sure he doesn't.'

'As though he were a fox and you were a gamekeeper,' Shelagh said. Both Theo and Breezer absorbed this announcement in silence.

'Well, a fox with wings, yes,' Breezer said finally. 'A fox with white feathers and an enormous fucking beak. You obviously do a lot of hunting, Shelagh.'

'Just don't hurt the heron, Breezer,' Theo said. 'Whatever you do, don't do that.'

'Couldn't we shut that window, Theo?' Shelagh asked, starting to shiver.

'It is a bit chilly, Theo,' the Breezer agreed.

'No, I think I'm going to have to keep it open. Must be starting to get asthma or something.'

'Amazing how many it's affecting. Half the people in London. Well, half the ones in London who get into my car anyway. Old Pete had that faraway look in his eyes again tonight, did you notice? Mind you, there a bit of a dearth of vintage dames. What did you think of the gig, Shelagh?'

'It was brilliant, really brilliant. You lot should be famous.'

'We are,' the Breezer said as he pulled over to let them out, 'it's just that not many people know about it yet.'

There was a reason Theo had looked uneasy. He had not been with a woman since that night in Fulham. This represented for him the longest stretch of uninterrupted chastity since he'd been inside. And the same thing happened this night that had happened on the last one: nothing. This recurrence so startled him that he couldn't speak. Even without romance, even without desire, the mechanical operation of the flesh had never before failed him. He had not expected to find himself so soon in this graveyard of expectation. Twice in a row.

'Maybe you preferred me dark-haired, Theo. I can't have aged that much, surely?'

'Maybe I have.'

Then later his dream came again. If only he could remember the numbers of that equation he felt as if he could save all those around him, or at least his mother, at least Jill, but he knew he must wake and that in waking he'd forget.

He would try to cry, even to scream, but he could neither speak nor move. Nor it seemed could he breathe. His lungs were paralysed. The rotten atoms were raging towards their nulliverse, a wasteland where no laws prevailed except the law of extinction and reversal. The brightly coloured atoms ate one another in an orgy of nihilistic frenzy as though matter had finally lost faith in itself; had abandoned any pretence at coexistence and turned to internecine predation instead. And his trapped spirit fought and fought, wrestling the collapsing universe of his bedsheets. Waking at last, face wet with tears, to discover that he had been kicking and shouting and throwing the pillows around. Shelagh was staring at him, a look of genuine alarm on her face. She spoke very quietly: 'I think you need a holiday, mate.'

After she'd gone that morning Theo found himself wondering whether he really might have left his manhood in that house in Wimbledon where his wife was now refashioning a life without him. His childhood dream and its demolition of the household's sleep had grown so unsettling, so relentless, that at one stage Vicki had arranged for him to see a psychiatrist. This had surprised Digby since he'd have thought someone in her family would have been more likely to recommend a Mediterranean exorcist. But Theo had been dutifully taken along to an address in central London. The psychiatrist, a stout middle-aged man with an unsmiling face and a sparse beard that he kept scratching, had attempted to elicit from Theo the reality behind the manifest content of the dream.

'Coloured balls, you say.'

'Coloured balls.'

'And you are trapped between them.'

'The balls are coming from all sides. Very fast.'

'And you believe they are going to crush you.'

'I know they are going to crush me.'

'But you have numbers in your head.'

'Yes. And if I could remember the numbers I'd be saved. Everybody else would, as well. My mum and dad. Everybody.'

'What form do the numbers take?'

'They're an equation.'

'What sort of equation?'

'One that balances everything out.'

'What colour are the balls?'

'Red, yellow and blue.' The psychiatrist thought for a moment.

'Tell me, Theo, have you ever played billiards?'

'No.'

'Snooker?'

'No.'

'Does your father have a billiard table in the house?'

'No.'

'Is it a game you've ever watched?'

'No.'

Various sessions of this sort took place, to no purpose as far as anyone could see. So given the fees involved, which Vicki had deemed scandalous, one week they'd simply cancelled Theo's appointment and never returned. Then at some point he'd stopped having the dream. Now it had come back.

Baiting the Firemouth

The non-frit paste which came to be known as bone china because of its admixture of calcined bones was originally marketed by Josiah Spode in 1794. Soft-paste porcelains flaked but this hard stuff didn't. Low cost, finely textured and of an enduring serviceability, it was immediately popular. For years afterwards demand outstripped supply. And so by 1800 others had joined in: Minton at Stoke; John Rose at Coalport; the Herculaneum Pottery at Liverpool. The throng of eager manufacturers was swelling and soon the names of Duesbury of Derby, and Hollins, Warburton, Daniel & Co. of New Hall were added to the list, which by 1812 expanded to include even the legendary Wedgwood. Ten years later there were another eighteen lesser-known Staffordshire potters all busily producing bone china, and one of these was Nathaniel Wilton, Digby's great-great-grandfather.

It was of a high quality and it endured. And it made Nathaniel Wilton's fortune. Sophistication of production techniques did not however necessarily imply subtlety of design as the examples from that period in Digby's glass case could testify, sometimes painfully. And subtlety of design was still hardly one of Wilton Bone China's salient characteristics when Digby was a youthful heir about to receive his patrimony, hence Uncle Freddie's periodic bouts of exasperation at the serviceable vulgarity upon which the family's wealth was founded. It sold, though. The ware of Wilton Bone China sold, making a reasonable living for all concerned. Uncle Freddie might not have wanted its latest range on the table before him but there were plenty who did.

Digby's conversations with Jakob after the war made it clear very quickly that none of the standard techniques employed in the factory as it stood could be used in the craft pottery they both wanted to create. Jakob wanted sgraffito or slipware, not printed lithographic illustration. He wanted hand-painting on the glaze, and most certainly no employment of the Murray Curvex which permitted those immaculately symmetric illustrations around the knops of covered dishes, such newfangled methods signifying not age-old craft but the unreality of modern technology. Jakob wanted asymmetry; he wanted rough textures and ragged edges to those textures. He wanted nothing to do with the latest machines of perfection because even the beautiful things that can be thus made had an air of separation about them, as if they had arrived from elsewhere without notice. The hand of the maker was missing. Everything, every single thing, that came out of the Potter's Hand would be different. And every item would take its final shape from the potter himself. The artist's own touch. Ruskin would have been proud and Digby felt exhilarated as he launched his beloved new project.

But that wasn't the way the world was going. The modern world had itemised its goods into artefacts it drank and ate from, sat in or slept in, and those it put on the shelf or inside museums. The world wasn't moving towards earthenware simplicity but plastic complication. In the face of this confusion Digby had embarked on his career of bewilderment, a career he had subsequently never entirely abandoned.

He had watched with a horrified fascination when in 1957 Roy Midwinter had launched a range of plastic tableware, believing that this was the material of the future. If you dropped it, it didn't break. There'd be no more of those subterranean shards from which we might piece together past civilisations, their feasting habits, their burial ceremonies, their dark gods. The age of convenience and hygiene had at last arrived. Midnight had given way to noon.

Plastic already provided the tough and brightly coloured laminated surfaces from which humanity was learning to eat its sundry pre-packaged foods. It provided the celluloid on which the latest moving icons were imprinted and the Bakelite out of which those small machines in the corner of each room had started to announce reality each day. The latest household gods.

But Digby had been wrong; he could acknowledge that now. In his yearning for apocalypse he had simplified things, as haters of an age so often do. It couldn't be doubted that plastic had kept pace admirably with modernity. Its raw materials, once produced by coal, were now by-products of petroleum instead. From steam to gasoline. A fine sense of chronology then in the exhalation of each main source of energy. The age's excreta kept up to date with the latest forms from which it might be ejected.

He had noted (who hadn't?) the impossibility of escaping from plastic. Buckets and pails, the insides of cars, the seats in cinemas, cameras, pens. All those boats with plastic hulls the ocean would never now be entirely rid of, and since then the dead computer screens, their artificial intelligence long-dormant inside them. Mutilated toys; ugly off-white knife handles; smashed video cassettes; so many billions of miles of ruined tape, intestines shrivelled, hanging loose from their brittle black casings; the warped vinyl of outdated dreams. Encoded memories of a past too annotated to replay even with an eternity before you in which to do it. Would anyone in the future really want to dig all this out of the ground in order to find out who we were? Was the high-tech dump outside Tokyo, rising steadily towards the sky with its burden of last year's camcorders, radios and CD players, worth the archaeological devotion that had sent men down into the Lascaux caves? Down into the womb of time. How much in the recorded archive of modernity was actually worth the hours it would take to observe it? And how much of it was merely stray murmurs from the noise of time? All those laptop computers and message recorders, bleating their electronic cries until fingers came and soothed them back to silence. Pressed their little buttons for them. Erased their short-term memories, wiped clean the disturbing cadences of human voices.

Digby had as far as he was permitted retreated from the world of noise and plastic to the world of silence and books, for it seemed to him that if computers dissolve time, books congeal it. While he had still taken a newspaper he remembered reading how twenty years before thousands of medical records had been discovered in London, encoded for computer storage. Sadly, no one could recall how the encoding had been accomplished and consequently no one could read the records. They had been duly burnt. This story had impressed Digby. It confirmed him in his view that it was in the nature of the computer to dissolve everything with the acid solvent of contemporaneity but it showed too what an impatient grasp of time contemporaneity has. Compare this with Da Vinci's journals, penned in a barely legible version of mirror-writing and painstakingly decoded over years of fastidious and unrelenting effort; or Coleridge's *Notebooks*, a concatenation of millions of words without apparent parameters or intelligible purpose. Random associations, unanchored allusions, arbitrary images. Transcribed, edited and annotated with love and scholarly intelligence over five decades. The unintelligibility of the medical records had been an immediate prompt to their destruction. Unintelligibility had disqualified them from preservation. The unintelligibility of Da Vinci and Coleridge had conjured lives dedicated to their interpretation. The medical records showed contemporaneity beyond its purchase date by years not centuries, memory's milk turning sour after only a few days. But the books had congealed time, solidified it, held it in place; inside them history had fossilised intelligent meaning. Nobody but a man hurrying towards death could want to throw away so much time. And there were still bibliomanes, fierce devotees of the cult of the book, who in effect claimed that there were no other historical facts that could ever be entirely trusted but the facts of books themselves, their rubric and publication dates. The mere texture of an old book, its ancient quidditas, turned you back towards the complexity and indissolubility of history. You held the past in your hands begrimed with years and realised how awkward and solid it was; how the precipitate of time was uranium-heavy. Computers could offer only an accelerated present which grew lighter by the minute. Many people had become books; no one ever becomes a computer. Its circuitry is as yet alien to that redemption which still troubles the sleep of the printed word.

That's why Digby had felt such a depletion of spirits the last time he had visited his local library to find a large sign saying BOOK SALE. It was after all the function of a library to retain books for consultation not to void itself of such vast numbers of them. So why was this happening?

'All that section over there will be filled with computers by next month,' the librarian had explained. 'We have to make space.'

'By getting rid of books?'

'Afraid so.' The librarian, a six-foot stick insect with a mournful grey beard, didn't look too happy about it either. He was evidently a bookman himself and so by definition superannuated, half-way to the pension and the grave.

'Are the computers meant to replace the books?'

'So they say.'

'But they can't do that.'

'I know they can't.'

And Digby had fumbled about amongst the volumes on the trestle table, with their scuffed plastic jackets, WITH-DRAWN stamped in blurred blue ink all over the inside front covers and free endpapers. Beautiful books, some of them (before their mutilation at the hands of librarians) printed in letterpress on creamy, acid-free papers. You could tell at a glance that many intellectual years had gone into their making. The footnotes alone were a miniature lantern show of learning. Selling for virtually nothing. As though they were of no use at all now for any institution travelling into the future under the name of library. Digby had bought one; a small volume entitled *Manufacture and the Industrial Revolution*.

Back home as he stared at the monochrome illustrations showing various industries scouring the earth and blackening the sky, as hungrily transformative as any tale in Ovid's *Metamorphoses*, he realised that time always keeps its mouth wide open, for how else can it continue to swallow the future? And an entirely open mouth makes only inarticulate sounds whether of hunger or rage or boredom. An open mouth is the sound of a mob howling or an infant before it chews on its first serious syllables. He stared at the words on the page but he couldn't read them. For some reason they refused to leave their typeset folios and enter his mind.

The next day he had returned to the library and asked a question that had been troubling him.

'What do you do with the ones you don't sell? You don't put them back on the shelves.'

'No, we don't put them back on the shelves. We're not allowed to, actually. We burn them.'

He had sat at home that day and thought back. He'd been wrong about plastic tableware; it didn't as he had feared take over the market. People still kept those cheap and unbreakable goods for picnics and children's parties. They had wanted their ceramic cups and plates after all and they'd wanted them made according to traditional designs. Traditional and recognisable; they hadn't wanted the ones that he and Jakob had laboured so hard to offer them, or not in a quantity sufficient to make them profitable. They hadn't wanted to go that far back in time in search of a true form uncompromised by either clutter or convenience. And as a result Digby had settled for an early retirement and a life of contemplation. Insofar as Victoria permitted it.

Oak and Mahogany

Anarchy. Digby looked up from the typescript he was reading and thought for a moment in silence. Then he walked over to his bookshelf and took down the A–B volume of the *OED*. *Anarchia* derived from *anarchos* and meaning rulerless. So that was what Howard meant, presumably: WITHOUT A RULER, NOT WITHOUT RULES.

Dictionaries. He couldn't even see them on his shelf without remembering Wilton Manor.

Uncle Freddie had had an obsession with dictionaries. And he thought it a disgrace that Digby's father wouldn't buy the first edition of the volumes now racked on Digby's shelf.

'The *New English Dictionary* is one of the wonders of the age,' he had almost shouted, 'it is one of the great creations of mankind and your father won't reach his hand deep enough into his pocket to buy one. Instead we have to make do with that –' He had pointed in disgust to the four volumes on the shelf, Ogilvie's *Imperial Dictionary of the English Language*. 'The last fascicle was published over ten years ago. There've been two full editions and one supplement. Over 400,000 words. And nearly two million quotations. Isn't that worth a few bob out of anybody's pocket? Well, not out of your father's, apparently, not out of my dear brother's. We are obliged to make do instead with Ogilvie, which is hardly the same thing at all if I'm still permitted to point it out. So if you and I, Digby, wish to consult one of the great works of the age we must make our way to the reference section of the Stoke public library. Which is precisely where we're going now.'

And off they would march. Once there, Freddie would spend hours turning the pages of a single volume. Sometimes he would find an entry so satisfying that he would bring it to Digby's attention by tapping him on the shoulder and pointing a thin finger, stained yellow from all the Turkish cigarette smoke.

'Read it out,' Freddie would command. People would be looking in their direction. Silence was strictly enforced in the reference section. Not that it bothered Freddie of course. 'Go on, man,' he would say and Digby would obey. Then they walked back home if the weather permitted. Freddie's monologue would be uninterrupted.

'James Murray is a hero of our time. His scriptorium in Oxford should be turned into a shrine. The man was a saint. The saint of lexicography.'

It was in the disparaged Ogilvie that Digby had one day come across a word that so fascinated him he'd learnt the definition by heart: *Nyctalopia 1. The faculty of seeing in darkness or in a faint light, with privation of sight in daylight – 2. The disorder from which this faculty proceeds.* A nyctalops, Ogilvie went on, was one afflicted with nyctalopia. What stayed in his mind then, and had stayed in it ever since he'd memorised the word that day, was the image of someone who has seen something so bright that everything afterwards remains dim in comparison. Dim and black-and-white. He was to meet one of those in the years to come, wasn't he? He was to have a nyctalops in his own life, someone who had gazed at a momentous eclipse and ever afterwards could see clearly only when the lights went out. And what she needed then was someone in the house, anyone in the house if the truth be told, who could burn brightly enough to light her up the stairs and warm her bed. He supposed he must have done it for a while anyway; waxed and waned until another burning soul arrived to take over the position. Digby the candleman brandishing his flame at the darkness. Victoria's darkness. Thus had another of Uncle Freddie's precepts been borne out: how the word usually arrives long before the experience that must be fitted into it.

As is the way with most of the manor houses of England, Wilton Manor's feudal obligations and responsibilities had disappeared through the centuries, shrouded in history's gunfire, fog and confusion, but mostly in the immemorial mists of custom and forgetfulness. Whatever manorial powers might once have been invested in it they had been happily forgotten by the time this particular building had risen on its site towards the end of the eighteenth century. A classical portico of the Doric order made a small stony salute to the Enlightenment but the interior spoke of Victorian comforts, for the house had been adapted and extended throughout the nineteenth century, its original classical ground-plan over-written by a rising edifice of modifications and accruals. The term manor was now no more than a vague geographical mnemonic, a fragmentary remembrance of former times.

What Digby himself remembered of Wilton Manor was oak, mahogany and dust. Hours clunked out elongated and remorseless from long-case clocks. The wood from tables, chairs, bookshelves and cabinets had been hewn from forests now dead. The upright piano never had its locked lid opened throughout the whole of Digby's childhood. It was a graveyard of tunes, sealed like a sarcophagus, though he'd heard it whispered that his mother had years before elicited Schubert and Chopin from those ivories. He had once found the key in a drawer and opened the stool lid to discover a ragged pile of sheet music. Preludes and sonatas long buried and forgotten along with her beloved nocturnes. All foxed and curling at the corners. At some point his mother had stopped playing, stopped singing. Why? Maybe she'd heard too much news from the twentieth century. Though surely art had been meant to provide some consolation and solace in the face of reality, rather than merely adding to its dissonance and discomfort? Either way, she'd quit. In the large front room, which looked out over the lawn, a vast oak table was surrounded by ten chairs, high-backed wooden chairs, all covered in old black leather. Brass studs would catch the light from the coal fire when it blazed in the evenings. Digby often ran his fingers over these studs and counted them while the grown-ups talked or bickered. In all there were one hundred and fifty gleaming convex studs and his little fingers had caressed each one many times. He thought of them as soldiers with shiny golden helmets, grouped in formation high in the black mountains of some distant country.

The dictionaries which so provoked Freddie's disapproval were always kept in that room and Digby would often take them down from the shelf so that he could lie prone on the rug by the hearth with one of them propped open before him. He didn't share his uncle's disapproval of Ogilvie's *Imperial*, for at the back of all four volumes were page upon page of line engravings which could entrance Digby for hours at a time. He would turn the leaves and murmur the words: axehead and flint; ibis, crane, woodpecker, hoopoe; the Virginian nightingale; Coptic monk and Marquesas islander; the Guarani woman civilised; Norwegian Lapp; Turk of Roumella; the sea bat, the sturgeon and a sinuous electric eel with a look of infinite menace in its eye. The body-whorl of the auger-shell; the anterior canal of the cowrie. These engravings and their Victorian taxonomies imbued him with a sense of the perfection of the world of knowledge: monochrome and diagrammatic, no superfluous detail anywhere. And in the inventories of Stone Age and Bronze Age remains he saw for the first time vital forms, undepleted by later sophistications and so consequently unsapped by the queries and parentheses of over-civilised design; forms of a sort that would echo in his mind when he later encountered, courtesy of Uncle Freddie and his passionate devotion, the modern movement in art, and later still when he discovered for himself the pottery of Jakob Kirk, which seemed to pay no attention at all to the century in which it had been fashioned. Here had begun Digby's own quest for the marvellous; he supposed that everyone must make his own journey towards it. It had taken him a long time to realise that the marvellous was what was left over when modernity's machines ceased whirring; it was by and large what the modern world discarded. The rejected bits and pieces; the debris. Although the modern world had produced more marvels than any other, it had also divested them of the quality of being marvellous. It had, as a matter of routine, demystified its wonders.

Back inside the pages of Ogilvie's *Imperial*, there were also the full-page illustrations of square-rigged ships, the ghostly outlines of their masts and spars making him think always of the Doré illustrations for 'The Ancient Mariner'. There was a little bookshelf which stood all by itself and was known in the family as Coleridge Corner. Digby suspected that these were the first books he had ever been shown as a child – the images were now so indelibly imprinted on his mind.

'Your great-great-grandfather corresponded with Samuel Taylor Coleridge, Digby, did you know that?' The question had been echoing around Wilton Manor for the whole of his childhood. It had been left to him to establish the answer, which in the process of writing *Wilton Bone China* he had done. But he still wasn't sure he'd fathomed what the answer meant.

Listed

The tape was pressed into the mouth of the machine. The black man with the wrinkled face and brilliant, large eyes looked up as the trumpet started playing. 'Who are these people?' The voice was American.

'Zeno.'

'But who *are* they?'

'Here's a list of pubs where they play,' his young Danish wife said, reading from the sheet in front of her. 'I heard them last time I was over and bought their tape.'

'Put them on the list. We've got to go see them. That trumpet's great. Just listening to it makes me feel young again.'

'You told me I'd already done that, Benny.'

Focusing

Misdirected urination. Erroneously navigated micturition. The spray of shame all over the bathroom floor of your hosts. The little puddles at your feet in the Gents at the public house. Worst of all, the return to a room full of demure guests with a whole trouser leg slapping with urinous waste like a loughing sail after a sea storm. Even if they could all manage to ignore it, you couldn't; couldn't taste the cocktails any more for the chilling sensation down your thigh, a sort of stinging frost, a piquant hint of acid medication, a dim memory of childhood's shame on waking. There was a unique humiliation involved in realising that after all the years of domestication, he was now barely house-trained. It was a sombre reflection: his own pisspoor performance in the small room of reflections. In his own home at least Digby knew where he was. He didn't have to stare at every drink he sipped, calculating its likely progress through his innards and out again at the other end. He could time himself and, in the event of a miscarriage of intention and chronology, change promptly into dry trousers, even sometimes, God help us, socks, such being the inescapable force of gravity. He had less and less inclination to go out at all. He and his bladder were happier at home. Like time and tide the urgencies of the prostate gland wait for no man, certainly not once the organ expands to the size of Digby's.

'Why not have it out?' his doctor had asked him repeatedly.

'Because I've grown attached to it, that's why,' he'd replied. 'We've grown old and unpredictable together.' Then that doctor had died, which gave Digby pause, as though his broker had gone bankrupt or his builder's house had fallen down. After thirty years as his general practitioner the fellow had simply keeled over without a single indication of a departure looming. It showed how few cards they really held in their hands, the medical profession, when faced with mortality's dealings. His temporary replacement was young, not over thirty-five. Digby felt he should have been giving *him* advice, had there been any real order to the scheme of things. One day he had asked Digby after a check-up if there were anything else troubling him and Digby had mentioned almost casually his errant focus in the passing of water; if only for something to say, to keep his side of the bargain by laying his ancient disabilities at the young man's door.

'Try pulling your foreskin further back,' the doctor had said. He was already filling in notes. Something in the insouciance of this remark grated with Digby. Why did the young always have to assume that every dilemma confronting the old was likely to be so facile in its resolution?

'Do you seriously imagine I haven't tried that? I mean, do you have any idea how long I've been at it?'

'It's very common,' the young doctor said, still not looking up. 'We tend to hold the penis as though it were a petrol pump nozzle we're inserting into a fuel tank and the natural urge then is to press the flesh forward, confusing the flow.' He looked up finally from his notes with a smile on his face. Blue eyes, black hair. Fresh complexion. Health and youth. Physical and mental well-being. He added a coda: 'The uneven fringe of a foreskin like yours prevents a steady stream forming its arc; that's what produces the promiscuous spray.' Digby felt obliged to reply to this from the lofty perch of his years, to point out that he'd been passing water for decades before this young fellow had even been born. Wisely though he'd kept his counsel and so the smile had continued, professional and tolerant. The infinite and seemingly ineradicable condescension of the young to the old.

'Try it,' he'd said finally. Digby did just that as soon as he arrived home and was both pleased and irritated to discover that the young doctor was absolutely right. 'Nozzle,' he'd muttered as he rebuttoned himself, 'inserting a petrol pump nozzle. Surprised he didn't have a rubber doll to show me where to find it. Can I really have spent the better part of a century peeing, without ever learning how to do it properly?' One more indignity then to add to his substantial collection. But it still didn't tempt him out, this freshly gained expertise in his own liquid-waste management. There remained after all the question of timing. This seemed to Digby to amount to something more than the quirks and vagaries of his own bodily senescence; it felt actively malignant and intentional, as though some minor demon inside were intent upon achieving maximum shame and inconvenience at his expense whenever the opportunity arose. So Digby was content to remain indoors. Or to put the matter more truthfully, being indoors produced in him a less radical discontent than being out of them.

And that explained his troubled expression now.

'I can't face it, Daisy. Exaggerated or not, my disabilities are my own affair and I prefer to tend them here in my own home.' Daisy seemed a little flustered.

'I made a mistake. I'm going to own up. I told them how kind you'd been, how neighbourly I mean, looking after my pussies for me. Jonty jumped on it straight away of course. So he does leave the house then, he said. In that case he can come to our next soirée – I've been wanting to have a chat with him about that latest catalogue of mine.'

'I can't face it, Daisy. Honestly I can't.'

'Then he'll be round here. You'll have your product sensitivity tested on your own premises instead of his – just don't say you weren't warned.'

And Daisy was right. Digby didn't turn up at the soirée that evening and Jonty arrived at his door the following morning, wearing a smile even more luminescent than his track suit.

'I hear you go to everybody's house now but mine. Tessa's most put out,' Jonty said, letting himself in. His hair, Digby couldn't help noticing, was now pure black, an anthracite gloss. Jonty had a curious habit of progressing from one room to another by peering round doorways and saying 'What's through there then?' And before the host or hostess could decide whether or not he should be given access he'd already be in. That's how, by means of three doors and a staircase, with buckled Digby only barely keeping up, Jonty stepped into the wunderkammer.

'My God, this is like a shrine.'

'I suppose it is a shrine,' Digby said, panting a little.

'To what?'

Digby felt invaded and defeated by this stage. There didn't seem to be much point trying to keep secrets any more. Throw the holy of holies open to the public; serve them chips and ice-cream.

'Oh, I don't know. One or two mementoes of the marvellous my family has acquired through the years.'

With his unerring instinct Jonty had already picked up the one item in the room that Digby least wished to discuss. It was a large dish and in the bottom of the bowl an aged sailor had been modelled in relief.

'Why's he got that white budgerigar round his neck?'

'It's an albatross, Jonty. That's the Ancient Mariner. That's why he's got a long grey beard and a glittering eye.'

'He hasn't though has he, really?'

'Not really, no.'

'It's more of an orange beard and a pair of bloodshot eyes. He doesn't look like someone who's just undergone an archetypal experience, more like a slightly demented farmer after the May Day celebrations. Or a pet-shop owner newly released on one of those Care in the Community schemes. I thought albatrosses were bigger than that.'

'I believe they usually are.' Digby had sat down. 'I think we might be looking at the representation of a very young one.'

'A sort of albatross in embryo, you mean?'

'That would be the generous interpretation, Jonty.' Jonty angled the dish this way and that as he squinted relentlessly into it.

'Looks like a fully fledged budgie to me, Digby.'

'Nobody's ever claimed that my great-great-grandfather's artists were very distinguished. The early items from my family firm have more of a curiosity value than anything else. But Nathaniel was very keen on Coleridge, you see. He revered him. They corresponded.'

'So you have some letters, then. In the family archive. They must be worth a few shekels these days.'

Digby blushed and turned his head towards the window. It was almost uncanny, Jonty's ability to ask whatever question you would choose not to have to answer.

'Well, corresponded is perhaps over stating it. My great-great-grandfather wrote expressing his great admiration for Coleridge, even sending him the set of bowls and plates he'd made to commemorate the poem. We have copies of Nathaniel's letters but no one's ever found the poet's replies.'

'Probably never bothered. Too snooty. It's a problem I've had myself a few times, to be honest. Artists and industry don't mix. You've given me an idea though. I'm glad I came. Do you have the rest of the set so I can have a dekko, out of interest?'

'No, that's the sole survivor in your hands. Don't drop it, will you?'

'What about the ones that were sent to Coleridge, then?' Digby could only shrug. Like son, like father. Jonty had elicited a Theo-like shrug out of him. The shrugging Wiltons.

'Probably pawned it and spent the money on drugs. He was a druggie, wasn't he?'

'I don't believe the term was current then, Jonty, but he certainly was very fond of laudanum.'

'Well there you are.'

Back downstairs Digby pointed to the vast portrait in oils of Nathaniel Wilton that hung on the wall above his fireplace. In the background behind the sitter's cane chair you could see through the founder of Wilton Bone China's latticed window the pottery chimneys industriously polluting the red and black sky, like a tiny illustration from a medieval apocalypse, while in Nathaniel's lap lay an open copy of the first edition of *Lyrical Ballads*. Something else that had unaccountably gone missing, along with the Coleridge letters. Time's undiscriminating maw had swallowed the lot.

'Commemorative issues,' Jonty was saying. 'I've developed my own theory as to why they're so popular, you know. Tessa reckons it's brilliant. Can you guess what it is?' Digby shook his head. 'It's how we get our own back at time. And you've just given me an idea. Now, why don't you make me a cup of coffee and tell me what you think of my last catalogue?'

Black-and-White

It seemed curious to Digby that he always thought of plastic as black or white, or just occasionally the feculent deep beige of Bakelite. But all other colours seemed like blemishes on its artificial skin. Was that because of the Midwinter ranges that he'd gazed at with such morbid fascination back in the Fifties? Some of those had surely had black patterns printed over white. He couldn't remember exactly. What he did remember was the black-and-white of snow settling on an industrial landscape, and how the blizzards of his youth had been swallowed by the dark veining of the canalways around Stoke.

A brief shuffle in the snows of memory had reminded him.

In the wintry morning light the swing creaked and rattled in the wind as Digby stared at it. How much of his life was now spent thinking either of his wife or his son? With Vicki there was nothing more to be done. She had been laid to rest, though very much not in the manner she'd specified. He still felt very bad about that. But what about Theo? Bloody Theo. What a poisonous slurry he left in the wake of all his relationships, but still the women kept coming. The world appeared to have an inexhaustible supply of them. He wondered if his son should have a health warning printed on his head, a creature like the little lions they used to stamp on eggs to show they were British and therefore beyond any hint of contamination. What a very long time ago that seemed. Maybe he should have a tattoo like young Desmond's. A sphinx, perhaps. How many legions of willing womankind had stepped forward to minister to his feckless offspring in the parish of his dissolution? He suspected that even Theo had long ago lost count. He still vividly remembered his Rumanian girlfriend, the viola player, a specialist in dirges and funeral laments who when not actually playing her instrument largely restricted her conversational gambits to uttering the word 'No' in reply to whatever question was addressed to her.

'Are you planning on going back to Rumania?' he had asked one day.

'No.'

'So you are going to stay in England?'

'No.'

'So you're neither going nor staying then?'

'No.'

Digby had soon tired of these exchanges as he had contemplated with dread the possibility of her becoming his long-awaited daughter-in-law. His son had seemed very keen for a while and did once insist that his father join them in some wine bar in central London so that the two generations might together hear her perform. It was the early evening; people in suits were arriving from their offices looking forward to a little laughter and a bottle of wine. Theo's Rumanian girlfriend, draped in black, stepped up to the microphone with a facial expression that suggested Cassandra during a particularly stressful prophecy, and proceeded to saw away at her viola, producing quite the most mournful noise Digby thought he'd ever heard in the whole of his life. You could almost make out the sexton's muffled bell behind her. It was music for a burial and it went on and on for the better part of fifteen minutes as her face, if that were possible, grew even more darkly melancholic. The swathe of her hair slowly sashayed back and forth like the short dark curtains coffins roll through in a crematorium chapel. Finally she was done. The whole place had by now fallen silent. Everyone stared at her with that combination of horror and fascination you can see in the eyes of bystanders gathering at the scene of a fatal accident.

'Good isn't she, dad?' Theo had said, with what appeared to be unfeigned enthusiasm.

'She's cheering the place up nicely, I can see that.' Digby could only assume that she had spectacular talents between the sheets. But where had his son met her, for God's sake? At the Samaritans? He could never bring himself to ask. And then one day she had uttered the mandrake shriek that all Theo's women uttered sooner or later, presumably on discovering that his recent sexual attentions had not been confined to herself alone, far from it, and she had gone. Theo had never mentioned her again. Where was she now? Back in Rumania? Or still making the rounds of the dimly lit wine bars of London, scratching away at her catgut, summoning the spirits of the dead?

My son, he thought, the Don Juan of Wandsworth. He had read somewhere that all Don Juans were in truth bona fide *noli-me-tangerians*, far more likely to detest the flesh, their own and others', than to celebrate it. Just one more classification of emotional cripple. He wondered if it might be a medical condition and if so whether it had been properly diagnosed: someone addicted to beginnings, so addicted in fact that he has to search for a new-found land every morning in order to rinse away his sadness, the unwanted weight of all life's onerous routines. As though the days of your time on earth could truly be written in fugitive inks. A fellow so besotted with beginnings, he thinks middles and ends are only ordained for the armies of the dutiful. Like Digby. Was that the seducer's true satisfaction, to know that every beginning was also an ending? That you were done as soon as you had got started? No sooner in one side of the bed than out the other. The early Church, he seemed to remember, had deemed obsessive adultery a type of chronic vanity; the wish to see your own image infinitely reproduced in every pair of eyes, a superficial parody of true fecundity.

Was Theo never sated with himself? Surely he had feasted too long on the pickings his mother's looks had made available to him? One day a black crow would spread its wings around his heart and he'd itch with the loathing of its infested feathers. The same moral laws apply, Theo, his father thought, clenching his teeth – they apply to everyone however lovely their faces. I tried to teach you that much at least. Now I wonder if I ever truly taught you anything. Who were those geniuses who proclaimed to your generation that sex could be a way of avoiding responsibilities, when it has always been the other way about? Sex has never been free; how can anything be free which produces new life? It is the cunning way nature arranged for us to acquire our liabilities, not dispense with them. Victoria, Vicki, my love. Your son is sacrificing all that is good in his life in pursuit of his infidelity. I sometimes wonder if I sacrificed all that was good in mine for the precise opposite. He thinks I killed you, my dear; but between us, the living and the dead, we know that's not true, now don't we?

The doorbell rang. That would be Theo, for it was Christmas Day and father and son had agreed to pass it together.

Two hours later, wearing a paper crown whose appearance on his head had made even Theo smile, Digby opened the oven door. The large turkey had been transformed from a corpse-shiver of white to an enticing golden glaze. He was transported back sixty years. If you could peer into the kiln and see the flames half-way to white heat, you could always think of hell. Certainly things do get destroyed in there. Any imperfections are found out and exploded, should the hardening skin for example be too tight for the raging heart of the heated pot. But it's possible to think of purgatory instead, a more comforting thought perhaps for an old man with a lifetime's sins on his head. There the atoms change their homes, substances switch structure and clay itself, that weepy underground sludge, becomes crystalline and ultimately precious. These are the flames of transformation, there to turn you into something new. Here's where metamorphosis begins. To believe in justice without mercy is to believe in a metaphysical prison, a universal torture chamber. Surely that couldn't be possible? Surely the Almighty looked upon His degraded, half-demented children with pity as well as anger?

'Is there any system of ethics you subscribe to?' he asked Theo as he sliced breast slivers from the bird, in an attempt to riddle out the mystery of his son's insouciance in the face of all that life had ever brought his way. Theo, as far as he'd been able to observe, simply seemed to have another drink and borrow another £50, before sauntering off whistling down the road. Not always whistling, to be fair. 'I mean, would you describe yourself as the adherent of any particular philosophy, now that you have abandoned your Catholicism?'

Theo pondered, but not for long. He took a single, thoughtful sip of his vodka and said: 'Elvis lives, but they still buried the poor sod.'

'You couldn't elaborate a little further, Theo, for the sake of the elderly?'

'Try not to join the living dead.'

Digby had an unpleasant feeling that the allusion was to his own good self. Just a jest, of course. One of Theo's little quips. My son, he thought, my son the humorist.

'Still don't believe in the battle between good and evil, Theo? You used to think that was altogether too black-and-white, didn't you?'

'I like black-and-white, actually. All my favourite pictures are black-and-white. Mother always said I'd inherited that trait from you.'

But in matters of spirit and morality he was holistic. Digby knew this, because his son had told him many times before. Like Pelagius he would put a smile back into the snake's features and make vegetarians of the lion and the wolf, for neither Theo nor Pelagius believed in Original Sin, only in primordial blessings and benedictions which were now obscured by man's inability to accept his own good fortune. The eyes that would see glory were obscured merely by the cuckoo-spit of scepticism, the smeared lens, the dark night of experience. Had Pelagius moved in the microscopic realm he would have anointed, St Francis-like, the spirochaete and tubercle, the cancerous cell and the ravenous virus, calling them brother and sister and other soft names, inviting them to share the feast of his flesh. Theo, like so many of his generation, was an unwitting devotee. So Digby reckoned, anyway. If only Uncle Freddie could have tutored him. Then at least his lack of belief might have had some precision about it.

They ate. They drank. They even pulled two crackers. A plastic pig for Theo; a plastic swan for Digby.

'Plastic,' Digby said. Theo suggested they switch on the Queen's Speech. His father wasn't sure whether or not this suggestion was ironical. In any case he pointed out, despite having paid his licence fee, since it was one of the totalitarian and inescapable strictures of our national life, he did not actually watch television. Ever. He put on some Mozart instead and poured the wine.

'All we need is mum here and it would be just like old times,' Theo said, with what his father thought was a definite air of malice. Digby thought for a moment before speaking with great deliberation. He had decided it was time this matter was put to rest.

'And I suppose you think she still would be, if I hadn't gone and killed her.'

'You must have known, once you'd driven her out from here, what would happen. Knowing everything you knew about her, knowing the way she was likely to live, it was unlikely to take very long. You made her leave. She told me. Quite a convenient way of signing her death warrant while avoiding any police charges.'

'I thought one of us should try to avoid them.' He hadn't wanted this Christmas to turn ugly. After all, he wasn't sure how many more he'd be having. He softened his voice. 'It wasn't black-and-white, Theo, because however much you might like those photographs of yours, and however much I might like them too, life usually isn't. She drove herself out, as a matter of fact. Or at least,' he said, with undisguised weariness, 'she drove me to drive her out. Not long after explaining to me what our marriage had been about.'

'What had it been about, then?'

He saw Victoria now in his son's eyes. The same bright look, the same vivid appetite for catastrophe. He could almost believe she was back here at the table with him. 'Her loving somebody else. A dead man.'

'Must have been hard to tell the difference sometimes.' His father flinched at this and Theo relented. 'I'm sorry, I shouldn't have said that.'

'Did your mother tell you that, out of interest, on one of your little trips to see her down in St Leonards? That it was hard to tell the difference between me and a dead man? She could tell the difference, all right. Anyway, it will be very hard indeed to tell the difference shortly, Theo, if that's any comfort to you. Then you can have all this.' Digby gestured vaguely at the house and its contents. Why not give me some now? Theo thought, but he said nothing.

'Then you'll be able to play the trumpet in comfort for a while. Even get a nice flat by the sea to do it in, if you like. Since you're so much your mother's son.' Theo didn't like him talking about his mother. It made him uncomfortable, even though he'd prompted it.

'You can't blame her for taking comfort from the bottle.'

'Choosing oblivion instead of me, you mean? No, I wouldn't dream of it. A choice between a dead man and a bottle is no real contest.' Theo raised his glass.

'To mum,' he said. They both drank and then sank into silence. After a while, Digby walked over and put another record on his gramophone. Cello suites by Bach. He always found those soothing but by the time the dark had returned Theo had announced he was leaving.

'You have plans for this evening, do you?' Digby asked. Theo shrugged his famous shrug. He didn't as a matter of fact but he couldn't face staying and his father couldn't face trying to make him. So much for Christmas at home this year. As he shut the door Digby muttered to himself, 'Why blame me for your mother's death, Theo? Why not blame Hitler or the Battle of Britain? Why not just have done with it and blame the twentieth century?'

Alone again Digby thought of Ruskin. He'd come to feel a strange sympathy with that man. He had hung a picture of him in old age on the wall. Now he took it down and stared at it, the eyes half mad with grief and anger.

Ruskin's admirable rage at what went on around him. Was it really that which had made him mad or a sexual dementia induced by the misfiring of his desire for Effie Gray and Rose de la Touche? The first went on to achieve a malignant triumph through Millais's tawdry and ill-bought celebrity, the second withered on the stem, poor anorexic Rose, bent finally all the way down to the ground. Ruskin in the Lake District, Digby had read with fascinated horror, continued to assert his lonely virility, ready to provide the proofs if necessary to fulfil any forensic requirements, even to establish his adequacy to the task through an onanistic performance duly observed and properly documented. But the vigour of his manly power, like that of his outraged prose, could find no other figure to assuage it. It had to stand up for itself, an assertion to which there was no reply. With his bouts of madness which were intermittent and the ravages of age and time which were anything but, he himself became a ruin at the edge of Coniston Water, the Gothic edifice of his own white-skulled desolation, remembering Rose's fragile beauty and the Jerusalem that England might have been, given the consent of its populace, rich and poor.

His life chronicled a translation from wealth to illth like the land he lamented. Daily he observed the fish of Coniston Water, for which there is neither day nor night but only the fluent freedom of the kingdom of shadows, terminated by a swift hooking and a slow suffocation. A shivering mirror thrown up on the bank, out of its proper element and gradually starved of oxygen. Meanwhile his enemies celebrated. What? The illiquation of his soul. By the end he even heard the fish complaining in his dreams.

When the doorbell rang Digby thought it must be Theo, having had a change of heart while heading back. It wasn't; it was Daisy. And she was laughing.

'I come bearing a gift for you from our venerable neighbour.' Digby opened the door wide to let her in. He would be glad of the company now. Daisy pressed the brochure into his hand as she stepped into the hall. Digby could just make it out in the shadowy light: *The Merriman Museum of Miniature Collectables. Special Christmas Catalogue.*

'God, he's done another one already.' He started leafing through it in his armchair a few moments later.

'He'll be examining you on your reaction to the contents this time.'

'Examining me?'

'He didn't think you two had a proper chat about the last one he gave you. He wants to test your product sensitivity.'

'My . . .' Digby faltered.

'Your product sensitivity, Digby. Very big on it, is Jonty. His own is apparently impeccable but he's worried about yours, what with you having been out of the swing of things for so long. He's hopeful though, don't get the wrong idea. He has indicated to me, Digby, on the quiet you understand, that he thinks there's a possibility your product sensitivity might turn out to be larger than any of us could ever have anticipated.' Daisy leaned towards him and winked. She was evidently a little drunk but then it was Christmas and it was nice to know someone had been enjoying themselves.

'Very gratifying, I'm sure, Daisy. And what am I supposed to do if we find it does correspond to Jonty's more optimistic predictions?'

'If we discover it's of elephantine proportions, you mean?'

'Exactly.'

'Buy things. Engage in the great race of consumption which, according to our good friend Jonty, makes the world go round.'

'Consumption.'

'Oh do stop pretending to be thick, Digby. Consumption. The purchase of merchandise. Cash. Credit. Debit card, hire purchase. Outright or on a month's approval, the individual item or the whole collection, off-the-page or at a retail outlet, but just don't imagine you can escape the fate of the consumer for it is Moses and the Prophets. It is the law of life according to our wealthy, healthy friend who appears to have won for himself, let's not forget, the undivided sexual attentions of La Merriman.'

'Moses and the Prophets,' Digby repeated disconsolately. 'What about smashing up that golden calf then?'

'Ah, now I think if Jonty could have been given half an hour or so with Moses after he'd come panting down from that mountain of his, he would have explained that his hostility to the golden calf was at best misplaced; that taboos were, frankly, taboo – from a marketing point of view, in the modern world of extended-credit finance and consumer durables. I think Jonty reckons the business with the golden calf was a pretty big strategic blunder for religion, if the truth be told. A setback in Judaism's overall management policy from which Christianity itself has inherited what I think he calls, now what was it . . . a *penumbra*-effect. Religion made the classic error of overestimating the strength of its unique selling point, probably suffering briefly from what Jonty calls the monopolistic mind-set, but I suppose you can see how the Almighty, given His uniqueness, might easily fall into that particular trap. Religion's ratings have never entirely recovered. But then, come to think of it, the celebrity potential of Sodom and Gomorrah could have been exploited with a bit more vim, eh Digby, as we in the performing arts have surely been proving ever since. God might have learnt a lot from Jonty, you know. Assuming He could have afforded his consultation fees.'

As Digby made the coffee, with Daisy humming quietly to herself in the other room, he remembered the time Jonty and he had attempted a serious conversation about the Potteries. His neighbour had seemed anxious to discuss Stoke-on-Trent, since they'd both been involved in a form of manufacture associated with the place. The only problem was Digby's growing conviction that Jonty had never actually been there.

'Where they make our wares with such care and attention,' he had said. 'Up in the north.'

'The Midlands, Jonty.'

'But that is the north, isn't it?'

'No, it's a bit south of the north. That's why it's called the Midlands. It's in the middle. Between the north and the south.'

Jonty could direct you round Paris without bothering to consult a map. Ditto Rome, Florence, Venice and a dozen other places where he had vacationed flamboyantly at some time or other in his life. He could recommend hotels in Palermo and what you must and mustn't eat if you ever went to Algiers. He could tell you how long it would take to motor from one Swiss canton to another and which months might be tolerable, given the heat and humidity, in Manhattan. He could itemise the beaches where La Merriman had been permitted to sunbathe topless and those on which she had not. But point him northwards in the British Isles and all was suddenly fog and confusion. He knew it all ended finally with cliffs, Scotland, oil, chilly islands and raging seas but he'd remained vague as to what precisely went on between Hadrian's Wall and Hampstead. He knew there were people up there labouring away at his Lilliputian products but he'd never needed to see them actually doing the labouring. His products manager simply brought the prototypes to the house and spread them out before him. In a gesture of cultural curiosity which Digby found profoundly unconvincing Jonty had asked, 'Is there a university up there yet?'

'Oh lot's of them now. Keele, Stoke, Wolverhampton. For every pottery or foundry that closes, a new university opens.'

'The poor should be happy, then.'

'I believe not, Jonty. They've had their grants taken away from them, you see. So to get through university at all, these poor people whom you mention, they have to do full-time jobs as well.'

'I do wonder what's gained by it all, Digby.' Jonty had

once more been rehearsing his tone of well-practised incredulity at the world's unfathomableness.

'I suppose the poor grow more articulate about their poverty, at least. So they can put their disgruntlement into words.'

'Asking for trouble, isn't it? In the long run, I mean.' Jonty really had no problem at all with the pornography of commodities or with the status quo ante. He simply wanted a lot more of both. 'Anyway, we'll have to go up there one day – the pair of us, I mean.'

Crash Landing

I didn't kill her, Digby thought with some bitterness. It wasn't me who killed your mother, Theo. I'm still not sure to this day what did, but it wasn't me.

Small secrets you can keep; nobody keeps the big ones finally. The small ones simply get lost amid time's debris. But the big ones are heavy and like all heavy burdens they demand to be put down from time to time. After a few drinks or while staring into the face of a new lover, you give up your big secret because that's the most expensive gift you can afford. And so it was with Victoria one day. After how many years of marriage? It might even have been vengeance that prompted her rather than the weariness that besets every veteran of secrecy if the game goes on for long enough; those tired wrecks of MI5 and MI6. He never knew. But one day, clinging as he always did to one of the very few things he could be sure was true, despite all the vicissitudes of their life together, he had said, after a spectacular row, one that had left him trembling with fury: 'You cried that first night we spent together. You told me to say nothing, not a word, but you cried for your young man in his uniform. And it must have meant something.' And this time, after only the briefest pause, she had replied.

'But you weren't the young man in uniform I was crying for, love. My tears that night weren't for you. I didn't want you to speak because I wanted to hear his voice instead.' And so it had begun, her handing over at last of the big secret she had carried for so many years, carried throughout the whole of their courtship and marriage. So it was that Digby had come to discover how one of the few things he knew to be true, one of the things he could hold on to when the foundations shook, wasn't true after all and he couldn't hold on to it any more. She had cried all right but not for him. 'It's the same salt wherever tears are shed.' Was that still more ancient Maltese wisdom? Salt in his mouth, vinegar in his wounds. Sniff on the onion and you'll cry. This fish-fryer's daughter had learnt her trade, all right. Her young love's name, it transpired that night, the longest night in his life, was Jimmy.

And then he had made love to her with a passion he had not felt for years. But it couldn't cure the complaint, for he no longer knew who she'd been in bed with during their marriage. It struck him that he had never known her happier than during that time when he had not shared her bed but Theo had shared her sheets instead. In the months after Theo had been born Victoria claimed that he couldn't sleep alone in his cot; that he was one of those children who'd squall the night away to his own discomfort and the fracture of any civility the house possessed. Digby felt the new arrival hadn't as yet been given nearly enough time to find out the extent of his gifts as a solitary sleeper. But with the boy in his bed Digby himself was soon expelled from it.

'You'll wake him doing that, love . . . We can't, not now

– don't you think it might be better if you slept in the other room for a while.'

It was true that they had occasional meetings in the other bed, but this required contrivance and intention, a schedule was involved, whereas it seemed to Digby that the flesh needed to work out its own intentions without a pre-ordained schedule, in separation from any rational procedures of the mind. That was what he most liked about the flesh; when it came right down to it, he sometimes wondered if it might even have been the only thing he liked about it: that as his brain fell asleep his body could come alive on its own terms. And he grew angry at the separation. They had already been married for ten years before Theo was conceived and he had certainly wanted a son, so he tried not to let his anger direct itself at Theo himself; after all, it could hardly be laid at the boy's door that his mother now seemed to have abandoned all physical contact with the father in preference for a close companionship with the son. But it rankled all the same. His bed, *his bed*, was, however temporarily, forbidden him. And he only saw his wife's breasts when the boy was sucking away at one of them, waving his tiny hands in the air in ecstasy. Milking the situation for all it was worth. The intimacy between mother and son struck Digby as frankly excessive and relentless. No good would come of it. In that respect, he had surely been proved right. Why else did the fruit of his loins, feckless orally fixated ne'er-do-well that he unquestionably was, now need either a trumpet or a bottle pressed to his lips for the better part of the day? And if any intervals should occur in this demanding schedule the same lips would soon be pressed to the lipsticked mouth of some bar-room floozie. So much, he thought, for the breast-is-best propaganda of the post-war years. Nobody seemed to have told Theo that you were meant to leave off at some point. Stop sucking; start earning. The alarm clock hadn't yet rung in his son's bedroom. Deferred gratification had still not been introduced to the hugger-mugger of Theo's murky life. He'd already been given enough years to perform Mozart's entire career twice over, and he was barely weaned.

Digby could vividly remember his departure for the pottery in the early morning, the snatched cinematic shots through slants in the bedroom door. Milkwhite glimpses of nursing flesh. Softness not proffered. Off to work then, charged with a brutal energy. To hack at the status quo, loot the tomb inside money's pyramid; lead men towards their fortune.

It had been six months after that fateful conversation about Jimmy that Vicki had suggested they went for a drive. She had written down the co-ordinates years before on an old canvas map, its creases now mostly broken into holes with the webwork showing through, its printed surface stained with years of use followed by years of neglect. Digby didn't understand her interest in that particular location, and she wouldn't answer his questions, but he drove her where she directed. Anything for a quiet life that day, a good day in any case for motoring through Kent. Digby still enjoyed a good drive. Finally they found the place. Nothing much. A field. A few hedges. A distant farmhouse. He still didn't understand.

'It's where Jimmy's plane went down.' So they had come at last to find Jimmy's memory. Beneath his rising resentment, Digby had made out the darkening pane of inevitability. It was a glass he could not see through as yet, not even darkly. Would he ever?

'His Spitfire.'

'That's right, Jimmy's Spitfire. It must have been in that field over there. He didn't die right away, you know, they took him to the hospital. But I heard from his mother afterwards that the burns were so terrible . . .' She had started crying. Digby wanted to reach out to her, take her in his arms and comfort her for losing Jimmy in the flames of war all those years before, but he couldn't. He couldn't move. He wished that she might touch him instead, but reckoned that an embrace was probably the last thing on her mind. He wasn't Jimmy, was he? So best to keep his mouth shut, the way he had that first night. For a moment he wished that he'd been the one to die back there and Jimmy had gone on living. He had grown so weary by then of being a substitute husband that – terminal symptom of weariness – he had stopped caring. They stood there, the two of them, man and wife, staring at the field where decades before a plane had come screaming from heaven to earth and Vicki's young love, the silent young man in the uniform, had been damaged beyond repair.

'Couldn't he have parachuted?'

'Didn't have time. He was at such a low altitude when he was hit.' She stared at the field for a while without speaking. Gradually her muffled sobs subsided. 'If we dug it up,' she said finally, with a brightness in her voice that he could barely endure, 'there might still be some of the plane there. A wing. A propeller. Something underneath the corn.'

'It's possible,' Digby said, before turning away and walking back to the car alone.

Still they had tried for a few more months. Married people default to the old pattern of their lovemaking; they turn to each other mechanically the way a horse finds its way home in the dark. But he felt like someone else now in her arms, felt as though he had always been someone else in her arms, presumably as she had wanted him to be, from that first night in Hastings on. He had not been that bright creature falling out of the skies, the one who had caused Victoria's nyctalopia. Just the candleman lighting the nyctalops to her bed in the days that came after. The link-boy after a night of debauchery.

The silent soldier boy then, holding his tongue so that the Maltese fryer upstairs wouldn't wake to hear his cries. Was that the way they'd done it? Then dying in the front line, the line that Digby had never even joined. The front line in the air. It was impossible. He'd realised that in Kent when he had seen her face bathed in its grief at the edge of the field. So they'd agreed to a 'trial separation', which was merely a way of saying, from Digby's point of view, that he couldn't yet face thinking about a divorce. Victoria didn't believe in them anyway. If it wasn't on the Vatican's agenda then it wasn't on Malta's either.

And in fact the subject was never to come up. He merely started to make payments every month into Victoria's bank account. They agreed on an initial lump sum, to grant her the independence she felt she needed, a figure of £10,000, a lot of money then. Why had he been so generous when in his heart he'd felt she had eviscerated him? Was it because he believed that she would one day come back? That she had no true home left except for the hole she had drilled in his heart? A hole that would have to be filled again one day.

It was Vicki's idea to stay separated in the same house. 'It would be so much easier on Theo,' she had said. 'The house is big enough for us to live our lives and meet in the middle.' But the first time she had come back home with another man, a much younger man, he had realised it was impossible. That's when he told her she'd have to move out. That's when, according to his son, he'd started pushing her into her grave.

The first thing she had then done with the £10,000 in her account was to rent a flat overlooking the sea at St Leonards in Hastings, with a dedicated garage round the back; and the second thing she had done was to buy an E-type Jaguar. That had cost £6,000. Digby had been astounded. She had only learnt to drive the year before. She drove up to London and parked it outside the house with its hood down, its vast bonnet gleaming in the sun. Primrose yellow.

'Four point two litre,' she had said proudly. 'It'll go up to sixty in first. Does a hundred and forty flat out. Would you like a drive? After all the driving you did for me, it's the least I can do.'

'No thanks,' Digby had said. 'Victoria, I do wonder . . .' But he had given up before even uttering what was on his mind. He knew it was futile.

That's how they'd started to live apart, and Theo had never since forgiven his father for the fact. For once his mother had settled into the flat in St Leonards and become conspicuous as the woman unencumbered with a husband, who drove around in a fancy drophead, she was soon taking up with plenty of young men, some of them not much older than Theo himself, in fact all of them around the same age Jimmy had been when he died, and Theo had then felt that he had lost his mother altogether. Lost her to distance and scandal. Lost her to brothers whose names he didn't know, whom she took to her bed. But he had never held it against her, only against his father – Digby Wilton, the ladykiller, whom she'd been confusing with a dead man for so many

· years. It was not until a long time after that the father was really able to speak again to his son. But he still hadn't got through, had he? Would he ever? Time was running out.

Crash: it had been one afternoon in Kent. I am a dead man, he thought, chosen to fill the space in a bed intended for another. Why did you have to choose me, Vicki? Why not choose another silent boy in uniform? Or become a nun and dedicate your life to Jesus? Or to some Maltese madonna, Our Lady of Valletta or the Virgin of Gozo. Could you not have been a dutiful and silent cemetery attendant in Hastings? Put flowers on their graves every day, mourned the passing of that brave generation who gave their blood so some good might come of it. Not like those of us who stayed behind for quartermastering duties at Aldershot. Real men, not lace-counters, sock-counters, boot-counters, button-counters, pen-pushing calculators in our uniforms. Digby had switched quickly from second to third and the hedgerows along the narrow country road had become a blur. He threw the car into the next corner without changing down. There was a mild shriek of complaint from the front tyres. He had come back to these roads once more; couldn't keep away from them. So every time you murmured your love words at me you were thinking of somebody else, were you? Was that why you used to shout so often, even in Theo's presence, I am living with a dead man? Because you were, weren't you? I'm nothing but his posthumous shadow. Bitch. You bitch, Vicki. You calculating, dishonest, little Maltese bitch . . . was I the nearest thing to a dead man you could find then? Was that what first attracted you to me? My ability to impersonate a corpse? And my money, of course. Mustn't forget the creature comforts, after all. His foot pressed violently down on the accelerator.

The fuel tanker was approaching the blind corner as Digby sped into it from the other side. Given the Wolsey's acceleration by now, and the narrowness of the road, a collision was inevitable. As the tanker's lofty cab filled his windscreen Digby slammed on the brakes and tried to steer the car in a hard swerve away from a head-on meeting, but the wheels immediately locked and then skidded and Digby, trapped in his silent metal cockpit, seemed to float for a second, a second that expanded to include everything that had ever happened to him or ever would as the tanker loomed ever larger and its horn, a strange noise of complaint from a faraway country, bleated its siren's wail at the top of its voice, then BANG. The metal crunch that celebrates all marriages of speed.

Green liquid sobbed and surged from the ruptured radiator of the Wolsey. Enough antifreeze there to get me through another winter, Digby had thought sadly as he stared down at it. Soon the tarmac where he stood was awash with the iridescent mix. A lizard's luminous guts.

'You all right?' the tanker driver asked sourly, looking first at his own mangled cab before he took in the damage to the Wolsey.

'Yes. As dead men go, I'm fine,' Digby had answered, then started to laugh to himself. Almost silently but not quite. Smoke was already rising from the Wolsey's bonnet. 'Sorry Vicki, my love, but I seem to have survived another little scrap. What does a fellow have to do to go and join your beloved Jimmy?'

The bonnet itself could have been repaired, the ruined headlights and sidelights replaced along with the demolished radiator. Even the windscreen, smashed from the sudden warping of the bodywork, could have been restored. But when it was discovered that the chassis was buckled, Digby was informed the car was a write-off. So he let proceedings take their course and waited for the insurance money. And he was never to buy another car. After all, he thought, Jimmy never bought himself another aeroplane, did he? Burnt and scalded beyond repair in that field in Kent, the poor bugger. Where do you need to travel to any more in any case? With his eyes the way they were, he should probably have given it up years before. Only one more car journey awaited him, only one more with him at the wheel anyway.

Angelology

They step through walls as if they were no more than a sheet of mist, they shape up like steam taking form briefly from a kettle's spout, only to disperse once more into the invisible. Such bright manifestations in the dark. Bright still though the brightest fell. Why imagine you can escape them? They come as they choose and their going is equally spontaneous. You listen and take note; you remember the messages they bring from afar or you forget. Your body will always remember. For how could your bones ever again be oblivious to such potent visitations, even if your cluttered and chattering mind moves on to find fresh distractions?

Digby's visitations. The first one as a rebuke, that fearsome slap across the face, later to become vast swaddlings of comfort arriving to cradle him in his room at night. A warmth like no other, wrapping him round and scorching irresistible potencies all the way through him, through the dialogue of past and present that now made up his aching flesh. As long as the presence was in the room then you knew you were healed.

A warmth for which the word warmth was insufficient, circling invisibly and penetrating everything. You knew briefly that no harm could ever come to you because such power was from a source that cannot be overcome by any demonic ravages. Its power is invincible. No way of proving this but no need to either. Digby simply let it travel through him at the speed of light, bearing its warhead of curative heat. He had lost count of these visitations but he had no doubt that without them he would have been dead a long time before, whatever the ministrations of the men in white coats. And when the spirit left he always lay still and uttered a prayer of thanks in his heart, a silent, impromptu hymn of thanksgiving for these annunciations.

Digby had tried hard to understand. If this was a messenger then what was the message? Nowhere beyond good and evil to escape to? Even no man's land was a combat zone. Modern physics was on to it: black holes and the unfathomable symmetries of cosmology made up heaven and hell for every second of our lives. Uncle Freddie had been proved right after all: no contradiction between science and faith, only a temporary falling-out. But first came the slap.

Vicki's absence brought home to Digby what he had always really known: the extent to which love is a function of place and romance another way of studying topography. So much of what goes into a man's heart arrives there through his eye. Women surely are nowhere near so ocular in their affections. Other organs play a greater part: the heart, the memory, maybe even the womb catching its whispers from the future. But if you took a man away from what he loved for long enough he simply stopped loving it quite so much. Not that she had ever left him, even in death. But her absence meant that she didn't fill his days the same way. Photographs and letters couldn't do it and what was later to be called virtual reality was no reality at all. So Vicki's place inside Digby's heart slowly shrank as the dimensions of his bed expanded to contain her absence. Ghosts need little space between the sheets but still they fill them. The more potent the presence had once been the more vivid and electric the trace of that absence now. And a ghost is not the person it once was. It's something different: an ectoplasm of grief. A white cry in the darkness, the single cotton shift hanging in an otherwise empty wardrobe.

Maggie had been Vicki's best friend, though it had seemed to Digby an unlikely friendship in many ways. Maggie had about her that air of casual omnicompetence which is one of the most striking features of a certain species of middle-class Englishwoman. Her hair and clothes were worn with insouciant authority though it never seemed as though she spent much time on either. She always looked right in whatever she wore, with her hair a dirty outdoor blonde, and her ancient tartan scarves and long-pleated skirts grown ragged at the edges. The geography of her face was dominated by prominent cheekbones and during the summer months her skin would brown until it had the mottled texture of a polished apple. Despite her exuberant laugh there was never even the mildest hint of hysteria about her, though there was often considerably more than a suggestion of psychic excess about Vicki, who was in temperament more Mediterranean than English, with her unpredictable upswings and sudden depressions. Her moods seemed to be all blazing sunlight or lethal squalls, with nothing much between, nothing of the temperate warmth or drizzle of these islands, the curious climatic restraint that seems somehow to reflect itself in the psychology of those who've learnt to live at peace inside the weather. When he had first met Vicki Digby had thought he'd escaped that restraint at last and was frankly glad to be out of it, but as he grew older he found himself craving more of his native birthright, and the specific form this craving took was an intense admiration for Maggie and her ways; her undemonstrative, beguiling ways; the frequency of her laughter, with no hint of menace in it.

She had come to commiserate after Vicki's departure and they had drunk a bottle of wine together.

'Poor Digby,' she had said, 'and you always seemed to try so hard too.' She had placed a hand on his arm and he had noticed that her crooked fingernails were still a little dirty from the gardening. It was probably an equal surprise to both of them to find themselves half an hour later sharing the large bed where Digby had until recently lain with Vicki, in the bedroom where so many of Vicki's things still hung in the surrounding cupboards. He at least was initially a little shamefaced at what they had done – it was after all the first infidelity of his married life – but they continued doing it all the same. And the size of his bed started to shrink again. With Maggie in his life he felt he could once more touch the edges of things without feeling he'd fall over them.

Maggie came over one evening when the chill was settling in and left the next morning with a bright sun shining, and that was probably why she left her white woollen sweater on the wicker chair in the corner of the bedroom. Digby had been given no notice of Vicki's arrival when the E-type swung into the drive two hours later.

'Just come to pick up a few more of my things,' she had said after kissing him briefly on the cheek. It struck him how happy she looked. The new car and her new separation were evidently suiting her nicely. She made her way upstairs without apology as though they were still her stairs, however far she might have chosen to live from them. And after she had loaded her few items of clothing into the boot she turned to him and said simply, 'I see you've been taking a little comfort with my best friend Maggie. Do give her my love, won't you?' Then she was gone, leaving Digby only with the sound of the Jaguar exuberantly throttling up the road.

He'd caught something in her eye. He knew that look. You couldn't spend all the years he'd spent with Vicki without knowing how certain expressions, certain angles of the mouth and narrowings of the eyes, promised serious trouble. It was only later when he made his way upstairs into the bedroom and peered round the door into the bathroom that he saw what she'd done.

Maggie's white pullover, the beautiful Aran rollneck that she wore for much of the year, had been sliced into small pieces with one of Digby's razors and deposited in the bath, covered with gobbings of blood. Had she cut herself by accident, or was this another part of the curse she was bringing down on Maggie and himself? The razor blade, blood congealing on it, lay on top of the shredded wool. He started to step backwards out of the bathroom, as though he had caught sight of some ritual in a forest, whispered prayers and smoky figures, anathemas in unknown tongues, something he didn't understand and didn't want to.

He had phoned Maggie and asked her to come over immediately.

'It won't wait,' he had said.

'I'm flattered,' she had said, not understanding.

When she walked into the bathroom, directed there by Digby, and saw her beloved Aran sweater slashed and bloodied, the tufts of white lamb's wool streaked with red, she slumped down slowly to the floor. So much violence, so much malice, dumped in that small bath.

'We can't go on with it, Digby,' she'd said later when she phoned him, 'not with that amount of hate coming after us.' And she had never returned to the house. Occasionally she had telephoned to make sure that he was all right but they were never to see each other again until Vicki's funeral, where they had arranged to meet for lunch the following week at a restaurant in Kensington.

The lunch was a subdued enough affair, for there was still something funereal in both their moods. Maggie had been explaining her latest project to him; the few acres in Cornwall she had bought and was preparing to farm, with what struck Digby as more of a nostalgic than an agricultural intent. Then she had stopped speaking, her face grown suddenly pale. Without warning she had lurched across the table, knocking over the bottle of wine in the process and with a mighty swipe she had slapped Digby across the face.

'That's from Victoria,' she had shouted before starting, very quietly, to weep. Digby sat and stared at her as the red wine dripped from the tablecloth down to the floor, its rose stain spreading stealthily over the stiff white linen. The restaurant had fallen silent around them. Waiters stood motionless, dishes still steaming in their hands. Then Maggie had stood up and left the room.

'Why did you do it?' he had asked her later as they sat in the back of the taxi. His cheek was raw.

'I didn't,' she said finally, staring out of the window as the streets of London concertina'd by. She drummed two fingers gently on his knee where she had placed her left hand with such gentleness a moment before. 'It wasn't me, Digby.'

Two months later he had returned to the practice of his

religion, after having set its rituals aside for over thirty years. And that was when he'd started his study of angelology in earnest. Not that it had helped him fathom anything much, but it helped him pass the hours.

At least the funeral had given Digby the opportunity to see his son again. Not that either of them had been in a very talkative mood that day. Theo had permitted his father to lay a hand on his shoulder.

Digby never knew how much Theo had seen of his mother's decline. Drinking heavily and being recklessly and publicly promiscuous before the onset of her disease, she had also apparently continued in the same vein for as long as possible afterwards. Her parents had stopped speaking to her. But finally the drugs had taken over where the drink left off and Sammy and his wife, old and frail by then, had forgiven her and taken her back to their home above the fish and chip kiosk, which was now run by Vicki's brother. The E-type had been locked away securely in the garage and the rented flat overlooking the sea relinquished; she soon began to spend the day in bed, surrounded by bottles filled with different coloured medicines, instead of those she had previously favoured, which had been filled with different coloured liquors. Medications, basins, bowls, towels, thermometers, charts. Some implements he didn't know the meaning of, and didn't want to: intimate incisors with minutely menacing points, spider-like metal ganglia, probes for the nether and the inner regions.

Digby had paid for a nurse to visit for an hour in the daytime and another at night. To do all that was necessary in the way of medications and injections. Her parents had been grateful. Having discovered that he had committed no acts of adultery or physical violence, and had been condemned merely for being who he was, an Englishman of predictably diminished emotions, they had sided with him in the marital conflict. But Vicki's final illness was to dissolve the conflict entirely for all of them.

Towards the end she had grown contemplative. He wasn't sure to what extent this was the drugs. He would travel down by train to see her every week.

'Do you think I invited him in?' she had asked one day. She was lying on the bed and Digby was staring out of the back window at the junk in her father's back yard. An old bathtub, a pile of tyres, a long-dead bicycle.

'Who, Vicki?'

'The one inside; the one that's killing me. I've invited a lot of others in, you know. A lot more than you ever knew about. Not just you and Jimmy. Do you think I invited him in?'

'Digby turned from the window and looked hard at her pale, wasted face. He had never seen flesh so white.

'I don't know, Vicki. I think he would have come anyway.'

'It's just that he acts as though he's been invited. He certainly makes himself at home. Never stops eating. Just like Theo when he was little. Munch munch munch.

'Now I know what it is to be truly loved. This one adores me. It'll never come out again into the sunshine, will it? Rather go down to the grave inside me. Shouldn't think either you or Theo would do that, now would you? Be honest, love. Not even Jimmy, probably. Time to go to sea again. When did we go last time?'

'Our honeymoon.'

'Water's the best thing. Goes along with things but goes

past them too. When it gets really cold it's still; and when it gets really hot it rises up for a while but it always comes back down again. You can rely on it. Water's the best thing: lets you see right through it. No secrets to hurt anybody with. No matter how hard you beat it, it doesn't change its shape or nature, does it? Always stays level with itself. Gets back together at the first opportunity. And it holds on to those inside it. The living and the dead. They all keep moving about in water.'

Digby often slipped into a kind of trance while she spoke. He had to rouse himself one day when he realised that she was making a request. Vicki was asking that she be buried at sea. Later Digby had mentioned this wish to her father and brother. They had said nothing but he had sensed in their silence some ancient Maltese prohibition.

She had known when the pain arrived that this was the final pain. She'd had plenty of pain before, of one sort or another, much of it rooted in her addiction, for the constant consumption of hard liquor generates at least as much agony as it soothes, even while giving a shape to a drinker's day and some control over the drinker's life, mixing medicine with poison, but this was something different. This had about it an intensity of purpose and a disregard for her whimperings which she had found startling in its purity. She had known right away that it had found its cave inside her, the one that it was destined for, and that none of the huntsmen of modern medicine would ever force it out again, for all their firebaitings and their sharpened, disinfected blades. It had come to stay – and she was the one who'd have to move on. And now the pain was quietly sucking at the morphine, a greedy baby at that breast inside as the whiteness of the drug took all the technicolor misery out of everything. She was glad they'd made the drug white. As a girl she'd had a glass paperweight that snowed whenever you shook it. How she had loved that snow, the way the little sky went crazy with it before settling on the village with its tiny street and bridge and river. Then all the coloured roofs would be hushed to white. She thought of the kindness in a good dog's eyes. For some reason she thought of that. The word fidelity loped on its four symmetric syllables slowly across her mind. Then something between her heart and her brain stopped happening, and she died.

Digby had been right about that ancient Maltese prohibition. They had all nodded in agreement at her request when they sat around her bed but they'd never had any intention of fulfilling it. Instead she ended up in a graveyard set so far back from the sea that the sea was forgotten. Its limitless greyness, its night-time rages, its soothing murmurs the morning after, all this was just too far away, along with the gulls' vindictive cries and the hungry bleating of slot-machines along the front. This Hastings graveyard was unsalted either by the sea's romance or its menace. It was merely a suburban dumping ground for defunct humanity, well enough kept to be sure under the supervision of the East Sussex County Council, its grass duly manicured, the stones largely upright and unfractured, unlike the subterranean remains they marked. But Digby now felt it to be one final betrayal to have let her be put down here encased in pine, where she had so fiercely elected not to be. He should have fought harder to fulfil that final wish of hers to be buried at sea. But there were problems, it appeared. You can only bury a body at sea if that is required by the necessities of sea voyaging. He could see the point of that: the prospect of

Victoria floating back on to the beach at Hastings after a few days bobbing about in the bay would have needed some explaining. The only way to do it, according to the undertaker, who appeared surprisingly knowledgeable on the subject, was for her to be burnt to a cinder then have her ashes scattered over the Channel. That procedure, though hardly encouraged, was permitted. It was not what Vicki had requested: to go to feed the fishes, that was the phrase she'd used. To hear the Maltese liturgy intoned one last time as she sank and then slowly to break up among the tidal surges. She had thought about it, even dreamt about it. It seemed to represent for her a kind of freedom. Jimmy had come falling from the skies in flames, she would break up slowly under the waves, drenched into oblivion. But cremation and scattering, it seemed, would have to do. He'd borne the message back. Her father and her brother were adamant they wouldn't have it. The old lady was largely beyond conversation by then but there was some instinctive horror in them all at the prospect of the flames. As though one were conniving with hell itself. So it was decided, Digby being too weary to fight over it any longer, that it should be inhumation. A standard inhumation in a standard Hastings cemetery.

Why was the Christian marriage ceremony so feeble in its promises? Till death us do part, indeed. The following week and the one after that he went down, with a floral bouquet to place against the headstone, and stood there with his hands crossed loosely on his belly as he thought of her body losing its flesh ounce by ounce as the worms meandered through her. He saw more and more why she might have preferred the waves. In his dreams she returned, a vacancy surrounded now only by bone and darkness. He woke sweating in the shroud of his memories. So what liar in the Church's hierarchy had come up with that absurdity then: till death us do part? Sex and love had their own eschatology. Buried in its tomb of syllables the word resurrection held the word erection inside it. So never say theology doesn't have its optimistic side.

Each time Digby visited the grave he walked down to the sea afterwards and crunched along the pebbled beach, sometimes talking out loud to himself as he went, sometimes even shouting into the waves' vast roar of incredulity. Victoria, he yelled, Vicki. The gulls caught his words on the wind and screamed with laughter. Then after a while he stopped going either to the beach or the graveyard. It all went silent inside him as though a thick coin had jammed inside the machine's slotted mouth and put an end to its bleating. As though the sea had swallowed the sun and quenched it and all the flames had finally gone out.

Noosphere

Howard had not come back to his mother's house on Wandsworth Common, but his father had. He had stayed for three days. Daisy wasn't at all sure what was going on but she found it amusing. For some reason Howard only communicated these days with his father, so to find out what he was up to, Daisy had to contact James. Now they spoke to each other on the phone each day. Except when he was off on one of his secret shoots. Why did these shoots have to be secret and even if they were secret, why couldn't he tell her about them? She couldn't help wondering if there was a woman involved. A young woman.

'But why doesn't Howard call me?' she asked after James had passed on his latest message.

'I think he wants to surprise you.'

'He's already surprised me enough. The little bastard.'

'Now he's not that is he, Daisy? I'd made an honest woman of you long before he was born.'

'Well you seem to be inviting me back to a life of shame now.'

'What, acting, you mean?'

'I'll ignore that. What's he going to surprise me with, James? Give me a clue.'

'They're working up to a launch.'

'Who is? A launch of what?'

'If I told you that I'd spoil the surprise, wouldn't I?'

'The son may not be a bastard but the father certainly is.'

'When are you coming to see me again?'

'When I find out more about this launch. If you're lucky, you old goat. I read the other day that in Afghanistan they still sacrifice goats.'

'And?'

'It's not all that far from Kabul to North Shropshire. So watch it.' How things do come round again, she thought as she put the phone down.

She had gathered up five or six of the small books and pamphlets strewn across Howard's desk, Bakunin, Kropotkin, Herbert Read, and a pile of the print-outs she had made by accessing sundry files from his computer. Digby had grown very effective at collating this material. Unless she was much mistaken and he actually was in love with her, he had become thoroughly absorbed in the task. Five minutes later the letterbox next door snapped open and Digby heard his neighbour's voice.

'DIGBEE. It's me.'

She crouched on the floor while he sat in his favourite chair by the window, turning over the pages of one of the pamphlets she had given him.

'Were you ever an anarchist, Digby?' He thought for a moment before answering.

'Only in regard to certain private matters.'

'When I first told James that his son had become one, he just laughed. Said all young men were anarchists at his age.

So I asked him if he'd been one and he said yes. But not you?'

'It always struck me as a little optimistic, to be honest, as a blueprint for humanity to live together, and I suppose I've never been over-endowed with optimism.' Digby almost thought he could hear Vicki's voice once more: 'Why do you always think everything will turn out so badly, love? Maybe thinking makes it so.' But then he thought of what had happened to her and what appeared to be happening to Theo, or for that matter the speed with which gin or chilled wine coursed through him these days, and reflected that everything does turn out badly, doesn't it, here in this sublunar region? All you have to do is hang on long enough. The paths of glory lead but to the grave. The Second Law of Thermodynamics often seemed to contain the same message as Uncle Freddie's teachings on Original Sin. Daisy was reading something out from one of the print-outs. It was quoting Shakespeare again. *Troilus and Cressida*. About how the appetite for profit, that universal wolf, had turned vegetarian animals into cannibals, and we had ended up eating ourselves away with profit as BSE had turned to CJD and we now had to watch as the brains of the young were gnawed away. Profit left to itself consumed everything, apparently. And that was precisely why, according to Howard, the principle of communication, while still remaining free, could prove so costly to our present masters. Digby didn't understand that part.

He couldn't help wondering if it were merely the Sixties again: those children whose birthright had been liberty, so much liberty that it had tripped without effort into libertinism. Meanwhile they'd prattled on about the glories to be achieved with arms, who barely knew the thump of a rifle's retort, let alone the sound that a man makes when a bullet enters his throat. They had spoken cheerfully of the spilling of blood but their own blood had remained secure inside their own scrubbed skins.

There'd seemed to be an enthusiasm amounting to glee for the prospect of mechanised slaughter in the service of revolution. In foreign places of course, as he remembered. These children of plenty would never see the rotting corpses for themselves or hear the screams in their own vicinity. Children's limbs would never fly past the windows of their salubrious neighbourhoods. The butchers round those parts would stick to pigs and cows, inside abattoirs inspected regularly by the Health and Safety comintern. Revolution, like free love, had been a term of utter and sublime liberation, untouched by the tangled depredations of humanity. He had remembered something his well-read uncle had told him: that when the Russian poet Osip Mandelstam had first heard the word progress as a little boy he had burst into tears, the stink of evil which the syllables gave off had been so potent. And the goddess of history had not by that stage even yet spat out the words Lubianka or Gulag, to which Mandelstam would be consigned soon enough, all in the name of progress of course. All in the name of cleansing the world of its evil. Daisy was speaking again.

'I'm not sure I've ever completely worked it out; anarchism I mean, the whole gubbins. When I was at drama school there was a student who was an anarchist. He was the biggest brute there by a long chalk, so I just assumed he fancied the idea of the survival of the fittest. If there'd been no laws at all he'd certainly have survived all right. He'd have eaten the rest of us. He once put his hand up my skirt when we were doing a reading of *Hamlet*. I told him if he didn't remove it I'd slap his face, and he told me I had an authoritarian personality. I never much felt like studying the subject after that.'

'You seem to be studying it quite a lot now.'

'Howard says all previous anarchists have failed because they needed to seize, or was it bring to a standstill, the means of production. Now for the first time anarchism's moment has come because the modern world is controlled entirely by communications, and the individualism of one figure in front of a screen can link up simultaneously with all the other individualisms across the globe. Individual protest and communal protest are now one and the same thing. One single virus could bring the world to a standstill if it was well enough designed. Anyway he told me the next revolution will be won in cyberspace; says the numbers are growing and at a certain point, a quantitative change will become a qualitative change. Because it always does.'

'I'm trying to understand all this, Daisy. Is he against globalisation, then?'

'No, he says he's for it. He says the only globalisation we have now is to protect the free movement of profits and commodities. Real globalisation would lift all restrictions on the movements of people. Then you'd never be able to apply the word illegal to a person again.'

'Where does the internet come in?'

'It represents a destruction of boundaries. You have to fight like with like. This treatment is . . . hang on, what does it say here?' Daisy searched amongst her sheets. 'Here it is. This treatment is homeopathic not allopathic.'

'My mother would have liked it then. Stoke's only German homeopath.'

'The Germans. That's another of the points here. We didn't fight the Nazis with warm beer and cricket, did we?'

'Not as I recall.'

Daisy was tracing words and phrases on the sheets she had laid out on the floor.

'We set about blitzing them back into the Stone Age. Treating like with like. There's enough of the global commodity on the internet to let it fight commodity globalisation. It's a sort of antidote.' She looked up again. 'Have you ever stayed in a Holiday Inn, Digby?'

'I don't believe I have.'

'They're exactly the same. Once you're inside it's impossible to tell whether you're in Slough or Kuala Lumpur. Exactly the same band of white paper protects the toilet seat, a sort of sanitised girdle, to show it's unused.'

'That must be a comfort to the hunter home from the hill.'

'And it's the same with McDonald's – that's why they all hate it so much. Brunelleschi's dome in Florence might be entirely different from those onion roof jobs in Moscow, but you can be sure of one thing: within two minutes of either you can buy a burger and fries which will be indistinguishable from the ones on offer in Neasden. It's become universal.'

'A constant like the speed of light. You must have spent a lot of time talking to Howard.'

'Correction, Digby: I have spent a lot of time listening to Howard. I barely got a word in edgeways, though I wouldn't mind listening to him again for a while. That's if he ever decides to come home again.'

She left the sheets and pamphlets with him and as he turned the pages Digby found himself remembering his mother. For a moment he was a boy, holding her hand as she scoured the moorlands and woods surrounding Stoke for comfrey and dittany, which she very rarely found. He still had some of them in the house somewhere, pressed into an old diary, his mother's precious herbs. She was either a late epigone of an earlier tradition or the harbinger of a later one, for she had been entirely holistic and homeopathic. The orthodox tradition of allopathic medicine, she believed, betrayed a fundamental hostility to the body, only serving to target it for attacks and commando intrusions by alien powers. Looking back he could see what a splendid oddity his mother had been, glowing so brightly in her quirkiness up there in the low light of the Potteries, with her German accent – all his aunts and uncles had said she'd only married his father to get rid of the umlaut over her name, but there was still an umlaut always hovering over her, along with the smell of herbs that accompanied her everywhere. She kept them in her pockets, so she could make her own tea and flavour her food. Her coat had been an enormous fur, and if the moorland winds blew hard she would open it up and take Digby inside too. He had loved it in there, pressed up close against her perfumed body. He could still remember the gentle chafing of the tiny buttons on her silk blouse, with their mothwing fabric. He had wondered sometimes if that's how he'd developed his taste for foreign women, the taste that had finally cost him so dear. Though Vicki wasn't exactly foreign; but then she wasn't exactly English either. The rest of the family had always thought that Digby's father had married an eccentric scatterbrain, who still hadn't mastered English grammar after twenty years on these shores. He had adored her until the day she died.

Now, he thought, I'd better make a list of all the words

Howard's using here that I don't understand. So he began to do just that. Taking out his pen and a sheet of blank paper he wrote his list, exactly as he had been taught to do by Uncle Freddie when studying a text in Latin or French:

Vocabulary

> People's Global Action
> J18
> N30
> Black Bloc
> Tute Bianchi
> Reclaim the Streets
> Affinity groups
> Vibe-watchers
> Fishbowls

Plenty of queries for Daisy there the next time she came over. There was one sentence of Howard's he kept returning to: *New Anarchism starts from this one tenet: the authorities we've agreed to place over us no longer enable but prevent.*

Spring

Since the day of his crash in Kent so many years before, Digby had never driven a car, except for that one ceremonial journey from Hastings to London. Once a week Desmond Turl, the son of his cleaner, arrived to pick him up and take him to the vigil mass at Westminster Cathedral on a Saturday evening. Digby would have preferred to go on Sunday morning but it had become all too apparent that Desmond's entry into consciousness could never be guaranteed much before lunchtime, certainly not on a Sunday. It was simply too haphazard gambling on the extent of Desmond's intake the night before. So now they went on Saturdays and when Desmond arrived in his clapped-out Mazda he was invariably sober. The car stank of cigarette smoke, it was true, but Digby suspected this might well disguise odours even more unacceptable so he didn't complain. By the time Digby came out of church, luminous as stained glass with his brief experience of a communion beyond words, the car always had a mild smell of drink too. Digby in affable mood one night had asked Desmond which watering hole he repaired to, only to be met with silence. Communication, he had come to feel, was not necessarily young Desmond's strong suit.

But when finally roused to wakefulness the boy seemed reliable enough. This might simply have been because of his mother's needling. She'd been cleaning and arranging deliveries of Digby's food for over a decade now. She constituted the only retinue the old man had, so they needed each other.

Digby's unreadiness to venture out much had been reinforced by his growing sense of the menace of the world, a menace brought home one day with such virulent force that he had never spoken of it to anyone. He had arrived back at Bolingbroke Grove after his stroll across the Common. The dog had been sniffing, sniffing and circling the grassy margin at the edge of the road. It was a mongrel, a hint of terrier spliced with any number of other breeds. This mangy creature was a repellent patchwork of white, black and another hue he could only describe as antique filth. Such miscellaneous curs were far from uncommon in these parts.

The car was throttling up through its gears. A Capri 2.8 Turbo with as many additions as a vehicle could reasonably carry. The windscreen bore a blue strip of plastic running along its top horizontal, and on this were lettered luminescently the names of the driver and his companion *du jour*. Suddenly the dog darted into the road and tyres scorched briefly as the brakes slammed on. The driver, an obese, tattooed man of about thirty, sweating with industrial vigour in his black string vest, had leapt out and rushed round to the front of his motor. He had taken off his mirrored sunglasses and run a finger gently along the chrome bumper, checking for dents. Satisfied that the vehicle had survived the encounter he had walked back and climbed in, glancing only for the briefest moment at the animal which now lay twitching but silent on the tarmac, dark blood oozing slowly from its snout. The car had backed up sharply, swerved around the dying dog then powered off up the road.

Digby had been left to stare in silence. He had knelt by the dog, its injuries evidently irreparable, its tiny whimpers unendurable to him. He had quickly crossed the road, entered his garage, taken a heavy hammer and a sheet of dirty cloth, gone back to the dog, stroked it gently for a moment to calm it, placed the dirty cloth over it so as to cover its eyes and then smashed in its skull. The blow had been swift and lethal. He'd heard bones shatter. He had left the dog covered in its cloth, the red patch slowly growing wider. After that day his appetite to go out had disappeared completely. There was a honk from his drive. It was Desmond. Young Des, his mother's pride and joy. Digby genuflected briefly before the little wooden madonna on his windowsill.

Desmond drove as he usually did, at a speed entirely unrelated to his competence, while Digby was flung hither and thus across his filthy back seat. Unspeaking, though you could hardly say in silence, given the blast of disintegrating sound that issued from his car radio. Desmond always seemed to look about him furtively whenever they stopped at a traffic light or had to park for a few minutes. Digby had often wanted to ask about the tiny tattoo on the back of Desmond's neck. As far as he could make out it appeared to represent a lion, though this interpretation could have been disputed. The lion's head had somehow transmuted into an ancient fellow with a square beard, and the whiskers had come out as two thin waving arms. It struck Digby as a curious place to have a tattoo.

As they drove along York Road Digby noticed a tree, its branches recently lopped and now festooned with ribbons, its base surrounded by flowers in their plastic film. Also what appeared to be a wreath.

'I wonder what that is,' Digby said, not expecting a reply.

'Jack Miller,' Desmond said without hesitation.

'Was there an accident?'

'Hanged himself. From that tree. They're going to cut it down next week as a mark of respect.'

'Any particular reason?'

'Drugs.'

'How old was he?'

'Twenty-seven.'

'Tragic.'

'Well, he was dealing as well as using. Probably topped himself before somebody else came round and did the job for him. Shouldn't get too sentimental, Mr Wilton.'

'Not something I'm often accused of actually, Desmond.'

Digby's return to the religion of his childhood had come late in his life, shortly after Vicki's death. She'd always been the devout one during the years of their cohabitation. As far as he knew she had never questioned the truth of her inherited beliefs, while he had for many years suffered a species of autism of the spirit, simply baffled into spiritual inaction by the complexity of the data.

His problems with the whole subject of God had been endearingly summarised once when he had gone with Vicki to see the ventriloquist Arthur Worsley at the Winter Gardens in Morecambe. Arthur was famous for never speaking at all; his dummy, the woodentop Charlie Brown, spouted an endless stream of eloquent abuse at his master. At one point the dummy had confided to the audience, 'All ventriloquists go nuts in the end, you know.' Then he turned slyly towards Worsley and said, 'He thinks I'm real – don't you, son?' Perhaps we'd invested so much energy in that fetish we called Father he'd finally taken to talking back. The chimera of our discontent had found a voice with which to instruct us in the catechism of our wretchedness; the dummy we'd fashioned for ourselves had taken to explaining, in book after mighty book, how unworthy we were even to address him. My boy here thinks I'm real – don't you, son? He thinks *I* made *him*.

But all that changed after his first visitation. It's a wicked generation that needs a sign, but Digby had needed one. And now the mass he attended each week at Westminster Cathedral was the one immovable feature in his admittedly sparse social calendar. Come, eat of my bread and drink of the wine I have poured. And he did, however guilty of dust and sin he felt. Then back home again with Desmond in his Mazda, in the back seat of which he seemed to spend most of his time thinking about either his wife or his son.

Theo had made it plain since the age of sixteen that he found organised religion ridiculous, the way they sashayed about in all their hieratic clobber, intoning their rites, crooning on about sin and redemption. Apparently, sin didn't strike Theo as all that bad. In fact what the men from the ecclesia called sin looked to him more or less indistinguishable from pleasure. This had led to some fierce arguments with his father once the old man had entered his late, religious phase, prompted at last by tragedy into devotion. He had once employed all his eloquence to try to talk Theo back round to the orthodoxy of his upbringing, but Theo was having none of it; he had merely responded to his father's talk by pointing out that the fall was the noblest episode in our spiritual history. Noblest: that was the word he'd used. The aboriginal calamity, Digby seemed to remember Newman had called it, when the monkey learnt to shriek and the lion to slobber over his food and the serpent's forked tongue first quivered in the morning air, and Theo simply wanted more of it, for nobility's sake. My son, he'd thought then, my son the theologian. Would he ever know what it really meant to be locked away in the tight room with the snakes and trumpets, the dark place where even the motion of your own breathing is a sound of terror? An endless line of women, an endless line of bottles, stood between Theo and the midnight hour. Concupiscence and bibosity were his spiritual prophylactics. What his physical ones were Digby had no idea, but they seemed effective enough.

Grandchildren, Theo, have you ever given a thought to procreation, if not for your own sake then for the sake of others? When it comes right down to it, have you ever in the whole of your life considered anybody's comfort but your own? All that coition and not a single swelling womb on the horizon. So much, thought Digby, for the contraceptive society.

Once more he sat in his favourite chair by the window and watched the seasons as they shifted into summer's *son et lumière*. A few months before there'd been nothing out there but evergreens. Now he could see spotted dead-nettle, forget-me-nots, bleeding heart. The hawthorn tree was in full colour. Over in the corner he could just make out French marigold and dwarf convolvulus. The garden, left to itself, had flourished. Spring had shed its skin and was now forming another, more colourful one. It always astonished him, this return of life with its rainbow of possibilities. It seemed so uncalled for, so gratuitous. He sat there in the early evening and tried to think of nothing but the flowers before him. Theo's old swing creaked very gently in the breeze.

Two miles away Zeno were reassembling in Wimbledon. Dove had just reminded Breezer of a joint acquaintance, another musician – you're employing that term pretty loosely, Dove, Breezer replied. The big man's face was already darkening at the recollection.

'You know when he does that . . . ?' he asked, unable for the moment to complete his sentence.

'Billy Deptford, you mean?'

'That is who we're talking about, Dove. When he does that . . . what would you call it? Tuneless warbling, I suppose.'

'It's meant to represent something, apparently.'

'What?'

'A protest against the sanitisation of music. All the studio engineering stuff. Sixty-four-track unreality. The marketing. The cleanliness of the modern image. He has a following, you know.'

'Does he still hit that electric guitar like he's trying to get something nasty off his fingers?'

'Mmm. But that represents something as well.'

'Well, good luck to him with his representations and his new-found following, but I'll stick to my original estimate, if it's all the same to you.'

'Which is?'

'Tuneless warbling; talentless strumming; doodlesome twaddle. Next you'll be telling me he's got a record deal.'

'He has. With Tumbleweed. Coming out next year.'

'Television appearances?'

'Not yet.'

'Give the meretricious little scumbag time. What a world, eh Dove? While the gold of Zeno goes unnoticed. While the likes of you and me play *My Way* in south Wimbledon.'

'With added vocals.'

'With added fucking vocals.'

It had been a sunny day and it was a mild evening and the band were reasonably relaxed during the interval, while they prepared themselves to impersonate a collective karaoke machine in the second half. Think of the money, boys: it was after all still their best-paid gig. Then Pete motioned to them to gather round and as they did he started to draw an inverted pyramid on the back of a sheet of music paper. They were smiling now; they always enjoyed this. Rudimentary though Pete's journalistic training had been he had taken great care to miss nothing on his way to his present editorial post. Which was why he could draw without thinking the basic geometric diagram every journalist learns before he learns anything else. Down the slant of one line of the inverted equilateral triangle he wrote the letters. W.H.A.T. Pointing to the W he looked up expectantly at the faces of the band. He'd explained these principles to them on various occasions before, with considerable care. He would have been disappointed if the boys in the band had not remembered them, but he was not disappointed. They had all made mental notes and retained them.

'What happened,' Reg said. Pete smiled and filled in that sector of the triangle with the words. Then he pointed to the H.

'How did it happen,' Paul said. Pete filled in that sector too, then he pointed to the A.

'Additional material,' Dove chirped. Pete duly wrote down the words. Now they were at the bottom of the cone, the bit where melted ice-cream gathers on a hot day. He pointed to the T. Theo felt obliged to show a little willing, to be a dutiful student: he found Pete so sweet in his explanatory mode.

'Tie it all up,' he said, and Pete duly completed his diagram.

'There,' he said, apparently happy with his work. 'You can all have a job at the *Streatham Clarion* any time you like, boys. Now, using this diagram let's recap the story of Zeno, shall we?' They carried on smiling but none of them had been expecting this, except possibly Theo, who'd been watching Pete with care over the last few months, wondering what exactly he had on his mind. *The future of the band.* He'd remembered that phrase. They all took gentle sips from their drinks and waited.

'What?' Pete said, his finger pointing to the top of the inverted pyramid as he looked into their faces one at a time as though daring any of the others to take over his explication. But they said nothing. 'What?' he repeated. 'What precisely is Zeno?' Again the expected silence. 'An unsuccessful band, that's what. Five years of going steadily downhill. We peaked three years ago with that Saturday night second billing in Reigate. That brief moment was our heyday. Despite our spread in the *North Putney Gazette* we failed to find lift-off. So what does life offer us now? Earning a pittance in the suburbs of London. A pittance divided by six. Can we all at least agree on this?'

'A bit harsh, Pete,' Reg said. Pete started scratching his chin with his blue asthmatic dispenser. He was priming himself for a blast.

'This is the newsroom now, Reg. There's no space for sentiment here. We're looking for headlines. We're after a splash. On to How.' He pointed to the second segment of the triangle. 'Not sure really. Nobody's fault. We rehearsed; we didn't miss gigs. Nobody was ever so pissed or stoned he couldn't play the notes. We even got through those nine months without Theo. There are nights out there when I'd have to say we are absolutely brilliant. I don't believe anyone's better. So what's the problem? I've come to think it must be our ghostly quality.'

'What's that then, Pete?' Paul said.

'Theo plays trumpet like Miles Davis forty years back. It's lovely, Theo. I wouldn't have believed anybody could do it. Shouldn't think even Miles would have thought anybody could do it. Reg plays drums like Buddy Rich forty years back. Paul plays bass like Mingus forty years back, Breezer plays horn like Coltrane forty years back and I try to play piano like Bill Evans forty years back. And Dove plays guitar like . . . who do you play guitar like, Dove?'

'Well, I'd have liked to play like Tal Farlow, but my hands weren't big enough. I'm not sure who I play like now, to be completely honest.'

'Dove: the one total original among us. Anyway, that's what I mean by our ghostly quality. We don't fit the requirements of the age, boys. They're all making different noises out there. We haven't even got a junkie in the band, not a real one, American-style. Nobody's shooting up; nobody's scoring crack. No one's freebasing on his riffs. We're moderate people. Even Theo gets soaked on English drizzles not tropical storms. If there's a climate for our music it's temperate. We avoid the tropics. We just tootle on in the old British way, and read about the heroes over the other side of the Atlantic. All our heroes went to jail at some point. Who's been to jail here?' There was an uncomfortable silence before Theo spoke.

'I've been, Pete. I went to jail for nine months. You just said so.'

'I meant apart from you, actually, Theo.'

'Sorry.'

'We're good, I've never doubted that, but we're devotees of a time already gone. And I've come to the conclusion that's all we'll ever be. We'll *never* give up our day jobs now.'

'So what's the problem?' Paul asked.

'The problem is that it's not enough for me, lads, which is why I'm quitting at the end of the month.'

This statement was so matter-of-fact, so definitive, so *ex cathedra* in its unruffled authority, that the rest of the band simply stood and stared at Pete without speaking. It was Theo who finally broached the topic they were all separately considering.

'But if you quit the band falls apart. I mean, you're the backbone, Pete, it's always been your piano-playing holding everything together.'

'That's right . . . no question . . . piano's the heart of the band . . . can't do it without you, Pete.' They all made their little murmurs of assent, their pleas to Pete that he realise his central importance in their lives. 'You can't go, Pete. Can't just desert us like that. Might have better times ahead. That piece in *NPG* was just the beginning.' But he simply shook his head as their entreaties continued.

'End of the month, boys. I'm sorry. Then I've got other plans. If you fellows want to carry on as Zeno, you're just going to have to get yourselves another piano player.'

★

Theo had felt so depressed after this that he'd turned down a lift from the Breezer and started walking. Wimbledon. After a few minutes he'd found himself at the end of Jill's road.

Jill had in fact had one relationship since Theo's departure. Her mother had guessed this when she stopped coming over to see them so often.

'Not a musician, is he?' she'd asked, with what appeared to be genuine alarm.

'No,' Jill had said, 'as a matter of fact he's tone-deaf.'

'Well I shouldn't think that would be any sort of impediment these days.'

'He owns the local video shop, mum.'

'Ah,' her father had said then, with a small look of victory on his face. 'A pornographer.'

'Is it serious?' her mother had asked.

'He's just a boyfriend.'

Boyfriend, her mother had thought. In her day that had meant a fellow you went to dances with, had a drive with, saw the occasional film with, occasionally held hands with, perhaps even bestowed the occasional kiss upon. But what did it mean now, when so many relationships appeared to last no longer than the time required between penetration and ejaculation, allowing for the prelude in the pub, obviously, by way of courtship and wooing? A little romance on the way upstairs, then the fellow would be off, before any tell-tale signs of impregnation could appear, any hint that he might conceivably have deposited his DNA as signature inside that particular evening's simper-de-cocket. She herself had been brought up to think that relationships ended with coitus; now they appeared to start with it then more or less tail off over the following few months.

Her mother had looked at her daughter's face over the last

year since she'd dumped Theo and had seen age, that slow eater, at last beginning in earnest on his meal. She'll never have a child now, she thought, whatever womb-related miracles were being reported in the press, whatever the latest gynaecologists might squirt in or take out to pop in the freezer. That's not my daughter's style, she'd thought, any more than it would have been mine. She's past it. The clock's already started chiming. Just as well her sister had married early and provided some grandchildren. They wouldn't be getting any out of Jill.

'Is he still your boyfriend, out of interest?' she'd asked.

'Not any more,' Jill had said, with a smile that spoke well either for her fortitude or her obliviousness these days. A spinster of the parish.

So this particular evening Jill was alone. The paper that she wrote for was open on the table before her and she was staring at one of the letters to the Media Page.

If you put an I, the erect phallic personal pronoun, into the word malevolence you turn it into male violence. The words sometimes know more than we do. They are penetrated too. Malevolence, to accept the I, has to break into two words: male violence. So there is a hole in the middle now, a caesura. Sound familiar, at all? Bobbitt the I, in its upper-case stiffness, and you get i. Turn that upside down and you have an exclamation mark: ! We all know what they call that in the press room, what the lads all call it of course: the dog's dick. Phallocentrism means that the language itself is invasive. Even the alphabet is penetrative and aggressive. Note the o in the middle of the word womb; note the ejaculating erectile in the middle of the word prick. Linguistically we are raped every day. Violation is inscribed inside us by the very words we use. Mother tongue, they call it,

*signifying the lickspittle of fellatio. Kneel down. Bow the head. Fill
your mouth with phallus as you worship.*

The chance would be a fine thing, Jill thought. Then Theo
knocked on the door. There he was with his trumpet case in
his hand and a weary smile on his face, just like the first time.

Nobody ever looks more attractive than they do in the
months after you ditch them – you start to remember why
you liked them so much in the first place. She gave him a
glass of wine and he sat at the end of her wooden table in the
kitchen with what she realised beneath the smile was a look
of total defeat on his face. It reminded her of the
conversation they'd had before he left. Then he had sat
looking exactly like that while she asked her questions.

'I'm sorry, Jill. I wish I were different.'

'You don't try very hard to be different, Theo.'

'I don't try at all, do I?'

'Do you know what I think? I think you save your heart
for the boys in the band. You want women, all right, because
you need to fuck them but you don't love them; it's the boys
in the band you really love. Sue at work says adultery's just
your way of mourning for your mother.'

And now he told her what Pete had said.

'It's the end of the band,' he said. 'There's no way we'll be
able to go on without Pete.'

By rights she should have laughed out loud. But the
thought of Theo without the boys in the band quelled her
mirth.

'Maybe you'll have to learn to start making do with
women, Theo.' Then he told her, very quietly, about his
impotence since leaving her. She wasn't sure whether to
believe him at first. But something about his whole sagging

demeanour finally convinced her. She felt genuinely shocked, felt as though she might have wounded him in some way. What was the point of Theo without a band to play in, a Theo who'd become impotent into the bargain? What were you supposed to do with him? It didn't seem right. When they had first started living together she had been intrigued to discover that anyone could have an erection for so much of the day. It had occurred to her that such a state of apparently permanent arousal could not have been entirely inaugurated by her arrival in his life, any more than one weekend's rain would have filled the oceans to the brim. She had comforted herself with the thought that her presence might satisfy his priapic urgencies, as long as he could get his hands on her at all the necessary times. Which, she reflected now, just goes to show how wrong a girl can be when she has the lovelight in her eyes. But impotence – it was almost as though she'd managed to notch into his consciousness a proleptic augur of his doom. She walked across and put her arm around him. He sank his face in her breast.

It struck her the next day at work that there might have been an element of quiet triumph in her succeeding where the whole *demi-monde* of Theo's doxies had failed. It had once seemed to be the other way round. She mentioned what had happened to Sue, to whom she told everything. Sue didn't like Theo. When she had met him she'd been waiting for him to turn on that famous charm she'd heard so much about but he hadn't done, had barely even registered her presence and she'd had no doubt why: her weight problem. Nobody needed to tell her anything about the likes of Theo. Why had someone as intelligent as Jill wasted years of her life with a creep like that?

'Well you make sure you get him out of there sharpish, Jill, or that's your decree nisi up the spout. Love's mission creep, remember: let them camp down for a night, they spend the rest of their lives consolidating the position.'

It hadn't even crossed her mind but it did cross it now: she didn't really want Theo back in her life, not permanently back in it, not irremovably back in it even if she had effected something of a resurrection in his nether regions. She brooded in silence for a few minutes. It had been such a palaver getting all that divorce stuff sorted out. She had a shrewd idea he'd still be in the house so she phoned. His voice was sleepy. He never had been an early riser.

'Out of interest, Theo, were you planning on going back to Wandsworth today?' He yawned.

'I was thinking I could prepare a meal here this evening. For both of us, I mean. No gig tonight, Jill.' There was a pause. Theo the chef. That was another new one. She almost faltered but not quite. She couldn't face the endless conversations with the lawyers, not to mention the hurricane of disbelieving sighs her mother would breathe all over her.

'I think it might be better if you went back to Wandsworth. I mean, I'm glad to have been of help with your little problem and, well, it really was lovely. I enjoyed it, believe me. But it's still over, Theo. Best think of last night as a postscript not a new chapter. Anything to help an old friend in trouble. Sorry, love.'

Illth

Digby's father had not been an uncultivated man, far from it, but his tastes had been restricted. He believed the function of art was to bring solace. Consequently he wanted neither his arts nor his artists discordant. He thought there were more than enough discords in life already without the artists joining in. If there did have to be discords then he wanted them resolved. As quickly as possible. He left the choice of designs at Wilton Bone China largely to others, intervening only if he thought a new range too daring to lure the largely unadventurous clientele. He had always had an instinctive understanding of what his customers wanted. The avant-garde was a phrase that simply made him shudder. His own brother Freddie's cosmopolitan indulgence in it was to him a characteristic symptom of the man's irresponsibility and moral squalor.

His solace was to produce once a year a catalogue of the company's products so beautifully printed that it was far more aesthetically gratifying than any of the items that actually came out of the kilns. He had made a meticulous study of typography and layout and realised quickly after the first issue that it was a mistake to use photographs. Photography in those unresourceful days reeked of too much reality. The grainy black-and-white was all too close to the range on the hearth. From then on he made sure he had drawings made of each item, at considerable expense. These line-drawings had a simplified elegance about them and they permitted the light of the paper to shine through. They could be simultaneously diagrammatic and luminous. They could lift off the page, defying the gravity of the footnoted prices.

One copy of this catalogue was sent to every customer who had bought at least three items during the previous twelve months. It was a successful manoeuvre, far more successful than its originator had anticipated. Many people ordered the latest dinner service or set of pots without actually seeing the product at all. They had seen the beautiful drawings instead and read the descriptions and that had been enough. Now Digby took down one of the catalogues that he kept on a shelf of their own. He turned the pages carefully and noted how every ampersand had been chosen with care. The typefaces, Garamond and Baskerville, had been selected by the same meticulous eye. Digby slipped the catalogue back between its neighbours and went slowly downstairs.

Once more Digby picked up the letter that had landed on his mat the morning before. He didn't like the sound of it. His dealings with Moffett and Son had been ritualised into a pattern over the years. Meetings were usually not necessary. So why was he suddenly being asked to go over there for one now?

Desmond came and collected him as arranged, then they drove over to the office in Victoria.

He had grown fond of old Jeremy but had never really established the same rapport with his son Tony now that the old fellow had retired. Tall and bespectacled Tony had a certain boyish earnestness which Digby found distracting. Characteristically he began to babble on almost as soon as Digby was in the room. Digby found himself listening in growing confusion.

'It didn't come completely out of the blue, Mr Wilton. It had already announced that its profits would be halved and that it would probably axe more than 10,000 jobs by the end of the year. There've been fears among the investors for some time that there might be a fire sale of assets. The dilemma itself is not unique, you understand, just the present size of the difficulties it's facing. Plenty of other groups have been cutting profit forecasts and jobs as well: Lucent, Cisco, Nortel, Motorola, Siemens, Ericsson. Nokia. Need I say more, Mr Wilton?'

'You need say a great deal more, Tony, because at present I have no idea what you're talking about.'

'Don't you read the papers? Watch the television? Listen to the radio?' The smile remained on Tony's face but only as a mass of water remains intact after a sheet of ice has formed upon it.

'No. None of those things as a matter of fact. Not for some years.'

'Not *ever*?' Digby remembered briefly the account of the auto-erotic asphyxiation of a popular singer which Daisy had obliged him to read out to her some months before.

'Well, hardly ever.'

'Ah. Then I'd best recap the goings-on, I suppose.'

'If you'd be so kind.'

Tony himself had spent more time than he cared to recall sitting before a screen watching share values floating down like confetti at a wedding. He had been truly astounded at the falling of the digits, the ceaseless cascade of numbers plunging to obey their new gravitation. All those zeros popping like ruptured balloons. There had been a spray of unreality across the screen. He had never known anything like this. Had his father? Too late to ask him. Each day brought more newly homeless employees and empty-pocketed investors muttering darkly about South Sea bubbles. By the end of the worst day of it Tony had felt giddy with unreality; light-headed with the realisation of how effortlessly the burdens of wealth could be dispatched. It hadn't cheered him at all to realise that most of the wealth he was watching evaporate belonged to other people. The ultimate burden of this unreality would of course have to be laid at their door. That's why he'd been making his way through the list. And today he had arrived at Digby.

'Remember, Waterhouse Coopers predicted the world's companies would grow from $20 trillion to $200 trillion in less than a decade. This is a quote from its report, Mr Wilton.' Tony read from the notes before him on the table: '"The years 2000–2002 will represent the single most profound period of economic and business change that the world has ever seen, not unlike the Industrial Revolution but much faster – at e-speed." What would you have done after reading that?' The implications of Tony's excited babble were only now starting to sink into Digby's mind. He moved uncomfortably on his chair.

'Would I by any chance have gone off to lose a lot of money?' Tony stared at him for a moment then the rush of words continued.

'So many unexpected factors have brought this about, you must remember that. To put it in perspective, the US economic downturn has left technology companies with overstocks of equipment. It started in the US but now it's

arrived in Europe. Marconi shares had already fallen from
£12.50 to under £2. The company had been cutting a lot of
jobs, outsourcing others. It's easy enough to see now that
George Simpson and John Mayo paid too much when they
forked out more than $6 billion for Reltec and Fore – those
were the US telecoms and internet equipment groups. It's
also easy enough to see that they shouldn't have got rid of
defence electronics; that had been such a steady source of
income over the years. But you have to understand the
amount of money everyone was convinced could be made in
telecoms.

'I fully realise that from your position you could accuse me
of irresponsibility, but what I'd like to remind you of is this.
You personally expressed the wish that an unusually large
part of your portfolio be invested in GEC.'

'That's GEC. What's that got to do with this other
company – this Marconi?' Tony looked genuinely startled,
unaware that any shareholder could really be living a life of
such unworldliness.

'But GEC *is* Marconi. The company was renamed.'

'Weinstock's not in charge any more?'

'In 1996 Weinstock made way for Simpson. Left him a
cash-rich company. There was never any discussion about
changing your portfolio; after all, it had always performed
well for you. In May 1999 Simpson and Mayo told two
hundred investors at a London conference that they could
double the firm's value in three to five years by transforming
it into a high-growth info-tech group. There was no reason
to doubt they could do that. The City believed them.'

'And so did you, Tony.'

'And so did I.'

'You believed them with my money.'

'I'll be honest: I invested some more on your behalf. It seemed worth the risk.'

'Thank you. So where are we now?'

'Marconi shares are suspended.'

Marconi shares suspended; dealing in GEC suspended; it barely seemed conceivable. Digby could still remember the approximate details of Weinstock's legacy, when he'd still paid attention to such things: a £3 billion cash mountain, largely the result of the defence interests Lord Simpson had, according to Tony, recently sold off to BAE Systems. GEC: nothing more solid in the world of defence and engineering. In business for one hundred and fifteen years. In Digby's day Weinstock had been legendary for demanding that the cash be counted at the end of every month. All the options, investments, predictions, market forecasts and whatnot were as nothing, so old Arnold Weinstock thought, compared to the cash in the cupboard when the shop doors closed. The young Turks sniggered behind his back: silly old bugger, living in a bygone age. But Weinstock knew that money is money and promissory notes, however highfalutin', something else entirely. It had been a company you could trust, proven by the number of its own employees who sank all their savings into it. Just as, it began to appear, Digby had done.

Tony threw his hands in the air and let them fall back down a little more slowly, fluttering his fingers as he went as though acting the part of a tree in autumn in a children's mime.

'Nobody could have predicted it, Mr Wilton, whatever some of the pundits say now. The amount of cash-burn in these companies has been phenomenal . . . they've been joining the ninety per cent club at an incredible rate . . .'

'Tony,' Digby interrupted him, 'I wonder if you would mind doing me a very great favour. Your father often uttered unintelligibilities while I was in this office: arcana about matters fiscal, indecipherable calculations about compound rates of interest, all the Masonic lore of your trade but as I recall he always restricted himself to speaking English. I wonder if you'd be so kind as to observe the same restriction.'

Before he left the office that day Digby had insisted that Tony give him the telephone number of his father.

'I don't think that's a very good idea, Mr Wilton, to be honest.'

'Just give it to me, Tony, if you'd be so kind. I think I'm entitled to that much if no more.' Tony had shrugged and written it down. And Digby had now dialled that number. It had taken some time to get past an uncooperative nurse but he had persevered. Finally he was connected.

'Hello Jeremy, it's Digby. Digby Wilton.'

'Hello, Digby.' The delivery was more ponderous than he remembered from their meetings of years before.

'Do you know what your genius of a son has done with my money?'

'Hello, Digby.'

'We've done the salutations, Jeremy. I'm asking you if you know what your son has done with my money. You placed me in his hands. You told me I had no cause for concern. You said you'd remain in the shadows behind the lad so as to ensure I was treated with the care and concern to which I would have thought I'm entitled after all these years of being your faithful client.'

'Hello, Digby.'

'Jeremy, if you say hello to me one more time I'm going to come round to that home you live in and give you a firm kick in your shrivelled old balls. Do you think it in order that the better part of my savings should be invested in high-risk shares? I had thought we had an understanding about risk. He didn't have the authority.'

'Hello, Digby.' Only gradually did it dawn on Digby that he was being treated to what was now the full repertoire of Jeremy's conversation. He kept on repeating the phrase even after Digby himself had long fallen silent. The nurse finally came back on the phone.

'Well, Mr Moffett enjoyed that, I think.'

'Is he senile then?' Digby asked.

'Oh, completely gaga. Didn't they tell you?'

Futures

Tony Moffett did have the authority. Digby had bestowed it upon him each year by signing the form he had received through the post and returning it as requested in the pre-paid reply envelope. And for a few years, while the stocks had been rising, nobody complained. Digby certainly didn't. As long as high risk was high growth everyone was happy. No one lamented the volatility of the market or the shakiness of its foundations as long as its volatility was pointing upwards. It was only when it stalled and suddenly turned nose down that the clamour to be out of it all began.

But Digby couldn't get out. Too much of his investment had gone south when Marconi crashed. His position, thanks to Tony's bullish optimism, was irrecoverable.

'I'm going to have to sell the house, Daisy,' he said. 'You'll have another neighbour soon.'

'Not one who'll stoop over my pussies the way you do, Digby. Jonty will be bereft.' She turned her head away. Finally she turned back to him wearing one of those smiles that shields whatever lies behind it. 'Is there anything I can do?' Digby shrugged; the Wilton shrug. He was getting into the habit. Like son, like father.

'But where will you go?'
'I haven't the faintest idea.'

If it's a terrible thing to fall into the hands of brokers and accountants, falling into the hands of doctors is surely no better. Digby wondered how much of his life had by now been spent in waiting rooms, listening for his name to be called, being zipped and pumped, needled, electrocardiogrammed and echo-sounded, handing over liquids to be tested, being smiled at and X-rayed or smiled at and auscultated or smiled at and told it would be best if he changed his errant ways somewhat. It was hardly as though his ways were *that* flamboyant. In the days when he still bought newspapers he had been astonished sometimes to read obits of characters who at the start of the war had suffered from such a cornucopia of complaints that one was surprised they'd even been able to walk unaided into the medical, and yet these armless or legless remnants of humanity would soon be hoodwinking the authorities so they could get behind enemy lines ASAP, parachuting in and hiking out, living on slugs and roots for months at a time and engaging in hand-to-hand combat with sundry rags, tags and bobtails of the enemy. In between they invariably drank bottles of whisky before lunch and trained themselves to smoke in their sleep. It not only made Digby feel valetudinarian; it made him feel as though he always had been valetudinarian. Anyway, whatever his initial clutch of complaints and disabilities, providence's cup of plenty had now added more. This was what the *Oxford English Dictionary* had recently informed him was now known as the Matthew Effect: to those who have, it shall be given.

So they kept probing and pricking and asking him to

come along with his usual medications and a sample of his urine, the mere colour of which was invariably enough to start heads shaking. Having one's bodily waste disapproved of so publicly struck Digby as a trifle unfair; after all, it was hardly as though he went about submitting the stuff for prizes. It seemed indecent that so many people wanted to peer at it so intently in the first place. Anybody'd think they were staring into an aquarium. And whatever stick they put in always changed colour. It always changed the wrong colour, signifying that there should be considerably less intake of something he liked considerably taking in. He would have thought the law of averages might dictate that once in a while the stick would change to the right colour and the doctor smile sweetly and say, 'Everything's fine, old chap. I should go back home and have a gin and tonic if I were you.' But no one had ever said it yet.

Desmond didn't like these trips. He flatly refused to stay put and would only arrange to return to a specified space at a certain time.

'Anyone would think the Keystone Cops were in hot pursuit, Desmond.' Desmond laughed a little queasily and always looked distinctly edgy by the time Digby returned to the car park.

'Don't like hospitals, Mr Wilton,' he would say as the Mazda's engine whined hideously in his hurry to be off. 'They make me nervous.'

'We all end up in them sooner or later, Desmond.'

'That's exactly what makes me nervous, Mr Wilton.'

By the time they arrived back at the house the For Sale sign was already up.

'Mum says you're leaving us.'

'That's right, Desmond. Put my money in the wrong place, I'm afraid.'

'Wouldn't have thought it of you.'

'Second time I've done it, all the same.'

An hour later, Digby stood in his wunderkammer and stared out over the Common. A boy was flying a model aeroplane on a string. Already three or four men had gathered to watch him, men who would walk obliviously along the road while in the sky above them an aeroplane travelling at hundreds of miles an hour carried a cargo of vulnerable human lives trapped inside its metal skin, and they would never even turn their faces upwards. But the boy with a model aeroplane one foot long, that can remain airborne for no more than a couple of minutes, with nothing but balsa wood for cargo, this had stopped them and held their attention. They gazed intently as he pulled it round him again and again. Maybe it was simply that the boy seemed more in charge of his portion of reality than the captain of the big metal pod so pregnantly seeded with humanity in the sky above them. Or maybe everyone preferred the great proportions of life to stay pocket-size, happy to leave pyramids to the pharaohs and the slaves.

The boys in the band had all accepted with stoically silent grins that their last gig would have to be in Wimbledon. It seemed appropriate somehow, just as it seemed appropriate that they should finish with *Amnesia*.

'We've got to end with that one, Pete.'

'All the rest of us drop out, leaving you on the stage. Beginning of your solo career.'

'End on a discord, while you're at it.'

'On the off-beat.'

'Born in the wrong place at the wrong time among the wrong sort of people.'

For once Theo was the last to arrive. He was in no hurry to join Zeno for its last performance. He had got off the bus early so he could walk the last mile.

Theo had never been a big band man. He didn't want a herd of horns suddenly blasting against the soft-shoe shuffle of the brushes, or the leader up there in his tux waving his arms up and down and smiling a menacing, public smile like Duke Ellington; not even Louis sweating out gallons of lyric perspiration as the boys blew and whooped behind him. Trios, quartets, quintets, sextets; jazz's own variant on chamber music. The intimacy of a conversation. That was Theo's number. The guffaws from the boys at the back, the ironic quips from the leader, Theo hated all that showbiz stuff. Miles playing with his back to the audience, leaving for the bar when he had no more notes to deliver; Monk sliding in from the car park, playing his concordant discords then sliding out again, not speaking a word for days at a time. Unannounced and understated genius, that was his true love. That was the only sort of music he really wanted to play. And now it seemed that not enough people wanted to listen. He wasn't going to stop loving it, though. Love can still be protected even if it's only by impossibility.

The traffic droned on along the Merton Road as he walked. On the other hand it wasn't raining. Look on the bright side, Theo. At least you won't be damp when you arrive.

Theo believed in songs. He didn't read novels or poetry; he didn't go to the ballet and he certainly didn't go to the opera. He couldn't see the point of anyone performing operas now that everybody lived inside songs. Songs were intense enough for modern life. They managed to be just short enough to tell the truth in before the lies got started again. He never seemed to have any time for symphonies and as for opera, well it was like keeping a butler in a caravan; like taking a full dinner service out on a picnic. He simply couldn't stand the way opera singers sang. He thought one of the great achievements of the popular song had been to cut out the warbling and vibrato, to make the delivery demotic, to make it feel as though singing was neither more nor less than a musical way of talking to your fellow man. As though, in other words, you actually meant it rather than just belting it out in front of kings and queens. Satchmo, Sinatra, Lady Day. They were human beings taking you into their confidence. Mentally they sang in a room not a stadium, even when they were actually singing in a stadium. This was one of the odd things about microphones: they'd made things more intimate, not less. Even the crooners had been phased out finally and they'd only wanted to take you to the bedroom, not the rally at Nuremberg. But opera singers still sang as if they were simultaneously addressing Queen Victoria, trying to remember the words of their mantra and holding a peacock's feather in position up their anus without benefit of manual assistance. It made the words seem irrelevant, as if the words were just the scaffold for holding all those high and mighty notes in place. Even the notes were dressed up in monkey-suits and dicky-bows. But Theo liked the words of songs – he had always learnt all the words of the songs he played and he always tried to play trumpet as though his instrument were singing the words for him. He'd made his trumpet learn the lyrics. *Pack up all my cares and woe, Here I go, singing low. Bye bye blackbird.* Miles had actually been able to *whisper* with a trumpet. His music knew how to keep secrets. When opera singers whispered they were still shouting. Get the music out of its tuxedo and into its jeans, that was Theo's motto. And if you should find there's still a cummerbund in the closet use it to wipe the spittle off your mouthpiece or rub the oily dribble from your gasket. Only ten minutes to go now and he'd be there. He'd give it everything he could tonight. Hadn't had a drink all day.

There was no doubt that when Theo hit it people stopped and listened: he left his signature in the air, for despite all the mannerisms borrowed from Miles there was something there uniquely his and it touched people the same way it had touched Jill. It usually happened on slow ballads. It's that curious moment when you realise that a song has briefly risen from the grave you have dug for it inside your own head. It could even be a mediocre song touched by the improvisatory magic of voice or horn and turning briefly to gold.

Theo had loved jazz from the first time he'd heard it. He loved the way, with every single song, the principle of order, fragile thing that it was, would be given a run for its money by the heavy weight of randomness all around it. The unprovided for; the unforeseen. Extempore. With no premeditation. Out of time. With no saving for the future and no malice aforethought. Dancing even as it goes down. Giving you the song by pointing to its absences.

You listen to a child playing a piano. A sharp where there should be a flat; a flat where there should be a natural. And in your mind the perfect shape of the song is formed as a ghost so that each time the child misses her landing you wish the note upon her, for her sake and the song's. Jazz has something to do with playing those expectations, playing for them and against them. The tune is there in your head. A thousand fractured fragments fly round your ears. And he loved them, the masters of this art, tightrope walkers with only the void on either side to buoy them up, aerialists inscribing space; cartographers of the darkness and the silence in the circus top. When they fell off it was usually into the grave. Artie Shaw hadn't played a note for fifty years. 'If I'd carried on doing it,' he said, 'I'd surely have died.' All improvisation rests on the essential thereness of the song, its quidditas, its ineradicable integrity. You hear the standard clear as you do when the child fumbles in her practice. You know the reckless manoeuvres can never eradicate the song – the song's the landing-strip from which they take off, to which they return finally. Trust the song. The song says it all.

And nobody sang a song more beautifully than Miles. That's why Theo was so utterly devoted to him. Satchmo was wonderful, the sense of high-octane celebration, the exuberant vibrato. But everything Miles said was true. That melancholy, slightly baffled tone on the trumpet, as if the melody had turned him down and he'd had to walk home alone, edging round the tune's memories with a mixture of love and anger. There was just something in the way Miles breathed the notes, the hesitant lyricism, the vulnerability. And then the age-old melancholy of the modes. He'd achieved that lyricism at least in part by leaving every unnecessary note out and Theo certainly went along with that. No point doing more work than was necessary. So many jazz players were Stakhanovites of note production, as if there were a bonus to be had for every extra ton of semiquavers dumped in the world's ear, unburdening on the air their fascicles of notes. So if Theo had learnt a number of Miles's improvisations by heart that didn't stop them having been improvisations in the first place, did it? Charlie Parker could play Lester Young's version of *Lady Be Good* note for note.

Theo had tried to keep up as best he could with the developments in modern music but many of them left him cold. He had spent hours recently listening to John Zorn and Masada, but when the noise emitted became too fractured and fragmentary, when melody was so comprehensively assassinated by the clamour of the modernity surrounding it, he switched off. It was the same with Anthony Braxton: when he played in the tradition Theo loved it but his great discordant chorales to the universe left him cold. He wanted to hear a song; he wanted to sing a song. Wasn't that what Gil Evans had said when asked why he'd been so desperate to work with Miles? Because he sang the sweetest song. Wasn't that what Lester Young had said on the bus when the young Turk blasted into his face with Be-bop relentlessness? 'Great, man. Now sing me a song.' He had even come to feel that Miles himself meandered too far away from the song sometimes. It could become a species of modal mathematics with a mute.

Really nearly there now. Theo stopped and looked at his reflection in the second-hand furniture shop window. Theo Wilton, he thought, trumpeter to Wandsworth and the royal boroughs. A travelling minstrel for an age that doesn't need them any more.

All the other boys had arrived. Breezer was holding forth.

'I was in Harrods trying to find a jacket. I found exactly the one I wanted. A black number, just the right cut. A bit on the small side for me but beautiful. I picked the largest one they had from the rack and tried it on. And the sleeves ended half-way up my arms. Flaps didn't even reach my arse.

And that was the biggest one on the rack. So I called the young man over.

'Haven't you got a bigger one than this? I said. No, he said, that's the largest size we stock, sir. What kind of clothes department do you call this then, sunshine? I asked him. We call it the boys' department, sir, he said. I was in the fucking boys' department.'

'Since when did you start shopping at Harrods, Breezer?' Dove asked him, puzzled.

'I was given a voucher, all right? For my fortieth birthday. I should probably have got that jacket for you, Dove; it would have fitted you like a glove. When are you going to be forty, my little man?'

'Been and gone,' Dove said. 'Long gone.' Ageless Dove, white-haired ancient of days. Breezer quickly turned his attention elsewhere.

'Why so gloomy, Reg? It's only our last gig.'

'I was listening to the radio. Chris de Burgh was on.'

'On what?'

'Just on.'

'Oh right.'

'Apparently an incredible number of people are buried every year to the sound of *Lady in Red*.'

'And how many of the poor buggers were still alive before Chris started singing, eh? That's what I'd like to know.'

How they blew that night. They even gave it all they had in the second half. They played the most demented version of *The White Cliffs of Dover* ever heard – Vera Lynn, the neglected surrealist – and Breezer's solo in the middle of *Daisy* would probably have had Coltrane covering it, playing his horn for all he was worth from the back of a bicycle made for two. They had free drinks all night courtesy of Old Ted, who had registered that the evening was by way of a valediction. That meant he'd now have to employ his Jim Reeves look-alike from Tooting three evenings a week instead of two. Cheaper though.

'The drinks are on me, boys,' he had said, to Zeno's collective incredulity. 'No spirits, all right?' Had to keep some sense of proportion after all. And then it was all ending with the boys walking off one by one leaving Pete alone at the piano playing *Amnesia*. There was something hypnotic, almost narcotic, in the signature of that tune. It wasn't jazz though, was it? Whatever else it was, it certainly wasn't jazz. Maybe that's how Pete was about to make his fortune.

They downed a few more of Ted's free drinks. They assured one another that they'd all be staying in touch. No doubt at all about that. And then they started to make for the door.

'Want a lift, Theo? I'm going that way.'

'Thanks, Breezer, but I'll walk I think. Help clear my mind.'

Ten minutes later he stood at the end of Jill's road. The last time he had knocked on her door she had taken him in but he had a distinct feeling he'd be wasting his time knocking again tonight. 'Ever thought of connecting up your prick to your heart?' she had asked him once. It was anatomically impossible of course so he hadn't even bothered trying. Now it seemed as though he'd finally managed it. And much good was it doing him.

When Louis Armstrong stared into the bell of his trumpet, what did he see? Maybe his own teeth, his own manic features, the contours of his smile celebrating the whole of creation. When Theo looked into the bell of his beloved instrument later that night he saw nothing but a circle of darkness. He had no idea how long he'd been staring into it when there was a knock on the door. A mild sense of alarm went through him but it was only Mrs Trevelyan from upstairs. Theo looked at her more carefully than he'd ever done before. Some old women wear cardigans but Mrs Trevelyan was a cardigan in which an old woman had taken up residence. It had grown along with her, adapted itself to her mountainous accrual of curvatures and protrusions. It had now become as pinkly organic as she herself was.

'Don't mind my asking, sweetheart, but have you paid your rent recently?'

'Not recently, no,' Theo admitted.

'He's after you. Been asking everybody today. Shouldn't leave your trumpet or anything like that in there if you're going out. Not if you owe him money, I shouldn't. He's got his own keys, you know. And he doesn't muck about.'

Beside the Seaside

So after an early start the next day Theo gathered up his few possessions and put them into his ancient holdall. The only thing that wouldn't fit in was the picture of Miles and Bird at the Three Deuces. He carried that under his arm. He took one last look at the pile of bills by his door.

'Forget it,' he said to the envelopes. 'Go back where you came from. I'm about to become no one living nowhere, all right?' He went and knocked quietly on Mrs Trevelyan's door. She took one look at him and didn't need telling.

'You off are you, sweetheart?' Theo nodded. 'Probably best. He's not the sort of person I'd want to pick a quarrel with. You take care of yourself then. It sounds lovely, the way you play that trumpet. I used to tell my friend in Southfields, I get a free concert here nearly every night. Wonder who he'll be putting in there next.' Then, as Theo was making his way down the stairs she called out, 'Where are you going, by the way? Don't worry: I wouldn't tell him anything.'

'Hastings.' But before he could go there he needed a little cash. He'd be heading up the Merton Road to where Reg worked at the second-hand car dealership.

When they'd first met, Reg had been a bus driver until

one day he had spotted in his mirror his girlfriend, the same girlfriend who only days before had turfed him out of her flat, attempting to board his vehicle with five or six ungainly plastic bags of shopping clunking and swaying at her side. Reg had marched around and ordered her off his bus.

'You're such an independent modern woman, Maureen,' he'd said. 'So walk.' Even his earring had flashed with anger.

'You tosser. I'm not shifting another inch,' she had shouted back showing the same fixity of purpose with which she had so recently ejected him from their home.

'Then neither is this bus,' Reg had said with a triumphant smile. They had both been inventive cursers and blasphemers during their time together and they now exercised their joint ingenuity, more and more loudly with each insult that passed between them. The conductor, a gentle and minute Bangladeshi called Ali, swivelled his head back and forth between the racketing verbal abuse but said nothing. He had still not been able to come to terms with white, western, secular sex and the curious froth of publicity it generated for itself. He also knew Reg well enough to realise that ringing the bell would count for nothing whatsoever, should Reg not be in an appropriate mood to drive.

Later that day Reg's girlfriend (now definitively ex, whatever doubt might still have lingered while she'd been standing at that bus stop prior to his arrival) had contacted London Transport and asked if they thought it in order that one of their employees should see fit to close down a bus route simply because he was being denied his marital rights — when he was in point of fact not even married. The authorities had had to admit that they did not think it in order. Maureen's complaint had seemed to them unassailable from the point of view of natural justice and Reg had been promptly sacked. It was then that he had made a crab-like career move into the second-hand car business. Theo sat on the top deck of the bus and thought briefly of Maureen. She had always seemed to him to have about her an air of invisible muscularity, a way of moving which suggested a mysterious tensile eroticism beneath her jeans and leather jacket. A taut tight body. Pumping iron.

Which was why, when they had bumped into each other a few weeks later and she had invited him round to her flat, he had gone. Once inside she had left him in no doubt about the location of the bedroom. But Theo had been troubled. It had been one of the few moral boasts that Miles Davis ever made that he'd never messed with another musician's woman. It was a matter of the greatest honour as far as he was concerned. Now, Miles tended to keep his morality to a minimum so Theo felt under the greatest obligation to stay in line on this particular score.

'I'm going to have to go,' he had suddenly announced. Maureen had stared at him in disbelief.

'Fuck off then.'

That had been an act of loyalty which hurt. Reg could now repay it by lending him some money in his hour of need. He felt he was owed one.

'A hundred pounds, Theo. Who d'you think I am, Father Bloody Christmas?'

'I'll pay you back, Reg, I promise. I wouldn't ask if it wasn't urgent, you know.'

Finally Reg went and had a word with Mr Thompson about taking half an hour off and they set off walking down the road together towards the bank.

'Where are you going, Theo?'

'Remember Christy?'

'Oh, I remember Christy. Mad as a hatter.'

'I just hope he's still working at that pub.'

'You going to ask him to put you up then?'

'His places tend to be run on a pretty informal basis. Might even pick up a few gigs somewhere. I've just got to escape these debts.' Reg stopped walking and turned to look at him.

'Not going to escape this one, are you Theo, this sub I'm about to take out of my bank account?'

'No.'

'Promise.'

'I promise.'

Later that day the train pulled in to the station at Hastings and Theo walked down to the seafront.

They used to go there for holidays. It didn't seem all that different. There was more traffic now as there was everywhere. But the same mythic creatures were still congealed into smiling metal and plastic contraptions and they still went round and round on tiny rails with children waving from inside. The slot-machine arcades were still bleating their imbecile invitations, if a little more loudly. The sea looked dirtier and the pebbles colder; the gulls in the air shrieked hungry hatred. Theo was hungry too. He couldn't remember the last time he'd eaten.

It was still called Sammy's though Sammy had long before gone to join his daughter on the farther shore. There was no longer any family connection that Theo was aware of. He ordered fish and chips and looked around him as the scowling young man served it up. He remembered how more than thirty years before he had stood staring at his reflection in the shiny metal fascias of the frying vats and how his blue balloon bobbed up and down above him like a vast bubble. Turning this way and that, he'd made faces like a fish while the real cod and haddock sizzled on the other side, translated from the ocean into the hissing aquarium of cooking fat. White slivers sinking and rising inside the rippling, scalding liquid. Sammy had lifted him up so he could see inside. What an ocean to end in.

'You want fish, Theo?' Sammy had shouted, calling out happily from the other side of the counter. 'You want fish and chips with lots of nice tomato sauce all over it? Your grandpa make you some, eh?' Theo always nodded gravely. Never said no to food. Invariably silent and worshipful back then in the face of his sustenance.

'Fruit of the ocean's loom,' Sammy had piped. Theo was now staring out of the window at the shifting salty acres on the other side of the pebbled beach, delivering their bounty to Britain's rainy shores. Always grey in the rain, an infinity of grey swill with an occasional tanker ploughing dutifully though it. He could still remember the sound of Sammy's voice.

'This fat fish swim all the way over from Malta,' Sammy had chortled as he scooped it out of the sizzle and into its paper. 'I can smell Valletta harbour on its tail.'

'That would be the oil, I should think,' Theo's father had said behind him, more to himself than anyone else but Theo had caught it.

'I said, take-away or to eat now,' the young man repeated.

'Eat now. Sorry, I was miles away.' He hadn't been miles away; he'd been right here. Years away not miles away.

Then he sat in a shelter chewing a chip and staring at the sea. Beside him an aged couple kept tugging at their weatherproof rigging to keep out the wind. 'That sandwich all right, love?' the old woman asked her husband. 'Not enough cheese in it to fill a tooth.' Just be there, Christy, he thought.

Christy was. At the end of the seafront, before the net lofts begin, before the road swings away from the sea and heads back towards London, leaving the coast to its ragged and overgrown cliffs, there's a ramshackle seaside pub where Christy had been barman for the last eighteen months. Whenever he applied for an overdraft, which was often, he called himself head barman but that was only because no one else ever lasted very long. He had his own room looking out over the sea and he'd learnt over the years how to keep a pub going. This suited the owner nicely because he didn't want to do the heavy work himself. Christy kept threatening that one day he'd go back to Ireland for good but nobody believed him any more, least of all himself. Instead he went back for one week each Christmas.

Short, wiry, curly-haired Christy was there behind the bar, his cheeks as reddened by wind and whisky as they had been the last time Theo had seen him almost a year before.

'Well, well, look what the tide has brought to our door. Flotsam or jetsam, sir?'

'Vodka and orange, Christy. A large one, I think. How are you?' Christy was already pouring.

'Not even a card for my birthday. How's the good lady wife?'

'Divorcing me.'

'Ah.' Theo leaned over the bar as Christy handed him his drink.

'Couldn't put me up for a while, could you Christy? I got into a bit of trouble.' Christy looked at him with his barman's practised shrewdness, tilting his head slightly to one side.

'Wouldn't be trouble with the law again, would it Theo? I can't afford anything like that round here. The old man wouldn't stand for it.'

'No, Christy, I swear. Just a few unpaid bills and an angry landlord in Wandsworth. He'd never find me here in a thousand years.'

'You'd have to share my room. Mattress on the floor.'

'Thanks, Christy.'

'And I suppose you'll be wanting another of those Russian bowel-warmers. Chilly out there today.' He took his glass and refilled it. 'You might lend a hand collecting the glasses. Only Yvonne here apart from me at the moment.'

The room overlooked the sea but the window was so caked with salt you could barely see out of it. Christy dragged a mattress down from the eaves and laid it on the floor together with some sheets, blankets and a couple of pillows. They didn't get to bed until well after midnight and Theo soon fell asleep, but not for long.

Christy's snoring surpassed all domesticity, the noise of a bull elephant on the point of orgasm, repeated with every single intake of breath. In Theo's intermittent shadowy dreamlands the room contracted to the labyrinth at Knossos with the minotaur bellowing in lust and incomprehension along its stony corridors; or swelled to the dimensions of the Channel beyond the window, shrouded in fog, with the *QE2* blasting all its horns simultaneously. During that first night in Hastings Theo slept little. He would dip into unconsciousness only to find that he had stepped inadvertently on the head of a rhino, thinking it a large scaly rock. The rhino had raised its head and opened its mouth; the vast gin-trap of its teeth about to close on Theo's naked ankle when it issued its roar, an equatorial roar signifying not so much the end of civilised life as he had known it, more the fact that such a life had never securely started in the first place, but then the African soundtrack would modulate once more into this seafront pub, which was to say Christy's intolerable soporific moaning, torturing Theo back to consciousness. He threw a pillow at Christy, who interrupted his wheezing bellows to bark briefly like a disoriented sea-lion before subsiding again into the public address system of his agonised groans. Badly oiled pistons; a peat bog imploding; the merciless machinery of one man's nocturnal complaint. And in the brief intervals when Christy didn't make a noise the gull did. The white gull on the roof screeching in outrage at the darkness. How long, Theo thought, am I going to be able to stand this? Not that he had any immediate alternative.

Christy rose early, leaving Theo to make a more leisurely start to the day. When he finally came to, he wandered about the room. He opened a cupboard door and contemplated the sadness of a pile of Christy's old shoes abandoned there. Never to be taken out for their walks again. He peered through the back window at the roof of the outhouse below. On its corrugated asbestos surface old canvas bags had been rotting over the years to reveal their contents to the weather: what appeared to be substantial portions of Christy's dis-carded wardrobe. Dead socks and decommissioned under-clothes loopy with eccentric apertures. Trousers no inside leg would ever slip inside again. Christy had come back upstairs with some coffee and saw Theo looking down at his life's makeshift dumping ground.

'That's right, Theo. Refuse collection round here is by arrangement with the Parachute Regiment only.'

'Wouldn't it have been easier to go down to the Oxfam Shop?'

'That would represent a walk.'

Months went by. After they had finished collecting the glasses and washing up at the end of each evening there would be an hour with just themselves and perhaps one or two of Christy's friends. Theo would sometimes play the trumpet. This particular night they were both sitting at the bar.

'Goodnight, you two,' Yvonne said, pulling on her coat before she walked across to Theo and kissed him on the lips. 'See you Sunday at half-past twelve. Don't be late.'

Christy looked at Theo carefully after she'd gone.

'Yvonne's a lovely girl. Always trusted her. The only thing is, Theo, she's looking for another husband, not to mention someone to be a daddy for her little boy. And I'm just wondering if you're sure, absolutely sure I mean, you're looking for another wife. If not there's going to be some sort of conflict of interest here. She's beautiful as well, which is guaranteed to confuse a fellow.'

'Gypsy loins,' he said after a moment's meditation. 'If you've got them it's no use pretending otherwise, is it?'

'Never been married have you, Christy?'

'Not exactly. Never could be bothered with all that finagling about.'

Later Christy lay in his bed and Theo lay on the mattress on the floor. They could make out the sound of the waves beyond the traffic.

'I blame my biology teacher, you know.'

'What for?'

'Gypsy loins. I never quite got over the disappointment.

He had these models he used to hand out, of men and women with their rudiments portrayed in a miniature sort of way. To explain the deed of darkness in the most up-to-date modern, rubberised fashion. I took them literally. I was a very literal sort of boy. So I was convinced their breasts were triangular and jutting. Like the pert little geometric buttresses on those models. Very gentle pyramids. The hours I spent caressing those hard outlines, I can't tell you. I even nicked one so I could take it home. God, I was so looking forward to it but I really hadn't expected all that sagging and asymmetry. When I finally got in there it distressed me, Theo. I felt cheated. I wanted my little rubber model back. I think I must have spent the whole of my life ever since looking for a perfectly geometric woman.'

'Why not build your own, Christy?'

'Now you're talking. Wouldn't work though.'

'Why not?'

'Never get the planning permission. Not with the East Sussex County Council. They're sticklers.' They both fell silent for a while. 'Found any work on the music front?'

'I've asked around. Doesn't seem to be any band I could play with at the moment.'

'You couldn't teach?'

'Teach?'

'Trumpet technique? Jazz? Debt-avoidance schemes?'

'Don't think so, Christy.'

'No, it's not easy. The old man's daughter taught at the college down the road until last year. Then they closed the whole department down.'

'What did she teach?'

'Applied religion.' Theo thought for a moment then he thought for another moment after that, but all the years of his

Roman Catholic education notwithstanding he could make no sense of it.

'What's applied religion, Christy?'

'Oh you know, the usual. Mondays turning water into wine; Tuesdays bilocation; Wednesdays healing the halt and lame; Thursdays raising the dead; Fridays efficient crucifixion – wood provided but bring your own Black and Decker. It's the practical side of the faith industry, Theo. Don't just kneel there like an unemployable cripple calling on the good Lord for mercy; roll your sleeves up and get something done. God likes self-starters. It says so in the Bible. Parable of the talents, remember.'

Searching for Theo

'So where is he then?'

'He said he was going to stay with Christy. The last time I ever saw Christy he was running that pub in Brighton.'

'What was it called?'

'Can't remember, Pete. I could probably still find it if I went down there.'

'So go down there and find it, Reg. We'll never get an opportunity like this again, will we?'

Reg travelled down to Brighton that Friday afternoon but the people in the pub where Christy once worked hadn't seen him for years. Somebody thought he might be running a pub in Rye but they couldn't be sure. Reg went back to London. He called round to see Jill.

'Christy?' she said. 'God knows. Try Pentonville.'

Reg even shuffled down to Theo's flat in Wandsworth. He found the old lady who lived above but she stayed tight-lipped. One look at Reg with his shaven head and glittering earring and she'd been in little enough doubt whose bagman this was.

'I've no idea where he went, my love. No idea.'

'There's something he really should know.' Yes, she thought, like where the nice policemen go to drink tea

before making their arrests. Must think I was born on a
Christmas tree.

'Actually, now I rememember, I think he might have
mentioned Birmingham.'

What Reg and the other boys in the band wanted to tell
Theo so desperately was that Pete had had a visit, as a result
of the telephone number of the *Streatham Clarion* being
printed on Zeno's tape. The visit, to his astonishment, had
been from Benny Milhouse, the famous old black trumpeter
and as of January of that year proprietor of Benny's Jazz Club
in Copenhagen. Having lived there for most of the last
twenty years, like a lot of other eminent jazzmen who
couldn't make much of a living in America, he'd finally
decided, with the aid of his young wife, to set up his own
establishment instead of working everyone else's. What he
needed now were a couple of bands to play there. He
couldn't offer a huge amount of money, so it couldn't be any
of the more famous names, but he could provide a three-
month residency, board, food and, most important of all,
audiences avid for decent jazz. With a very good chance of
other offers following on. And who knows, maybe even a
record deal with one of those Danish jazz labels. He'd loved
Zeno's tape. He particularly loved the trumpet-playing,
being a trumpeter himself. He really hadn't expected to hear
such quiet lyric urgency, it was a sound he felt he'd not heard
in years and one he wanted to hear a lot more of, now that
he had his own club.

'So where the fuck is he then?' asked the Breezer.

'He's with Christy, wherever that might be.'

Utility

The houses along Bolingbroke Grove were much in demand and since Digby had a particularly large one he had a substantial offer within a fortnight, one he decided to accept. Might as well get the whole wretched business over with. But he still had no idea where he would go. Daisy arrived as usual around lunchtime.

'I've had a thought, Digby,' she said as she buttered the bread. 'Now don't just dismiss it before you've even listened to what I've got to say, do you hear? I think I might have the solution to your problem.'

'You have a proposition?'

'I have a proposition.' So Digby listened as Daisy explained.

'It was last weekend when I went to see my father in Shropshire.'

'And your first ex, Daisy. You've started seeing a lot more of your father since you started going to stay with James again.'

'It's the only way I ever get to find out what Howard's up to. Odd that he never phones when I'm there, though he seems to phone all the time when I'm not. Don't you find that odd? Anyway, none of this is relevant. He lives in a rather beautiful residential home, my father I mean. Just keep an open mind for one moment will you, Digby,' she said seeing the expression on her neighbour's face. 'It's not what you think. Everyone has their own rooms and some of them are really quite substantial. With views out over the valley. My father who is, how can I put it, as demanding in his way as you can sometimes be in yours, has settled in there. Wouldn't go anywhere else. They'll even bring your meals to you I believe if you can't face the dining room.'

Digby was thinking, she could see that. He hadn't dismissed it out of hand. She pressed on.

'The advantage is that you have all the independence of a place of your own, with everything provided. You don't even have to go to the doctor; the doctor comes to you. Makes a visit once a day. All you have to do is point him in the direction of whatever latest bit you think is dropping off. And you're left to your own devices unless you actually ask for help. You could read all day. Or write all day. Or watch videos of me.'

'How much does it cost?'

'Well I mentioned your circumstances – in a discreet sort of way of course – to the owners. The sale of your house would be more than enough to cover you, well, for ever really . . .'

'I think for ever sounds optimistic, Daisy, but I catch your drift.'

'It would be the same arrangement my father has. You pledge your capital to provide for the rest of your future. You still have access to your own cash as long as it stays above a certain figure, but from that point on you'd never have to look at another bill, never have to worry about making another doctor's appointment. They guarantee you a lifetime's care.'

'I dare say they're gambling on the lifetime not lasting all that long, but there must still be quite a queue to get in.'

'Ah, now that's the point. The room on the other side of the corridor from my father has become vacant. The old gentleman there . . .' She faltered.

'Made alternative arrangements with regard to his future. Yes, I think I get the picture, Daisy. No need to be too delicate. Go on.'

'It's free now but I'm not sure it will be for long. It's a lovely room with a wonderful view of the river and the valley. I had a look around. On your behalf, you understand.'

Digby sat in silence as he thought. He had been baffled as to where he could go next. He'd even briefly considered whether the old Roman way with blades or the Eskimo route out into the cold mightn't have had something to recommend them, but that counted as a capital sin in his religion and he didn't want to take on any more of those at this late stage. Daisy's suggestion therefore came closer to being a credible scheme as to what might be done with him than anything he'd managed to think up for himself.

'Are any of them mad?'

'Maybe one or two. Don't think the lunacy statistics would be much higher than round here, frankly.'

'I must visit the place, obviously. As soon as possible. I'll have to see if Desmond can drive me up there.'

Sadly, Desmond couldn't. As he explained while scratching the top of his shaved head with some discomfort, short forays into town were one thing but a three-hundred-mile round trip involving motorways and suchlike was quite another. It appeared that Desmond, rather like Theo, had unfortunately forfeited his licence some time before so without any tax or insurance and carrying a two-year ban a trip to Shropshire and back really was out of the question. Digby understood for the first time the young Turl's wish never to dawdle at traffic lights or park anywhere within the possible field of vision of a passing policeman.

'It was very good of you to put yourself at such risk on my behalf then,' Digby said, imagining he was being humorous.

'My mother didn't give me any choice, Mr Wilton.'

'Do you mind if I ask a question, Desmond? Something that's always intrigued me. What is the tattoo on the back of your neck?'

'A lion-centaur. It's a benevolent demon from Mesopotamia, Mr Wilton. Used to bar the way to all the forces of evil. The one on my neck's based on a stone relief from the royal palace of Assurbanipal.' Desmond pulled down his collar at this point and turned his back on Digby, thus enabling him to take a closer look.

'I wish we'd had more chance to talk over the years, Desmond. In the car, I mean. But you never seemed very forthcoming.'

'Always had to keep a look out for the law, Mr Wilton.'

'Yes, that must have been distracting for you.'

In the meantime Digby continued clearing out. Men kept coming and going, purchasing this item or that. Desmond and his mother gathered things up, packed them and then disposed of the packages from morning till night. Digby himself kept swaddling the more treasured items from his collection in bubble-wrap and working his way through the long-forgotten contents of his cupboards. One day he found in the bottom of a closet an old wooden abacus. He held it in his hand and suddenly had a vivid memory of Theo sitting at the table as a six-year-old with the abacus before him. Tears were coursing down his cheeks. The red, yellow and blue balls had been stationary on their metal wires.

'It's really not that difficult, Theo,' Digby had shouted before picking up the primitive calculating contraption and shaking it violently. Then he'd slammed it back down on the table in front of the boy before walking out of the room in disgust. Probably been in a state of emotional warfare with Vicki at the time – it wouldn't have been unusual. Her fleering scorn. He could still see her face at the window, the storm of her disapproval; still remember his returns to the stony dolmen of her table, the cormorant swoops of her appetite for hard-beaked recrimination. His tongue would turn to suede in his mouth, then something colder, more solid. Even as he shouted back he tasted the worst taste in the world: the rancid metallic bite of acrimony, the mineral poison of a hateful home. Locked into the tight room as the snakes and trumpets started up their terrible noises. Hardly surprising if he'd taken it out on Theo sometimes, Theo who had in any case developed the facility for exasperating his father early on in life. What goes around comes around. He dropped the abacus into one of the boxes Desmond would be taking to the charity shop later that day.

The house soon started to look stripped. And Digby at last knew the time had come to enter the garage.

After he'd removed the covers he sat in the driving seat and remembered that last journey.

'The car must be taken away, Digby,' Sammy had phoned him to say. 'The rent on the garage runs out next week. Can we leave it to you please?'

'Yes, leave it to me,' he had said. And he had travelled down to Hastings that weekend, collected the keys from Sammy and gone to get the car. He'd had to adjust the seat from Vicki's position, to give himself leg room. He'd been a little alarmed at the roar of the engine when he started it up but he'd soon found himself on the open road heading for London. The first time he had driven since his crash. He had begun to realise as the miles went by what an extraordinary machine the E-type was. It had been built with great love and devotion and behaved accordingly. Had Digby been able to see further along the road through his glasses he would have driven much faster but he drove fast enough as it was. At one point he even started laughing at the sheer exhilaration that the car afforded. Three minutes after starting to laugh he pulled over into a lay-by in the middle of Ashdown Forest between Uckfield and East Grinstead and wept uncontrollably. He sat there in the car with the hood down sobbing away until some local rambler walked over to the side of the car. He had tapped Digby very gently on the shoulder.

'Anything I can do, my friend?'

'No, nothing, thank you,' Digby had said, wiping away the tears with a handkerchief and wishing he'd been left alone.

'Wouldn't see me crying if I had a car like that,' the man had said as he'd wandered off again. Digby had sat there for the better part of an hour, alone except for the little wooden madonna on the passenger seat beside him. 'It's from Malta,' Sammy had said. 'Vicki wanted you to have it.'

He was still sitting in the driving seat with the past speeding about his head when Jonty's face appeared around the garage door.

'Ah, here you are. My God, I didn't know you had one of these. You're a dark horse, Digby.' And Jonty proceeded to examine it and stroke it and murmur his assent. 'What a beauty. This is the original 4.2, the best of the lot. Always wanted to drive one of these.' A thought struck Digby.

'How much have you always wanted to drive one, Jonty?'

'A lot.'

'If I were to get it properly looked over and serviced over the next couple of days how would you fancy a trip to Shropshire at the weekend? With you driving.'

'What me and Tessa, you mean?'

'No, you and me is what I mean. I need to go and look at a place called Valley Prospect. Well, what do you say, Jonty?'

'Our little trip at last. You're on. I'd have to check with Tessa first, naturally.'

'Naturally.'

On his return to the house Digby made a phone call about the car and later that day his trusted old mechanic arrived with his son and towed the Jaguar away.

'Should be back by Saturday,' he said. 'I'll change the hoses and whatnot, but if I know this car the way I think I do, there won't be too much wrong. Not with that mileage. And all the loving care I used to give it.'

So it was that the following Saturday morning, Digby was driven away from Bolingbroke Grove in the primrose yellow E-type with Jonty at the wheel.

'God, what a car,' Jonty said as they finally reached the A5. 'I'm going to have to get one of these.'

'Why not make me an offer on this one?' Digby said.

'You selling?'

'I'm selling.'

They had to slow up once. They could see at the side of the road the shards of charred and twisted metal and the circle of black ash where a car had exploded into flames. Finally they arrived at Valley Prospect. In Digby's mind it had already become Twilight Mansions and that was how he had started to refer to it with Daisy. The building was Victorian, an old vicarage with minor castellated corners and ridges, in the ludicrous pseudo-Gothic manner of the time. Given its size, they'd evidently expected their rectors to be philoprogenitive: you could have billeted a small army there. Anyway it was more than capacious enough to house the thirteen inmates it now accommodated, in various stages of mental and physical decomposition, Daisy's father Mr Eric Gresham, retired solicitor, amongst them.

And Daisy had been right; he soon realised that. He wouldn't do any better. They showed him the room. Airy and spacious and with a view over the valley below; he could pass his final days here, surely? London would soon get over his departure.

Conversations were held, hands were shaken. Digby signed a form. The matter was settled. As they were leaving a small man, as bald and bent as Digby himself, blocked his way.

'Wilton?' he asked. 'Digby Wilton?'

'That's me.'

'Gresham. Eric Gresham. Daisy's father. She said you'd be coming.'

'How do you do?'

'Are you joining us?'

'It seems so.'

'Look forward to it.'

As they drove away Jonty was smiling.

'You don't really want to travel all the way back to London today, do you Digby?'

'What else did you have in mind, Jonty?'

'A night in Stoke-on-Trent. We'd always planned it one day, just the two of us. Remember?'

'A boys' night out. Where would we stay?'

'At the North Staffordshire Hotel. I've already booked us in.'

And Jonty had his route worked out. He'd obviously studied everything in some detail. Digby was amused. After all, he'd just signed up to his future, all the future he was going to get anyway, so he might as well relax.

'Stoke,' Jonty mused as he drove. 'Is it called that because of the ovens?'

'No,' Digby said, as Uncle Freddie's lectures came fluently back to him. 'No, it means a place, that's all, from the Saxon word *stowe*. Stoke on Trent: a place on a river. Though it's got confused in many minds with stoking furnaces, which is appropriate enough really, given how many of the local lads used to follow their fathers into the pot banks.' He could hear Freddie's voice in his ear: 'A smoky fate awaits them, my boy. You too, I suppose, though your office will have cleaner air than theirs down by the kilns and, looking on the bright side, you will be able to retire from all that smoke every evening. To Wilton Manor, that haven of culture and rusticity. You'll be able to replace the heavier paintings with modern ones. Something a little less in awe of Queen Victoria and her seemingly infinite progeny, not to mention the antiquated laws of perspective. Buy yourself a proper dictionary. And get rid of those bloody carpets.' I did try, Freddie, he thought; I really did try.

'A place on a river. Then it became a place on a canal.'
Jonty drove and Digby explained how, despite the proximity
of large coalfields, Stoke hadn't been stocked with all the
necessary resources to continue providing tableware for the
nation. Its local clays offered a severely impoverished
selection. But they'd started building the Trent and Mersey
Canal in 1766, so those artificial waterways soon connected
the smoky urban smudge to the major ports it needed for
import and export. Flint and animal bone could now be
shipped with relative ease to the pot banks and the pots in
their glazed and burnished splendour shipped out to Liverpool which had opened its own watery maw on the world at
large. All cargoes passed through Liverpool, human, organic
and mineral, everything a soul could desire or a body could
crave. Landlocked Staffordshire had made it to the sea.

Jonty asked about bone china and Digby explained how
bone from the slaughterhouses would be ground to fine
powder in the mills. What had kept the slaughtered creatures
upright only days before was now employed to keep the
pottery white instead. Digby's monologue continued until
Jonty suddenly announced, 'I think we're here.'

It was hard to tell. Stoke now felt as much like a road
junction as a town.

'Just remind me where I'm going?' Jonty said.

'You've never actually been here before, have you Jonty?'

'Not Stoke as such, no.'

'Where's the nearest you've been to it?'

'We had a weekend in Norwich once.'

'That's not very close, you know.'

'It's a lot closer than Wandsworth Common.'

'True. I don't really think I can help you. It's so long since
I drove round here and everything looks so different.'

So Jonty found the nearest place he could to park and they started to walk.

'Not too far and not too fast, Jonty, if you don't mind.' Things soon came back to him. They stood before a church, St John the Baptist, which Uncle Freddie had pointed out to him as one of the very few steel-framed ecclesiastical buildings ever erected. It was now an object no one had any use for at all, it seemed, not even the indefatigable heritage industry. Windows left unboarded had been comprehensively smashed – a lot of stones and many hours of vigorous activity had obviously been expended on the clerestory, out of reach of any but the most accurate stone-throwers. The breeze-blocked porch had been wallpapered in posters advertising long-gone rock concerts and records. Most of these were now peeling – tearing and decaying in their turn. Digby and Jonty walked on past Bethesda chapels, their noble Greek façades half demolished, silent and neglected on the sites where they had once proclaimed their mysteries.

Hi-fi warehouses. Video exchanges. One Ann Summers sex accoutrements boutique, in the window of which the female manikins flaunted their clasps and frilly garters in a state of wax-like suspended animation. Their bright artificial eyes, sky blue and amethyst, stared manically into middle distance with a mystical intensity. Outside the police station a young girl, maybe twelve or thirteen, ginger-haired, bespectacled, touchingly obese, wept and wept as her mother and father attempted to comfort her. What had happened? An assault? The theft of her mobile phone? She seemed inconsolable whatever it was. Minutes later another girl walked up to them, older than the weeping child of a moment before, this one indisputably touched already by sex and debt. Her face was death-pale and alarmingly thin. The bones were visible beneath it like balsa wood behind the doped tissue of the model aeroplanes he'd built with Uncle Freddie.

'Could you give us twenty pence, just for the phone?' The voice was insistent, as was the hand on Digby's arm, fingers a white Gothic tracery of crookedness.

Jonty reached his hand into his pocket and handed her a pound. They stopped before another once-mighty building sinking into ruin, not without dignity, its stonework pecked away by the weather, its cast-iron guttering flamboyantly rusted, the void of its rose window now a hutch of metal gauze, all rotting quietly in a few shafts of sun before the rain of Staffordshire returned to asperse it.

Then they went back to the car. Jonty drove until he found the little factory that made his miniature collectables. It was now late on Saturday afternoon and it had closed. But Jonty was still pleased. He had visited the site of his own production without having to become too tiresomely involved in any of the minutiae. Then Digby directed him to Wilton Manor. They stared through the iron gates up the drive. It had become some sort of management centre.

'So this is where your illustrious forebear was born?'

'No,' Digby said, 'no, he wasn't born here. He was born in a crooked little house above a filled-in shraft and marl pit. Subsidence caused the foundations of the house to lean, Jonty, and to slant so much it looked very scenic indeed, I'm told, until one day the whole house tumbled into the pit, taking one of its inhabitants with it.'

'Not Nathaniel obviously, since he ended up in this one.'

'He did indeed.'

'Progress. You were born here anyway?' Jonty said.

'It's where I was brought up. You see the squat little building over there in the bushes. That was our ice house.'

Then Jonty had circled around the roads outside town. The long primrose car revved and braked. Digby stared out at the fields. He remembered visiting them with his mother. Flat fields they had seemed then, with cows mostly slumbering, seldom lumbering. He remembered days when summer had seemed nothing but a vast, lethargic rehearsal for extinction. If you went closer you'd see that each cow had a shimmering mandorla of flies around its twitching ears. Then they were back amongst defunct warehouses at the side of railway lines. Unemployment: he remembered the menace of the word and the striking miners of his youth scavenging for fuel around the tips, their dirty faces an unfathomable mixture of impertinence and terror.

Then they had driven back to the big hotel near the station where Jonty had booked them in for the night.

During dinner, a three-course affair which Jonty insisted on ordering with an exuberance that exceeded Digby's appetite, Jonty quizzed Digby relentlessly as to how exactly he had come to relinquish his role in the family firm.

'Irreconcilable aims; irreconcilable methods.'

'Come on, Digby, you'll have to be a bit more specific than that.' They were eating their oxtail soup.

For some reason Digby's mind went back to 1950. He started trying to explain. In Stoke-on-Trent that year there'd been an exhibition of Picasso's ceramics, all the work he had done at Vallauris. More sculpture than pottery in any sense normally understood in the Potteries, this work was asymmetric, uninterested in exquisite finish, wildly expressive. It was also sanctioned by the government-backed Council of Industrial Design. Digby had loved it. It was modern art at its best, which was to say that, like all modern art, it had largely dispensed with the clutter and complication of modern life. Modernity in art has little to do with modernity in life. It was primal, in the same way that Jakob Kirk's work was. It saw the shape of the woman beneath the steam-ironed pleats, the unchanging shapes life makes beneath the candlewick bedspread.

Manufacturers in Stoke had been suspicious. They'd felt that alien styles were being foisted on them. They were being discouraged from their love of the figures and colours of art deco; instead they were meant to embrace the International Style. But they didn't want to embrace the International Style. Exactly the same argument had produced the same effects in 1943 when Utility Ware had been imposed on all the potteries except those like Wedgwood and Royal Worcester, which were allowed to continue producing their highly decorated and very traditional goods for the American market, simply because Britain needed the dollars. For everyone else it was Utility: it had to be white and entirely free of decoration. The Potteries didn't like it and they liked it even less when the government attempted to dictate the designs themselves. They weren't having that and as soon as possible after the war they'd all reverted to the highly coloured commodities they'd been producing before. The trouble was that Digby almost uniquely *did* like Utility Ware. He liked the cups and saucers and dishes and plates that Wilton Bone China produced during the war more than anything it had produced before or anything it was to produce immediately after. In its brusque simplicity, in its refusal to pander to a craving for ornament and its eschewal of all gimcrack devices and polychrome distractions, it seemed to him to have a dignity missing in the other Wilton lines. He made the mistake of expressing this view during a boardroom meeting when one of his colleagues had taken it upon himself to denounce the current exhibition of Picasso down the road.

'That's not pottery. You can't imagine that on a family table.'

'I'd be happy enough to have it on mine,' Digby had said. This particular colleague, a man called Thomas, bored him intensely. Digby only came to understand later, too late to repair the damage, how much he had underestimated him.

'But then you have a bigger family table than the rest of us, don't you?' Not for long, as it turned out, though even Digby had laughed at the time.

At the end of that meeting he'd announced his plans to set a substantial part of the factory aside for the production of pots designed by Jakob Kirk and other new artists of a similar scope and intensity. The Potter's Hand.

'The whole of Shed A?' Thomas had said, astonished. 'But that would be nearly a third of Wilton's total capacity.'

'This isn't a sideline, Thomas. This isn't just a little craft shed. This is going to be central to Wilton's future identity.'

'It's not bone china, which is what we make, what we've always made, how Wilton made a name for itself; what we *understand*. It can only be completed when the potter's actually here to do the magic with his fingers. So if one of them catches a cold we'll have no production figures at all that month. It's completely untested.'

'Most things are until someone tests them.'

'Forgive me,' Thomas had said, 'but in my understanding of the term it's not even manufacture, is it?' Digby had then made a mistake, one that he had had plenty of time to mull over ever since. He had smiled and said, 'I think Thomas that if you look in the dictionary you'll find it is precisely manufacture. Which is to say, something made with the hands. It's what we normally call manufacture that isn't manufacture.' He should have remembered the fate of Uncle Freddie: how easily logolatry leads on to logomania. Thomas's face had reddened.

'Well, for those of us who don't have either the time or the money to live inside dictionaries, the word has another meaning. Namely, things made to a certain quality in bulk. Maybe with a certain amount of hand-finishing, but certainly without the designer there in person on a day-by-day basis to sign it off. What you're talking about is craft, Mr Wilton, and what we do here is manufacture. That's what most people understand by the term. Trying to mix the two things up is bound to lead to trouble.'

'I've never even heard of him anyway, this Jakob Kirk,' another colleague had said. Digby had brushed this aside.

'That's your loss, Malcolm, believe me. But it won't be for long.'

He might as well have stuck a scarlet letter on the back of his dark jacket, for he would hardly have been more conspicuous. From that day on he was a marked man. Like many a fellow whose name has been wrought in iron on the factory gates, he hadn't realised that its presence there was no guarantee of his permanent presence behind them. The family representation on the board no longer constituted a majority, since Uncle Freddie had sold his shares and headed for Europe to spend his murky final years in Venice. And six years later almost to the day, with his new scheme in financial ruins, Digby Wilton had been separated for ever from Wilton Bone China via a generous but very final settlement. Two centuries of family tradition.

Jonty was staring at him intently as he nursed his wine glass.

'But your colleague was right, wasn't he?'

'What?'

'Your chap Thomas was right, surely: you did confuse two different types of product and two different types of production. First rule of business, Digby: never confuse your pleasure with your livelihood. I mean, some people have produced avant-garde tableware in bulk and made money.'

'Who?'

'Rosenthal, for a start. But they were always quite clear in their minds what they were doing. And they certainly understood that they were manufacturers, not craft potters. Anyway, like father like son, eh Digby?'

'How do you mean?'

'You inherited some wealth from your father's business and used it to subsidise your life of scholarship. And now you help subsidise the musical life of your son. You must help him, presumably? It's admirable in a way. That was how the Victorians did it, wasn't it? Industry finances the arts.'

Digby brooded for much of the journey back to London the next day. As they drove up to Bolingbroke Grove Jonty said, 'How much do you want for it, Digby?'

'For what?' Digby asked, still pondering what his neighbour had said the night before.

'For this car, Digby, for this wonderful example of something beautiful that's also at the cutting edge of technology. For this modern marvel.'

'The Jaguar. I don't know what it's worth.'

'I've got a shrewd idea, I think, but I'll have to check. Can I have a discount? For my role as chauffeur and facilitator.'

'Yes, as long as you pay me in cash.'

'Cash.'

'There's someone I need to get some money to in cash.'

'You do realise you're talking about a lot of cash here, Digby.'

'Those are my terms, Jonty.'

'You're a hard man. I'll see what I can do.'

Money

The last of the pictures were being taken down from the walls. Daisy walked in; the door was now left open as Desmond and his mother heaved boxes in and out. Daisy handed him the invitation.

Wibley and Holinshed
Invite you to the launch of
Stone And Shadow
By James Oldham and Crispian Hale
At the Gallery Bookshop
Covent Garden

Digby looked at the date.

'It'll be one week after I go to Shropshire.'

'Yes, I thought it was unlikely. Anyway I'll be coming up just before to make sure you're settling in, and I'll bring you an advance copy. Courtesy of the family firm. Managed to get in touch with Theo yet?'

'No.'

'Absolutely no idea then?'

'Oh, he's probably holed up with some blowzy slattern.'

'I don't think they do blowzy slatterns any more, Digby,

to be honest; they discontinued that particular line some time back.'

'What did they replace them with?'

'Old slappers; little tarts.' She paused. Surfing the internet the day before she had discovered a cyberspace journal called the *Twathopper's Companion*.

'It's a less genteel age than when you were young, Digby, when a girl could opt to be either a lady or a blowzy slattern.'

Later she phoned James. Before she could ask the question she now asked every day he'd already replied to it.

'Howard will be there for the launch.'

'For your launch?'

'For *the* launch.'

'How do you know?'

'He phoned me again yesterday and told me.'

'He seems to phone you several times a week, James.'

'Yes, he does.'

'Odd that he never phones me. Even odder that he never phones while I'm there with you.'

'Wants to surprise you, I think, Daisy. In any case, he's glad that he's helped bring us back together.'

'*He's* helped bring us back together?'

'Well, he did, didn't he? And he'll be over from New York for the launch.'

Jonty had gone off and made the proper checks in the all proper places. The car was in exceptional condition, with a very low mileage. Apart from a few outings up and down to London Vicki had largely used it for short trips around Hastings and it had always been garaged each night. In the early years of keeping it, Digby had had it checked over each year. The tyres had been maintained, the oil periodically

changed. It had only been in the last few years that he'd let
the matter go. Even so, he was astounded when Jonty told
him.

'I'd say it's worth £32,000.'

'£32,000,' Digby repeated.

'Give or take a few hundred. It's the most sought-after
model. Not quite as fast as the 3.8, but much better handling.
And it's still got those sleek, hungry lines it had before they
started fattening it up to meet all the latest safety requirements.'

'£32,000,' Digby said again. 'Do you still want it then?'

'Oh yes.'

'Make it thirty and get me cash, Jonty.'

'Done. Don't mind my asking, Digby, but you're not
planning on wandering round the streets with this stuff in
your pocket, are you? That kind of folding money could
make you an object of considerable interest in some parts of
London these days.'

'No. There's a fellow I owe a favour to, you might even
call it a subsidy, and he always prefers cash.'

'Who doesn't?'

Once Jonty had the car and Digby had the money, he felt
he could pursue Theo in earnest. Now that he'd escaped
from his own black hole, though only at the cost of losing his
house, he wanted to try to help Theo out of his. He had
taken Jonty's point. Why shouldn't he help subsidise Theo?
He had in his own way been subsidised, hadn't he? In any
case, he felt it only proper that Theo should receive the
proceeds from his mother's car. So all he had to do now was
find him.

He couldn't, though. He had Desmond drive down to
Wandsworth and knock on the door of the flat, since the

phone was never answered. Desmond returned to say that an old woman on the floor above had informed him that the nice man with the dark hair and the trumpet had done a moonlight flit.

'Are you a friend of his?' she'd asked in a low voice.

'A friend of his dad's,' he'd confided.

'I think he's gone to the seaside, sweetheart. He's probably playing that trumpet of his on a pier somewhere.'

When Desmond conveyed this to Digby the old man had had to go and sit alone in his wunderkammer for a few minutes. Then he resolved to do what he would have preferred to avoid and call Jill.

'I'm sorry to trouble you, but I have something for Theo and I can't get hold of him.'

'No, I haven't heard from him for a while either.'

'I've heard he's gone to the seaside.'

'He'll be with Christy,' she said without hesitation.

'I beg your pardon.'

'He has a friend called Christy. Whenever life used to get too hot for Theo to handle he'd go and stay with Christy for a while. One more way of avoiding life's onerous regime: Christy's nearly as feckless as he is.'

'Do you know where Christy is?'

'No, but I gather the boys are out searching.'

'I don't think he'll be coming back; not to that flat in Wandsworth from what I hear.'

'A pile of bills?'

'I believe so.'

'Good old Theo. Nice to know some things in the universe remain constant, apart from the speed of light.'

'The thing is, Jill, I'll be leaving London shortly.'

'Going away for a while?'

'Going away for good, I'm afraid. And I wondered if I could give you something for Theo. He will contact you, I suppose?'

'Well he always has before but then I suppose we were never getting divorced before.'

'I have a feeling he's a lot more likely to contact you than he is me. Do you have somewhere to keep an item of great value?'

'I have a safe. A big old heavy one.'

'So would you mind if I left the package with you?'

'No. But you must understand I've no idea when I'll see him again.'

Desmond drove Digby down to Wimbledon where he handed over the taped-up envelope containing £30,000 in cash. On the front it simply said Theo.

'You will put it in your safe?'

'I will, as soon as you've gone. Would you like to come in for a coffee?'

'I can't, I'm afraid. Desmond is waiting in the car and he never parks anywhere for long. Another fugitive.'

'What if Theo wants to contact you?'

'I've written my new address and telephone number on the back.' After a pause he said: 'I'm sorry, by the way.'

'What about?'

'Theo.' She shrugged. 'And I didn't, in case you're still interested.'

'Didn't what?'

'Kill his mother. I didn't keep her alive, I grant you, but that's a different thing.' Then he made his stooped way to the bottom of her path and climbed into a waiting vehicle so clapped-out that Jill hesitated in her doorway for a moment, just to be sure it would start. What a family she'd married into.

Two weeks later Digby was installed in his new home: Valley Prospect in North Shropshire.

Sitting on Top of the World

Daisy was true to her word. Five days after Digby's own arrival, she turned up.

As she motored through Shropshire she was once again astonished at the beauty of the landscape, the constant presence of the hills at the edge of her vision, and asked herself as she always did on these trips why she stayed in London. It never took her too long to answer this question. Still she always enjoyed the greenery, the unmediated weather, the quiet side roads with their promise of seclusion. But she also enjoyed her return to the metropolis. She'd spent enough years in Wem in her youth to understand the perils of peace. But she thought Digby was probably ready for it. She doubted her father had even noticed the difference.

Finally she arrived at Valley Prospect. She parked her Morris Traveller in the gravel driveway and made her way in. Deva was as usual hovering behind the door. This ninety-year-old Yorkshirewoman with advanced Alzheimer's had now reverted almost entirely to her northern childhood. Her orange hair had been recently cropped in the punk style. Daisy noted that the hacking was quite effective in a theatrical sort of way, Ophelia seventy years on, having survived the drowning but still firmly stuck with the madness. Her strong hand gripped Daisy's arm. Her voice was low and confidential, powered by mania.

'You just wait till my mother gets her hands on you,' she said. Daisy smiled uneasily. There was as usual a hint of menace in Deva's complaint. 'Dragging me up and down that front all day without me cardie on.' So much anger, so much real anger underneath the knitwear.

'Come on now, Deva.' The voice of Margaret arrived a second before her person. The voice like the body from which it emerged was comforting, heavily fleshed. Deva was led away gently – 'It's your birthday today, Deva, so let's have no tantrums now' – and Daisy made her way to her father's room. It was always Deva's birthday whenever she arrived. She walked past the rank of folded wheelchairs, which made her think briefly of a Formula One race. An old lady was slowly descending the staircase in the automatic chair. She smiled gracefully at all who came within her view like a queen sitting in a state limousine. Daisy smiled at an old man on the corridor but his face registered nothing. Her nightmare was to confront a first-night audience where every face remained like that throughout the whole of the first act, then the second . . .

Her father was sitting over by the window. She stepped across the room with feline discretion and bent down slowly over the bald head with its blue veins protruding. She smoothed her hand across his scalp and then kissed him at the topmost part of his dome. He looked up without smiling.

'Arrived at last then?' His traditional greeting. She stared past him to the bottles ranged across his table: Warfarin, Digoxin, Atenolol, Zestril, Bendrofluazide. My father, she thought, the micro-pharmacy. She tried to remember all their different functions; there were pills to thin his blood and lower its pressure, others to help his misshapen kidneys in their ageing functions. One to ease his urine's flow and another his temper's eruption. But there in the middle of them all stood a plastic tower with SLUG PELLETS written on it. She lifted it up and held it close to his face so he could see.

'What are you taking these for, dad?'

'I've been helping with the gardening.' She looked down at him, bent into his chair, and a mild expression of bemusement crossed her features.

'Directing activities from the herbaceous border, you understand, rather than actually leading them in the field.'

'Ah. I was going to say, I couldn't see matron letting you loose on that self-drive mower out there.'

'Who exactly do you mean by *matron*?'

'The smiling lady with ample breasts who comes to minister to your needs, dad.'

'I've never noticed anyone with apple breasts. I certainly hope you're not suggesting I should start plucking them, not at my age. Cox's Pippins.'

'Ample breasts, dad,' she said, raising her voice a little, then she raised it a little more. 'AMPLE.'

'I suppose,' he said, in a tone of Olympian sarcasm not much modified over the decades, 'shouting is now *de rigueur* on the London stage, is it? Shouting and smut.' Daisy was pouring herself a glass of his mineral water.

'Hope you choke on your slug pellets, you cantankerous old sod,' Daisy said *sotto voce* as she sipped. He looked at her sharply.

'What was that, Daisy?'

'And raised my soul to God.'

'Raised your soul to God? What are you jabbering on about, child?'

'Just some lines from a new play.'

'Your friend Wilton's here.'

'Yes, I'm going to see him in a moment.'

Only as she was on her way out did it cross her mind to ask her father the question she had by now asked everyone else, for he had been a much-travelled man in his time. She'd really grown bored with the subject and would find out everything soon enough in any case.

'Ever heard of Thailand Great Anakh, dad?' She didn't think for a moment that he would have done. He gave her another look of contempt before finally opening his mouth again.

'You're speaking to a fellow who has completed the *Times* crossword puzzle every day for sixty years, my girl,' he said, 'and don't you forget it, just because I'm spitting-distance from the grave.' She stared at him, startled.

'You know where it is, dad? Thailand Great Anakh?'

'Of course I know where it is. I'm rather surprised you don't, as a matter of fact. And I can't help thinking your enunciation . . . I sometimes wonder if I might ask for my money back from that famous school I sent you to. Could it be method acting, I wonder . . .'

'Where is it, then?' she interrupted him.

'You're raising your voice again, Daisy. I do wish people wouldn't shout. It's at the end of Book Four of *The Dunciad* by Alexander Pope, that's where it is.'

A minute later she went over and tapped on Digby's door. When he opened it his face looked genuinely bright with joy to see her. So she could still make at least one old man very happy. She kissed him on the cheek.

'Come in, come in.'

'Digby, this probably sounds very strange but I have to go and find a library before it closes. I'll be back to see you tomorrow.'

Sitting in her car Daisy opened her dog-eared map book and located the nearest town where she might find a library. She drove there as fast as her Morris would permit, arriving twenty minutes later. From the poetry section she pulled out an edition of Pope. She flicked through the pages rapidly until she came to the last page of the last book of *The Dunciad* and read the last lines. After scanning them three times she knew the couplet by heart.

That night at James's farmhouse she asked if she could use his computer.

'You are on the internet, I take it.'

'Have to be, living up here.'

After he had switched her on and closed the door, Daisy keyed in four words and activated the search. The announcements and indexes that flashed on the screen before her now confirmed her in her dark suspicion: that she'd been well and truly conned.

Shortly before dawn on 17 January 1994, California was woken by the Northridge earthquake. Electrical power, the sustaining food of the modern city, was disconnected. All the bright city lights went down and in that sudden darkness the stars came back on. The Milky Way became visible again and the inhabitants of that land looked upwards in wonder. All they had seen since their childhoods were the artificial stars of LA. Now the stars upon which men had once calculated their fates and sailors had navigated home by, were burning in all their glory. A few of the panicked citizens realised then, perhaps for the first time, that every action has an equal and opposite reaction.

Two centuries before, the lunar societies only ever met close to a full moon so that members could find their way home again after the celebrations. In those days a full moon meant a full diary. So who on earth could have opposed the introduction of light? To do so would have been perverse and antinomian. Light in all the dark and sordid corners would surely help expunge the sordid and vicious, the diseased and the depraved. Link-boys, those luminous villains, would no longer be needed to lead the unwary traveller to his ruin. But as the city lights grew brighter and brighter so did the heavens slowly fade. By that morning in January in California some of the people staring up at the brilliant stars had never seen such a sight before in the whole of their lives, except in cinemas or late at night on television, catching an educational programme about astronomy after the end of the news.

Digby had largely forgotten about the stars too. Light pollution in London had diluted them into a liberal wash close to invisibility. Some instinct had guided him to pack the astronomical telescope and bring it with him all the same. He had given it to Theo on his eighteenth birthday in one last desperate attempt to interest the boy in anything other than drink, women and jazz. It had, needless to say, remained in its box. Now it was resting on its tripod over by the french windows of Digby's new home. And Digby could barely get himself to bed for the pleasure he took in viewing the stars. He was reminding himself one by one of the names of the constellations.

The next day he kept checking his watch to see how long

he'd have to wait for the darkness but before its arrival came Daisy's. She banged on his door. As Digby let her in she pushed straight past him.

'Have you got a television, Digby?'

'Yes, they've plugged it in over in the corner there. I still don't use it of course for anything but . . .' Daisy was already in the corner fiddling with the switches. I think I might have escaped from this woman in the nick of time, Digby thought to himself.

'I'm switching it on.' Digby stared at her from across the room.

'But I really don't *want* it on. This is my home now after all, Daisy. I mean to say . . .'

'Oh do shut up, Digby.' There was something definitive in her tone. 'I've just been listening on the car radio.' Daisy was already kneeling before his set, which flashed into life as she turned up the volume. She sat back on her haunches on the floor and stared at the screen. Digby dropped into his armchair, defeated.

It was now late in the afternoon of 11 September 2001. They both remained silent as the images on the screen were played over and over. The first aeroplane crashed into one tower of the World Trade Center, then another crashed into the second. Both planes, it seemed, filled to the brim with human cargo and high-octane fuel. Amidst the babel of confused voices trying to make sense of the sudden flames and smoke, the commentators battled to retain an air of calm authority, attempting to pick out a pattern in such dark events; such fierce and sudden annunciations.

'God,' Daisy said as the first tower collapsed, then she muttered something Digby couldn't make out as the second one went down shortly afterwards. Clouds of smoke like debris from a volcano surged vastly through New York's canyons of concrete, glass and stone. The voices of the commentators and their words soon became a seamless shroud of desolating information. Information nobody wanted and nobody could switch off.

'Four planes hijacked simultaneously . . . no possible survivors . . . the Pentagon also attacked . . . the number of dead impossible to calculate at this stage . . . we know that thousands of people would have been inside those offices . . . these twin towers were the symbols of the world's free trade and were presumably attacked for precisely that reason . . . Lower Manhattan has now been completely sealed off . . . resembling a scene from the last war rather than the commercial capital of the world's only superpower . . .'

They sat for hours like this, watching, saying almost nothing. Later, after the rush of televised images, after the endless visual recollections of the actual moments of disaster she turned to him and said in a subdued voice, 'I think my son's somewhere in New York at the moment – but I couldn't tell you where.'

Then the cameras were roaming the still world of the aftermath, cyclops lenses scanning the surface of a ruined planet. White dust from the eruption had settled over the roofs and bonnets of Mercedes and Cadillacs and the black tarmac surfaces of the roads and streets had been bleached and powdered. Pompeii the morning after; a moondust mausoleum; the day New Yorkers looked up to see concrete and fire falling from heaven. A giant had shaken this bright glass world and made the snow fall. Hot white snow. People wept into microphones. An occasional mobile phone emitted its SOS from beneath the tangles of ruptured metal, the lunar mountains of rubble. The counting of the dead had begun.

No one had the faintest notion at this point when it might end.

For no good reason he could fathom Digby remembered the white dust of Giacometti's studio in Paris which he had once visited with Jakob. Fashioned figures striding grandly into a vastness that might turn out finally to be nothing at all. And others who simply stood, impassive at the void opening up before them. There had been white dust everywhere. The plaster figures seemed to have covered the floor with the dust of their flesh. There was hardly anything left of them. Gaunt, skeletal, solitary. When they were put side by side they looked even more alone than when they were left to stand in isolation. The distance around each one was absolute.

Digby remembered the first time he had ever flown over New York. Through the aeroplane window as it started banking he had surveyed the buildings of Manhattan shining in the orange evening sunlight and marvelled at the mighty makings of man. Hadn't the plaque on the WTC building been cut to read *One World Financial Center*? Could that really be true? Or was it another of those false memories, a feather caught in the same blast that's generated whenever the gates of Eden bang shut? A feather from a fabulous bird that lives for ever in the land of memory but isn't real enough even to become extinct elsewhere.

Over the next few days the television, switched resolutely off for so many years, was on from morning till night. He couldn't take his eyes off it. So that's what the new age looks like, he thought. I lived long enough to see it after all. The stories started to leak through: the final messages, the last telephone calls. All of them facing death spoke of love; of their great love for those they were about to leave for ever.

Digby thought of Vicki and his eyes filled with tears. He picked up the telephone and called Theo's number. He knew there'd be no reply but he let it ring and ring all the same before replacing the handset gently in the cradle, so gently, as though there might be a creature in the house he would not wish to wake; a vulnerable creature whose cries he would try at all costs to avoid.

Mad as a Fish

Theo's cellmate Lee might have been as mad as a fish in a tree but he'd had a firm understanding of what was going on around him. He had complimented Theo on his ability to do his bang-up. A certain passivity in Theo's nature, an innate sense that circumstances were if not exactly unchangeable then at least best left to take their own course in their own sweet time, had helped him there. Many an untutored contemplative is held over at Her Majesty's discretion. They're the ones who get through the easiest. Iron bars in every window between you and the sky can often induce a certain fatalism, a relinquishing of the will to a greater power. And from time to time Theo would catch sight of the heron.

The other great thing about being inside is that nobody sends you any bills for being there. How the bills of life do mount up. Without Jill to stand between himself and officialdom's displeasure he'd started to realise how hard it was to concentrate on maintaining a contemplative equilibrium. *Pack up all my cares and woe, Here I go, singing low.* But you couldn't always be packing up and going, could you? And another of Lee's phrases had started to echo in his mind of late: there's always a padmate, Theo, always a cellmate – only way you ever avoid cellmates is by doing solitary. For six nights a week now Theo's cellmate was Christy; only on the seventh, when even the Almighty rested from His labours, did he get to sleep with Yvonne instead.

'Did you ever . . . with Christy, I mean?'

'He sized me up one night. I don't think I was geometric enough.'

'You're not made of rubber either.'

'We could probably have come to an arrangement about the rubber bit, but the geometry presented a real problem. Needs women designed by Euclid, our Christy. Anyway, I don't want a fly-by-night fellow. Getting jealous, by any chance, Theo?' Maybe he was. There's always a cellmate, Theo. He couldn't stand solitary any more and he surely couldn't spend the rest of his life sleeping on Christy's floor and listening to Christy's roar. 'You're going to have to make a decision, you know. Sooner rather than later.'

Theo liked Yvonne but then he'd liked Jill too. Theo liked lots of women. He wasn't sure he'd ever before felt quite the desolation he felt these days, between the dark wastelands of Christy's snoring, the storms coming in from the Channel and the dream where the great coloured globes were all hurtling along to crush him. He never had the dream when he was sleeping with Yvonne; just as well really since he'd have woken her son Jack. He didn't have the other problem with Yvonne either. So did that mean she'd already become his wife? In the dark in bed she felt like Jill in his arms. He felt, for the first time in his life, too old to just move on again. Now that he was by the sea he seemed at last to be wearing a diver's lead boots: it was hard to shift his feet anywhere else. Yvonne didn't want Theo to move on, she wanted him to move in – with her and Jack but not in the studio flat where she lived. 'We'd all go mad with another body in here, Theo, I'll promise you that.' She had seen a bigger flat she very much wanted to buy to replace the small one she was renting but Theo would have to make a contribution to it or she wouldn't be able to manage the mortgage. Theo would have to hand over some money every month. And that, as Jill would have been happy to confirm to anyone pursuing such enquiries, would have represented something of a new departure for him.

'It's up to you, Theo, but I'm not hanging around for ever. Jack deserves better and so do I.'

'He invents things.'

'That's a shame.'

'What do you mean?'

'Can't take people seriously who invent things. You need to know where you are when you're talking to somebody.'

'No, he invents things; he's an inventor, for fuck's sake.'

Theo stared at the men standing at the bar for a moment, drank off his vodka and left.

Yvonne had been explicit. He could either get a job so that between them they could afford the mortgage necessary to buy the bigger flat or they could split. He would share her bed no more, not even once a week. Each day would end instead on Christy's floor, listening to his curious monologues and waiting for the minotaur bellow to begin once his eyelids closed. To avoid that fate he was making his way now to his appointment at the Job Centre. Yvonne had noticed the card in the window: night-watchman needed for a local electronics firm.

'You never get up till half-way through the day as it is, Theo. You could probably even practise your trumpet; not likely to be anyone else around in the middle of the night, is there?' She loved his playing but she couldn't help wondering how much money there was in it. He didn't seem to have made a fortune so far.

He had to sit at a desk and fill in a form listing all the jobs he'd had over the previous few years. Theo dutifully did so, running out of space by the end. When he was summoned to go through to a tiny room with one table and two chairs, the interviewer read out what he'd written.

'Barman, brickie, commentator on a Thames cruiser, ceramics curator, jazz trumpeter, shop assistant, minicab driver (one week), hotdog vendor, fairground tout and road resurfacer. You sure you haven't left anything out here? I mean, that is the lot, is it?' Theo shrugged.

'As far as I remember. Might have missed one or two highlights.'

Something about the place, its plastic chairs and air of enforced depression, and the large young man jammed into the narrow space behind the table, even the way his spectacles perched on his sweaty little nose beneath the striplighting, debilitated Theo and sapped his will in the grand endeavour to find himself a new career. They'd once asked Duke Ellington why there was so much dissonance in his music. Because there's so much dissonance in the world, he'd said, that's why.

'Oh sorry, I just remembered. There was also nine months in Wandsworth for drug dealing.' The fat young man stopped staring at the form in front of him and stared at Theo instead.

'Recently?'

'Pretty recently.'

'Ah. Now, that's not an insuperable barrier any more, of

course. But we will need some special references, especially for a security post like that of night-watchman.'

'You think we should leave it for the moment then?'

'Let's say I wouldn't be in a position to put you forward straight away.' The interviewer's eyes were now fixed on the trumpet case on Theo's lap.

'Only popped in between gigs,' Theo said by way of explanation.

Five minutes later Theo stood at the corner of the High Street. *Pack up all my cares and woe, Here I go, singing low.* He played for the better part of an hour. He heard coins intermittently clinking into the cap at his feet. His eyes were as usual mostly closed. When he opened them Yvonne stood in front of him, Jack at her side holding her hand.

'That's good, Theo,' Jack said. 'That sounds really good.' Theo smiled at the little boy in his coat and muffler.

'That's right, Jack,' Yvonne said. 'Highly paid work this, on the street corner. Just look at all those coins Theo has in his cap. If you practise hard enough on your recorder you'll be able to make a living like this one day.'

I'm wasting my time with you, Theo, aren't I? Yvonne had been trying hard to convince herself, just as she'd spent the better part of five years trying to convince herself with Jack's father, but this was the moment she finally stopped trying. She looked hard into Theo's eyes and he knew exactly what her hard eyes were saying. He knew that from that day on he'd be spending all seven nights on Christy's floor.

Stone and Shadow

The book was beautiful. James had made it a condition of publication that it should be printed on the finest paper and to the highest standards. This had pushed up the price but it would still sell with his name on it. Daisy had left a copy with Digby and even that fastidious old connoisseur of exquisite typography had felt obliged to remark upon its quality.

James turned the pages with pleasure sitting in the passenger seat of Daisy's Morris as she drove them both towards Covent Garden for the launch. He'd been working on it for years with his old plate camera but only eighteen months before had he realised there was a book in it. That's when he'd brought in Crispian to put a text together. And now here it was. All in glistening black-and-white. His tenth book since 1968. The first one had had two shots of Daisy but he thought he liked this new one best.

Naves with the morning light flooding through them. Monks' heads grimacing on misericords. A ruined chancel with its tracery of stonework. Wide-angle shots peeping down from the triforium. Vined vaulting in the chapter house. Tiny organs with their misshapen ivory keys. Tomb-weepers resting on monuments. Stooks and posies from the harvest festival. Weathered gargoyles and memorial slabs, their recessed incisions cutting through a glaze of light. A few piscinas the hammers of the Reformation had failed to demolish. Carved pews, wooden bosses, crooked grave-stones. Scrolling capitals in the crypt and ambulatory. A mournful Lazarus rising up reluctantly from death. Chantries and lecterns and screens and ancient fonts. He liked the silence he'd captured in every image. Doing the book had brought out a patience in him he really hadn't known was there. A patience that had paid off in regard to Daisy too. Good old Howard.

Suddenly she startled him.

'So we're launching two books tonight then?' James half-turned to look at her, then turned back resolutely to stare through the windscreen at the road. They were crossing one of London's painted iron bridges. He didn't know what to say. Daisy continued in a sing-song voice:

> *'Thy hand, great Anarch! lets the curtain fall;*
> *And Universal Darkness buries All.'*

Silence in the car, a noisy silence.

'How did you find out?'

'My father told me, funnily enough.'

People were milling around inside the shop when they arrived. There were piles of *Stone and Shadow* on a table which Crispian was already signing. But there were also piles of another book entirely. Daisy picked up the paperback and stared at its title page: *Storm the Citadel. Photographs by James Oldham, Text by Howard Oldham.* She turned to look at the imprint and was not surprised to read: *Published by Thyhand-greatanarch.com*. Hadn't they been doing a lot of work, though.

'Hello, mum.' She received his kiss, even half returned it. 'How nice to see you again.' He looked well. He'd been eating.

'Sorry I haven't been in touch. Been busy.'

'Obviously.' Despite her irritation she pulled her long-absent son towards her and hugged him tightly. James had assured her of his survival and well-being but she was still glad to have him in her arms. She spoke into his ear: 'Don't you ever do that again, understand?'

The place was soon filling with people and Daisy resolved to keep it all bottled up until later. But then the speeches started. And there was her son, whom she had not seen for the better part of a year, laughing as he spoke about the scheme he'd concocted with his father.

'When I first asked James if he'd be prepared to do this book with me I thought I'd get a pretty dusty answer. These days he spends most of his time creeping round empty churches in Shropshire. The thought of smuggling him in to secret addresses so he could take photographs of some of these demonstrators – and sometimes it could get pretty hairy, believe me – might have looked like pushing my luck a bit. But it turned out that the old dissident from the Sixties is still lurking behind his lenses . . .'

The old dissident from the Sixties, Daisy thought. It was now James's turn to stand up, smiling away, and treat the crowd to his own recollections.

'I suppose it all did sound a bit uncomfortable to begin with, I'll admit, but by the end I was enjoying it. It was obviously something worth doing. Crouching behind walls and trying to hide my cameras while the forces of law and order cleared the streets out there. It soon became evident that they wanted to clear them of everything and everyone that might even whisper a criticism of those who've taken it upon themselves to rule our destinies these days . . .'

They were so pleased with themselves. Daisy had already realised that Howard and James had been collaborating on *Thyhandgreatanarch.com* and its publishing outlet, for she had been clicking on with great ferocity since her chat with her father, but she had simply not recognised the extent of the connivance. She only understood now that when James had been away on his mysterious shoots, the ones he said he couldn't talk to her about, he had in fact been photographing the black bloc or whoever else it was, with Howard in attendance at his elbow, scribbling away at their joint book while the pair of them continued with their systematic deception of Daisy. As the queues started forming to buy the books, some signed by James, some by Howard, and some of course by both of the men in her life, she flipped.

She walked up to the front of the shop where father and son were smiling away in acknowledgement of their joint triumph, all their hard and secret work over the last year. Half-way through the swing she'd started aiming at Howard she changed her mind, didn't want to disfigure her only son and heir when all was said and done, so she shifted angle enough to land her fist instead on James. She still packed quite a punch, and James promptly keeled over backwards into the trestle table sending books crashing all over the floor. Her son and her first ex had been assiduous between the two of them in making sure the press was in attendance so the cameras were obediently flashing as all this took place.

After a silent journey the three of them finally arrived back at Bolingbroke Grove. Daisy turned on them as soon as they were all inside the kitchen. Her eyes flicked between her son and first husband, quick as a lizard's tongue.

'It was cruel and thoughtless.'

'Cruel maybe, mum,' Howard said, with what struck her as a remarkably insouciant tone, 'but it certainly wasn't thoughtless.' And then James chipped in from behind the handkerchief he was clutching to his eye.

'Quite a lot of thought went into it, Daisy, to be fair.'

'You bastards. You calculating bastards. I'm disowning the pair of you from this day on.' But Howard was obviously in combative mode.

'Why did you and dad ever get divorced? Tell me that.'

'Ask your father.'

'I'm not asking my father. I'm asking you.'

'Then I'll ask your father for you. Do something useful for once in your life, Howard, and pour me a drink. The claret – it's over in the cupboard – the wine at your launch was quite disgusting by the way. James, why did we ever get divorced?'

James was still clutching his white handkerchief to his face.

'Because of your fame.'

'What do you mean, because of my fame? You were famous as well, as I remember. You were famous before I was.'

'But I wasn't as famous as you were becoming. Anyway I was famous because I was talented. You were famous for being beautiful.'

'Are you trying to say I wasn't talented?'

'No, you were talented all right but the fact is you only became quite so famous quite so quickly because you were beautiful *and* talented. If you'd been ugly and talented like a lot of other people I could mention we'd have heard a lot less

333

about you. I mean I can still remember it: there were pictures of you in every magazine I picked up. Pictures on billboards.'

Daisy had by now accepted a glass of wine from her son.

'Some of those pictures were by you, I seem to recall.'

'Some might have been. But a lot weren't. Some of the photographs of you minus your clothes were by me and a lot were by other men who weren't me. Other *young* men, Daisy, who weren't me. I know what photographers are like and I couldn't cope with it.'

'So you started going with all those other young women just to show me you weren't coping?'

'That's one way men have of not coping,' he said.

'Well that's very handy, James, I must say.' She took a sip of her claret. 'I just want to know what it was you decided between the two of you.' Howard had remained uncowed. He hadn't taken his eyes off his mother's face.

'Just that to find out anything about me, to communicate with me at all, you'd have to do it through James.'

'I do wish you wouldn't call your father James, Howard.'

'That's his name.'

'His name's father or dad, or it should be. You're his son. Show some respect.' She took another swig of her wine. 'And during all those shoots with all those anarchists you two were meeting up, weren't you? Working on your little book. Going out for meals in foreign cafés. And lying through your teeth to me about it all the time. Having a good old giggle while I lay awake in bed at night worrying myself sick.'

'I didn't lie, Daisy. I said I was going off on work I couldn't talk about.'

'But you *could* have talked about it.'

'Not without spoiling the surprise.'

'Oh, the surprise. Daisy's little surprise. I should have put my party frock on tonight, I suppose.' Howard now spoke again, quite fiercely.

'Look, I've always known ever since I was little that you two should be together not apart. That's all. Mum, you were completely miserable with that other wanker you married. Asking me to call him dad, for Christ's sake. I knew who my dad was. He was the bloke chasing around his studio after models young enough to be my sister, as though he was trying to prove something. Well, who was he proving it to? You're a pair of fucking lunatics.'

'Don't swear, Howard,' Daisy said.

'That's right, Howard,' James said. 'Just because you're now a famous anarchist with your own website and publishing house does not give you the right to swear. You're in your mother's house and your mother's never sworn, have you darling, despite all her years of mixing with insalubrious, foul-mouthed, theatrical types. She'll happily beat the shit out of you if you step out of line, like she's just done with me on the evening of my latest book launch, but she never fucking swears, any more than I do. Where does he get it from, Daisy?' James removed the handkerchief to reveal an eye already puffed up. Howard whistled.

'You punch above your weight, mum, I'll give you that. Muhammad Ali would be proud of you.'

'Not bad is it?' she said with a hint of pride as she made her way across the kitchen to peer down at her wounded first ex. She looked a little closer then turned away and started laughing uncontrollably before making for the medicine chest.

The next day the newspapers were full of it. Coverage was guaranteed: FILMSTAR FLOORS DIVORCED HUSBAND. ANAR-CHIST FRACAS IN COVENT GARDEN. DAISY GRESHAM DECKS

JAMES OLDHAM. THY HAND, GREAT ANARCH, ON JAMES OLDHAM'S FACE. Howard couldn't have contrived a better launch if his mother and father had been leased under contract to him.

James had shrewdly calculated that *Storm the Citadel*, unlike *Stone and Shadow*, should be published as a cheap paperback and that the only other place where anyone could see his photographs of the demonstrations here and there across the globe was on *Thyhandgreatanarch.com*. His name was still weighty enough to have people searching out his work. That way either route led people to Howard's website, Howard's internet journal or Howard's cyberspace publishing house, that freshly built mansion in the skies.

Slaves of the Visible

In April 1986 Captain Michael Hatcher finally salvaged the *Nanking Cargo* from the South China Sea. It had sunk some time around 1750 on its way to Europe where it had become fashionable for men in periwigs and dusty-faced women with hoops around their thighs to sip Chinese tea from blue and white porcelain. This cargo, so long a domicile for coiled eels and silent fishes, was painstakingly retrieved. Chamber-pots wreathed in the fragrance of their floral designs; plates with fan-tailed carp swarming among lotuses; pagodas by still lakes. A scholar on a bridge with a pavilion behind him. Terraces by rocky rivers where poets retreated into lonely meditation with their scrolls. There was an all-too-contemporary hullabaloo in the press and a major auction at Sotheby's in Holland.

The curious thing was, as Digby realised the moment he'd set eyes on the pictures in the newspapers, that the porcelain had evidently been designed and made in Jiangxi Province specifically for the western market and then transshipped through Nanking. It was destined for the East India Company since it was of a quality far too low for the Chinese themselves. Although transcending anything likely to be produced in such quantities to such a standard in Europe, it would have remained unimpressive to the authentic oriental eye and touch. It was thick and clumsy, manufactured merely to the standard required for occidental vulgarity.

Every lot at the auction had sold for prices far above the estimated markers. The West had once more been supplied with the version of China that it needed and could afford. The mysteries of trade.

These reflections came to him as he worked to finish 'Wilton Bone China in the Age of Coleridge'. There was no point hanging around any longer. He'd evidently arrived at his final destination: time at last then to clear his desk.

Coleridge hadn't died until 1834 so the age of Coleridge took *Wilton Bone China* well into the nineteenth century. And what an age it had been. He'd had a pleasant afternoon once discussing it with Theo's jazz-playing friend Paul. He'd liked Paul. He'd even asked Theo if he could see him again. Theo had said he would arrange it. He hadn't of course. What he and Paul had agreed on that afternoon was the astonishing vigour and confidence of those people who'd refashioned the earth they stood on. Telford driving his canals and roadways through the most inhospitable terrain, with aqueducts and viaducts left striding the hillsides by the time he'd gone. Brunel standing before the massive chains of the *Great Eastern*, having a quiet smoke before the next grand scheme was started. Joseph Paxton taking time off as head gardener to the Duke of Devonshire to design the Crystal Palace. At the end of every train line a grand hotel had soon sprouted like a vast stone blossom on the railway's stem. The resorts themselves, originally cultivated in the most Georgian mode of modest gentility, now bloomed in brash imperial splendour at the edge of the sea, even the sea itself seeming for a while to be British since the British ruled it, bringing foreign goods and foreign personages to those massive country houses built for the newly rich and recently ennobled. Digby could still remember the map on his father's study wall, engraved and printed by Dexter's of London, splodged with pink from Egypt to the South China Sea and signifying empire – British Empire. London gathered the world's money into its widening vaults while boats sunk to their gunwales with sundry cargoes were filled on their return with smashed stone to pack the veining roadways. The world had been filled then with British possessions. To some it had seemed as if the world itself was a British possession. Now who was it Paul had been obsessed by? Titus Salt. Northern millionaire and philanthropist.

'Wilton Bone China in the Age of Coleridge'. He probably returned to it so often because it was his favourite chapter and the one period of his ancestral company's history for which he could feel unambiguous enthusiasm, but one of the great sorrows of his life had been his inability to trace any mention of Nathaniel Wilton in the life or correspondence of Samuel Taylor Coleridge. The letters from Stoke that the company's founder had sent had been of sufficient importance to Nathaniel that he had copied them in his own hand and placed them in the company archive, but the lengthy epistles from the poet which they solicited or to which they responded had vanished. Digby could only conclude that these characteristic chapter-length disquisitions on Spinoza, on the trinity, on nightingales, griffins, krakens, the aurora borealis, the fugitive breath of the divine spirit, had been of such importance to his great-great-grandfather that he had kept them in his pocket.

There appeared to be a hint in one of Nathaniel's letters that he had actually sent Coleridge money. This would not have been so unusual – the Wedgwoods had after all done the same thing at more or less the same time but Digby always felt a surge of pleasure to think that some of the proceeds from his family firm had once gone into the pockets of the creator of 'The Rime of the Ancient Mariner' even if, as was more than likely, the money had done no more than feed one of his insalubrious habits.

So for the purposes of his book Digby had needed to reconstruct the correspondence from the one side of it still in existence. He had been forced to resurrect what Coleridge had actually written from its echoes in the words of the man he had written to. The correspondence had begun in the late 1790s, the time of the making of *Lyrical Ballads*, and the addresses still flared with those legendary times: Alfoxden, Nether Stowey, Bristol. There had been brief descriptions of the Quantocks, with cirrocumulus flying eastward from the Channel, and Coleridge's now sardonic account of how he had once become Silas Tomkyn Comberbache so that he might enter the Fifteenth Light Dragoons and thereby escape a mountain of debt. (He had apparently imagined the cymbal-crash of battle, steel shafts wincing about him as the bugles trilled. He'd not actually seen himself mucking out stables.) And there were languid memories of the scheme of Pantisocracy, the location in America chosen by Coleridge purely because of his delight at the sibilants in the word Susquehannah. Then the various Sarahs who arrived to torment and delight him. And, of course, laudanum. For a while the hours would melt as gently as butter on a griddle. He would see in the candle's blue and amber flame Krishna's wheeling arms before Arjuna or Lord Brahma enthroned in silence on the lotus.

On its appearance 'The Ancient Mariner' had evidently

fascinated Nathaniel to the point of obsession. And yet Coleridge had been happy to confess to hearing these thalassic surges and murmurs, these savage pursuits over the liquid and shifting mountains by the vengeful numen of the equatorial zones, while gazing across the Severn estuary for he'd never actually yet put to sea. The imagination, then. Inhabit it and you inhabit the world. Coleridge of all men had certainly known that well enough by the end, when the good Doctor Gillman in Highgate had tried to help him quell the wired veins of affliction. The last letter Nathaniel ever received seemingly spoke of the city Coleridge looked down on from Gillman's highest window. He spoke of the smoke of time, its tainted breath already darkening the sky over London. On Hampstead Heath the poet had seen a squirrel's spine snapped in the jaw of a mongrel and this had made him think of that Bacchic frenzy men and women don feral masks for in Euripides. And not long after he had died.

The Wilton letters had presumably been sufficiently insignificant at the Coleridgean end to be dispensed with swiftly, never to be even mentioned in any of the editions, and the Coleridge letters had conversely been so significant at the Wilton end that he had kept them with him always. If that had been so then it would have explained how the exploding kiln that killed Nathaniel in 1840 would have turned them to ash as well. All that was left were the Wilton letters, so carefully and scrupulously copied out and deposited by Nathaniel in the company archive. And a copy of the pro-forma invoice that accompanied Wilton Bone China's set of plates and dishes commemorating 'The Ancient Mariner', which had been sent to the poet, and whose shards were now presumably scattered somewhere under the earth.

Digby, in devotion to his own ancestral voices, had even

approached the Oxford editors of Coleridge's *Collected Works* to see if some mention might not be made, if only in a footnote, of Nathaniel's correspondence with the poet.

A dignified and scholarly lady who, Digby calculated, could not be more than a decade younger than himself had gone with care through the copies of Nathaniel's letters which Digby had sent to her. At their meeting in Oxford he had stared at her lined face and the grey hair she pushed back fearsomely from her brow whenever she'd leaned forward for a moment. She appeared to choose her words with great care.

'There is no evidence here, no material as it were from the Coleridge end as reported by Nathaniel Wilton, which could not have been gathered from other sources. Don't get me wrong – I'm not suggesting your ancestor was a fantasist. But all we have are these accounts of things in STC's letters, not the letters themselves. And all of that material could have been acquired from elsewhere. Coleridge at the time was corresponding with the Wedgwoods, for example. Presumably Nathaniel might have known them socially.'

'He did know them.'

'What I'm trying to say, Mr Wilton, is that without some exterior verification, it would appear impossible at present to establish whether Coleridge ever actually communicated with your great-great-grandfather, though it would obviously appear to be the case that your great-great-grandfather communicated with him.'

Digby had then taken from his case the one remaining item from Wilton Bone China's 'Ancient Mariner' collection.

'He sent him a full set of these,' he said. 'I have the pro-forma invoice to prove it.'

The female scholar took the large dish between her delicate fingers and peered into it.

'Why does he have that white budgerigar around his neck?'

'It's an albatross.' She stared over the bowl at him in undisguised amazement.

'This is the Ancient Mariner?' Digby nodded. A second later the editor put the dish back on the table and walked out briskly, shutting the door behind her. When Digby tiptoed over to the closed door and leaned his ear against it he could just make out her muffled sobs from the next room. Sobs of barely stifled laughter. So Wilton Bone China had been definitively relegated to whatever lies beyond the footnote.

When he sat down now to write his final draft he began with this sentence: 'Nathaniel Wilton undoubtedly knew Samuel Taylor Coleridge; whether Coleridge ever knew Nathaniel Wilton must remain one of history's unanswered questions.'

Daisy had returned. Her father sat in the chair with the *Times* crossword on his lap before him, almost completed.

'Brass monkey,' he said, after she had said hello. 'Could that be right?'

'The nether regions shrivelled up against the cold, dad.'

'That's right. How did you know?'

'I was in a play once that used the words. I also read books, as it happens; you're not the only literate one in the family. Brass monkey weather. It certainly is at the moment.' She lowered her voice. 'How are your nuts, you old tyrant? Haven't fallen off yet then?'

'What's falling off?'

'Never mind, dad. *I'll* be off soon enough. I'm going to see James.'

'James who?'

'James Oldham. You remember – my husband.' Her father's face underwent a brief flicker of genuine perplexity.

'But you divorced that one, surely?'

'Yes. But we seem to be getting back together again.'

'What an extraordinary generation. I haven't seen young Howard for a long time.'

'No, he'll be coming to see you soon though, don't you worry, I'll make sure the little bugger comes back with me the next time.'

'I do wish you wouldn't swear, Daisy. Your mother never saw the necessity of swearing.'

'Oh yes she did,' Daisy said as she turned away, 'the minute you were out of the bloody house. And you were the one she was always swearing about, though I can't for the life of me think why.'

A few moments later Digby opened up and let her in.

'It seems to be easier to gain entrance here than it was in London.'

'Fewer people knocking on the door asking for money, but then I suppose they've already got it all, haven't they? How's Bolingbroke Grove?'

'Much more exciting now that Tessa's started driving up and down in that yellow E-type.'

'Tessa drives it?'

'Jonty gave it to her. A marital gift. Didn't he tell you?' Digby seemed to brood for a moment. How things come around.

'And the other night we were treated to her ceremony of the coconut.'

'Go on.'

'Apparently, she picked the idea up at a Hindu festival she attended last year somewhere in India.'

'Do they have coconuts in India?'

'I don't know, Digby. They can import them, surely. Maybe they used gourds. In any case, Tessa uses coconuts. There was a hole in the coconut, and through this hole we were invited to project all the darkness and failure and resentment inside us. Each one of us in turn. We had to make a statement. As though we were in a Salvation Army meeting. Or Alcoholics Anonymous. We had to itemise all the dead lumber of our psyches.'

'And put it all in the coconut?'

'It all went into the coconut.'

'What darkness and resentment did you put in, Daisy?'

'Something about my husband and my son, Digby – you don't really need to know.'

'What happened next?'

'Tessa goes off with the coconut down to the pond on the Common and throws it in. We all had to follow along the pavement. Thus did we dispose of our evil spirits.'

'I hope she didn't hit the heron. It lives on that pond. My son's very fond of the heron. Says it got him through his stint inside.'

'Has he been in touch?'

'He has not.'

'You're settling in then, Digby?'

Digby confirmed that he was, though he took the opportunity to describe his most recent source of distress. He had developed a curious propensity to yawn and belch at the same time. He thought it might have something to do with the disruption of his routines involved in the removal from

London. He had brought the matter up with Valley Prospect's doctor. Digby's heart had sunk when he'd seen him. A young Welshman, healthy and smiling. What use is a young and healthy doctor to anyone? You want someone old and battered and withered, enduring some notion from the inside of what it's like when the horn of life's plenty turns into an army of ailments billeted inside your intestines. It was the usual situation: a doctor too youthful to respond with any sensitivity to an old man's problems.

'You've already told me before that you drink spritzer,' he had said. 'Plenty of gaseous liquid there. The yawn provides your body with the opportunity it needs to get more oxygen and the belch then seizes its chance to get rid of the gas. Carbonated water mixed with wine is probably your problem. Try to cut it out.'

'I can assure you that gin and tonic's no better,' Digby said.

'So don't drink that either then,' the doctor had replied.

As simple as that. Another roundhead, Digby thought, determined to expunge the vestiges of our cavalier traditions. Once he'd have whitewashed the walls of churches and smashed statues of the Virgin to bits. No respect for tradition.

'You're talking about the habits of a lifetime, doctor.'

'So carry on belching and yawning then,' the doctor had said, already on his way out, probably to the rugby pitch. 'No need to add the sound of bellyaching to the chorus, is there?'

By the time Daisy had left it was already dark. After receiving with gratitude his toasted sandwich and tea he made for the telescope. He soon found his planet and started focusing, hearing Uncle Freddie's voice in his ear as he worked.

'Slaves of the visible, Digby. Our panoply of lenses makes us slaves of the visible. We abolish distance and nearness. But there's no lens as yet through which you might see God and his angels, is there? *Ergo* they can't exist, can they? *Quod erat demonstrandum*, my lad. If it isn't at the end of a lens, then it simply isn't there as far as we're concerned. The measure of all things, indeed. What a clever fellow Swift was with his Lilliput and Brobdingnag. Think how helpless Gulliver's size made him when he was a giant but think of the disgust he felt at the gigantism of others when he was a midget. The only difference is that unlike Lemuel Gulliver we live in both realms simultaneously. Microscopic or gigantic at the turn of a screw, the twist of a focusing ring. And like all benefits it also has to be a demerit because the only thing permanently out of focus now is ourselves. We can see everything large or small but the agency doing the seeing has become a bit of a blur.'

Ah Freddie. *Requiescat in pace.* You couldn't escape lenses though, could you? Even Digby couldn't. So after he'd finished scanning the heavens he poured himself a drink – who was there to care whether he yawned and belched or not? – took his video from the shelf and pushed it into the black slot.

It was well over an hour later when Mr Gresham put his head around the door after the briefest of knocks. Daisy had just divested herself of her last item of clothing and her father stared at the screen for a moment.

'That wouldn't be my daughter, by any chance?'

'Yes,' Digby said, considering whether he should dart over and switch it off, but he wasn't entirely sure he'd retained a dart amongst his present repertoire of movements.

'Her mother never wanted her to go on the stage in the first place, you know.'

'A child in the arts is always a worry,' Digby said with unfeigned sincerity. Theo. Dear bloody Theo. Daisy on the screen had started moaning. It was a simulacrum of sexual ecstasy, obviously, but a startlingly authentic one.

'Must have got jolly chilly sometimes, I shouldn't wonder,' her father said. 'Should have had a vest on. Or at least a liberty bodice.' Then he tapped his stick sharply on Digby's door.

'See you at breakfast then, Wilton.'

'Yes, God willing.'

And Digby was left by himself to watch as the end of the film came nearer, so that even the irreproachable body of Daisy Gresham had to melt in the glare of man's intractable and implacable anger: with others, with himself, with the condition of being man at all. The soundtrack started up once more:

God gave Noah the rainbow sign
No more water, the fire next time.

Seneca's Grin

Thus Uncle Freddie: 'The only thing you ever learn from time, Digby, is that it's always now. But *now* is drenched to the bone in *then*, from the second after you've been born. This condition, shall we agree to call, if only for the sake of convenience, Original Sin; it is incidentally the source of all humour, which is no more than that curious glimpse of itself which the psyche occasionally finds in the mirror of the world: the hilarious images of a displaced ego in an alien landscape, the dissonance appetite encounters when it meets an objectivity not designed to cram its greedy maw with all it requires but rather to thwart it at every evil turn. Humour, I think you'll find as the years go by, is neither more nor less than a series of glosses on our fallen state, fractured reflections on how and why nature turned against us like a spouse we've irreparably wronged. Postlapsarian then, which is merely to say, after the honeymoon. If astrology was the way we once comforted ourselves with the illusion that the planets were sympathetic to our tragedies and trials, that they still bent a drooping eye in our direction if only to condemn us to a dreadful fate, humour is the wry face of stoicism; philosophy's dark anarchic secret; Seneca's grin. When you stare out at the universe you see only distance and denial, light-years of icy indifference, however symmetric the constellations. We might believe in a personal Creator, but what He created was an indifferent universe.

'I do wonder sometimes whether the curious grimace formed by the face when we laugh immoderately might once have been the shape of a primeval howl as we called out into the recession of darkness for an answering voice, but received none. Maybe anguish only modulated into mirth to stop humankind's wits from coming astray. So you've got to laugh, after all; otherwise you'd spend the whole of your existence shouting and crying and people who do that are so tiresome we lock them away and forget their names. And when they say they are hungry we feed them poisons that take their words and memories away. Remember though, Digby: angels are bright still though the brightest fell.'

Vicki. Theo. There could be a more benign interpretation placed upon it all no doubt. Perhaps there were those who believed humour was our way of tuning ourselves in to the cosmic benevolence. Ah but the darkness, Pelagius, think of the darkness. Think of the moonblind men and their nyctalopic women.

He remembered how he and Jakob Kirk had left Giacometti's studio that evening and walked along the river. Digby had spoken of the parallel between the ravages to which the sculptor's fingers subjected the faces of his sculptures and the ravages to which time and anxiety had already subjected the face of Giacometti himself.

As they had approached Notre Dame Jakob had said, 'Most sculptors work from the outside in; he works from the inside out. Do you want to go to a brothel? I know a very good one.'

'I'm a married man, Jakob.'

At this point Jakob had laughed so hard Digby thought he might tumble into the Seine.

'You're an English man, Digby,' he had said finally as his laughter subsided. His eyes were still bright with the absurdity of it. 'An Englishman.'

dot.com

When Daisy got back to the farmhouse in the hills above Oswestry that evening she was soon enough connected up to *Thyhandgreatanarch.com*. She still wanted to know precisely what it was her son had been doing, with her first ex's connivance. She scrolled with great rapidity through the texts until she landed on sections that interested her. She halted briefly on *Economies*:

> *Special reductions on all travel to any May Day demonstration, WTO summit, World Bank conference, etc. With advance block bookings substantial savings can be made whether the journey is to London, Gothenburg, Seattle or Genoa. Why give money to the same institutions you're setting out to protest against? Thyhandgreatanarch.com can arrange your travel. Ten per cent of all profits from Thyhand goes to fund a portfolio of anti-capitalist organizations and ecological investments. Conference facilities are also provided on all booked trains.*

So he was a travel agent, then – an anarchist travel agent. Obviously a good business to be involved in. Anarchists need to get about a lot.

Summaries in digests of no more than twenty-five pages of all the great works of anarchist and anti-capitalist literature. Acquaint yourself with the full tradition of international dissent at a fraction of the cost and in a fraction of the time: Bukharin, Herbert Read, Kropotkin . . .

Then she found *The Poetry of Dissent*.

Ginsberg, Ferlinghetti, Corso. Blake . . .

Blake? Was Blake an anarchist then? She wasn't sure. Better keep going. He even had Coleridge in there, though admittedly that was under the section *Environment and Profit*:

> *Oh lady, we receive but what we give*
> *And in our life alone does nature live*
> *Ours is her wedding-garment, ours her shroud.*

What Coleridge might have added is that there are of course no pockets in a shroud.

And then there was this under the heading *Corporate Theft*:

Exposés of all the major corporations and the dealings they would prefer not to have disclosed. Immediate access to all the latest information world-wide.

Daisy kept clicking on her mouse.

Global. They have internationalised profit and loss, but then they had done that a long time before; they've just decided to give up any further pretence on the subject. A country now equals the cost of its

*labour and the pliancy of its government in collaborating with big
business. Justice has been internationalised too but only insofar as a
mythical creature called the International Community can now bomb
from a great height any people it decides are not worth protecting.*

At the end there appeared to be a little personal column by
Howard.

*Today let's offer a brief salute to those captains of the occult, the
hackers. Listening in to the heart of the system with their nocturnal
auscultations they've helped us all establish an intimacy with that
surreal calculating machine some people refer to as reality. If every
person really is hardwired at birth to be this or that, then the world is
hardwired for oppression and so can only go one way round the
circuit. There are men in shackles in solitary confinement today whose
crime was to listen in to the world. Simply to take account of what's
going on and pass the knowledge on to the rest of us. Simply to
explode the secret.*

'Can he really make a living out of being an anarchist?' she
asked James as he prepared dinner.

'It's been done, I believe.'

'Not many people do it.'

'Not many people make a living out of being a photographer or an actress either. But I think we might have hit upon
the secret, Howard and me.'

'Which is?'

'The website actually works. You can always get through.
If you order something you'll get it. That's quite a change
from most of the sites with the word anarchy in them,
believe me. They still need things, don't they? They still
read, they still travel. Just because they're against the world

doesn't mean they don't live in it. Somebody has to supply them. So why not Howard?'

'Keeps him off the streets, I suppose.'

'Well, yes and no, Daisy.'

Syllabus of Errors

Theo unshaven for three days was a Sicilian at a funeral, one of the dark figures at the back of the church, heads bowed, dark collars up, who would never come forward however much the priest beckoned. Keeping their tongues away from the host and their guilty fingers well clear of the holy water stoup, just in case. Was he a mourner then, come to pray, or an executioner here to gloat? Both perhaps, life being full of such complications.

He had soon found a supplier downstairs in the saloon bar. He tried to keep up his normal intake of vodka. Occasionally he even helped himself to a bottle. Since he'd stopped seeing Yvonne he didn't eat much. Even Christy thought he'd started to look pale and fragile.

'Isn't there someone in London you could stay with for a while? That landlord must have stopped looking for you by now. I'm not sure life down here is the best thing for you at the moment, my friend.' But Theo just shrugged.

He woke this day to a chaos of voices, all inside his head. His father had once asked him outright whether he punctured his epidermis with needles or risked his septum rotting away from snorting white powders, and it was true that Theo had certainly tried what William Burroughs always called God's Own Medicine, but while hardly excelling in self-knowledge he did have just enough of it to realise that if he repeated that operation often enough he'd be gone beneath the earth's blanket a little sooner than even he had planned. And yet despite this abstinence he didn't feel at all good at the moment.

He slipped out of the pub and went down to the little café. He sat at the table by the window and stared out across the promenade. The man and the woman at the next table had obviously been arguing.

'Just tell me one thing. Why do you dismiss everything I say without even listening to it?' The man stirred his tea before answering.

'I suppose it saves time, that's all.'

Theo stepped outside into the rain. He felt anointed rather than assaulted; felt like taking off his clothes instead of buttoning them tighter. Why not step along naked beneath the leaking tide of the skies? It wasn't as though he had anything more to lose, was it? He watched a boat out there in the Channel and wondered if he might have turned his life in the wrong direction, then oversteered in an attempt to correct his mistake and was now enduring the yaw.

He crunched across the pebbles on the beach with the Dictaphone held to his mouth. Pressing the button mechanically he started to speak into the little square grille in the metal that was the microphone. A red light was glowing.

You used to ask me what I believed in, dad. I think I believe in songs. They're true and they don't go on too long and you can do them any number of ways. If I could come back in another life I'd like to be a song. Imagine knowing you're so much shorter than an illness or a marriage. You cost almost nothing and people carry you around in their heads without noticing. You don't have to pay any bills and you never get cold.

You were always asking me about jazz. What's so special about jazz that you won't do anything else, Theo? Maybe you thought it was the devil's music, just like those old American preachers used to. Badmouthing creation, intoning the devil's paternoster. I think maybe what I like about it, dad, is that you can't work out everything beforehand. One unexpected harmony, one individual chorus, might just alter everything. It never abandons the random. It rides the wave.

Theo stared out at the sea. And that's what I'll have to do now, isn't it? Ride the wave. But where exactly is this tide going?

Back at the pub he sat with his vodka at the bar, listening in as usual.

'They say this Osama bin Laden's got four wives and fifty-seven children.'

'The four wives makes sense anyway.'

'How's that then?'

'Well, on average I'd say men want sex about four times more often than women.'

'I didn't realise they wanted it at all.'

'They probably don't with you. Are you still chasing that Jennifer from the post office?'

'Leave it out.'

'No, go on, are you? Do you love her? Do you?'

'I love her more than I love you.'

'Two of us you're not shagging then.'

Christy was beckoning him over.

'I'll be going away next week, Theo. My annual trip to Ireland. You can stay in my room if you've really nowhere else to go. But use the side-entrance, all right – the old man doesn't know anything about you being here and I'm not sure he'd take to the idea. Just stay well out of the way. Probably better if you drink in another pub to be honest, and only use this place for sleeping in. Yvonne seems to have decided that she's not that keen on you after all. Oh, and don't steal any more bottles of vodka from down here, is that clear? Or you'll be out.'

If old men stare hard into the past it might be because they have no reason to throw fond glances at the future since the future, when all's said and done, is death. If not tomorrow then the day after that.

With his breakfast of grapefruit juice and toast, Digby sat in his chair by the window at Valley Prospect and found himself once more recalling the town of his childhood. Picture an L.S. Lowry painting slowly coming to life, except that instead of tall industrial steeples coughing out smoke, there were dirty canals at the side of which stood pottery chimneys, each looking as though a goose's neck had started to swallow an ostrich egg, an egg now stuck in its brick gullet for ever. These were the fat smoking throats of the Potteries.

China. He had thought as a child that they actually lived there; thought that the Wilton Factory of Stoke-on-Trent *was* China. After all that's where the china was made, so this must be Chinatown. Only years later did he learn that it was in fact a place unimaginably far away, so far given the curvature of the earth that by the time you reached it you were already on your way back home. Thus do things proceed in their circle. So China wasn't after all the stained glass window bearing the lettering GENERAL OFFICE, through which light streamed to form the same letters once again in shifting shadows on the floor. He had knelt there and traced them on the dusty stone with his finger, begriming his knees in the process. Nor was it the sign at the gate which read: STRANGERS NOT ALLOWED ON THIS WORKS. ALL ENQUIRIES TO BE MADE AT THE LODGE. Who were these strangers and how strange were they? He had stood for hours and waited for exotic creatures to arrive but all he had observed were the workmen and drivers coming and going in their overalls. Then back inside to see the cups and pots in their serried rows after they'd emerged from the kiln. The first day of creation before the breakages began.

Digby had now finished his book. He had risen at last from the wearisome task of composition. The slather of the weather at the window was a bluster of imprecisions. He peered through the swerve of the rain to the river beyond, the little banks carpeted with their sluggish, sodden sere and yellow. The year's fall, he thought. House sold, book done, new millennium entered. What else remains if I'm to set my lands in order? Where's my egregious scapegrace of an heir? What showers of things passed through his mind these days. What a detritus of joys and sorrows. Odds and sods of the soul.

He phoned the small publisher in Staffordshire who'd expressed an interest in his work. He announced that it had been completed and they gave every impression of being wholly uninterested, but he noted the address to which the manuscript was to be sent in any case. Then he phoned Jill.

'I'm sorry, Mr Wilton, but I haven't heard a thing.'

'So you still have the package?'

'Yes, do you want it back?'

'No. It's safely locked away, is it?'

'In my safe.'

'It's just . . . it contains something I think might make quite a difference to Theo's life.'

'Money.'

'Is it so obvious?'

'If it's going to make such a difference to Theo's life, then yes.'

'I wish you'd been able to keep him as your husband.'

'Theo always said he wished you'd been able to keep his mother as your wife. It's nearly Christmas, so I suppose he's bound to contact one of us.'

Bright Still

After Christy left for Ireland Theo was on his own. He played as many hours as he could endure out on the street, since that was now his sole source of cash. It was mid-December and people had already started feeling generous, so he had enough money for drink, none for food. He had come back early and let himself in quietly through the side-entrance. Christy's room was suddenly very cold. He tried to work out if the heating had been switched off but he couldn't fathom it. And he certainly couldn't face going down below to ask the old man or Yvonne. Either of them might have turned him out of doors there and then. So he piled the blankets high and listened to the waves as they broke on the pebbles. He took another drink from the bottle. He really wasn't feeling very good at all. A storm was now louring out there. By the time it had broken through and the windows were weeping the music had started up from below. Both the guitarist and the fiddler were playing through too much reverb, a dungeon of hollow echoes that made their notes melodramatic and imprecise, so it was impossible to say if they were playing truthfully or not. There's whiskey in the jar, the fellows sang. There probably was too; Christy would be drinking it over in Cork.

Theo took the bottle underneath the blankets and tried not to listen but it wasn't possible. He could never not listen to a song. He climbed slowly out of the bed and put his clothes back on. Every movement seemed to cost him too much effort.

Down in the shelter he stared at the sea and tried not to feel the cold. He had brought the bottle with him and took a drink from time to time. There were big boats with their navigation lights ploughing through the waves. He wished he was on one of them. He shivered and felt as if his nerves were wired up to the moon. Pity they weren't; then he might shine from head to foot with bright electric ecstasies. Become a light to himself and to others. A beacon for all shoreline insomniacs and misfits.

If he had nothing else in common with his father Theo did believe in benedictions and curses. Believed in their power. The world he understood wasn't as innocent as his father imagined. Benedictions and curses. Particularly the curses of women. Had he brought too many down on his head? Was that why there was a knot of dirty seaman's rope tied up inside his chest?

Back at the pub Yvonne took the call. The boys had finally got hold of the right number. 'Theo Wilton?' she said, having to shout over the sound of the music. 'No, he left here weeks ago.'

He watched as the large man lumbered across the car park. He pressed an invisible button in his pocket and the Volvo estate, like a long metal beast crouching in the dark, suddenly lit up. Four yellow eyes, two at the front and two at the back, flashed in joy as they registered the return of their master. A home to go to.

The weather was getting serious and Theo knew that he

would have to heave himself back to the pub soon. He felt so tired that he thought he'd sleep now whether or not the boys were still digging their tunnel of reverb under the Channel. He took one last good slug of his liquor and rose from the wooden bench. He was surprised how unsteady he was. Theo never got drunk, so the slumbrous and uncoordinated condition of his legs confused him. He held on to the side of the shelter and stared upwards. Dark breath of the clouds coughing over the moon. Sky like a spittoon. Back to the pub. Must get back to the pub. Straight over the road he went in a swerving blur, not even seeing the car. The car was just another smear of moving lights along the front.

The horn blared as Theo rolled over the bonnet and hit the windscreen, then dumped down hard on to the road. The impact had sobered him and he was back on his feet in seconds and moving quickly away from the sea.

'Are you all right?' the driver was shouting as he climbed out of his car, but Theo was already hobbling off. The man looked down at the front of his car to see the smashed vodka bottle.

Later that day Daisy arrived with a gift.

'It's from Jonty,' she said, 'for Christmas.'

'Should I open it now?'

'I'm certainly not going till you do.'

Digby tore open the envelope as Daisy watched. It appeared to be some sort of voucher or an immensely ornate and elaborate certificate. His name had been written in ink in the middle. They both stared at the words printed on it in silence.

Bright Still

★

The Ancient Mariner. A tribute in bone china.

From the Merriman Museum of Miniature Collectables.

25 unforgettable collector's items reprising the whole of Coleridge's great poem, with original illustrations designed specifically for this collection.

The items to be sent to you at the rate of one per month.

They both stopped reading at the same time and looked at one another.

'He said he owed it all to you.'

'I suppose he does in a way.'

'Yours, he assured me, would be the only free subscription.'

'Very neighbourly of him.'

'And he's not even your neighbour any more. He's expecting it to sell out. Would you like to come over to the farmhouse for Christmas?'

'I think, Daisy, now that I'm here I'll just try to settle in.'

'I knew you'd say that. I'll pop over anyway to see dad.'

'I'll make sure there's some claret for you.'

'My father's very fond of crème de menthe.'

'I'll have a word with Margaret and see what we can do.'

That Christmas Jill spent in Kensington with her parents. Daisy and James and Howard were all together in the farmhouse. They went over on Christmas Day to see Daisy's father and Digby. Presents were exchanged. Kisses were bestowed. Yvonne and Jack were with Yvonne's mother in St Leonards pulling crackers and opening parcels. Christy was drunk in Ireland. The boys in the band were in their respective homes in London with their kith and kin, all except one.

Theo did not know what he'd hurt inside when that car hit him but he knew he'd hurt something. The influenza he'd already contracted had in any case weakened him to the point where he could barely climb out of bed. The noise below from the pub was riotous, but no one down there knew that he was above them. Anyway he had to stay well clear of the old man. Those were his orders and he couldn't afford to be falling out with Christy at this stage. He thought sleep would soon restore him. But now every breath brought another harsh cough. There was sharp glass in his throat, that was how it felt when he breathed; it must have been that which brought the blood up when he retched. He only lost consciousness between coughs for a fraction of a second. In fact influenza and the cold between them had now induced pneumonia and he'd been bleeding internally for days from the accident.

Monk at last in the apartment with the piano draped and the countess providing for his every need. Sunk into a silence no one could recall him from. Not worth the effort of resolving those discords any more. Let the world of harmony lie unfractured. The chord voicings stay unvoiced. Let Thelonious lie where the end of his music had dropped him. Where the black-and-white of the keyboard ends and music turns into a blur of chaos again.

Something was refrigerating his chest and belly. So cold. He had never in his life felt so cold. His bones were sticks of ice and his white flesh was snow that wouldn't melt. Sometimes he shook hard enough to make the bed-frame rattle. Just as well they were making so much noise downstairs or they'd have heard him. The little Dictaphone was still in his hand. He pressed the button and spoke as best he could into it, his lips pressed close to the metal grille.

Jill handed Digby the Dictaphone along with Theo's trumpet.

'I thought you might want these. I shouldn't think you'd have wanted any of the other things. They were soiled. I had them burnt.' She had still been next of kin, even though she wouldn't have been a few weeks later when her divorce came through, so the police had given Theo's things to her after she'd identified the body.

The ceremony at the crematorium had ended an hour before. They were now standing about in Jill's house. She'd felt obliged to have a little reception of some sort. The boys in the band stood in a sad little circle, each clutching a beer.

'And there's the other thing, of course.' Jill left the room for a moment and when she came back she had Digby's package. She handed him that too, and Digby said, 'I suppose, if he'd received this, he might still be alive.' Jill shrugged.

'I suppose he would. If the boys had found him he'd still be alive too. They've been given a residency in Copenhagen. For three months. Theo would have been in seventh heaven. The rest of the band have had to arrange sabbaticals, though they're all hoping they'll be extended for ever. Theo wouldn't have needed to bother. Sad the way some things don't connect up in life, isn't it? I still think Theo was lucky in some ways, even though I couldn't tame him.' Digby looked at her in silence before speaking again.

'Lucky?'

'To be driven on like that the whole of your life. Never

stalling. It's a kind of luck, isn't it? And he was a wonderful trumpet player. However many lies he might have told himself or the rest of us, he never lied when he was playing the trumpet, you know. Did you know that?'

'I was never sure. But for some reason I'm glad you said so.'

Then he spoke to the remaining members of Zeno, particularly Paul.

'How's your book going, Mr Wilton?'

'Finished. And yours?'

'Abandoned.'

'I'm sorry.'

'Don't be. Leaves more time for playing double-bass in Copenhagen.'

When Reg made his way over to Digby he looked even more uncomfortable than he usually did. He asked if he could have a word in private, so they went into the front room. Reg was staring at his shoes as he spoke and Digby couldn't take his eyes off his earring, which was catching the light and gleaming as he bent his head.

'I know this must seem pretty insensitive at a time like this but . . .'

'What is it, Reg?'

'Before Theo went down to Hastings I lent him a hundred pounds.'

'Stay there,' Digby said and went to get the package from his bag. He cut it open and gave Reg two of the notes from inside.

'Thanks, Mr Wilton. I didn't want to bring it up but I'm trying to get everything sorted out before we go off on our gig – it's a pretty long gig.'

'I'm glad you did. I wonder if I might ask a favour of you in return, Reg.'

'Anything I can do.'

'Would you be able to get me one of those tapes of Zeno, with Theo playing the trumpet?'

'I've got one in the car. I'll go get it for you now.' When he came back with it he said, 'Benny Milhouse couldn't believe that Theo's dead. It was listening to the trumpet first caught his attention. He thought it was brilliant.'

'So who'll take Theo's part then, in Copenhagen?'

'Benny himself. Theo would have laughed. I mean . . . I'm sorry . . .'

'Don't be, Reg. I'd like to think of him laughing. We should both have done more of that.'

So it was that when Digby Wilton returned to Valley Prospect he had in his bag a tape of the legendary Zeno and a package containing £29,900. Also one trumpet and a small and battered Dictaphone. But he didn't have a son any more.

Household Gods

The warmth had returned. Digby lay still and let it penetrate him.

'They sent you my new address then,' he said to the darkness. His face was wet with grateful tears. Victoria and Theo. Theo and Victoria. Wherever they were he'd not be too long joining them.

He could never think of Victoria now without remembering the war. Old men often go back to the beginning of things in their minds. For a while the war had been unreal in much of the country, even with the menace of Hitler blaring out of the radio but then the bombs started falling, the houses started caving in and the children evacuees lined up in their sorrowful queues with name-tags and gas masks. It had started to feel real enough then.

It was only afterwards that they had understood the full horror of what they had been fighting, even those like Digby who never actually saw combat. The translation of humanity into statistics, statistics not disquieted by screams nor altered for the worse by them. It was as though Swift's dreadful vision in *A Modest Proposal* had come true: those children of history we wouldn't feed we'd eat instead. Or at least our machines would eat them for us and all our love would go into repairing the machines. The great machines of the regime were to be oiled by the unanimous devotion of the people. A small fire in the engine's heart could be the light of the world, together with the spirit's breath when the gas starts to hiss through the nozzle. Doors shut tight as they always are in any tabernacle. So who were these coming to the sacrifice? Mechanics. The mechanics of the new world order.

Digby hoped the figure of history might be like the concentration camp number on Otto Rosenberg's arm, never removed. Instead this inmate of Belsen, this gypsy vagrant who'd once cleaned Dr Josef Mengele's shoes and even smiled into his affable smiling face, had had an angel tattooed over that emblem of statistical non-identity so that the forces of good could be seen to triumph over the forces of evil. Staring at his seven children late in life he'd said, 'God is making it all up to me.' History as palimpsest then, the good script over the bad, hell forever erased by the signature of paradise, the mysterious language of redemption covering the curses of the damned with hallelujahs. It was all a question of fathoming the riddle. Contained within the poisoned baffle of Mengele's name was the German word for angel: Engel. Had some of them heard its mystic murmur when the guards yelled his arrival; was that why the subjects of his diabolic science had dubbed him the Angel of Death? A doctor who was himself the disease medicine was meant to cure. He was to Hippocrates what antimatter was to matter: the mandrake-shriek of reversal. But Providence might still be asserted if you could only believe that Mengele could be shorn of history's sadism, of Hitlerite nihilism, and transmute once more entirely to angel. The number itself didn't disappear, couldn't disappear, but at least it no longer piped its victory. History's mountain of statistics, its pyramid of skulls, settled in one beautiful equation: seven children, a candelabra in the living temple, small candles blazing in the sun. Knowing that any one of history's catastrophic winds could extinguish all those flames merely by breathing in the wrong direction once more. The bad breath of tragedy. Climb inside the mighty maw and study the dragon of history's dentition for yourself.

Digby was well aware that if you look on the dark side things can start to look very dark indeed. If you crouch down there in the shadows long enough then when you do look up even the light will blind you. The sun itself turns black. Nyctalopia. So he was trying to find things he could celebrate about Theo's life. Once more he pressed the tape of Zeno into the machine. *Pack up all my cares and woe, Here I go, singing low* . . . When Daisy arrived she said, 'I didn't know you liked jazz, Digby.'

'Neither did I.'

Jazz in its modern incarnations had so often struck Digby as a demolition of age-old melodies, another of modernity's assaults upon the antique. Of course in his time he'd liked modernity's assaults on the antique in the visual sphere, but in music he hadn't been at all sure. He had often thought there might be something there he wasn't hearing; the instruments seemed sometimes to be employed primarily as weapons. But then maybe people had felt like that on first hearing Beethoven smashing his hands down on a piano keyboard, breaking strings, announcing his unprecedented discords. Digby didn't even try to judge it, for how could he judge it? When Theo had played him the record of his beloved Miles Davis's *Kind of Blue* he had found the trumpet-playing hesitant to the point of incompetence, sometimes seeming to die on the note, but Theo had said no, he had said that what Digby heard as incompetence or inadvertence was in fact intentional; a refusal of overstatement, an admission that the instrument was an instrument and not an extension of the voice. They both heard the same notes, Digby and his son, but Digby had been deaf to the intention behind the delivery. If there *was* any incompetence then it lay in his own ears. Still, he had no problem now with Beethoven, did he, so maybe *Kind of Blue* needed another two hundred years to mature. He wouldn't be the one judging it when the time came round, that was for sure. In the meantime he was warming to Zeno and wished now that he had made an effort to hear them live while he'd had the opportunity. Not that he remembered ever having been invited.

'Neither did I, Daisy, but I'm trying to develop and adapt as much as possible in the time left to me.'

'It's very good.'

'I know.'

She had picked up the trumpet from the mantelpiece.

'Was this your son's?'

'Yes, and that's him playing on the tape.' Digby felt a great sense of gratitude to Daisy. Her readiness to take him down to the funeral and bring him back again had placed him even more firmly in her debt. He wished there was something he might do to express his gratitude.

'There's an item missing from my life, Daisy.'

'All this business with Theo must be very difficult for you.'

'No, I didn't mean that. Whatever I feel about Theo, it's hardly as though I miss his visits each week. He only ever dropped by once or twice a year to accuse me of murder.'

'Then what?'

'All those things Howard wrote that you used to bring round . . . is he still doing it?'

'Oh, very much so. Now it's on-line. Now you can even key into the secret bit.'

'You finally found out what it meant then, Thailand Great Anakh?'

'*Thyhandgreatanarch.com.*'

'Why did it say *Greetings to the law* whenever you went in there?'

'My son and his colleagues were protecting themselves from any unwanted curiosity from the authorites. Though I can't see how they'll protect themselves any longer. He says he doesn't need to. Says he's an anarchist not a criminal. The new anarchists apparently are not fighting for lawlessness, they're fighting against it. The lawlessness of large corporations, the lawlessness of states armed to the teeth and looking for trouble. That's what they say.'

'It sounds as though he's convinced you.'

'Let's say I'm a lot more convinced than I used to be. He's an interesting fellow, Howard. Doesn't accept anything on authority, particularly not on mine or his father's.'

'So how would I key into it, Daisy? I miss it; miss the way it helped me clarify so many of my own foggy preoccupations.' Daisy looked at him for a moment and smiled: Digby the new anarchist. Well, she wouldn't put it past him. Not now that she'd started learning the ropes herself. And it was really no stranger than her return to the bed of Howard's father, with the boy already in his thirties.

'You'd have to have a computer. Then you'd have to become a subscriber.'

'I agree.'

'Agree to what?'

374

'To both things. I mean I can't be dawdling about, can I, not at my age? I must get on. So could you ask Howard to arrange it, do you think – and I'll pay whatever's necessary.'

'Well, he'll be coming up next week. I'll have a word, Digby, and see what I can do.'

A week later a slightly bemused Howard arrived to install Digby's computer. He needed all the subscribers he could get, though he very much hoped he'd not have to set up a complete computer system for each one of them in turn, but his mother had been characteristically firm about it.

The tall athletic young man with black curly hair needed to lean over a little to greet the stooped figure of Digby. He'd never expected to be signing up such an aged recruit.

'It's very good of you,' Digby said. 'You'll have to show me how to use it, of course.'

'Shouldn't take long.' And it didn't. Two hours later they were up and running and Digby was double-clicking on his mouse as though he'd been at it for years.

'Well I shall look forward to seeing what you've got to say. I always found your pieces,' he hesitated briefly, 'refreshing. Yes, that's the word. I want to know what it looks like, you see.'

'What it looks like?'

'The age. This time we live in. The new millennium. Never expected to survive into it but since I'm here I want to recognise its features. Stare into the whites of its eyes. Have you seen what it looks like?'

'I've caught a few glimpses.'

'Did it have its mouth open?'

'Difficult to tell. It had its visor down and its baton raised.'

'I must owe you some money.'

Howard took the receipt for the computer from his pocket, then he took out another piece of paper and wrote a figure on it for the price of the subscription.

'That seems very reasonable,' Digby said, going over to the drawer where he kept the large envelope he'd once prepared for Theo. He took some money out and handed it over. 'And how's it all going?'

'Not too bad. Could do with a few more investors.'

'Investors.'

'A bit of cash to help with the start-up costs.' Digby barely hesitated before going back to the drawer.

'Can I be one?' he said. Howard laughed.

'Can't think why not, if you want to be. As long as mum approves. She might think I'm corrupting you.'

'You're not old enough to corrupt me.' Digby counted out £10,000 in £50 notes and gave them to Howard.

'I'm in.' What am I saving up for at this stage? he thought. And with Theo gone it's not as though there was anyone else left to pass it on to, even beyond this stage. He was happy with the idea that the money was going to Daisy's family. Howard counted out the money note by note. There was an edge of bewilderment to his smile.

'I suppose I'd better say that we're likely to have a slightly quirky way of working out the annual dividend.'

'It can't be any quirkier than Marconi's way of doing it, I can assure you, Howard.'

'I'll confess that I'd thought of today as a bit of a chore, Mr Wilton, but I'm very glad I came.'

And later Digby sat down before his new, brightly coloured plastic wunderkammer, which dissolved both time and distance, to see what marvels it might bring him from afar and to try to fathom whether such dissolution might help

him at last trace the lineaments of his age. *So Where Are We Now?* began Howard's editorial:

They globalise trade not justice. They no longer call themselves East and West but the international community. They declare war on undemocratic regimes unless the families in charge of such regimes happen to live in a palace built over a sea of oil. Oil supplies still rate higher than a sweetly smiling populace. But Newton's third law of motion applies beyond the world of mechanics. To every action there is an equal and opposite reaction. In consequence terror too has been globalised. The one language the whole world now understands, the esperanto of the new millennium, is violence. If you have the power to bomb and poison, to terrify and maim, then you make the front pages. But if you are merely subject to those with such resources, without having an equal and opposite amount of them yourself, you are one of history's footnotes, doomed to a roofless home inside parentheses. Your land is stolen, your children dispossessed, your houses bulldozed into rubble, while men in suits shake hands thousands of miles away and settle what is left of your fate. Smiling as the cameras click. So whenever the dispossessed see missiles flying through the air in the opposite direction they cheer, thus provoking even more violence and terror; more ruined homes, infected water, flattened cities. Wherever the bombs and missiles start out from they always seem to land on them. The rich from both sides bomb the poor in the middle and call any complaints that rise above the smoke sedition. And this, they have declared, is the end of history; this is the new world order.

Later in the darkness Digby sat by the window with Theo's little Dictaphone in his hand. He pressed the play button again. He had listened more than ten times now, but he still didn't know what Theo had been trying to say between the coughs.

Why does my mouth taste of salt, dad? . . . (coughing) . . . the window's closed . . . (coughing) . . . so how can the ocean get into my lungs? Why . . . (now there was a lengthy spell of coughing, harsh, grating, uncontrollable) *. . . why . . .* (more coughing as Theo made a desperate effort to finish his sentence) *. . . why . . .* (there was the sound of something crashing, after that only the whirr of the tape).

I don't know why, Theo. My old china. Country of opium dreams and distant wars. I couldn't answer your questions when you were living and now that you're dead I still can't answer them. All I can do is keep asking my own until the next time we meet. Bye bye, blackbird.

O Lady! We receive but what we give,
And in our life alone does nature live:
Ours is her wedding-garment, ours her shroud!

Samuel Taylor Coleridge